Montana
CHERRIES

Books by Kim Law

The Sugar Springs series

Sugar Springs

Sweet Nothings

Sprinkles on Top

The Davenport series

Caught on Camera

Caught in the Act

The Turtle Island series

Ex on the Beach

Hot Buttered Yum

Two Turtle Island Doves (a novella)

The Holly Hills series

"Marry Me, Cowboy" novella, *Cowboys for Christmas*

Montana
C H E R R I E S
Kim Law

Montlake
Romance

Published by Montlake Romance, Seattle

www.apub.com

Amazon, the Amazon logo, and Montlake Romance are trademarks of Amazon.com, Inc., or its affiliates.

ISBN-13: 9781503944831
ISBN-10: 1503944832

Cover design by Shasti O'Leary-Soudant / SOS CREATIVE LLC

Printed in the United States of America

To my street team. You guys are the best!
I hope you enjoy my venture out West.

chapter one

"Twenty cupcakes, purple sprinkles, princess wand," Dani Wilde muttered to herself as she peered into the box on the counter, the homemade treats aligned with military precision. She closed the lid and laid her niece's sparkly wand across the top. "Perfect."

Turning from the cupcakes, she surveyed the rest of the kitchen to ensure that all was in order. Only to find a pile of women's dry cleaning dumped on one end of the ten-person table. She stared up at the ceiling as if she could see right through it. Most likely, Michelle would claim another headache and wouldn't be able to run her own errands again today. Including delivering the cupcakes to the preschool for Jenna's last day of day camp.

Dani sighed, grabbed the pile of mail for her clients and the flyers for the summer sale at The Cherry Basket, and shoved it all into her Cinderella tote. Jenna had given her the tote last Christmas. The four-year-old loved Cinderella above all else.

Then Dani headed for the stairs.

When her father had moved into town six years earlier, stepping aside and leaving her brother, Gabe, to manage the family orchard, Gabe and Michelle had taken the opportunity to move into the master suite. But having Michelle in her parents' room often reminded Dani of her mother. Carol Wilde had suffered from headaches, too. Only . . .

Dani shut off her thoughts. Possibly Michelle really had migraines. Who was she to say?

And if they were anything like Dani's mother's had been, then driving a car was the last thing she needed to be doing. That had been proven by the accident that had brought Dani back home from college.

Reaching the far end of the hallway, Dani knocked on the closed door and waited for a reply.

"Yes?" a muffled voice answered after several seconds. Dani cracked open the door to find the Vera Wang bedspread pulled over a slim mound in the middle of the bed and the shades drawn on the windows.

"Do you need me to take the cupcakes to the school?" Dani asked quietly.

"Do you mind?" Michelle didn't even lift her head.

Guilt tugged at Dani. The woman was probably experiencing severe pain, and here she was being judge and jury. "I don't mind," she admitted. And she didn't. She loved being there for Jenna. "There's dry cleaning on the table . . ."

"Gabe took it down for me. Can you drop it off?"

Michelle rarely left the house in anything that didn't need to be dry-cleaned.

"No problem." Dani glanced at her watch. "I need to run in to see Mrs. Tamry anyway."

Mrs. Tamry was one of their best customers at The Cherry Basket, but had been unable to come in for the last few weeks due to chemo treatments. Her husband would be happy to stop by for his wife's favorite treat, but Dani preferred to take the fresh cherry scones herself. The weekly errand was the least Dani could do.

There wouldn't be a lot of time for visiting with the Tamrys today—not with needing to drop off Jenna's cupcakes—but adding in a run to the dry cleaner wouldn't cost her more than a few minutes.

"Anything else I can do for you while I'm out?" Dani asked.

Several seconds of silence passed and Dani decided that Michelle had gone back to sleep, but then the covers shifted and she peeked out from behind her silk sleep mask. "Will you take care of Jenna tonight? I don't want her coming in here and bothering me."

The words cut Dani in a way that almost bent her over. She so wished she had the power to do something about Jenna's mother. That was the only worry she had about her upcoming move from Montana to New York. She would be leaving her niece on her own. And this request wasn't uncommon in the girl's life.

Dani had never understood why Michelle had decided to conceive if she didn't want to be a mother.

"Sure." She nodded, even though Michelle had already disappeared back under the covers. "I'll make sure we do something quiet once we're back at the house."

Everything about that sentence bothered Dani.

She shouldn't have to keep Jenna quiet. She shouldn't *have* to take care of Jenna.

If Michelle were a decent human being, she'd have an actual interest in seeing her own daughter grow up. But so far, that didn't seem to be the case. What Gabe had ever seen in his wife, Dani had no idea. Or any sense as to why he continuously put up with her.

Dani backed out of the room, pulling the door silently shut as she exited, then shoved her tactless thoughts out of her mind. She checked her email as she hurried back down the staircase, one hand holding the phone up in front of her as the other slid along the stair rail. There were five emails from local marketing clients, three more from potential clients she simply didn't have the time to take on, and one from San Francisco.

Similar to the marketing firm she'd be joining in New York City next month, she'd done freelance work with the San Francisco company for the last three years. She hated the thought of giving up any of her clients, especially considering the potential attached to the one in San Francisco, but the contract she'd be signing with her new employer would force her to do just that. Not to mention, she'd likely have zero time left over for anything else. She had to prove herself when she got to New York. That was priority number one.

She stopped by the kitchen to scoop up the cupcakes and clothes, then headed out the back door. Peering across the field, she wondered if her brother was within cell service, and couldn't help letting her gaze hang on the Salish Mountains on the far side of Flathead Lake. She'd lived in Montana her entire life except for the eight weeks of freshman year at Columbia University. She'd made it to New York City briefly. And she *would* do it again.

She'd miss this place, of course. A lot. But New York was her dream. She had to do it. If not for herself, then for her mother.

Not seeing any sign of her brother, she settled the desserts into her car before sliding behind the wheel. She dialed his cell as she turned the vehicle around and headed down the long drive.

"Yeah?" Gabe always answered as if he had no time to talk.

"Michelle's in bed, I'm taking the cupcakes to the school."

He didn't reply at first, then grunted out a single "Thanks."

"You know she eventually has to do these things herself, right? I *am* leaving, Gabe. In a month."

She'd discussed making a permanent move to New York for so long, it had crossed her mind that her family might not believe she'd really do it. She'd been a constant for them, here for the last fourteen years. But things were different now. Jaden had just graduated college; everyone else had their own lives. They didn't need her anymore.

In fact, of her five brothers—all younger—Gabe was the only one still at home. And that was because he ran the farm. He'd been one year behind her in school, and where she'd come home from college to take over responsibility for the house, he'd gone *off* to college to ensure he had the most up-to-date knowledge to run the farm. It had been a given since childhood that he'd one day take over for their dad, and since graduating, he'd done an incredible job. Production on the farm had increased—they now rivaled any of the other orchards running along the coast of the lake—and they'd introduced two new cherry varieties in the last five years.

"I know," Gabe said in her ear, bringing her back to the present. "And she will. I promise. I'll talk to her."

What went left unsaid was "again." He'd talk to her *again*.

And what Dani didn't respond with was "It won't do any good." They both knew it wouldn't.

"Jenna needs her," she said instead.

"I know," he bit out.

And you do, too.

But she wouldn't say those words. That would really set him off. He'd been snapping at her for weeks, a situation she attributed mostly to whatever was going on in his marriage. Things had been going downhill for a while there.

But she'd also wondered if her upcoming departure didn't play into his bad mood, too. They'd struggled once, around the time their mom had died. They'd fought a lot. But things were good between them now. They had been for years. And she didn't want that to change because of something she might do.

"I *do* know, Dani," he reiterated, this time more polite. "I'll talk to her."

That's all she could ask. "Want me to stick around until the party is over and bring Jenna home?"

"Could you? I need to get this tractor working or we'll be short one come harvest."

Harvesting the fifteen acres of cherries on their farm would start in about two weeks, lasting for another two weeks, into the first days of August. Then she'd board a plane and start her new life. "Will do," she confirmed.

She disconnected and headed down the road. Due to the mountains immediately to their west, the climate in the area was more temperate than in the rest of the state, making it the ideal location for the many orchards running along the eastern coast of Flathead Lake. Dani loved how the whole community came together at this time of year. The Cherry Festival was next weekend, migrant workers would soon move in, then picking would commence up and down the entire lake region—weeks filled with roadside stands and trucks weighted down with cherries, all heading to the packing plant.

Because of the cherries, the lake, and the fact that the town curved around the most gorgeous bay in the state, Birch Bay became a popular little tourist attraction in the summer months.

Pride swelled in her as The Cherry Basket came into view. Her days of living here might be coming to an end, but just because she was leaving didn't mean her past accomplishments would disappear with her. The Cherry Basket had been her creation from the ground up. Not only did they serve fresh-baked items made with fruit from their very own orchard, but they had mixes, cookbooks, jams, jellies, and pretty much any culinary delight one could want. They held cooking classes, and they'd even partnered with a big-name chef to develop their own line of kitchen utensils. It had been a proud moment for her when the doors had opened for the first time.

But it *would* continue without her. She'd made sure of it.

She'd worked hard to ensure that only the best employees were in place for both the local and online businesses. It was a well-oiled machine. Plus, it's not like she wouldn't check in on them. She wasn't cutting Montana out of her heart. Just her everyday life.

❀

Later that afternoon, after a roomful of four-year-olds got buzzed on cupcakes and sugary drinks, Dani turned her reliable four-door sedan into the winding driveway of the Wilde Cherry Farm. She glanced in her rearview mirror at her niece. Jenna was waving her wand in the air in front of her, her pink tutu bunched up in her lap.

"Your teacher told me how great you did this year, did you know that? She was very impressed with how smart you are."

Jenna's blonde head bobbed up and down. "She liked me."

"Yes," Dani said, chuckling. "She liked you a lot. Because you're such a great little girl."

"I know," Jenna said almost matter-of-factly. Then the girl's gaze darted in the direction of the house and the joy on her face lessened. "Do you think Daddy's done working yet?"

"I'm not sure." Dani readjusted her own gaze, taking in the house and the land beyond it. Her dad's truck was parked behind Michelle's car, alongside a black SUV she didn't recognize.

"Mommy might not feel like playing," Jenna murmured from the backseat.

"That's okay." Dani winked at her niece as she shifted the car into park and took in the California plates of the SUV. There was a car seat in the back of the vehicle. "I'll play with you all afternoon. How about that? We'll play in *my* room."

She made the proposition of playing in her room sound exciting. Instead of saying that she didn't want Jenna to go upstairs because it might upset her mother.

"Who's here?" Jenna asked as she unbuckled the seat belt and climbed from her booster.

"Looks like Pops is," Dani said. Which didn't surprise her. Max Wilde and his longtime girlfriend, Gloria, often showed up for Friday-night dinners. "But I'm not sure who else."

Shooting a final glance at the shiny, new-looking SUV, Dani took the little girl's hand and they headed for the back deck of the two-story log home. Her parents had built the house after her fifth and final brother had been born, but only guests and strangers approached by way of the wide-sweeping front porch. The back deck led directly into the family room and had become the main entrance years ago.

As she stepped inside the house, she released Jenna's hand. Gabe was, indeed, in from work, and Michelle had even made it downstairs. She wore a flattering pair of designer jeans and a silk top that, if Dani remembered correctly, she'd picked up on a weekend anniversary trip to Seattle last fall.

The elder Wilde sat in his favorite recliner near the stone fireplace with Gloria perched in another chair close by. And on the sprawling leather sofa sat a little girl about Jenna's age, back straight and looking scared.

Beside her was a man Dani hadn't expected to ever see again. Outside of magazines.

Benjamin Browning Denton.

Dani's pulse let her know that she was still very much a woman, and very much alive, as she took in the insanely gorgeous man who stood at the sight of her.

With slightly rumpled hair a shade darker than hers, and casual jeans with a white button-up, the man came from good stock and he wore it well. He'd rolled up his shirtsleeves to reveal toasty-warm skin, and both jeans and shirt looked made to fit.

Despite the testosterone practically waving like a flag, his smile was uncertain.

"Ben—"

"Dani—"

They spoke at the same time. He inclined his head in a half nod, fondness radiating from his green, green eyes. "It's great to see you, Dani."

It had been ten years since she'd seen him. Ten years since she'd lost her virginity.

"You too." A short laugh came out of her, tight and higher pitched than normal. A fact she attributed to the embarrassment that suddenly flooded her. Good grief, she'd thrown herself at this man.

She shot a questioning look at her brother, who'd moved to her side and picked up Jenna. "What's going on?" she muttered to Gabe.

It wasn't that she didn't want the others to hear the question, but she was confused. And she didn't like being caught off guard. Ben had returned to Los Angeles after he and Gabe had graduated from Montana State, and as far as she knew, he hadn't been back in Big Sky Country since.

He hadn't even made it to Gabe and Michelle's wedding. He'd been at a shoot on one of the Pacific islands.

Ben was a photographer to the stars, mostly models, and often showed up himself on the pages of national magazines. Usually with some of the same beauties he captured through his lenses. He'd even been romantically linked with a foreign princess at one point.

"Didn't I tell you?" Gabe asked while Jenna giggled at his nuzzling kisses.

"Come home anytime he wants," her father added from across the room. "I told him that years ago."

Only, it had never been Ben's home.

Though it had probably been closer to a home than anything else he'd ever had. He'd spent three summers and two Christmases there during his college years, due to his A-lister movie-star mother rarely being in one place for very long. And Ben wanting to be around her even less.

"So when he called," Gabe continued, "I invited him to stay for a few weeks."

A few weeks?

"No." Dani gulped, trying her best not to look upset. She wasn't. Merely shocked. And wishing she'd taken more time that morning with her appearance. "You did *not* mention it."

Had a houseguest been mentioned, she would have prepared a room for him.

Or for *them*, she corrected herself as she took in the child not quite by Ben's side. Clearly this was the daughter recent tabloids had rumored to exist. She looked just like him. But with such a gap between the two, both physically and what seemed like emotionally, it wouldn't be hard to imagine they'd never met.

She pulled her gaze from the dark-haired, terrified-looking child and turned to Ben. He remained standing, an overly large, bright-pink stuffed bunny in his right hand. "So the rumors are true?" she couldn't help but ask. The tabloids had recently claimed that a model he'd hooked up with years ago had shown up on his doorstep last month with quite the surprise.

"The rumors are true." He tipped his head toward the girl, but didn't look at her.

Dani glanced back at the child, and though she didn't say it, all she could think was *Wow*. Ben Denton had a kid. That would surely put a damper on his globe-trotting-bachelor ways.

Jenna's dog, Mike, chose that moment to come barreling down the stairs and race for his mistress, still high in her daddy's arms. At the same time, Michelle pulled a photo album from the shelves between the two sets of floor-to-ceiling windows, and glided across the room. She set her sights on Ben and sidled in close. *Too close*, actually.

"Tell me about Hollywood," Michelle purred, her eyelash extensions fluttering as she looked up at him. "What's it like working with models every day?"

Gabe had met Michelle in LA when he'd gone home with Ben during spring break of their senior year. They'd dated long distance for a couple of years before he'd married her and moved her to Montana. She'd been whining about wanting to return to California ever since.

"Well," Ben started. He glanced at Michelle's French-tipped nails where they'd landed on his bicep. "It's a job," he added, sounding uncomfortable. "Lots of travel, long hours. But there are perks."

Dani almost snorted. She'd just bet there were perks.

Ben gave a subtle shrug of his shoulder, and Michelle's hand slid from his upper arm . . . to his forearm. She goaded him to the couch, where she settled in beside him and opened her album.

"Let me show you pictures of when I lived there," she cooed, "and you can tell me what's changed."

Pictures of *her*, no doubt. That was pretty much the only thing in that particular album.

Dani looked at Gabe, who was hunkered down now, he and Jenna both accepting Mike's sloppy kisses while the dog's tail slapped wildly against Dani's legs. Gabe seemed oblivious to the fact that his wife was coming on to his friend.

Finally, Jenna looked up from Mike and the two of them marched determinedly across the room to stand in front of the other girl. The newcomer's hair had fuzzed into a knot on one side, looking as if it hadn't been combed in a couple of days, and her top didn't match her shorts. Her gaze had silently followed every movement Jenna and Mike had made.

"My name is Jenna," Dani's niece announced. "And this is Mike."

Uncertain eyes darted to her daddy. When she got no help, she finally whispered, "I'm Haley." She bit down on her lip and dropped her gaze to her lap.

Poor kid.

Michelle didn't pause from her story while the two kids introduced themselves to each other, but Dani did notice a wrinkle in her brow like she was annoyed with the distraction.

"Did you wanna play with me?" Jenna asked.

Mike nudged his nose into Haley's lap, and she glanced at her daddy a second time. This time Ben looked back, but that's all. No nod of encouragement. No pat on her shoulder to show a bit of support. He did wear a similar uncertainty in his own gaze, though. As if he had no idea what he was supposed to do when his daughter looked at him like that.

And he once again shifted the arm nearest Michelle, this time succeeding in easing her hand away from his body.

"How about all three of us go play," Dani jumped in. She was unable to watch the fear on the little girl any longer without trying to help. Moving forward, she held a hand out for both children. "We'll play in Jenna's room while the grown-ups have silly grown-up talk," she said. "And we'll take this wild and crazy dog with us."

Haley almost smiled at that, and slid off the couch to reach for one of Dani's hands.

"I'll fix the guest room for you," she told Ben as she edged past him. Though there were three unused bedrooms upstairs, her remaining four brothers would soon return for the harvest.

All Wildes did their best to make it home every July, even their father's sister—though she was now in her seventies. Aunt Sadie, who'd lived in Colorado since before Dani had been born, normally took the guest room on the main floor across from Dani's bedroom, but since she and her husband had recently taken a fiftieth-anniversary trip, she'd decided to sit this year out.

As Dani and the girls moved toward the hallway, she looked back at the sound of a feminine laugh from the far side of the room. Her dad and Gloria were leaning in toward each other, talking softly, both wearing tender expressions of affection. It was sweet. She supposed.

She only wished her mother were still around so it could be her *mom* and dad cuddling like that.

Before turning back, Dani took one more peek at Ben. He was watching her.

Her pulse ratcheted up once again as she thought about the past. He may have been Gabe's best friend, but something different had happened between them over those summers. Not romantic—

Well . . . no.

Though she did have sex with him that one time.

The bigger thing had been the friendship that had developed. Not buddy-buddy as he'd been with her brothers. And not simply looking for a good time the way he'd done with the other girls in town. What had been between them was more akin to him being able to see inside her head. Or maybe her heart. As though he'd been able to simply understand who she was.

Which was funny, because at that time in her life she'd had no idea *who* she was.

She'd just been sad. And missing her mom. And certain that everything that had ever gone wrong in her life had been her fault.

She turned back to the girls. Possibly what had been between her and Ben during those summers had simply been about her going through losing her mom while he'd been busy avoiding his. Whatever it had been, the two of them as friends had worked.

And that's what she'd missed when he'd left that last time. Her friend.

chapter two

Ben watched Dani walk out of the room, a kid on either side of her, and wished he was trailing along behind her. She was the reason he'd come to Montana, he realized. He hadn't thought about it when he'd called Gabe, but Dani was the person who'd shown him what a family could be.

The entire Wilde clan had.

But mostly Dani.

She'd been only twenty when he'd first met her, but she'd jumped into the role of surrogate mother to her brothers with an enthusiasm he hadn't been able to understand at the time. At first glance she'd seemed riddled with anxiety and strung a bit too tight. But then he'd begun to watch her. She'd been good at it. She hadn't been her brothers' actual parent, yet no real mother could have taken any better care of them.

Witnessing her make this house a home had forced him to understand what he'd been missing all his life. Or most of his life. He'd spent his first seven years living a couple hundred miles from here on a small cattle ranch with his uncle and grandparents. He'd had a normal life then. He'd seen his mother a few times a year when she'd come to visit, and that had worked for them. Sure, he'd occasionally wondered why he didn't live with her, but she hadn't ever lived on the ranch so it made a weird kind of sense. But his uncle had left when Ben was seven, and the next thing Ben knew, he was on a plane to LA. To live with his mother.

His priorities had been forced to change then. As was his mother's norm, everything became about being seen and auditioning for high-profile parts, even for him. Parts he'd never wanted, nor asked for. In front of the camera never interested him. He'd desired to be behind it. And not films, but stills.

When he'd finally convinced his mother of his interest in photography, she'd bought him his first SLR at the age of ten. And the rest, as they say, was history.

Dani's footsteps disappeared up the stairs, her murmured voice slipping down to the main floor, followed by his daughter's soft giggle. The sound lifted the hair on his arms as he realized it was the first time he'd heard Haley laugh.

Her mother had dropped her at his apartment three weeks ago, and he'd been doing nothing but floundering since. Most likely only making things worse. From what he could tell Haley hated him and would prefer to be anywhere else. Even with the mother who hadn't wanted her.

Nothing he'd done had made it any better, and he'd run out of ideas. So he'd come here.

Which had been the right decision. He was certain of it.

The Wildes were good people. Montana was good living. And if he did nothing else right as a parent, he'd introduce her to a different lifestyle. He didn't want Haley growing up in LA the way he had. It was no life for a kid. But he had no idea if he should stay here, either.

It *was* a great town, though. If nothing had changed, there was a closeness among the residents that he'd often craved as a child. He hoped Haley might like it, too.

An additional question that had haunted him over the past three weeks was what in the world would he do with himself? His job involved traveling the world. Without a kid. And he loved it. He was like his mother in that way.

He liked the notoriety that came with the job, the doors the position opened.

He liked the income. And he liked the perks.

When he wasn't shooting for a paid contract, he spent his time capturing the world for himself. Could he give that up? Recording the way he saw places and people had pretty much been his only ambition in life.

He *could* take Haley with him. He'd traveled with his mother; Haley wouldn't be the first kid to do so. And he had loved discovering new places.

Only . . .

He'd hated it more.

The nannies, the loneliness.

Having no real roots.

Another giggle hit his ears, matched by a second child's laughter, and he knew what he *needed* to do. He needed to give it up. All of it. He had Haley now.

He clenched a fist around the pricey stuffed animal he'd bought that she had yet to pay attention to, and wondered if he could really make this work. Three weeks ago he hadn't known he had a daughter, and now he'd canceled contracts, traded in his expensive sports car, and traveled from the Pacific coast to near the Canadian border.

Yet, his daughter still hated him.

Could he learn *how* to be a father? Or was he too much like his mother?

Whatever the answer, he had to accomplish at least one thing. He had to erase the fear he saw in Haley's eyes every day. He couldn't live with himself if he didn't do that.

❀

"Amazing meal, Dani girl. As always."

"Thanks, Dad." Dani didn't look directly at the man, but gave a small smile to the table as a whole. "I enjoyed cooking it for everyone."

"Yes," Gabe added. He leaned back and patted his stomach proudly. "Terrific as always."

Dani gave another tight smile as Ben took everything in. She'd been mostly quiet through dinner. But then, Michelle had done the majority of the talking.

Jenna leaned back, mimicking her father's actions by patting her own stomach, and piped up with a thanks of her own, and Haley even squeaked out a shy "Thank you" herself. The latter touched Ben's heart. Jenna and Haley had gotten along like long-lost friends all afternoon. She'd even smiled a couple of times throughout dinner. And she'd eaten most of the food on her plate.

This was apparently what he'd needed the last few weeks. Another child for his daughter to feel comfortable around. Hopefully by being around Jenna, Haley would eventually feel more at ease with him.

"As far as I can tell," Ben started, glancing at his daughter as he spoke and going for a teasing tone, same as he'd heard earlier from Dani, "she's some kind of meat loaf whisperer."

Jenna laughed at his words. Haley merely blinked.

Damn.

"What's a meat loaf whisperer?" Jenna asked.

Ben pretended his daughter was as interested in his answer as her friend was, and included them both in his explanation. "It's someone who can take a pound of beef"—he lifted both hands and moved them like he was molding and shaping a block of clay—"and work it, and coax it into this magical"—he wiggled his fingers and waggled his eyebrows—"amazing meal we just ate."

Jenna laughed again, her chuckle lighthearted and fun, and Haley *almost* lifted one corner of her mouth. He let the air out of his chest. It would have to do.

He snagged Dani's gaze over Jenna's head as her blue eyes locked in on him. He'd caught her watching him several times throughout the meal, and he couldn't help but wonder what was going through that brain of hers. Had she picked up on just how much his daughter hated him?

Or was she thinking about the past? About them?

Whatever had been running through her mind, he was appreciative of the warm welcome from everyone. Being included brought him back to good times. He'd always enjoyed being here. It felt like family.

And he'd always enjoyed the pleasant scenery that was Dani. That hadn't changed.

Her dark hair, piled on top of her head, formed a soft halo around her features, and her soft gray shirt had a way of accenting her eyes. He hadn't thought about her too much over the years. He hadn't let himself. But sitting here, sharing a meal with her tonight, had flooded him with memories. She'd always done the cooking. She'd always done the cleaning. And she'd never once complained.

Dani Wilde was a sweet, hardworking, amazingly capable woman.

Whose innocence he'd taken the last time he'd been here.

Guilt closed his throat as he glanced away from her. That night had crossed his mind about a thousand times over the last week. He'd known, if he planned to come back here, he would have to face what he'd done.

Not that she'd been innocent in all of it.

She'd come on to him first. Then she'd showed up at his room later that night and practically stripped naked just inside his door. But he should have at least called after he left. Or something. Sent a thank-you card? An "I'm sorry" card?

Made sure she didn't leave his room that night?

Or . . .

He glanced down at his plate. He could have not slept with her at all.

Heaviness sat in his chest as Max began telling a story about a trip he and Gloria had recently taken to the East Coast. Ben tried to focus on the words, but his mind wasn't through playing with the past.

Dani had been a virgin. At twenty-two.

He never would have imagined that.

On the other hand, he should have known. Hadn't she told him during one of their many talks that she hadn't really dated in high school? She'd been too focused on getting a scholarship. Then her mother had been killed in a car accident and after only two months at college, Dani had come home to help her dad finish raising her brothers. When would she have had time to sleep with anyone?

And what right had he to take that from her even though she *had* offered it? After all her family had done for him. He'd felt like a heel.

And he *hadn't known* she'd been a virgin.

"Dani will have to check it out after she moves. See if she likes it as much as you two."

Gabe's words brought Ben out of the past, and he let his mind replay what Max and Gloria had been saying. Something about a museum . . .

In New York.

He turned to Dani. "You're moving to New York?"

He remembered how badly she'd wanted to live there—to live in the middle of that kind of excitement. That's why she'd worked so hard for her scholarship. She'd dreamed of it, just as her mom had.

"Next month," she answered. Her face lit with joy. "I have a job waiting on me."

Warm delight filled him. "Congratulations."

"Thanks." When she bit her lip in a fashion similar to Haley, it had a completely different effect on him.

Damn. He still wanted her.

"What kind of job?" he asked, forcing his mind away from her mouth.

"Marketing. I finished my degree a few years ago, and will be hiring on with one of my long-term clients in the city."

He was dumbfounded. "You have clients in New York City?" Of course she'd have clients in New York City. Probably all around the world. The woman didn't do anything halfway.

She glowed from her seat. "Several," she announced proudly. "Though only one on a large scale. I targeted BA Advertising for the full-time job potential, and it paid off. They've been trying to get me out there for over a year now, but I didn't want to leave until Jaden graduated college. He's traveling right now, but will be home before harvest. He'll take over the books when I go."

"You do the books for the farm?"

She nodded. "That's one of my jobs."

"She's always got her nose stuck in her laptop," Michelle butted in.

Ben saw Gabe slide his hand under the table and put it on Michelle's leg, and Michelle shot him a nasty look. But it did shut her up. Dani didn't let herself be goaded by the other woman's words, though her shoulders did tense. Ben had gotten the impression throughout the afternoon that Michelle didn't care for her sister-in-law at all. He was thinking the feeling was mutual.

"She's right," Dani said casually, not so much as granting Michelle a look. "If I'm not working on the books, I'm putting in hours for a paid client, or brainstorming new ideas for the farm or the store we opened a few years ago. Or playing Dora the Explorer games." She winked at Jenna, and the young girl tittered happily on her seat. "Jenna loves to play games with me," Dani added.

Jenna nodded enthusiastically. "I'm good at them, too."

Dani finally glanced at her sister-in-law before returning her attention to Ben. "I spend a lot of time with my niece."

Michelle's eyes narrowed. Then she rose from the table.

"Come along, Jenna." Her tone was sharp. "It's time for your bath."

"Mo-om," Jenna whined. She edged back into her chair. "But I didn't get dessert yet."

"You don't need dessert. It'll make you fat."

Ben caught Dani stiffening once again, but she didn't respond to Michelle's words. Gabe went as still as his sister. However, the instant Michelle reached for Jenna's hand, he spoke up.

"Let her stay and have dessert."

The air in the room grew thick.

"Excuse me?" Michelle's tone iced over as she turned to her husband.

"We have company," Gabe explained. "She has a new friend. She's staying for dessert."

"I don't—"

"I don't care," Gabe interrupted. His eyes were hard. "She's having dessert with the rest of us."

Dani quietly rose and moved to the counter, her back to the group. She began slicing a pie and sliding individual pieces onto plates while Michelle and Gabe had a stare-off. The next instant, as if she realized they were arguing in front of a crowd, Michelle's posture eased and a bright smile flashed across her face. Her chin tilted at a haughty angle.

"Well, I, for one"—she shot Ben a look—"won't let a silly dessert ruin *my* figure."

With those words, she headed out of the room. Ben caught Jenna's fork shaking as she reached up and placed it on her plate, and Haley had slunk back in her seat, identical to her new friend. Gabe apologized to the room, his voice low and strained.

"Well." Max cleared his throat. He scratched at his neck, then cleared his throat again. "Before we lose anyone else, Gloria and I had something we wanted to say tonight."

Dani paused in her movements. She turned back to the table, and Gloria—who had to be well into her sixties—blushed. She took Max's proffered hand.

"No sense beating around the bush," the elder Wilde stated. "Gloria and I are getting married."

Dani appeared speechless, while Gabe barked out a chuckle and a hearty "Congrats!" He slapped his dad on the back.

"Congratulations," Ben said from the opposite end of the table. "You're a lucky man."

"Please." Gloria let the word roll out as she smiled up at Max. Love shone across her face. "I'm the lucky one. I've been trying to tie this man down for years."

"Well, you finally caught me, darlin'." Max kissed her hand, and she blushed again.

Laughter and chatter filled the room, and Ben couldn't help but keep an eye on Dani. She was laughing now, saying all the right things, but her expression had gone blank. Did she not like Gloria? The older woman certainly wasn't like Michelle. She'd been nothing but pleasant company all evening. And she seemed to genuinely care for Max.

"How about we do dessert and coffee in the family room?" Dani suggested. She quickly lined the saucers up on a serving tray while the rest of the adults filed into the connecting room. Ben, Jenna, and Haley remained sitting at the table.

"Can I go back to Jenna's room now?" Haley asked hesitantly.

Dani looked around at the question, and at Ben's seeking glance, she answered, "Don't you want dessert?"

Haley shook her head.

"I don't either," Jenna mumbled. She didn't look up from her plate.

"Me either," Ben decided on the spot. There were some weird dynamics going on in this household, and he hoped to help ease at least one of them. "How about you and I"—he spoke to Haley— "help Miss Dani clean up the dishes instead?" He'd heard other people refer to adults as "Miss" whoever around their kids. He hoped it was the right thing to do.

Jenna nodded. "Can I help too? I like doing dishes."

"Of course," Dani answered.

She glanced at Ben, her gaze hanging on his for several seconds. The look in her eyes reminded him of the summer they'd first met. And the word he'd often thought to himself to describe it. Broken. It had been a year and a half since she'd lost her mother, and from everything he'd learned, the woman had walked on water. She and her daughter had been close, and Dani had taken the loss particularly hard.

"Thanks," she murmured now.

He gave a small nod, wondering if she was remembering all the nights he'd stuck around back then to help clean up after dinner. He hadn't done so at first, instead heading into town with Gabe each evening. But during the last week of that first summer, he'd been hit with the realization that Dani always cleaned up after them. By herself. And that hadn't seemed fair.

Their time in the kitchen had been the beginning of many conversations between them. Not that first week. He didn't think anyone had ever offered to help, and she'd tried her best to send him out of the room each evening. But by the time he'd returned for Christmas, insisting once again that he would stick around for cleanup, the air in the room had eased.

They'd talked while doing the dishes. And laughed. About mundane things at first, but by the next summer they'd been onto topics with more substance. Their hopes and dreams. College. Careers. Eventually, their mothers.

He'd also started following her down to the small stretch of beach late in the evenings. The Wildes' property contained one hundred feet of lakefront access with a private boat slip, and Dani had made a habit of stealing away by herself.

Until Ben had begun joining her.

He looked at Haley again, forcing himself away from the memories. "What do you say?" he asked. "Want to help with the dishes?"

After a few seconds of silence, she solemnly nodded.

She didn't look at him as she climbed down from her seat, but as she and Jenna both carried their plates to the sink, she laughed softly at something the other girl said, and the sound was as gut wrenching as the first time he'd heard it.

It also gave him renewed determination to have her someday laugh with him.

chapter three

After Dani doled out the desserts to everyone in the family room, she and Ben fell into the easy rhythm they'd once shared, him clearing dishes from the table, her loading the dishwasher. She passed a handful of silverware off to the girls and showed Haley how to place the pieces one at a time into the plastic basket, then bit the inside of her lip to keep from smiling at the focused expressions that appeared on both faces.

She turned back to Ben for another plate, only to catch him watching her with his own contemplative look. Its intensity sent a tingle of awareness through her. Not that he was looking at her in a longing way. More like he was simply *looking* at her. Which was something no one had done in a long time.

And was only fair since she'd spent a generous portion of tonight observing him, as well.

He'd changed, but not so much. He'd filled out. Aged a little. But more than his physical appearance seemed different. When he'd come to their home all those years ago, he'd been a celebrity's son. He'd known it, and he'd understood the power that gave him. He hadn't been a jerk about it, but he'd walked with a privileged swagger.

Today he seemed more like a man trying to figure out his place in the world.

Granted, he still reeked of money. But if Dani were to guess, finding out he had a daughter had set him back a step or two. It had most likely made him see the world differently. Though exactly how he now saw it, she wasn't yet sure.

She lifted a brow when he continued to stare at her.

"You don't like Gloria?" he asked with a muted voice.

Her expression dropped and she glanced toward the great room. It was a large space, but there wasn't a wall connecting the two rooms. However, no one seemed to be paying attention to them.

"I like her fine," she muttered. "Why?"

"You didn't look happy with the announcement."

She snatched a plate off the table and bent to load it. Of course she was happy. Her dad had been with Gloria for a long time. He'd been without a wife for even longer.

She was happy.

When Ben still didn't hand her another dish, she finally looked back at him. "What?"

"You didn't look happy," he repeated softly.

"I'm happy," she said through gritted teeth, giving him a wide, toothy grin.

He snorted at her response, and she let her fake grin turn into a real one. This was what she'd missed for the last ten years. Someone to talk to at the end of the day. Someone who saw beyond the outer parts.

That ability of his had frightened her back then, yet at the same time it had comforted.

She found that it still comforted today.

"I am happy," she said, nodding her head in the direction of her family, where her dad was now laughing at something Gloria had said. She tried to picture her mom and dad in a similar situation. Laughing and enjoying the moment. She couldn't do it. "It just made me think of my mom," she told him. "I still miss her."

And she was certain her mother *had* once made her dad laugh. Even if she couldn't remember it.

"I'm sure you do." He handed the girls the last of the silverware. "But he deserves to be happy."

"I know. And really, I'm thrilled. Gloria is a great person. She's great for him. It's all . . . great," she finished lamely, lifting her hands, palms up.

"That's a lot of great." He scraped the remains of Michelle's half-eaten food into the garbage disposal and turned on the motor. When it stopped he passed over the plate. "Jealous?" he asked.

She made a face. "Of what?"

"I don't know. Gabe's married, has a kid. Your dad is getting married. Your brothers are all off doing their things. Living their lives."

"I'm living my life. I finished my degree, I told you that. I have a business. I'm moving to New York."

"Where'd you get your degree?"

She paused at his question—why would it matter? "U of M, Missoula. Mostly online, but I drove back and forth when a class demanded it. Why?"

"Not quite Columbia."

Her throat went tight. He remembered well. She'd worked so hard for that scholarship. Then regretted ever taking it. "It's a perfectly fine school," she pointed out.

"Only, you could have done more. You could have been Ivy League."

"Really, Ben." She rolled her eyes, wanting to change the subject. "Do you charm all the girls this way?"

He smiled then. A real smile for the first time that day. The curve came slow, and as she remembered it, it formed deep creases alongside his mouth. It was hot, naughty, and *definitely* loaded down with charm. "I try," he murmured suggestively.

She gulped.

He was teasing. She knew it. And she knew that he knew exactly what that smile could do to a woman.

Still didn't lessen the impact.

"Stop it," she murmured.

He laughed then, his eyes smiling along with his mouth, and handed her the last dirty dish. Then he propped himself in the corner of the countertop and crossed both arms over his chest. "So what about men?" His gaze flickered quickly over her. "Date much? Ever marry?" He glanced at her ring finger.

"Definitely haven't married." Her thumb rubbed over the bare spot on her finger as if it were missing a ring. "I have a career to get to."

"Aunt Dani doesn't like boys," Jenna supplied helpfully.

Both Dani and Ben gaped at the blonde as she put a spoon in the basket with great precision, then Ben slowly turned back to Dani. His eyes asked the question that neither of them voiced.

She burst out laughing. "Not like *that*," she assured him. "I *like* boys."

"I didn't think I remembered it that way," he murmured.

Heat touched her cheeks as she ignored his words and bent to load detergent in the dishwasher. She'd tried hard not to think about *that* all afternoon. She had lost her virginity to this man. He'd seen her naked. His hands had been on her body.

"Your mom would be proud of you," he said when she stood back up. "New York."

She appreciated his change of subject. "I'm counting on it."

New York was the main reason she'd rarely dated over the last ten years. Why she'd never considered long-term when she had.

And why Jenna thought she didn't like boys.

"You should be proud, too," he added.

She looked at him as she considered his words. Of course she was proud of herself. Right? She'd worked hard to get here. And she was darned good at her job.

She nodded. "Yeah," she said. "I'm proud of me, too."

But the conviction in her voice seemed to be missing.

"You deserve all your dreams, Dani. I'm glad you're getting them. I'm thrilled for you."

"Thanks." She smiled tightly, and wanted to lean in and give the man a hug. Or, more precisely, she wanted him to lean in and give her one. Just hold her. Because she didn't get held a lot.

"We done'd all the dishes," Jenna announced, yanking Dani's thoughts away from the comfort of hugs. Her niece stepped between them and looked up. "Can Haley sleep in my room tonight?"

They'd redone Jenna's room over the summer, adding an additional bed for sleepovers. So far it had gone unused. Dani glanced at Ben. "If it's okay with her dad," she said.

Both girls turned inquisitive eyes to Haley's father.

"But there's a cot in my room for you," Ben began, and Haley's excitement visibly faded. "You would have your own bed," he finished.

"She could have her own bed in my room, too," Jenna informed him. "I got buck beds."

Dani bit her lip at the mispronunciation.

When Ben raised his gaze to hers, she nodded. "She has 'buck' beds. It'll be fine."

"Michelle?" he mouthed.

Dani shook her head. "It's fine."

He looked back down at Haley then, who was still staring up at him. Her eyes were solemn and direct; her expression emotionless. The sight twisted Dani's heart. The child's mother had dropped her off with a virtual stranger, and that stranger now controlled every aspect of her life. He could also leave it as quickly as he'd appeared. As quickly as her mother had.

Dani could understand that desperation for something just out of her reach.

"Then I guess you're sleeping in Jenna's room tonight," Ben answered his daughter.

The child's entire face changed in an instant, and even better, Ben's changed along with it. Haley beamed at her daddy. And he beamed back.

It was stunning to watch.

"You both go on up and play," Dani told the girls. "I'll come up soon and help you take a bath, then read you a story before bedtime."

Four feet scurried out of the kitchen, and when Dani turned back to Ben, she couldn't miss the marvel in his eyes.

"How long has she been with you?" she asked.

He didn't answer until they heard footsteps overhead. Then he let out a long, slow breath. "Three weeks," he answered.

"She smile for you much?"

His Adam's apple moved up and down as he swallowed. "Only tonight."

Dani came darned close to giving him that hug she'd so wanted for herself. "You planning on keeping her?" she asked instead. He was here with her. Dani had questioned all afternoon whether that meant he was trying to figure out how to make it work, or if he was somehow looking for an out. *He* had been dumped off on a ranch in Montana as a kid, after all.

"I'm keeping her," he said. The words came out as uncertain as he looked.

"Her mother?"

He shook his head. "Not coming back."

Dani wanted to find the woman and rip out her throat. "Then I'm glad you came here," she said softly. "And I'm glad I got to witness the first of what I've no doubt will be many smiles aimed your way."

He nodded absently, rubbed his hand over the day's scruff on his jaw, and looked in the direction of the stairs. After several seconds, as if only then registering her words, he brought his gaze back to hers. "You're okay with me being here?"

"Of course."

"I was planning to stay through harvest," he said, leaving the sentence hanging like a question. Four weeks at the minimum.

"If Gabe's good with it." She nodded. "I have no problem. You're his friend."

"I was your friend too."

Oh. She glanced away. He meant because of *that*. She grabbed the dishcloth to wipe the table down.

"I was more," he said behind her.

She shook her head, but didn't stop what she was doing. "It was just a thing, Ben. No biggie."

"Right," he agreed. "But it was a *thing*." When she edged within reach, he nudged her foot with his. She ignored him and kept wiping at the now clean table. So he did it again. If they discussed it now, they could be done with it for the future. She got the point he was trying to make.

Stopping her movements, she clenched the cloth in her hand and turned to face him.

Solid green eyes burned steady on hers. "We never talked about it after," he said.

Which had been her fault. She'd been a coward and had been out of the house the next morning before he'd gotten up. She stayed gone all day, and he'd returned to college that afternoon.

She'd seduced him, plain and simple. He'd never once shown that kind of interest in her, and she'd felt shame for what she'd done.

She'd felt like her mother.

The thought froze her for a full three seconds. Why would seducing Ben have made her feel like her mother?

She shook her head in denial. "We didn't need to talk about it. It was just a thing."

He stared at her for a moment longer, the power of his concentration reaching deep inside her, but she refused to blink first. She would not let him see her nerves.

Or know how much that night had actually meant to her.

chapter four

"And Cinderella and the prince lived happily ever after." Dani lowered the book and peered down at the two four-year-olds snuggled in tight, one on either side of her under Jenna's pink comforter. The girls both wore matching smiles of contentment while their eyelids drooped with much-needed sleep.

This was the fourth night Haley had stayed at the house, and as on every other night, the two girls had crawled into the same bed before talking Dani in with them.

Ben had spent the better portion of his days in the orchard with Gabe, leaving Haley with Dani. Which was okay; she'd offered to keep an eye on the girl while he caught up with her brother. It gave Jenna someone to play with, and Michelle less time to complain that she had to do anything for her daughter. With Haley and Jenna keeping each other company, it even allowed Dani to get more work done than she'd anticipated. She had several projects needing completion before she left town, so she'd been working steadily to wrap them up.

But Dani got the feeling Ben was doing more than remembering good times with his friend. She thought he might be avoiding his daughter.

She supposed that was the easy thing to do. He did seem overwhelmed with his new responsibilities, and Haley certainly hadn't made it any easier on him. No matter what Dani had caught him saying to the girl when they *were* in the same room together, the child had yet to crack another smile for her father. She barely even spoke.

It had to be frustrating to be getting nowhere with her, but he had to keep trying. They needed to form a connection. Haley had to learn she could trust him. Leaving her with someone else all day, or sitting her in front of a kids' movie, was not the way to win over his daughter.

Closing the book she'd just read, Dani wrapped an arm around each child and squeezed tight. "Did you like *Cinderella*?" she asked them both.

Not that it was the first time either had heard the story in the last few days.

"Yeah." Jenna sighed out the word. She pressed both palms to her cheeks, and her mouth puckered in between her two hands. "But I wanna prince."

"Me too," Haley agreed. She snuggled deeper into Dani's side.

Me three, Dani thought. Then she twisted her mouth into a sarcastic smirk. No. She didn't. She had no time for a prince.

But she could use a temporary stand-in.

She added an eye roll to the smirk. That was a crazy dream, as well. Ben wouldn't likely be interested, even if she was.

She leaned back and stared up at the ceiling as the girls listed princely qualities, and thought about Ben. The last few days she'd barely spent any time with him, but her hormones had been wildly attuned to his every move. A warm, outdoorsy smell trailed along behind him whenever he walked through a room. It left her yearning to bury her nose into the side of his neck. She'd just bet it was warm there.

And then there were his jeans. Those babies should be outlawed.

Heck, his *jeans* had even showed up in her dreams.

But other than the quick conversation that first night about him staying here, there had been no further discussions about "that."

Which was good. He had a daughter to concentrate on.

And Dani had plenty of other things to occupy her time. She did not need a quickie with Ben Denton.

She tweaked her niece's nose, before doing the same to Haley's. She shouldn't even be thinking about Ben like that. "Silly girls," she teased. "What would you two do with a prince if you had one?"

Blue eyes very similar to her own peered up at her in a fashion suggesting she'd lost her ever-loving mind. "He would play with me whenever I want, Aunt Dani."

"Even Barbies?" Dani winked. If there was one thing Jenna loved as much as Cinderella, it was Barbies.

Wide eyes grew so round they seemed to fill Jenna's small face. "Of course. He'll haf to since you won't be here no longer."

"Any longer." Dani corrected without thought, but couldn't stop the sadness from creeping in at the thought of how much she would miss this child. She wished she could take her with her.

"I'll play with you, Jenna." Haley's soft voice spoke up from the other side of the bed. "I never played with Barbies before I got here, but I love it."

Her innocent statement made Dani wonder what Haley's life had been like before she'd met her dad. She'd never played with Barbies? Hard to imagine. But then, equally hard to envision a mother dropping her daughter off and never looking back. For someone who'd been through that, Haley was actually doing remarkably well.

Except for the not-speaking-to-her-father part.

"Thank you, Haley," Dani said. "I'm sure Jenna would love to play Barbies with you."

"I would," Jenna agreed around a yawn. "Just like we did today. I like playing Barbies with you."

"And with Mike," Haley added. At the mention of his name, the dog lifted his head from the foot of the bed. His tail thumped the mattress, and Haley giggled.

Jenna patted her hand on the bed. "Come up here, Mike. We need you to lay with us."

Right. Like two munchkins and one adult didn't take up enough space across the width of the twin bed. But like the good dog that he was, Mike roused himself and scooted closer to his owner. He stretched out along Jenna's legs and rested his snout on her hip, and Dani let her head sink deeper into the pillow. She closed her eyes. She loved this time of night. Gabe occasionally put Jenna to bed himself, but it was more Dani's ritual.

Michelle rarely saw the need for more than a simple "Good night."

If Dani ever had a daughter, she would make sure to—

She stopped herself midthought. She couldn't imagine that she'd ever have a daughter, so there was no need to let the hypothetical go any further. Not that she wouldn't love a daughter. A son, too. But given the fact that she was already in her thirties and her career was just now about to start, she didn't hold out hope. By the time she'd made a name for herself, she'd probably be too old to birth a child, much less find a man who wanted her.

She'd have to be content with the role of aunt, and having cared for her brothers over the years.

It was enough.

Because she wanted New York.

Her broker had forwarded a link for an apartment today, with the email address of the woman already living there. The place was a bit pricier than she'd hoped, but with a roommate, Dani would be able to juggle it. It was definitely a possibility.

Then there was the job.

And the energy of the city.

It had been nineteen years since she'd first visited New York— Aunt Sadie had taken her on a girls' trip, just the two of them—but Dani still remembered every detail. She wanted that life. And it was finally at her fingertips.

Both girls inched closer, and Dani's elation waned. She would miss this a lot.

She pressed a kiss to the top of a silky blonde head, then to the top of a silky brown one, the scent of baby shampoo filling her nostrils, and she sent up a prayer that she was making the right choice. She worried so much about leaving Jenna.

"I like this." Haley's soft voice floated up to Dani.

"Like what, honey? Sleeping in here with Jenna?"

"Yes, but . . ." She lifted one of her hands, let it hover momentarily in the air, before touching a single fingertip to Dani. "I like you."

Dani's heart pinched. "I like you too, baby. A whole lot."

She reached out and clicked off the lamp as she felt the two bodies at her sides growing heavy with sleep, and stared up at the stick-on stars glowing from the ceiling.

No amount of logic about stars and constellations had been enough to sway Jenna from what she'd wanted. Dani and the little girl had spent hours this summer planning exactly what would twinkle down on her every night, and Dani had to admit that Jenna's ideas were far better than anything that could be seen nightly from outside their back door.

There were the "constellations" Pumpkin Carriage and Cowboy's Hat. And of course, The Big Heart and The Little Heart. Jenna was a dreamer. Dani hoped that never changed.

"I still wish I had a prince," Jenna whispered.

"Me too," Haley echoed.

Dani stared into the darkness and admitted something she hadn't let herself acknowledge for a long time. Being alone hadn't been part of her plan.

Her gaze traced the outline of Cowboy's Hat. "Me three," she admitted softly. A sigh slipped out with the word.

"What's the matter, Aunt Dani?" Jenna asked. "Are you sad?"

"No, baby. Not sad. Just thinking about princes."

"Oh." Jenna grew quiet, then spoke in a hushed voice. "I hope you find one."

Dani kissed her niece's forehead. *Someday.* Right now she had something else to do.

Lifting the covers, she shifted Haley so she lay right next to Jenna, and Mike flipped his tail as though acknowledging he was on watch duty. Instead of leaving immediately, though, Dani lay back down, this time on top of the covers.

She perched on her side. "It's time for you two to go to sleep, don't you think?"

The light filtering in from the hallway made it easy to see Jenna shake her head back and forth. "I don't wanna until my daddy gets home. I need to give him and my mom a bedtime kiss."

Gabe and Michelle had gone out to dinner for date night. "They'll be out for a while longer. How about you kiss me, and I'll pass it on to them?"

After a slight hesitation, Jenna agreed. She puckered her little mouth and Dani leaned in to accept the kiss. She then caressed Jenna's soft cheek. Soon there would be no more times like this. Logically, she'd known that, but it seemed to be sinking in hard tonight.

Haley lifted up on her elbows and pressed a timid kiss to Dani's cheek as well, catching her slightly off guard. "Will you give that one to my daddy?"

Dani's thoughts shot instantly beyond a kiss on the cheek to something very, very different. But explaining why she would *not* be kissing Ben in any fashion seemed harder than simply agreeing. "Sure, sweetie. I'll give it to him."

She'd at least tell him about it. Maybe that would loosen him up a bit when it came to his daughter.

"Thank you," they said in unison.

"Go to sleep now, sweethearts. When you wake up, we'll play Barbies for as long as you want."

"Okay," they returned, and Dani began to rise.

"Aunt Dani . . ."

She paused. "Yes?"

"I'll miss you lots when you're gone."

Tears suddenly appeared and slipped over her cheeks. "Me too." She leaned down and gave both girls one last hug. "Lots."

Straightening, she headed for the bedroom door, needing to get out before more leakage occurred. She wiped her face and stepped into the hall, pulling the door shut behind her.

And when she turned, Ben stood waiting for her, an unreadable expression on his face.

After several seconds, he finally muttered, "You're great with them."

Embarrassment crashed over her that he'd caught the moment. She looked away, ending up fixating on the woven rug running the length of the hall, as she worked to get a handle on her emotions. "Thank you," she mumbled.

"You're close to Jenna."

She nodded.

Several more seconds ticked by as she waited, wanting nothing more than to escape to her room—certainly not to stand there with her heart open and Ben looking in. But she found herself unable to kick her feet into gear.

His hand reached out, and he swiped at a tear with his thumb. Two more followed in its path.

"Can I ask you something?" he said.

She nodded again, still keeping her eyes averted, and rubbed at her cheek.

There was a long pause before his voice came out so low and quiet that she caught herself leaning closer to hear it. "How'd you learn to do that?" he asked.

She peeked up. "Do what?"

A slight inclining of his head toward the closed bedroom door was all the information he gave. She focused on the shellacked wood separating them from the girls. And then she got it.

He wasn't avoiding Haley because he didn't want to be around her. He had no idea what to *do* around her. "Let's go back in," she said. She reached for the doorknob, but he caught her hand before she could turn it.

"Don't." His voice was barely audible. "Don't bother them."

"But she would love it. Don't you want to tell her good-night?"

"Nah." He gave a quick shake of his head, his eyes wearing a quietness that strummed a sad song through her heart, and took a small step back. He didn't let go of her hand. "She didn't ask for me."

"Yes, she did, she . . ." Dani clamped her lips shut when she realized what she was about to say. *She wanted me to kiss you.*

Electricity filled the space as his gaze tracked to her mouth. "I heard what she said."

Dani swallowed. "So you see? She *was* thinking about you."

"Sure." He released her hand. "She thought of me." He took another step back and motioned toward the room again. "What I want to know is how all that is so natural to you. How do you know what to do? What they need from you?"

How completely precious. This was powerful stuff.

"She just needs to spend time with you, Ben. That's all. Read her a story, talk to her. Show her that you love her. Jenna's been around me since birth. It gave me the advantage here."

He nodded, hanging on her every word.

Show her in more ways than sitting in the same room with her while she watches a Disney DVD, she wanted to add, but suspected he got it without her voicing the thought. She touched his arm, the muscles below the skin bunching. "She just wants to know you're there for her."

"Of course I'm there for her, but she . . . you . . ." He shook his head, frustration etching his features. "She laughs and talks to you. I can barely get her to look at me."

Her heart completely flattened under the weight of his pain. "It's new for you both. You're as scared as she is and she can sense that. She's already had one parent disappear on her." She lifted her shoulder in a shrug. "She's not comfortable with you yet. That's all."

"But with you—"

"With me she knows I'm not the parent who's supposed to stick around forever. It makes it easier to relax. To accept me for exactly who I am. I'm the fun aunt. The one who plays Barbies and reads stories." She paused. "I'm not a threat."

Her words removed some of the strain from his face, but the rest of him remained coiled tight. She waited while he digested her words. He seemed to turn them over in his mind and study them.

He was a thing of beauty to watch, even when the only thing he was doing was thinking about his daughter.

Especially when the only thing he was doing was thinking about his daughter.

Finally, he nodded, slowly at first, then with more certainty. "I see what you mean. I'm a threat."

"Only because she's scared. It's not you personally."

"I get that," he murmured. "I just have to prove myself."

"Exactly. You can start putting her to bed at night, if you'd like. That would help." It would also mean that Dani wouldn't get to do it for Jenna since the girls were sleeping together.

"Include her in things." He nodded. "Talk to her."

"Yes, right." She smiled up at him. "You're already a good father, Ben. You let her into your life. You brought her here. Soon you'll be a terrific one."

He locked his gaze on hers. "You really think so?"

"I know so." Her head felt almost too heavy to nod.

He glanced at the door again, before coming back to her. "Will you help me?"

The plea punctured her heart. "However I can."

"Just teach me how to be a good parent."

They stood together, mere inches separating them once again, when a noise on the stairs pulled their attention. Turning together, they saw Michelle come around the bend. She eyed Ben as if he were the dessert she never allowed herself, then reached behind her and unzipped her dress.

At the same time her foot touched the landing, the material dropped from her shoulders. It hung at her waist as she passed them, her fingertips skimming Ben's shoulder blades along the way, and at the bedroom door, the dress hit the floor. She stood in nothing but four-inch heels and a matching thong and bra.

Then she disappeared behind the door.

It had all taken a matter of seconds, but it was enough to ease the moment. She and Ben turned to each other, and both burst out laughing.

"I'm not imagining that, right?" he asked, motioning to the master bedroom. "She's been flirting with me?"

"Well, I'm no authority on flirting, but that's what it looks like to me."

"Why?"

Dani shook her head, out of ideas concerning Michelle. "Heck if I know." But it bothered her greatly. Her brother didn't deserve that for a wife.

They both stared at the closed door once more, and Dani decided that Michelle's interruption marked a good time for her to make her exit. She had a couple of hours of work to do before she went to bed, and she also wanted to get started packing up her belongings. Harvest would begin next week, and she'd be leaving immediately after. She didn't want to worry about cleaning out her room while the rest of her family was home.

"So you're good?" she asked, putting a foot of distance between them. "About Haley?"

"I'm good." He gave a small smile. "At least, I know where to start."

"'Kay," she breathed. His smiles got her every time. "I'll see you tomorrow then." She headed for the stairs before she was tempted to strip out of her own clothes, but stopped at the sound of his voice.

"Dani." The word was spoken quietly.

She turned back. "Yes?"

"What about what Haley said?"

"What do you mean?"

In two strides he was back in her space. "She gave you something for me."

Haley hadn't—

Dani sucked in air. "The kiss?" Her eyebrows shot up.

Ben shrugged, his shoulders practically rippling under his shirt, as mischief played in his eyes. "It *was* meant for me."

She laughed and shook her head. "Not going to happen, Hollywood. Our kissing days are over. You'll just have to *tell* her that I gave it to you."

"Now what kind of a parent would I be if I started off by lying to my own daughter?" He shook his head and tapped a finger to his lips. "I want my kiss."

He gave an exaggerated pucker. The truth was, she wanted a kiss too. Only, not the one his daughter had given her. But if he wanted to play, she could play.

In fact, she suddenly felt very much like playing.

"Well." She drew the word out in her most sultry voice. "Since you insist."

She rested her hands on his chest, and his teasing expression turned instantly to heat. The overexaggerated pucker disappeared, the change catching her off guard, and she was left with the understanding that she wasn't alone with her attraction.

Which she did *not* need to know.

Unsure why she continued stoking this particular fire, yet unable to help herself, she lifted to her toes and slid one hand up to his face. He stilled, and with a patience she did not feel, she turned his cheek to her mouth, and she leaned in for a soft peck.

Just barely grazing his cheek.

A shiver ran the length of her body at the feel of his rough whiskers under her lips, then she pulled away, breathed in his heady scent, and said softly, "Good night, Daddy."

Dani disappeared down the stairs as Ben watched with his tongue hanging out. *Damn.*

He wanted to chase after her and drag her to her room, assuming she didn't smack his face simply for suggesting it. But doing so would surely complicate his already complicated life.

It didn't last time, his overeager self informed him.

And no, it hadn't. Not really.

He hadn't seen her the morning after, nor had he returned for Christmas that year. Neither of which had done anything to ease his remorse. But they *had* seen each other at his and Gabe's graduation ceremony the following spring. Pleasantries had been exchanged, and Dani hadn't seemed in the least angry. It had been cordial.

No complications.

Yet something told him that this time around would be different. He was no longer a cocky twenty-one-year-old just looking for a good time. He had a kid now. He needed to figure out what to do with his life.

Stripping Dani of her clothing simply to see if she still moved the same way underneath him would not, necessarily, help him with any of that.

But good Lord, did he want to.

Footsteps once again fell on the stairs, and his body went on red alert. Was she coming back?

But it wasn't Dani. Instead, Gabe appeared.

He glanced at the girls' closed door. "Everyone asleep?"

"They just went down," Ben told him. "Jenna was asking for you."

A faint smile touched Gabe's face. "She likes to get a kiss every night."

Though the smile was there, Ben didn't miss the soberness that remained in Gabe's features. The same sense of defeat Ben had noticed every day since he'd been back. He had yet to ask about it.

Then Gabe's gaze landed on something at the far end of the hall. Michelle's dress.

"What the hell?" he muttered.

Ben tensed. *Shit.* How was he supposed to explain to his buddy that his wife had just stripped in front of him?

But he didn't have to. Gabe got it. "She took it off out here?"

Ben nodded. *Double shit.*

"And I take it that *you* were out here when she did?"

"I'm sorry—"

Gabe's harsh laugh cut him off. "*I'm* sorry. She likes to make a point when she's mad."

"Ah," Ben murmured. He thought he understood. "The night out didn't go well?"

"The night out went as good as every other night for the past six months. Three hours of nonstop complaining about how she hates Birch Bay and wants to move."

"Damn."

"Tell me about it. If we don't relocate, I think she might leave me."

Ben didn't ask if that would be such a bad thing. He knew nothing about their marriage or their relationship. He only knew that the wife was a flirt.

"Don't say anything to Dani, will you?" Gabe scratched at the back of his neck as he once again stared at the far end of the hall.

"About the possibility of you moving?" Ben asked. "Or a divorce?"

Flat eyes turned to him. "Either. I just need to hold it together until she's gone." Gabe looked at the dress once more, shook his head, and muttered, *"Sonofabitch."* Then without another word, he slipped into the girls' room.

Ben could hear him telling both girls good-night before he exited, gave Ben a nod, and headed for his wife. Leaving Ben once again staring at a closed door, knowing that his daughter was on the other side of it.

He stepped forward.

He hadn't really thought about it since he'd first learned of Haley, but he'd once wanted to be a dad. He hadn't been in any hurry, assuming it would happen when the timing was right. When he met the right woman. But he had wanted it.

And now he had it.

And it scared the living shit out of him.

What if he did it all wrong? Screwed her up?

What if she never grew to like him?

He cracked the door open, but instead of going in, he remained just outside of the opening, his biggest fear making an unwelcome appearance in his head.

What if he was no better at parenting than his mother had been?

He leaned his forehead against the doorframe, listening to his daughter talk. She was explaining to Jenna that her mother would be coming back to get her soon. And Ben knew for an absolute fact that she would not. He'd made sure of it.

But what was he supposed to say to that?

Feeling even more inept than usual, he silently pulled the door back to him. Right before it closed, the pink stuffed rabbit he'd bought at the trendy boutique near his apartment caught his eye. It was lying on the opposite side of the room, shoved half under a dresser.

Forgotten.

chapter five

The rip of tape filled the air as Dani secured another box. Then she stood back and surveyed the damage.

Unlike fourteen years ago when she'd packed up her clothes and only her favorite items before heading to New York, over the past couple of days, she'd gone through thirty-two years' worth of memories tucked away in her bedroom closet. She'd found more than one forgotten item. It had been fun sorting through everything, only now she wanted to take even more of it with her.

But wherever she ended up, her apartment would no doubt be tiny. Space would be at a premium. Therefore, the majority of her belongings would stay here, stored in the attic until she found a more permanent, and larger, place. The other boxes would ship out when she did.

She glanced at the open closet, at the condensed amount of clothes hanging on the rack. She had three weeks left here, but she'd kept out everything she would need. What remained would go into the suitcases she'd be taking with her.

Eyeing the remainder of the room, an overwhelming sense of sadness engulfed her at the distinct lack of *stuff*. There would soon be no traces of her left.

Her bed and dresser would be shipped out, as well, along with a few pictures from the walls and a couple of other pieces throughout the house. But other than that, that's all she'd be taking with her. Maybe a few dishes. But those had been her mother's, and Dani didn't feel right taking much. This had been her mother's house, and Dani had never pushed to change much up. Her dad and brothers hadn't either. It seemed more respectful to keep traces of their mom around. A way to honor her memory.

Studying the dressing table, then the antique desk in the corner, Dani decided to go ahead and sort through the desk tonight. It had been her grandmother's, handed down to her dad and then to her, but she hadn't used it since setting up her office in the study years ago. Curious as to what she might find tucked away inside, she settled into the chair.

Pulling open the bottom drawer, the first thing she saw made her smile.

It was a square box, deeper than it was wide, and almost too deep for the drawer. She tugged it out and removed the lid. A rhinestone tiara sat cushioned on a swath of black velvet, the topmost jewel having dulled after years of no use. She'd won the title of Miss Cherry Blossom as a senior in high school, and had worn this crown with pride.

Until her mother made her feel insignificant.

She paused with her thumb caressing the stones. What?

But the memory was gone. She closed her eyes and tried to bring it back. Her mother had . . .

Dani shook her head. Nothing.

Absolutely nothing came to mind. But she couldn't believe her mother had done anything that would make her feel bad about winning the crown. Her mother had been the one to encourage her to enter the competition. Miss Cherry Blossom was part beauty contest and part academic, and though not as gorgeous as her mother, Dani had held her own with her classmates. Winning this title had added much-needed money to her scholarship.

She lifted the crown out of the box and moved to the mirror at the dressing table. And as if she were still eighteen, she placed it on the top of her head and struck a pose.

The sight made her think of Ben and all the models he'd met over the years.

And the fact that he'd even had his own princess. Who no doubt had a *real* crown.

She made a face at herself in the mirror. Good for him. While he'd been living the life, she'd been stuck here in Birch Bay having one crappy relationship after another.

Not that she'd wanted a forever relationship. But she would've liked to have had one that didn't end up with her waiting on the guy hand and foot. However, every single man she'd gone out with for more than a few weeks had somehow ended up getting her to run around more like his servant than his lover.

That's the reason she'd eventually quit dating.

She returned to the desk, leaving the crown on her head, to see what else she could find. And what she found was a hot-pink boa.

Her legs folded underneath her as she sank to the floor. Tugging the boa from the drawer, she smoothed her fingers over the soft feathers and let it trail over the back of her hand. This had been a birthday present to her mother when Dani had been seven. After saving up her allowance for over a month, she'd spent thirty minutes at the school's fall festival picking out the perfect gift—pink had been her mother's favorite color. Dani had been certain her mother would love it.

But she hadn't.

She wouldn't even put it on.

Which seemed so contradictory to everything else Dani remembered about her mom.

Yet the memory was strong enough that it threatened to cut off the oxygen to her lungs. She pressed a hand to her mouth, sucking in a deep gulp of air as she worked to recall the specifics of that day. But all she got was that her mother had not liked the feathers, and that she'd refused to put it on.

In fact, she'd wanted to throw it away, but Dani had . . .

Dani lifted her chin and stared at nothing as another memory crashed over her. Her mother *had* thrown it away. Dani had snuck into the laundry room in the middle of the night and retrieved it from where it had been crammed in with handfuls of lint from the dryer. She'd hidden it in her backpack for weeks after that, terrified her mom would find it.

Dani wasn't sure where she'd stashed it after that, but clearly, it had eventually made it into the drawer with her crown.

The open drawer mocked her now, as she wondered what else she might find in there. And if she even wanted to know. So far, the two things she'd pulled out had retrieved painful memories she hadn't known existed.

And that she couldn't explain.

Why be so cruel as to throw away a gift from a child? Granted, it was tacky, and Dani could see that now. No woman in her right mind would want to wear a hot-pink boa to run errands in town, sure. But a seven-year-old wouldn't get that. And to toss it into the trash?

She ripped the crown from her head and shoved both it and the boa carelessly into the open drawer. Then she slammed it closed and clambered to her feet. The room seemed stifling all of a sudden.

Yanking open the door, she headed for the kitchen.

Only to stop short at the sound of Ben's low voice.

"Did you want to use the red one?" There was a pause before he asked, "Blue?"

Another pause.

"Green?"

Several seconds of silence ticked off before Dani heard Haley's soft voice say, "Pink."

"Sure. Pink is nice."

Dani tiptoed down the hallway until she could see what was going on. Ben and Haley were sitting at the kitchen table, and Haley had a page from a coloring book in front of her.

"You're supposed to stay inside the lines," Ben explained.

Haley shifted very slightly in her seat so that her shoulder pointed toward her dad. She was trying to block him out.

The sight broke Dani's heart once again. He'd been trying so hard the past couple of days, but the child wasn't budging. He'd put her to bed the night before, and had even taken her into the orchard with him earlier today. Dani had seen them leave together, him carrying a camera and her clasping one of Jenna's dolls to her chest. They'd come back less than thirty minutes later, and Haley had spent the remainder of the day playing with Jenna and Dani.

"Did you want me to show you how?" Ben asked, trying yet again to get the girl to respond.

"Hey," Dani said, forcing cheer to her voice, as she entered the room. She shoved her own issues aside.

Ben looked up, but Haley remained focused on the page in front of her. She wasn't exactly coloring, but the tip of the crayon *was* on the paper.

"I see you two are coloring. Can I join you?"

"Sure," Haley mumbled. She pushed the paper to the empty spot in front of where Dani had pulled out a chair. Dani sat and took a careful look at the page, as though she were studying a great piece of art. The princess had a blue swipe over her face and a green one on the lower portion of her dress. There was no pink anywhere on the paper.

"Can I go to Jenna's room now?" Haley asked, the question directed at Dani.

Dani didn't immediately answer. But neither did Ben.

"How about you color with me instead?" Dani suggested. "I don't like to color by myself." She scooted her chair closer to Haley's, tucked in next to the girl, and picked up the blue crayon. "I think I'll start here." She positioned the color right on the outside of the line.

As she did, Haley's body tightened with anxiety. Dani ignored the nervousness of the child, coloring with wide, sweeping strokes on the blank corner of the page, and discreetly cut her eyes up at Ben. His were trained on her.

"He said that was wrong," Haley whispered.

"Nah." Dani shook her head. "Your dad just hasn't colored enough. He doesn't know that some of the prettiest pictures are made when you stay *outside* the lines."

"Really?" Haley asked. She bit her lip and clenched her fingers around the pink crayon.

"Sure," Dani said. She inched the paper back toward Haley. "Try it. I think this picture needs some pink on it."

And so she did. Haley first swiped a couple of streaks on the top left corner of the page, and when her father didn't say anything, she scrunched in her shoulders and began working in earnest.

A few of the marks made it onto the princess's dress, but most of them did not.

When Haley exchanged the pink crayon for an orange one—and pulled the paper all the way back in front of her—Dani once again took a peek at Ben. He gave her a tiny shrug as if to say he hadn't known what he was doing, and mouthed the words "Thank you" above Haley's head.

"You're welcome," she mouthed back.

She watched Haley continue to color, while letting her mind return to what lay hidden in her desk drawer. The thought of retrieving whatever else might be tucked inside made her feel ill.

"What's wrong?" Ben's terse question brought Haley's head up, but seeing that her dad wasn't talking to her, she swiveled to Dani.

"Nothing," Dani denied. How had he known something was wrong?

His eyes narrowed on her, and she felt locked into place. As if he didn't intend to free her until she answered his question truthfully. The man had always been excellent at seeing inside her head. She sighed.

"It's nothing," she reiterated. "I was just packing up some things in my room. Thinking about the past." She shrugged. "Brought up a couple of unpleasant memories, that's all."

"About?"

"Ben—"

"What about?"

She glanced at Haley, who had not returned to coloring. The girl was watching with curiosity, her eyes wide.

"My mom," Dani finally admitted. She let the words hang there as she brought her gaze back to Ben's. If he remembered much about their past conversations, he'd know how guilty she'd felt when she went off to college, leaving her mother here to handle everything by herself.

"How bad?" he asked.

She shrugged again. "Bad enough. Things I hadn't thought about in years. Since before we lost her."

Haley blinked. "You lost your mom, too?"

Oh, geez.

"Yeah, baby." Dani patted Haley's arm. "She . . . went away a long time ago. But that's okay. I have a really great dad."

The words only served to make Dani feel worse. She and her dad hadn't always seen eye to eye, and she'd been known to give him a hard time over the years. They'd been closer when she was younger, but things had shifted at some point. Though she couldn't quite put her finger on when, or even why, it had happened.

Haley took a quick peek at her father before refocusing on the picture in front of her, and Ben rose and went to the refrigerator. A smile formed on Dani's mouth even before he opened the freezer door. He remembered. And he understood the reason she'd come to the kitchen in the first place.

When he pulled out the gallon tub of chocolate ice cream, Haley perked up. "Do we get ice cream?"

"I think Miss Dani could use some," Ben told her.

Haley looked at Dani again, and all Dani could do was nod. Ben had not only seen that something was bothering her, but he remembered her go-to for crappy days.

"Two scoops?" he asked, and Dani almost wept.

One scoop was a not-so-perfect day that she just needed to unwind from. Two meant there was trouble. Add crumbled potato chips on top, and she needed to crawl under a rock and hide.

"Please," she answered.

He shot a questioning look toward the pantry, and she mutely nodded.

"Can I have two?" Haley asked.

"One is probably enough for you," Dani answered, not wanting Ben to have to be the bad guy, but also knowing that the child did *not* need two scoops of sugar.

Ben expertly crumbled a handful of chips over the ice cream and set Dani's bowl in front of her. He winked at his daughter when her mouth hung open at the sight of Dani's dessert.

"Looks gross, doesn't it?" Ben asked.

Haley wrinkled up her nose.

"Dani's had a bad day," he explained. "Two scoops is *only* for when you've had a bad day."

Haley's green eyes shifted to Dani's. "I'm sorry about your bad day," she said sweetly. Then she reached over and patted Dani on the hand, and once again, Dani was almost brought to tears. The child was adorable, and Dani wanted to hug her up. Actually, she wanted to hug up both father and daughter. The man had gotten her ice cream.

Instead, she pulled her gaze back to her bowl and dug in.

After Haley got her own bowl and Ben returned to the table without any for himself, he picked up the green crayon lying in front of him and ripped out another sheet from the coloring book. Haley watched with interest as she scooped creamy bites into her mouth, half of each spoonful dripping down her chin, and when Ben very purposefully began coloring everywhere but inside the lines, Dani witnessed a gorgeous smile break across the girl's face.

"Do you like coloring that way?" Haley asked her dad. Her tone was both hesitant and hopeful.

Ben sat back, studied the paper before him, then nodded with great authority. "I do. And I think Miss Dani was right. This is the prettiest picture I've ever made."

Haley giggled then, and Dani's heart skipped a beat.

"Mine is the prettiest, too," Haley declared.

"I do believe it is," her father agreed.

Both Dentons proceeded to color more pages, doing their best to hit nothing inside the lines, and though Dani's heart still clenched, it eased its grip as she watched them. After several more minutes, she quietly rose and took the rest of her ice cream back to her room. This was bonding time for father and daughter, and she didn't need to be in the middle of it.

chapter six

The laptop beeped as Ben inserted the media card from his camera. He'd made quite a few good shots as he'd roamed the grounds throughout the week, and he wanted to get a closer look at them. The area was as beautiful now as it had been when he'd been here as a college student. And if today was any indication, he thought it might grow on Haley, too.

He'd taken her into the orchard once again, and this time—thanks to something so simple as Dani subtly pointing out yesterday afternoon that four-year-olds didn't need rules to color by—Haley had actually talked to him. She'd also been mesmerized by the cherries hanging from the trees and the fact that she would soon get to eat them. He'd promised that when the time came, they'd all get their bellies full.

And as he usually did, he'd snapped pictures while they walked. In fact, he was pretty sure he'd captured one that he suspected would rank as one of the best of his life. His daughter. With honest happiness as she laughed up at him.

Of course, that hadn't lasted long. He'd been overconfident with his newfound parental skills, and had taken her into town for dinner and shopping. It had not gone well.

He moved the files from the card over to his hard drive and connected to the Internet to make a backup. As he waited for the copy to finish, he took in the study. This was Dani's domain. She spent a lot of her time in here, either doing administrative work for the orchard or creating magic for her clients. Some of that marketing magic was framed on the walls throughout the space, but the centerpiece of the room was a photo of the skyline of New York. It hung over the mantel.

It was the picture he'd given to her the second Christmas he'd been here.

He could do better today, but for a shot taken by a sixteen-year-old, it was pretty good. And she'd kept it. He didn't know if that was because *he'd* given it to her, or because New York had been her focus, but if he had to guess, he'd say the latter. She'd never struck him as the clingy type, and he doubted she would keep something just because it reminded her of him.

The computer finished copying, and he loaded the photo of his daughter.

Her face filled the majority of the frame, with a blurred background of cherry trees.

And man, was she gorgeous. He already knew he'd be fighting the boys off when she got older. It wouldn't merely be playing a part, either. A protective layer a mile wide had settled around him the instant he'd looked into her face for the very first time. Protectiveness and worry.

The worry had shocked him. He'd been so long on his own, he would have thought caring about someone else would require more of an effort. But thoughts about her consumed him. Would she be happy if they stayed here? Would she be able to make friends?

And if not here, then where?

Haley's mother, a woman he'd dated only long enough to take a trip with around the holidays five years ago, had shown up at his apartment declaring Haley his, and it had been abundantly clear that the child had never been a priority. Lia's career had had more downs than ups over the years, but she'd finally landed her big break. Or so she claimed. And their daughter had been in her way.

"She's yours," she'd told him. "It's your turn to play parent."

What an unbelievable thing for someone to hear, much less a four-year-old.

So Ben had taken Haley into his life. He'd shielded them both from public view, wanting to come up with a plan first, and had immediately started legal proceedings for full custody. Without visitation.

Lia hadn't hidden the fact that she didn't care to ever see Haley again, therefore he'd seen no point in drawing it out. Haley didn't need anyone like that in her life, and he intended to make sure she never experienced that kind of ugliness again.

Continuing to let thoughts of his daughter roll through his head, he clicked through the other pictures from the week. As he studied them, past phone calls came to mind. He'd been approached by publishing houses more than once to do a book, but he'd never put more than a passing thought into the idea. It hadn't been the right time.

However, now might just be the time. He could do a book from anywhere.

And surely he already had enough decent photographs to pull something together.

He'd traveled the globe since he was a kid, and had seen some of the most beautiful places in the world. What had caught his eye as a minor, he'd returned to as an adult, and replicated his earlier attempts. Only with a professional's eye and ability.

But now that the opportunity to seriously pursue the idea had arrived, he had no clue what kind of book to do.

Landscapes? People?

He had a talent for both.

He did make his living with people, though. Probably he should stick to that.

The thought brought to mind another of his favorite pictures, and he went in search of it. He clicked, perusing folder after folder until he found what he was looking for. It had been more than ten years since he'd taken it, but if he went with a book of portraits, it would have to be included. Possibly even the cover.

With a quick double-tap, he opened the file and immediately realized that no, in fact, he could *not* use this image in anything he might publish. This shot was only for him.

The vision instantly returned him to those summers.

He'd chased every girl he could find that first year, enjoying his freedom, not wanting to be too serious. But after he'd finally noticed Dani, he'd struggled to have interest in anyone else. They'd paled next to her.

During the day she'd worked hard to come across as tough and in control. Competent. She would have done anything for her family, and once her mind was set, she wouldn't let her brothers or her dad get in her way. But Ben had always watched her eyes. They'd told the real story. And what they'd told him was that she was sad. Strong and there for everybody during the day, but at night she'd slip away.

To recharge? To meet a local boy?

He hadn't known at first.

She'd always waited until the house had settled down before slipping out the back door. Assuming it to be a boy, jealousy had eventually driven Ben to follow. When he'd found her stretched out on the dock, he'd been unable to walk away. She'd done nothing but lie there, hands clasped behind her head, studying the stars.

After that, whenever she disappeared, he silently followed.

Finally, he couldn't stop himself. He went to her. That was when their friendship had taken a new turn. Their talks had deepened, and he'd often felt as though he could see to her soul. He'd shown her his, as well. He couldn't keep it from her. That had been the cool thing about them. He held nothing back.

He'd even told her of his loneliness as a kid, as well as the indifference of his mother.

Everyone assumed that being the son of Angelica Denton gave him a leg up. That the advantages made life one great adventure.

But not everyone liked the kind of benefits that life came with.

Pulling his mind back from the past, he brought the computer screen into focus and studied the shot. The photograph had been taken in the dead of night, his camera and tripod a good distance away.

One night, after Dani had settled in, he'd turned on the camera with a delayed shutter. Since she always lay so still, he'd known he would get a good photo, even with the extra length of the exposure.

He hadn't been mistaken. Dani, in jeans and a tank, was painted across the platform in the moonlight. As on every other night, her hands had been clasped behind her head, her hair fanned out around her, and her small breasts reaching for the sky. The background was a blurred, but shining lake. He'd captured the lost look of her, yet in the moonlight she appeared angelic.

And now he wanted to kiss her twice as badly as he had when he'd teased her upstairs earlier in the week.

Damn.

He'd been doing so well with not thinking about that. But he slept in the room across from her every night. He heard her moving around after the house had quieted down. Watched her throughout the days, and stood side by side with her in the kitchen at night.

It was simple. He wanted her.

A knock sounded and he diverted his attention from the monitor.

"Hey," Dani said from the door. And as if his fantasies had materialized right before his eyes, she wore snug jeans and a tank top. But sadly, an open button-down covered the majority of her shirt. "You want any tea?" She held up a cup. "I just brewed a pot for Gabe and Michelle. Thought I'd see if you could use any."

"No, thanks. I'm good." Except he wanted to strip her bare.

Instead of leaving, she fidgeted in place. Finally, she lifted a shoulder and wrinkled her nose. "Missed you at dinner tonight."

Her awkwardness amused him. "Missed me helping with the dishes?" he teased.

But she only shook her head. "I don't mind the dishes. Just wondering how things went with you and Haley today. I saw one of the pictures she'd colored hanging on the refrigerator. That was a good move."

"Thanks," he said. "And yeah, we did a little better today. Thanks for your help yesterday. She even talked to me out in the orchard. Smiled, too. But then I took her shopping and . . ." He quit talking as he replayed his daughter's meltdown in his mind. He blew out a frustrated breath. "I don't know. I thought girls loved to shop."

Dani did a half snort, half chuckle. "Usually they do. I take it things took a turn for the worse?"

"That's putting it mildly."

"I'll be glad to take her with Jenna and me tomorrow. We're going for manicures. A girls' day."

He could picture his daughter in that scenario. "I'm sure she'd love it."

It would also give him a break. This parenting thing was exhausting.

Dani took a sip of her tea then, and his eyes lingered on the slope of her throat. The lines of her body ran graceful and sleek, whether it was her neck, fingers, or even her toes. Then his gaze lowered to her chest.

And he remembered what her breasts had looked like in his hands.

When she moved toward him, his brain froze for a split second before it kicked into gear and pointed out two highly relevant things at once. One, he still had the picture of her open on his computer, and two, he'd suddenly sprouted an erection the size of Montana.

He quickly shifted so he was more fully under the desk.

"Are you sick?" Concern flashed across her face as she reached his side. "You're flushed." She put a hand to his forehead, and he jolted at her touch. But he did manage to click the photo to close it. Only, instead of shutting down his viewer, he brought up another picture.

At least it wasn't another one of her.

He forced the tightness in his neck to release. "I'm fine," he scratched out.

Her smell surrounded him. He'd noticed it several times over the past week; she still smelled the same. He inhaled through his nose, pulling in the light scent of flowers, and wondered if it would be better to know if she also still *tasted* the same, or to constantly be wondering.

Geez, he had to get a grip. Leaning away from her fingers, he gritted his teeth. "Did you want something else?"

"Oh, I'm sorry to bother you." She took a step back. "I wanted to—"

She stopped talking as her gaze landed on his laptop.

"Oh my," she breathed out.

He looked at the screen. His grandpa reclined in a rocker, the wood older than the old man had been at the time, and the chair one he'd made as a much younger man. He'd been sitting on the raised porch of the ranch house where he'd lived until the day he died. A worn cowboy hat was perched far back on his head, and a graveness echoed from his eyes down through his body.

As withered as he'd been at the time, the man had still made an impressive sight. And at sixteen, Ben had captured it exceptionally. He shrugged. "I've improved since then."

Dani turned wide eyes on him. "This isn't recent?"

The blue of her eyes was as deep as they'd been the night he'd made love to her. "No."

"But the hat . . ."

They both looked at the rack by the door where the very same hat currently hung on a metal hook. Ben had inherited the hat along with his grandfather's ranch house. He'd taken the hat. Sold the house.

"I took the photo years ago."

"Oh, Ben." She grabbed a straight-backed chair from the corner of the room, and settled in close beside him. Her body heat muddled his brain as she leaned in and stretched out a hand as if to touch the photo. She stopped before her fingers brushed the screen. Her nails, with their light-pink polish, hovered over his grandfather's leathered face. "This is amazing. No wonder you've won awards."

She knew about his awards?

Eyes sparkling, she turned to him. "It's your grandfather, isn't it?"

He nodded. He couldn't have denied who the subject of the photo was if he'd wanted to. Not with Dani looking at him like that. He wanted to keep that excitement directed his way.

He wanted more.

His gaze trailed to her lips . . .

Ben's heated gaze on Dani's mouth rendered her motionless. Except for pulling *her* attention down to *his* mouth. Was he going to kiss her?

Did she want him to?

Stupid question.

But valid point.

Kissing him was the last thing she needed. She had too many other issues on her mind. She still had no good leads for an apartment—that last one hadn't worked out—she'd taken on a new project earlier today that she had zero time to devote to, and her brother's marriage issues were getting worse.

Gabe and Michelle had been arguing more than usual lately, and neither seemed to care that the entire house was aware of it.

But darn it, she wanted to kiss Ben.

She licked her lips, her breath swirling hot between them, as she contemplated whether one tiny little kiss would hurt anything.

It wouldn't.

She was certain of it.

Only . . . she flicked her gaze up to his and told herself the truth. It wouldn't stop at one kiss. And she was leaving soon.

She didn't want to risk confusing Haley. Or Jenna.

Or Ben.

Or *herself.*

So no kissing. That's the way it had to be. Better safe than sorry.

Ben waited patiently, seemingly content to let her make the decision, and she knew what she had to do. She ignored the electricity snapping between them, slowly leaned back in her chair, and returned her focus to the picture that had captured her attention.

With Ben's same eyes and sure posture, Dani could easily imagine Ben looking exactly like that in fifty years.

She tilted her head and studied the details. The New York landscape hanging at the front of the room was beautiful, but this photo made it obvious he had more of a knack for capturing people's essence, even years ago. The man in the rocker had not only experienced life, he'd lived it. His sadnesses, joys, even the pain of aging, were all exposed in that one click of a shutter.

She squinted at the picture, then, as something occurred to her. From the looks of the rustic porch and the wide, blue skies, this photograph hadn't been taken anywhere near LA.

"Didn't you once tell me you didn't see your grandfather after you went to live with your mom? And you moved to LA, when?" She glanced at him. "When you were five? Six?"

"Seven." There was no heat in his tone. Certainly no indication that he'd just been thinking about kissing her.

His hand reached for the laptop.

"Wait," she urged. She set the cup of tea down and rested her fingers over his. "You couldn't have taken this picture when you were seven."

One corner of his mouth moved as though tugged upward from an invisible string. "I can see why you were valedictorian of your high school class. Impressive deductive skills, Ms. Wilde."

"And you're avoiding the question."

"I didn't hear a question."

She fought the urge to roll her eyes. He reminded her of her brothers. Were all men experts at evading when they didn't want to talk about something?

She slipped her fingers between his, holding his hand on top of the desk and her palm flush with his skin. "How often did you see him after you moved? You were probably what . . . fifteen, sixteen when this was taken? Did you spend time at the ranch that summer?"

A muscle ticked in his jaw, and he looked away. The hand under hers twitched.

Finally, some of the steel in his spine melted, and she heard a hiss of air slip past his lips. "Sixteen. It was the only time I saw him alive after my mother bought a plane ticket and sent for me."

Sent for him.

He'd once explained that meant she'd paid extra for a flight attendant to chaperone him from state to state. With her assistant waiting on the other side of the flight.

"Okay," Dani said, intuitively knowing that she needed to step cautiously. But she *was* going to take that step. "It must have been something important you'd gone back for?"

Ten seconds clicked off until she was certain he had no intention of answering.

She loosened her grip, ready to admit defeat, but he surprised her by flipping his hand over and threading his fingers through hers. He squeezed tight.

"This was made about thirty minutes after putting my grandmother in the ground."

"Ben—"

A short shake of his head cut off her words. "Grandma had suffered with Alzheimer's my whole life, yet Grandpa never left her side. He loved her until the day she died, even though the last eight years of her life, from what he told me that day, she never once knew who he was."

Dani studied the picture with a new light. Knowing the man in the photo had just buried the love of his life explained the look in the old man's eyes. It had reeked of hurt before, but now it was almost unbearable. "That's incredibly special, you know. Finding a love like that."

It made her wonder about her own parents. Had they loved each other the same way?

Did her dad love Gloria like that?

Ben gave a simple nod. "I struggled with him letting me go when I was seven. No longer wanting me. But I understand now. He was seventy-two the day I left. My uncle had moved away, and I didn't get that Grandpa couldn't care for both a child and an adult by himself. Not when the adult needed more care than the child. And my mother never bothered explaining it. I was simply told one day that it was time I lived with my mom. I packed a bag, and Grandpa took me to the airport. I actually hated him when I left."

Dani held her breath as she listened.

"When the call came that Grandma had passed, I bought a ticket, and was back in Montana by late that afternoon. Mom came out a couple of days later for the funeral, but only to make an appearance. She'd never been especially close to her parents, and a camera crew showed up with her. So . . ." Ben shook his head before picking the story back up. "Mom went from the funeral back to the airport, and I spent another week with Grandpa. He was so worn down from the years of caring for my grandmother, he barely had anything left."

"I'm sure your being there meant a lot to him," she spoke softly, and a few more pieces of Ben clicked into place. "You couldn't resume your relationship at that point?"

A fleeting look of regret washed over his face. He released her hand, and clicked the picture closed. "He passed away three weeks after I returned to LA. I went back by myself to bury him beside Grandma."

What strength he'd had as a teenager. She was impressed.

The look on his face said it was time to end the subject, but she couldn't make herself get up and leave. She clasped her hands together in front of her, hurting for him. "Will you show me more pictures?"

Maybe that would take his mind off the family he'd once thought he didn't have, only to find out later that it had merely been circumstances out of his control.

His fingers stilled on the computer, then tapped out a short staccato along the edge. Finally, he nodded.

"Okay." With the single, gruff word, he relaxed back in his chair and reached for the mouse. He clicked and another picture filled the screen.

With a soft gasp, Dani leaned forward once again.

"This was a first-time mom," he shared. "She'd been told she would never conceive."

The picture was of a mother and child, the mother's arms encircling the baby and her breast providing nourishment. Both had their eyes focused on Ben's lens.

He couldn't have portrayed nurturing and protection any better. Or so she thought.

As he clicked through picture after picture, one thing became clear. It wasn't merely people Ben had a knack for, it was capturing a nurturing essence. There was the occasional beautiful landscape or close-up of inanimate objects, but when he turned his sights on people, the shots left her breathless.

"I'm sure you've been told this numerous times, but you have a beautiful skill."

"Beautiful?" Ben tapped her on the nose. "You romanticize things, babe."

She shifted in her chair and faced him straight on, then pointed to the photo on the screen. "Tell me that isn't beautiful." And she most certainly did not romanticize things.

He shrugged. "It's a good one."

"Has it ever won an award?"

"I don't win awards for photos that no one sees." He shot her a look. "No one except you. And the mom in that first shot. I gave her that as a gift."

He didn't share these with other people?

The idea of getting a private peek into this side of his work—his personal collection—gave her a thrill. But surely she wasn't the only one who'd seen them. His talent deserved to be showcased. She studied the photo again. "What about the others?" she asked. "Has anyone seen those?"

"Most are just shots I've made in my downtime."

"You've got to do something with them. They're too good not to share."

He grew silent and clicked back through several of the pictures they'd already viewed. "I'm considering compiling a book," he grudgingly admitted.

"Yes." That idea was brilliant. There was no doubt, with his notoriety and skill, all he'd have to do was announce he wanted to publish and he'd be snapped up in an instant.

"I can't figure out how they all fit together, though. I've got some good landscapes." He grew silent once more as he continued looking through the photos. "I've sold a few of those over the years. They seem popular."

"No." She returned her hand to lie on top of his harder one. The skin was rougher than hers and she fought the urge to trace her fingers over each dip and rise. "You've got to use these. The ones of people."

She stopped before saying *the nurturing ones*. She wasn't sure he had any idea that was inside him. He'd always told her he was like his mother. Of course, the way he'd taken Haley in proved otherwise. But Dani was somehow certain he'd rebuff the idea if she pointed it out. He was just getting used to being a dad. He didn't need her highlighting the fact that he was already a softie.

Realizing she once again had moved too close, and that her gaze had returned to his mouth, she removed her hand and stood. "Thank you for sharing these with me."

"You're leaving?"

"I thought I would, yes." She wouldn't have believed such a lost tone could come from him if she hadn't just heard it. "I have a few things to do before turning in."

"Oh." He nodded and motioned to the computer, ignoring her words and looking as alone as he'd just sounded. "You really think the people, then?"

"I definitely think the people." She slowly lowered back down. "They show a side of you that's not always obvious," she explained. "A very good side."

A hint of color painted his cheeks and she couldn't help but smile. "Are you blushing?"

"I'm sure I'm not." He didn't look at her.

The man clearly didn't accept compliments easily. Although . . .

She studied him now, and thought about the stories she'd read about him over the years. Women fawned over him all the time. That had to be complimentary. And she doubted he blushed each and every time it happened.

So it must be that these photographs meant something more. Something personal. And he'd shared them with her.

She liked that.

Nudging his shoulder with hers, she looked back at the computer. "Now that you've kept me here, got any more I could see?"

Chuckling under his breath, he began scrolling through the folders on the drive. His voice, when he spoke, had lightened considerably. "Maybe I wanted you to stay for a whole other reason."

Whoa. She rose once again. "You are a flirt, Ben Denton. And a tease."

His eyes followed her movements. "And if I'm not teasing?"

The space in the room seemed to be sucked right out until all she could focus on was each individual breath coming from Ben and her own pounding heart. She edged toward the door. "I think keeping it at teasing would be best," she said.

"Best for who?"

"Ben." The single word was all that came out.

He stood from the chair and crossed the room then, and when he reached her, he tilted her face up to his. Barely inches separated them, but he didn't cross the line.

"I want to kiss you, Dani. I'll put it out there and let you deal with it. I probably *shouldn't* want to kiss you, I know that. I'm here in your house, accepting your hospitality. I shouldn't want more. Especially considering what I took the *last* time I was here. But I do. It's that simple. I want to kiss you."

"Or that complex," she suggested.

"Does it have to be?"

His green gaze roamed over her face as she digested the question. Did it have to be? They could kiss. They could have sex. They could have a really fun few weeks.

But there was something about Ben that was different than the other men she'd been with. And it frightened her. It made her scared for her dreams.

It warned her to keep her distance.

"I actually came in here to remind you about the Cherry Festival this weekend," she said instead of answering. Best to keep things as they were. Not to mention, she didn't want to simply be his "downtime." He'd been with plenty of women over the years, and no doubt had far better options at that very moment than her. This was boredom on his part, plain and simple. And that was insulting.

His hand lowered to his side. "Gabe mentioned it," he said. "The whole family is going?"

Dani nodded. With so many orchards in the area, practically everyone in the community turned out for the festival. The event represented their whole town. "The twins should be in Saturday morning. Hopefully Jaden will make it before the day's over."

"Cord's not coming home?"

Though the unspoken rule was that everyone came home for harvest—which, depending upon the weather, usually kicked off within days of the cherry festival—that rule had been shaken lately. Nate, one of the twins, hadn't been home in a few years, and Cord, who was one year younger than Gabe, was sporadic. "He's a doctor in Billings now," she told Ben. "As far as I know, he'll be here before harvest is over, but his time is more limited. He won't make it in for the festival, for sure."

Thankfully, her other brother, the remaining twin, Nick, came home on a more regular basis. But then, he also lived the closest. As part of the Montana Pro Rodeo Circuit, he was only three hours away.

When she looked at everything as a whole, her family seemed to be crumbling around her. And she couldn't figure out how to stop it. Her dad was moving on, getting married to someone else. Gabe's marriage was teetering all over the place. And everyone else did their own things. She'd struggled even to get them on the phone lately.

Given the fact that she'd been in charge of a huge chunk of their upbringing, she took the problems personally. Her mother would have held the family together better.

Ready to get out of the room, she took a step back, landing her on the other side of the doorway. "We'll leave at nine Saturday morning," she told him. "I hope you'll go. Haley would love it."

"I'll be there."

"Good." She nodded, suddenly unable to leave. While at the same time desperate to go.

Desperation showed its hand. She fled down the hallway and hurried into her room.

Once inside, she leaned against the closed door. He wanted to kiss her. Which meant, he wanted to do more. There was no doubt in her mind.

Her subconscious did a happy dance, while at the same time shaking in terror. The first time she'd been with him, she'd wanted to not be a virgin anymore. That's pretty much all there'd been to it. Lose her virginity. Yeah, he'd been hot and sexy, and after three years of overhearing stories of his escapades, she'd wanted to see what it was all about.

Plus, she'd been mesmerized by the guy. He talked to her. He listened to her.

But she hadn't been prepared for him to sleep with her.

He'd been shocked to discover that she'd never been with a man, and she'd even thought he might stop. In fact, he'd offered to—of course, the deed had been done by that point. She hadn't taken him up on his offer, and instead, he'd slowed. He'd made love to her. He'd treated her like she was the most important person in the world.

After he'd fallen asleep, she'd escaped back to her room and stared at her ceiling for the rest of the night. No one had ever made her feel that special.

And if she kissed him now, she feared he might make her feel that way again.

chapter seven

They'd been going strong since arriving at the festival that morning, the energy and excitement of the crowd seeming to pump enthusiasm into the kids as they ran from one exhibit to the next. Not to mention what it was doing for Dani.

Ben watched as she hurried from inside the Main Street Bakery with yet another cartful of pies. The cherry pie eating contest was set to begin in thirty minutes, and when one of the organizers came down with a last-minute family emergency, Dani had jumped into action.

Of course, she'd also been chatting up everyone she'd come into contact with.

If it wasn't talking to Mr. Tamry over at the Co-op about which brand of feed was best for horses—as if Dani owned a horse—it was exchanging recipes with the Women's Auxiliary Club, discussing quilt patterns with the owner of All in Stitches, or laying out quick marketing ideas with various shop owners.

In a word, Dani was the center of the crowd here as easily as she was the center of her family. Drop her into the middle of something—the bigger the better—and she flat-out fit.

She would thrive in New York.

"Daddy, look!" Ben's attention returned to his daughter, who stood twenty feet away, one hand clasped with her best friend's. She'd taken to calling him Daddy the day before, and those two syllables did something to him every time he heard them. Something that made him forget what life had been like before her. "Check me out!" she shouted again.

She and Jenna were on a small platform two feet high, with one of the Wilde twins standing just behind them. Nick had arrived at the house before they'd headed into town that morning, but Nate hadn't shown up with him as planned. Nate was a crab fisherman off the Alaskan shore, and had decided at the last minute not to come home. He'd sent word of his change of plans through Nick instead of giving his sister a call. Dani had not been pleased.

Ben waved a hand at Haley to let her know he was watching, and she turned back to the waiting crowd of onlookers. She then wiggled her mouth, scrunched up her face . . . and spat.

The cherry pit dropped at her feet.

"I did it!" she shouted. Her arms pumped in the air.

Ben laughed out loud. "You most certainly did." Kids in a pit-spitting contest were a sight to behold.

He remembered taking part in the adult contest years ago, when he'd been twenty. A contest in which he'd won. Haley would need a little direction in learning the fine art of spitting the pit, but with this particular action, Ben felt he was up to the task.

In fact, he was feeling more up to the task of parenthood every day.

"She's changed this week." Gabe spoke from beside Ben. The two men had been deserted at the arts and craft booth when everyone else had scattered for attractions seemingly better than hanging with them.

"She's happier," Ben agreed. "Doesn't seem as scared."

"Coming here was a good decision." Gabe looked to Ben. "You seem like you're getting a handle on things."

"I'm trying." Ben watched as his daughter took another stab at it, only to have the pit land on her chin, and he couldn't contain a smile of pure joy. He didn't remember ever feeling this way.

"I hope you'll stick around," Gabe added. "I think it's good for her. And you."

He'd been thinking the same thing. "It's possible."

"I just hope I stick around too," Gabe muttered. The words were spoken under his breath, and didn't seem to be asking for a comment, so Ben didn't offer one. No additional words had been exchanged concerning Gabe's marriage since Michelle had paraded almost naked down the hallway Monday night, but it was clear things were snowballing fast. Michelle had been out with friends every night this week instead of at the house, and when husband and wife *did* talk, everyone in the room grew nervous.

Ben saw Max in line for the adult pit-spitting contest, with Gloria by his side. They wore matching T-shirts and baseball caps advertising the Wilde orchard, and the smiles on their faces would have given away their newly engaged status if the gigantic ring on her finger didn't do it first.

They'd been at the house again the night before, sharing dinner with the family, and Dani had been more herself. Ben only hoped that meant that she was coming around to her dad marrying another woman. If not, she'd done an excellent job faking it.

But then, he *had* witnessed her heading out to the beach later that night, a bowl of ice cream in hand.

He hadn't followed her, but he'd wanted to.

Of course, he'd wanted to follow and do more than ask about her need for ice cream. But she'd said no in the study the other night. Kissing wasn't what she had in mind. Which was a bummer.

Someone appeared behind them, and Ben turned to take in the newly arrived brother. It had been ten years, but Jaden Wilde hadn't changed much. Glasses, a full head of dark hair, and still several inches shorter than his older brothers. He needed a shave, and intelligence shone from his eyes. He also had a gorgeous woman with him.

The brothers shook hands, and Jaden slapped Gabe on the back. "Old man," he said with a grin.

"Pain in my ass," Gabe returned.

Both brothers laughed with fondness and Jaden turned to Ben. "I'd heard you were back." He held out his hand. "Good to see you."

"You, too. Congrats on the diploma."

"Thanks." Jaden took a half step back, and the brunette he'd walked up with eased in front of him. "This is Megan."

She slipped an arm around Jaden's waist, and fired off a wink. "I came with the degree."

Both Ben and Gabe chuckled.

The four of them talked for several minutes, Jaden explaining that he and Megan had met in psychology class as freshmen, but hadn't started dating until this past year. They had several interests together, and had been going strong ever since.

Eventually, Gabe pointed out Max and Gloria in the crowd, and the younger brother headed off. But before he reached his dad, his sister approached him. Dani launched herself at her youngest sibling, her smile wide and eyes shining. After finishing with Jaden, she enveloped Megan in a welcoming hug. Ben forced his attention back to his daughter.

Haley had moved on with Jenna to the face-painting booth. She smiled freely up at something Nick said behind her, and Ben lifted his camera. It had been riveting to watch her come to life this week. She was so different than even a few days ago.

In the background of the shot, Dani returned to the bakery and once again exited with a cart full of pies. He lowered the camera to watch. She slid the cart to the waiting crowd of helpers, said something to them, and had them all laughing. She was totally in her element.

"So . . ." Gabe spoke up again. "What's going on with you and my sister?"

"What?"

At Ben's glance, Gabe nudged his chin toward the tables set up for the pie-eating contest.

Ben shook his head. "Nothing."

"Right," Gabe replied. He crossed both arms over his chest, and widened his stance. "You help her with the dishes every night. I hear you in there laughing."

The words sounded accusing. Which didn't sit well with Ben.

"The better question is," Ben began, "why don't *you* help with the dishes every night?"

"What?" Gabe looked honestly shocked at the idea. Ben just shook his head.

"You never do," Ben said. "Why?"

"Because I . . . well . . ." Gabe stammered, finishing with "She likes to do them herself. I've heard her say it."

"Are you sure about that?"

"Yeah, I'm sure." Gabe sounded offended. "I've lived with her my whole life. She's always been that way."

"You ever offered?"

"Listen, where's this coming from? You're just trying to change the subject. There's something going on between you two. I see it. I'm simply asking what it is."

Ben shrugged, trying to act casual, but that protective streak he'd discovered with Haley had reappeared. Only, this time with Dani. "And I see that she does everything at the house. Have you ever actually paid attention to her? The dishes, laundry, cleaning. Hell, she made you and your wife a pot of tea the other night. She even takes care of your kid."

"Hey, she's taken care of your kid this week, too."

"Yeah." Ben nodded. "Some. But I'm trying. I'm figuring it out. And I'm serious, man, cut your sister a break. She has a full-time job, too."

"Her job doesn't start until next month," Gabe grumbled.

"Are you kidding me?" Ben's voice rose. He was full-out pissed now. "She has her own marketing business. How many clients does she have? How long has that been going on while she's been managing everything about the house, too?"

Gabe went silent, as did the people around them. The two of them were causing a scene. "Shit," Gabe mumbled under his breath. They moved away from the crowd before Gabe continued. "I know she works hard. I'm aware of that. She just makes it look so easy that I forget sometimes."

"You take advantage of her, is what you do. How much does she do for the orchard?" Ben prodded. "Please tell me you do handle *some* of the paperwork yourself?"

"I do plenty, asshole."

But Gabe's words lost their heat as Michelle wound through the crowd, only about ten feet away from them. She'd dressed to the nines that morning, and though she'd smiled and greeted people upon their arrival at the festival, holding Jenna's hand and looking like the perfect little parent, she'd since forgotten her husband and child existed and had been mugging for any camera she could find.

Including Ben's.

He'd ignored her every time she'd come near.

Ben watched Gabe as he watched his wife, and saw the light dim in his friend's eyes when Michelle didn't so much as glance their way. That was one shitty marriage going on there.

Turning back to Ben, Gabe picked up their conversation, conveniently leaving out the part where Ben had pointed out the man's shortcomings. "She's more vulnerable than you realize," Gabe told him. "That's all I'm saying. Don't hurt her. Be friends with her all you want, just don't sleep with her."

"I wasn't planning on it." Which was a big fat lie. He'd sleep with her in an instant if she gave him so much as an opening.

"I know you did before," Gabe said, his tone grave.

"I didn't—"

"I *know*." Gabe drilled him with a look. "I was looking for you that night."

"Fuck," Ben muttered to himself as a shiver slid over his shoulders. "Please tell me you didn't see us."

"God, no. But I did . . ." Gabe looked away, his jaw hard. "I overheard some things. You guys laughing. Other stuff." He shook his head. "Look, it doesn't matter. I knew she didn't date much, and you were heading back to school. I didn't see the harm. But she's about to leave now. Finally. Don't give her an excuse to stay."

Their conversation from Monday night flitted back through Ben's head. "That's why you don't want her to know how bad things are between you and Michelle?"

"She'll try to fix it." Gabe gave him an imploring look. "She'll think she needs to stay in Montana to take care of things. And she'll be worried about Jenna."

"Should she be?"

"Hell, no. I'll take care of my daughter."

"Your wife doesn't."

"I'm aware of that. It's why I have to do something. Only, I want Dani to have her own life first. After all this time, she deserves it."

"Yes. She does." Both men grew quiet, each in his own thoughts, then Ben offered all he had. "I'm sorry, man. Sometimes life can be a bitch."

"Ain't that the truth."

Jenna and Haley shouted for their fathers, and both men looked around. Jenna had two cherries with stems painted on one cheek, and Haley's entire face was red.

"I'm a cherry!' Haley shouted happily.

"I see that." Ben laughed at his daughter. She was amazing to be around.

Nick eyed the two men as though he understood the seriousness of the conversation going on, and quickly steered the girls to the next booth, where they all met up with Jaden, Max, and the women.

"You're planning to change things after Dani leaves?" Ben asked Gabe, seeing the path of the conversation.

"I have to. If I don't, Michelle will divorce me."

"Who'll run the orchard?" he asked.

Gabe faced him, his look dead on and serious. "You want the job? Looks to me like you could use one."

"I don't need a job managing an orchard."

Gabe shrugged, but the move didn't come off as casual as he might have liked. "Can't blame me for trying."

"How about one of your brothers? Jaden looking to take on more?"

The silence that followed Ben's question raised the hair on the back of his neck.

"What?" Ben asked cautiously. He didn't like the look on Gabe's face.

"Jaden isn't staying."

Jaden was supposed to take over the accounting. "You've got to be kidding me."

"You can't tell her," Gabe said.

"You can't keep this from her." Though Ben did understand her brother's reasoning. She'd want to stay. Give up her dreams yet again. Because if there was one thing that woman was overprotective about, it was her family. And her *family* included the orchard. "How do you think it'll make her feel when she does find out? Knowing that you've been keeping secrets from her."

"We're protecting her."

Ben looked away from his friend, and his gaze landed on Haley. Behind her stood Nick, Jaden, and Max. All three men were watching them.

"Who knows?" Ben asked. He suspected he could guess.

"Everyone."

He shook his head. "You're making a mistake. She deserves to know what's going on before she moves to the other side of the country. And she deserves to be a part of figuring out the solution. She's put too much of herself into this to be excluded from it."

"But that's not how it's going to happen. We've been protecting our sister for a long time. I don't intend to stop now."

Gabe's words didn't make a lot of sense. It seemed to Ben that if anyone had been bending over backward to watch out for people, it was Dani. From Ben's point of view, her dad hadn't even manned up when her family had first fallen apart. Max was a good guy, and he'd worked hard for what they had. Ben had seen that back then.

But it had also been clear that Max stayed to the side and let Dani run the show.

What hadn't been obvious was whether that was Dani's doing, or Max's.

But he couldn't point out any of that right then. Nick had exceeded his ability to keep the girls away. They ran over, both talking faster than Ben could keep up, followed by the remainder of the Wilde clan. Gloria and Megan brought up the rear.

Ben would keep his mouth shut about the family secrets. For now.

But he didn't know how long that would last. Somebody had to think of Dani.

chapter eight

"Cotton candy?"

With the question, Ben waved the sickly sweet treat-on-a-stick in front of her face, and Dani peeked over the top to find him grinning at her. He'd been doing that a lot more lately. Grinning. It probably had to do with his daughter seeming to enjoy his company once in a while.

Or it might go along with him wanting to do naughty things with Dani. She wasn't sure.

She also didn't plan to ask. She had to quit thinking like that. She was not going to sleep with him. That had been her decision after they'd danced all around the subject in the study the other night. Sleeping with him wasn't smart. She didn't need that kind of distraction in her life right now.

Therefore, no sleeping with Ben.

Which meant no flirting with Ben. No matter how many heated grins he tossed her way.

"No, thanks." She ignored the thrill of being close to him and pushed the cotton candy away. "You can tempt all you want, but I just polished off a huge cherry tart at that last booth. Nothing else is going in here." She patted her stomach.

"Your loss." He popped a large pinch of the sugary fluff into his mouth. "Mmmm."

She made a face at him, and turned her attention to his daughter.

Michelle and Gabe had stuck around long enough to see the parade before returning to the house, leaving Jenna to spend the afternoon with her uncles, so Dani had decided to hang out with Ben and Haley. She wanted Jenna to have that special time alone with Jaden and Nick. She didn't get it often enough.

Dani only wished that Nate had come home, too.

She'd called when he hadn't shown up that morning, but had only gotten his voice mail. Which was so like him to avoid her like that. So she'd reminded him that she *was* moving over two thousand miles away in a matter of weeks, and it would be nice to see her entire family before she left.

She hoped he'd get his crap together and come home, but she'd learned long ago that with Nate, he would do whatever he wanted. Even if "whatever he wanted" landed him in either jail or rehab. Both of which had happened in the past. And the boy was only twenty-four.

Nate hadn't been the easiest brother to raise.

She and Ben continued wandering through the kids' section of the festival, trying everything they could think of to get Haley to perk up. They'd had a struggle separating her and Jenna, and since then, Haley had refused to leave their sides. She hadn't been interested in making her own butterfly at the kids' craft station, in having a dog balloon that she could walk on her own, or even in the regionally famous magic show featuring The Amazing Lolo.

Dani supposed sticking by Ben's side was to be expected, though. Haley wasn't used to strangers, and clearly remained nervous around them. But what got to Dani was the fact that it wasn't Ben's side so much as *hers* that Haley was clinging to. The attachment being formed had begun to worry her. It could end up hurting the girl in the end.

She shoved the pink fluff out of her face once again when Ben silently held out his arm, and decided it was time to broach the subject. She nudged her head in the direction of Haley, who'd finally taken more than two steps away. She'd squatted down to look at a toy box made to look like a giant cherry, and was actually talking to the woman manning the booth.

"Do you worry she's building too close an attachment to me?" Dani asked quietly.

Ben stopped eating and bunched his eyebrows together. "She knows you're leaving."

"Yes, but she's a child. I'm not sure she really understands. I worry it'll hurt her when I do go." She stepped closer to ensure only he could hear. "Like her mother did, you know? I don't want to make things worse."

Concern slipped quickly over Ben's features, and the cotton candy was forgotten. He tossed it into a nearby trash bin and took his time wiping his hands. Dani suspected he was delaying in order to think over what she'd just said. Because she had a point. Haley was sensitive to people leaving, even if she "knew" up front they would be.

Dani really should have thought of that sooner.

To help matters, she voiced a suggestion. "I could spend less time with her. Distance myself a little."

Not take her for manicures and fix her hair every morning.

"No." The answer came fast and harsh. "You're good for her, even if you are leaving. And . . ." He paused. "You're good for me too. You've already done more for both of us in a matter of days than I'd accomplished in three weeks."

"It wasn't all me. You would have gotten there."

He took her hand in his. "Don't lie to either of us. It was you, and we both know it. No," he said again, and she struggled to focus on his words instead of the heat from his palm. "We'll talk to her. Make sure she understands that you won't be here forever. We'll find her more friends to fill the void. But right now, you're bringing a life out in her that I didn't know she was capable of. Certainly more than I've seen since Lia left her standing there staring up at me."

Dani couldn't bring herself to argue. Because she didn't want to pull back yet.

They stood in the middle of the street, both watching Haley, each deep in their own thoughts, and in her heart, Dani knew she needed distance. From both of them. She kept finding herself making excuses to spend more time with Ben. And she loved Haley to death.

The little girl wasn't the only one who would be hurt when Dani had to leave.

Yet, she said nothing.

She did tug at her arm, though, intending to free her hand. But Ben's grip tightened. He didn't say anything, didn't even glance her way. He just didn't let go.

Fine. She'd hold his hand.

Mostly because she liked it.

But also because she didn't want to cause a scene. She was not a fan of drawing unwanted attention to herself.

With a squeal, Haley left the booth and skipped back to them. "Do you like it?" She held up her hand. On the back was a tiny butterfly tattoo. "The lady gave it to me. Isn't it beautiful?"

Haley went into an excited jump, and relief rushed through Dani. Ben's daughter seemed to be getting back to her earlier self.

"Absolutely," Dani and Ben said in unison.

Dani smiled her thanks at the mom of three she recognized who'd put the temporary tattoo on Haley, and without additional comment, she and Ben each caught one of Haley's hands and the three of them continued down the street.

A lively bagpiper passed them, his music entertaining the crowd, and his "funny skirt" making Haley laugh. It was a good day—a beautiful day—to live in Birch Bay.

Ten yards later, Ben stopped at the booth for The Cherry Basket, and Dani watched him study the assortment of items. Quilts, cookbooks, jams, and jellies. All spread out before them, each displayed in either red, cloth-lined handmade baskets, or on cases a local carpenter had built for the store. The manager had done a beautiful job setting up the booth as if a section of the store had been plucked up whole and plopped down in the middle of the street.

"This is your store?" Ben asked.

Dani smiled with pride. "Not *my* store. But the family's, yes."

Haley's eyes widened. "You have a store, too? Will I be able to eat cherries there like I will at your house?"

Laughter rose from Dani. She loved what children found important. Though Haley had eaten her share of fresh cherries throughout the day, she was certain they weren't nearly as good as the ones that would come from Wilde Cherry Farm.

Dani squeezed the small hand inside hers and winked. "Absolutely."

"But you started the store?" Ben prompted as if Haley hadn't interrupted them. "It was your idea?"

"Yeah." Dani turned back to the setup. "I did. The idea began when I was a kid. I'd just talked my dad into my first cherry lemonade stand."

She pointed out the fresh cherry lemonade that was for sale at the stand, and Ben said, "You're going to slay them in New York."

"Thank you." The gravity of his statement affected her. It wasn't that her family hadn't expressed the same confidence, but they were her family. It was their job to say things like that.

But to hear Ben say it helped soothe the fear that occasionally arose. She knew she could do a good job. She knew she *had* done well. But no matter how aware of that she was, no matter how many of her own awards she'd won, a consistent nagging voice sat inside her head, leading to worry that it might not be enough.

She stepped to the booth and greeted the manager with a handshake. "How are you, Sara? Everything going okay today?"

"Terrific. We just sold out of the new mixes that came in last week. I sent Brandi to the store for more, and to grab up a couple more boxes of brochures. We're making sure everyone who stops by the booth walks away carrying something with our website printed on it."

"Good deal." Thousands of tourists passed through the festival every year, and there were many booths set up along the walkway, all representing different orchards throughout the area. But Dani and her family had something they didn't. A thriving store and online business. Ensuring that a large percentage of the attendees went home aware they could order additional product online was key to keeping that a reality. "The samples going over well?" she asked, and Sara laughed with enthusiasm.

"You know they are. The team is continuously running fresh batches of the scones and muffins over from the store."

They talked for several more minutes, Sara offering a cup of cherry lemonade to Haley, before Dani and Ben moved on down the street. The afternoon slowly slipped away. They took in the boats bobbing out on the bay and the water-skiers off in the distance. The festival bumped right up against the water, and the way the sunlight glistened, the lake could look blue or green, depending on the time of day.

Ben pointed out a group of girls about Haley's age waiting in line by the carousel, and suggested they go over so Haley could talk with them. Haley wanted no part in it. So when they came upon the oversize bounce house, with loud shouts coming from inside, Dani instantly knew it would be too much for the girl.

But she didn't have time to warn Ben.

"Look at that." He pointed to the blow-up structure. "That looks exactly like a place you'd love."

Haley's grip tightened and she took a step closer to Dani. "Is Jenna in there?"

"I'm not sure," Ben said. He craned his neck as though he were checking to see if the other girl had made her way to this end of the street. "But plenty of other kids are. Come on, let's get you inside."

"Ben," Dani tried to warn him.

"It's okay." He took a step forward, Haley's hand in his, but Haley leaned back and dug in her heels.

He glanced behind him, and when his daughter didn't budge, he smiled down at her as if all was right with the world. "Dani and I will be right here the whole time," he assured her. "I'm sure you'll find a new friend in there. Don't you want someone new to play with?"

Ah. He'd apparently taken Dani's earlier words to heart and was intent on resolving the issue right this moment. "Ben," she tried again.

Haley inched closer to Dani.

When Ben pulled at the child's arm once again, Haley released her daddy's hand, and wrapped both arms tightly around Dani's leg.

"I already have friends," she declared stubbornly. "Dani and Jenna will play with me whenever I want."

Crap. Wrong answer.

Dani untangled the girl from her leg, but she could see the damage was done. The child had retreated into her shell. She was scared. Additionally, Ben seemed just as determined.

Stooping to Haley's height, Dani soothed with her voice. "You don't have to go in if you don't want to, Haley. That's okay. But remember what I told you before? I won't always be here. Making new friends might be a really good idea."

"It is a good idea." This came from Ben. He'd apparently decided that coaxing wasn't going to work because he lifted Haley in his arms without waiting for her to respond. "Come on. You'll love it."

"Ben—"

Dani started to protest once more, but stopped when Haley went into a screaming fit. Arms and legs stiffened, then flapped in the air as if she were fighting for her life. Her small face turned bright red, and fat tears streamed from her eyes.

She reared back with all the strength one small child could muster, and Ben froze where he stood.

"Don't put me in there! Don't put me in there!" Haley screamed.

Everyone within earshot turned in their direction, looks on their faces like they were trying to decide whether to offer help or request that the three of them keep it down.

In the next instant, Haley lunged for Dani. Without thinking, Dani pulled her from her daddy's grasp. The child was terrified. She twined slim arms around Dani, her whole body shaking, and buried her damp face in the crook of Dani's neck. Her sobs lowered in volume fairly quickly, but the tension in her body was slower to ease.

Several moments and a couple of loud sniffles later, most everything had returned to normal. Except, Haley still clung to Dani.

Ben stood in front of them, arms hanging at his sides.

Everyone else's attention had refocused on their own kids, and Ben's gaze lifted from Haley to Dani. And that's when she noticed there was more than shock lurking inside him. He was angry.

And carrying not a small bit of pain.

Dani studied him as she patted Haley's back. Her taking his daughter away from him had hurt. Or better yet, Haley pulling away had more likely been the culprit. But whichever had caused the problem, Dani wasn't sure what else she could have done. The child had been terrified. Dani couldn't stand there and let it continue.

That didn't seem to matter to Ben.

"You can get her back to the house," he ground out.

He walked away then, leaving Dani and Haley staring after him.

chapter nine

Dani peered over the pull-out map in the adventure book, and smiled down at Haley and Jenna. Nick and Jaden had already been in, and each read a book to the girls, but the excitement of having uncles in the house had led Jenna to beg for more. Haley had been right there with her, only her "excitement" had more resembled unease. All thanks to her daddy walking away from her at the festival earlier that day. And then not coming back to the house.

"So you see," Dani began, returning her mind to the map, "I'll be way over here in this state."

"New York," Jenna added.

"That's right, New York. And where will you two be? Haley, do you want to show me?"

After running Nick and Jaden out of the room, Dani had finally gotten the girls to settle down, and the three of them had looked at the map and read about both states twice. Following the episode at the fair, it seemed a wise thing to find a way to explain the situation so Haley could better understand.

The little girl lifted up off the mattress and pointed to the state of Montana. She gave a tiny smile when Dani praised her, and Mike joined in with his own congratulatory lick to her face.

"That's Montana," Jenna filled in. Jenna and Dani had done this same exercise several weeks earlier when Dani's plans had first come together. "And we'll come visit you sometimes," Jenna added, "and you'll come visit us."

"Will I get to visit you, too?" Haley asked.

That was a toughie. Because . . . probably not. Dani didn't see Ben packing up his daughter and making a cross-country flight to see a girl he'd once had a one-night stand with.

She leaned in and gave Haley a big hug. "I don't know, baby. I think your daddy's probably going to be too busy."

Tears welled up in Haley's eyes. "But I wanna come see you."

Oh, geez. This really wasn't going the way she'd planned.

"When my daddy and I come to visit," Jenna said, "we'll bring you, too."

Thank goodness for Jenna. Except, Gabe and Michelle might not agree with the suggested plan.

But Dani didn't really care about that at the moment. "That sounds perfect to me."

It would have to do, because Dani wasn't prepared to argue the point. She was strung out from the afternoon. Haley hadn't calmed down after Ben walked away from them, and after hunting up her brothers and Jenna, Dani had hurriedly strapped the girl into the car seat she kept for Jenna and headed home. Only to find that Ben hadn't returned to the house.

Dani had gone red-hot with anger. She hadn't let it show, though. Haley didn't need any additional stress to come from the afternoon.

So instead of spending a few hours working, Dani had set aside her plans and taken Haley for a long walk. They'd checked on the cherries before heading down to the beach. Both of them got their feet wet along the shoreline, picking out the prettiest rocks, then practicing the fine art of skipping them across the lake. Sadly, Dani's skill was at about the same level as Haley's.

The entire time they'd been out there, Ben had been remained absent.

She stood and clicked off the top part of the lamp, leaving the smaller, bottom half on as a night-light. Haley had asked earlier if they could sleep with the light on tonight, so this had been the concession.

"Will you tell my daddy I'm sorry I cried?" Haley asked from the bed. "I didn't want to go in that thing, but I'll try the next time."

Haley had been worrying about upsetting her father all this time?

Dani was going to kick Ben's butt.

If he ever showed back up.

She returned to the edge of the mattress and took Haley's hand. Jenna and Mike watched in silence. "I'll tell him, sweetie, but you know he didn't mean to upset you, don't you?"

The night-light allowed Dani to see Haley's nod. "He wants me to have friends."

"Yes." Dani nodded encouragingly. She also tried to smile. "Because he doesn't want you to be lonely after I leave, and because Jenna may not always be around to play with. But if it takes you a long time to be ready to go into the bounce house, then all you have to do is tell your dad you aren't ready, okay?"

"But it might make him mad."

"No, baby." Dani hugged the girl tight, squeezing so hard Haley lifted up off the bed. "It won't make him mad, and it didn't make him mad today. He just doesn't always understand little girls, so he didn't know how bad you didn't want to go in there. All you need to do now is tell him with words, okay? He'll listen. I promise."

She would make sure of it.

Ben couldn't push too hard or Haley would fight back every time. If for no other reason than so much of her life had been upended in the past month, and she needed to have some amount of control over it.

But also, Dani had no doubt that still in the back of Haley's mind lay the fear she'd felt when she realized her mother hadn't wanted her.

Dani stood once more.

Her emotions were right on the edge, and she needed to get away. It was time for ice cream. After wishing them a good-night, she quickly stepped to the other side of the door. And as had happened several nights before, Ben stood there waiting for her.

His gaze glanced off the closed bedroom door before coming back to hers. "Take a walk with me."

Not *will you* take a walk. Simply, *do it.*

No concern for his daughter? No apology for leaving the two of them and disappearing for hours?

Oh, hell yes, she'd take a walk with him. She was ripe to take a walk with him.

Without saying a word, she moved quickly past him and down the stairs. In the living room were her three brothers and Megan, all watching a ghost hunter show. Gabe looked up as she entered the room.

"Can you keep an ear out for the girls?" Dani asked. "Ben and I need to talk."

"Sure." Gabe tossed a look at Ben, but no one in the room said another word.

Continuing her controlled march, Dani exited the back door and headed down the stairs. When she reached the ground, she whirled. "You asshole," she shouted, all the anger from the afternoon exploding out in the single word. She punctuated her point with a finger jabbed his way. "You ungrateful, selfish, good-for-nothing *ass.*"

"Dani." Ben grabbed her elbow and pulled her away from the house. She jerked out of his hold. "Calm down," he urged.

"Don't you dare tell me to calm down," she yelled. She did move her feet, though, because he had a point. They probably had four pairs of eyes watching them through the windows lining the back of the house. Every one of them was aware that she'd come home with Ben's daughter—but without Ben—and that she hadn't been especially pleased about it.

Not wanting to put on a show, she followed Ben.

He had deserted his daughter today. What was wrong with the man?

His steps were long and sure, and when Dani realized he was leading them to the beach she jerked to a halt. "Not the beach," she snapped out.

He looked back. "Why not?"

"Not. The. Beach." She pivoted to her right, leaving him to follow. Thank goodness it stayed light until late this time of year or she'd probably smack her head on one of the branches of the many cherry trees. Because she was not going to the beach with that man. The beach had once been their spot. It had been their *friendship.*

It had also been where she'd launched herself at him, seeking a kiss.

Which he'd turned down.

"Dani," Ben said behind her.

"Shut up, Ben. I'm not ready to talk to you yet."

Wisely, he complied.

They walked for several additional minutes, Dani burning off steam until she finally began to slow down. She pictured Haley again as Ben had walked away from them that afternoon—Haley had done nothing to deserve that. Heck, *she* had done nothing to deserve that.

And Ben should have known better.

Finally, she ran out of steam and stopped.

She didn't turn to Ben, though, but instead tilted her head back and stared up through the branches of the trees to the darkening sky. The world was so big out here. So peaceful. It had always been the thing that kept her sane, to come out here and stare up at the sky.

Until that moment, she'd thought those late-night sessions on the dock had started after she'd come home from college. She'd thought it had been about losing her mother.

She would come outside to reset for the following day, maybe to speak to her mother, to search for guidance. And to remind herself that she was lucky to have the family and the life that she did have. It didn't matter what she'd had to give up.

But standing in the middle of the orchard right that very moment, angry on Haley's behalf, and on the verge of tears due to the emotions assaulting her, Dani also remembered coming out here *before* she'd gone away to college. Sometimes she'd walk through the fields alone, while other times it had been straight to the beach. Her dad had figured out she was sneaking out late at night and had tried to put a stop to it, but she'd begged him to let this be her thing.

He'd seemed to understand that she needed to have her own quiet space. And he'd agreed; it could be her thing.

"You won't tell Mom?"

Dani closed her eyes as the question echoed through her head.

"*I won't tell Mom.*"

He'd hugged her then. Long and hard. He'd *loved* her then.

And yes, he still loved her today. She knew that. Just as she loved him. But things had changed at some point in their lives. A distance had formed between father and daughter, and it had never completely closed.

"Dani."

She jumped and spun around, having forgotten she was out there with Ben.

"What's wrong?" he asked.

"Haley," she answered bluntly. Was he seriously that blind that he didn't get that?

"I don't mean with her. I know that. We'll talk about that." He motioned toward Dani. "I mean with you. What just happened? Where'd you go?"

"Nowhere." She shook her head.

She'd gone into a past that was different than the one she remembered.

With some of the anger having evaporated, she could now talk to Ben rationally. "You hurt your daughter today."

"I know." He looked completely repentant. "I handled things badly. My only excuse is that I don't do rejection well. When she wanted you instead of me . . ." He shrugged. "It felt personal."

"She's a child, Ben. Grow up. She didn't reject you. She was terrified. She's had a crappy month, and you tried to shove her into an oversize balloon filled with strangers. I would have run from you, too."

"I know. I'm an idiot. Hell, Dani. I don't know what I'm doing with her. Half the time I think things are going okay, and the next instant I'm drowning. I'm in completely over my head, and the person who has to pay for that is Haley."

"You can't walk out on her like you did."

He glared at her as if he thought she were an idiot. "Don't you think I know that?"

"No." She glared back. "As a matter of fact, I don't. Because that's exactly what you did today. Just like her mother. You walked out on her." She could see that her words had an impact.

"Fuck," he muttered. His shoulders slumped. And for the first time since they'd started arguing, Ben seemed to see past his own issues. Beyond the difficulty of having parenthood thrust upon him. He saw how *his* actions could affect *his* daughter. "Christ, Dani. I didn't even think about it like that."

She didn't want to soften at the destroyed look on his face, but she couldn't help it. She softened. She began walking once again, more slowly than before, and Ben followed along beside her.

"She's scared, Ben. And the worst part . . ." Her voice cracked as she relived sitting in the bedroom with Haley tonight, hearing her apologize for crying. "The worst part is that she asked me to tell you she's sorry."

Ben stared at her. "For what?"

"For upsetting you. She's sorry for upsetting *you*, Ben Denton. She doesn't want you to be mad at her for crying."

"My God." The look on his face was pure horror. "I screwed up and *she* feels bad about it?"

Dani nodded. "That's pretty much the way of it."

"I just wanted to help." His words came across as pleading. "To get her more friends. Jenna won't—"

He pressed his lips into a straight line and gazed toward the setting sun, its orange glow just beginning to stretch toward the mountains. "Jenna may not always be around," he finished. "I know what loneliness feels like, and I don't want that for Haley."

Dani put her hand on his forearm, and they both stopped walking. They remained shrouded in the trees, the almost-ripe cherries heavy on the branches and a light wind drifting through the night. It was a peaceful scene, but inside she could see Ben's torment.

"She'll get there," she assured him. "With the right support. But her mother deserted her and you can't forget that. Ever. She's probably terrified Lia's leaving was due to something she'd done, and she won't want to do the same with you."

"Of course it was nothing she'd done. Lia is a selfish—"

"I get it." Dani nodded. She squeezed his arm. "Not mother material. Some people aren't. But Haley is four. She's confused and scared. It'll take time before she's secure again."

Pain etched over Ben's face. "What if she never had security to begin with?"

❦

"You think that was the case?"

Ben eyed Dani as she voiced the question, and silently ran through what he knew of the first four years of his daughter's life. She'd been raised by a grandmother who'd had one foot in the grave and a mother who'd dashed in and out of her life.

The grandmother had passed away a couple of months ago, leaving Haley with Lia. It was very reminiscent of his own childhood. Which answered Dani's question.

"I think being with me is as close to security as she's come."

And he'd blown that big-time. Because he'd been mad at *himself.* What an idiot.

He sighed and turned away, and he and Dani continued on their walk. He captured her hand and tucked it into the crook of his elbow, and when she didn't pull away, he tightened his fingers over hers. It felt good to have her close.

He didn't immediately return to talking, though, and she seemed to sense that he needed time. Instead, he listened to the quiet sounds of the night settling around them. He'd spent the past several hours driving around the perimeter of Flathead Lake, questioning each of his decisions made over the past month. Had it been a mistake taking Haley in the first place? Coming to Montana? Would Haley be better off with someone who had a clue of how to raise a child?

But if so, who?

Then he'd gotten a phone call that had seemed to come at the perfect time.

Only, now it seemed the call had merely been a test.

They emerged from the canopy of trees, and up ahead was a worn path through the grass that led to the beach. At his glance, Dani nodded and they moved in that direction. They walked for several minutes, stopping only when they reached a rise that provided a brilliant view of the lake. The sun had almost touched the mountains by now, and the sky was layered with long stretches of clouds striated with color. Orange was the most prevalent, mixed with purples and reds. The calm lake tempted the same feeling to grow behind the wall of Ben's chest. This entire area spoke to him. It always had. As had being with Dani.

"I've got to go to New Mexico tomorrow," he told her.

Dani straightened beside him. "I thought you'd canceled your contracts."

"I did, but I can't get out of this one. The backup bailed. I got a call this afternoon."

She looked at him for a minute before removing her arm from his. He let his drop to his side.

"You *can't* get out of it?" she asked. "Or you don't want to?"

105

Truth was, he hadn't tried to get out of it. But he couldn't call back now and change his mind. It was too late. He had a flight to catch in the morning. "Maybe both," he admitted.

The silence from her was deafening as he waited for her reply. She'd always been able to understand who he was before. He was curious if she still had that ability today. She didn't disappoint. "You miss your old life."

Yep.

He crossed his arms over his chest, feeling ashamed for spending the afternoon wishing he had his life back, and concentrated on the smoothness of the lake. It was late, so there were no boats to be seen. No Jet Skiers, no fishermen. Just nature. Just reality.

"Yes," he answered truthfully. He turned his head to look at her. "Everything feels out of control right now. I thought maybe being 'normal' for a couple of days might help. Might put things more into perspective."

The look on her face said she understood what he was feeling. The need to run. "It feels like your life is spinning out of control," she said. "I get that. Okay." She nodded. "I can watch her while you're gone."

"I'm not asking you to." He captured her hand again.

"What're you going to do then?" A ghost of a smile crossed her lips. "Ask your mother?"

Her question made *him* smile. She did know him well.

His mother had come up in conversations with Dani several times in the past, and he'd shared his frustrations that she had not, exactly, been "motherly." In fact, she'd never been. That had been difficult after spending his first seven years with his grandfather. The man had let Ben trail along behind his every step. He'd taught Ben to explore life, to live it. He'd also taught him about others, and how to respect the people he came into contact with.

And he'd done his level best to show him what love was.

But then Ben had gone to live with his mother, and he'd discovered that love came in all shapes and sizes. Which was what worried him now.

His mother hadn't been able to love the way Grandpa did. She'd provided. She'd taken him on trips. And she'd never seemed especially put out by having to do either.

But he was merely a task on her assistant's to-do list.

His mother had also never once looked at him like she was *happy* he was a part of her life.

He'd lived with that kind of love a lot longer than he'd experienced his grandpa's, and that fact always made him wonder which flavor *he* was capable of. Or if he believed in love at all. Because it wasn't as though he'd been sitting around pining for the woman of his dreams to come walking by these past few years. Nor had he wanted anything more in his life.

He'd been happy and content. His life had been good.

"You messed up today, Ben," Dani spoke softly at his side. "You made a brilliantly bad move, but you know it was wrong. You feel awful about it." She cut her eyes over to him. "You're not like her."

Her words meant a lot. As did her ability to follow his thoughts.

"Mom's not a bad person." He truly believed that. She did a lot for those less fortunate, and had been recognized as a Goodwill Ambassador for the United Nations. She donated both money and her time for charity appearances. She was a good person.

Her focus had just never been on raising a kid.

"I'm not saying she is," Dani said. "But she wasn't the greatest mom."

He chuckled. "No, she was not that."

Dani went quiet for another moment before forcing him to face facts. "You came out here intending to ask me to watch Haley for you, didn't you? You wanted to go away, pretend she didn't exist for a couple of days?"

He nodded. He was an ass. "Pretty much."

But that had quickly changed.

He turned to her, the need urgent for her to understand. Because he didn't want to be like his mother. He wanted to be a good father.

And he wanted to believe in love.

"I won't do that to her, though," he said earnestly. "I made a mistake. Big time. I see that, and I won't do it again. I won't desert her—I'll take her with me." The idea of taking Haley was suddenly exciting. Not because he wanted her on location with him, but because there were so many things he could introduce her to.

The world had a lot to offer, and for making him aware of that fact, he would always appreciate his mother. His childhood hadn't been a total waste.

"There are always extra people on-site," he pointed out. "I'll get someone to keep an eye on her when I can't."

Dani's eyes softened. "Make sure it's someone nice, will you? She needs nice."

"Definitely." Then he shot her a teasing wink. "Or you could come with us? Watch her while I work?"

"Not on your life, Hollywood. You created this mess, you handle it."

She slipped her arm back through his and rested her head on his shoulder. Both of them let out heavy breaths as they turned as one to face the water. It was so much like it had been in the past, only they weren't lying side by side on the dock.

"Do you really believe I can do this?" he asked. "Without screwing her up?"

She tilted her face up. "The very fact that you ask the question tells me you can."

He wanted to kiss her in the worst way. "Thank you," he said, instead of leaning down and putting his mouth to hers. "I hope so."

"I know so. But I do have a suggestion that might help."

"What's that?"

"A therapist," she told him. "Will you consider taking Haley to see someone? I have a friend with an office here in town. She's great with kids. I think it might be good for Haley."

That wasn't a completely bad idea.

It was humiliating to admit he might need help. But he wasn't simply talking about *his* life these days. This was his daughter's.

"I'll think about it," he promised. He lifted Dani's hand from his arm and pressed a kiss to her fingertips. "I believed I could do this on my own, but after today . . ." He shrugged. "I'll think about it."

"You're a good guy, Ben." She touched his cheek. "You're changing your life for her. She's a lucky girl."

He just hoped he didn't keep screwing it all up.

His phone chirped, and, aware they'd asked Gabe to watch Haley, he pulled it from his pocket.

He checked the text. "I've got to go. Haley's asking for me."

chapter ten

D ani closed the lid of her laptop and slumped in her chair in relief. After a long day of work for a client she'd picked up at the festival over the weekend, she'd just finished a video chat with a potential roommate. Their conversation had gone well. The other woman was a product manager for a financial company, and had lived in New York City for three years. She'd recently broken up with her live-in boyfriend, regularly worked sixty hours a week, and though not desperate for a roommate, she was certainly in the market.

She seemed normal and capable of paying her bills, and that was pretty much what Dani was looking for at this point. Signing a lease—much less agreeing to live with someone—sight unseen was nerve-racking.

Pulling the lease agreement off the printer, Dani spread it out in front of her to reread it.

This was such a big step. Which was a silly thought, because it was a step she had to take. It wasn't like she hadn't already made the decision to move to New York. Yet reading through the language of the contract, and seeing the glaring blank line where her signature would go, had her heart racing. She was really about to do this.

She was about to have the life she'd always dreamed of.

It was both exhilarating and completely frightening at the same time.

A door in the back of the house opened and closed, and she lifted her head to listen. It wouldn't be Ben or Haley. They'd both left the morning before and wouldn't return for another day.

After rushing back to the house Saturday night, Ben had not come out of Haley's room. Dani had peeked in on them before going to bed to find Ben asleep on the top bunk, his feet hanging off the end. The sight made her smile. And also warmed her heart.

He really was a good guy. She couldn't imagine going from the life he'd had, to suddenly being thrust into single parenthood of a four-year-old girl, but Dani was confident that both man and daughter would come out the other end of this okay.

And she was slightly sad that she wouldn't be around to see it unfold.

More than one set of footsteps moved through the family room, and Dani closed her eyes to focus on the patterns of the movements. One sounded like Jaden. Another was softer, probably Megan, given that wherever Jaden went, Megan followed. And vice versa.

The girl seemed sweet and very down-to-earth. And Jay was smitten. Big-time.

Which made Dani wonder what Megan thought of Montana, and if she might be considering moving here with Jay.

Heavier footsteps moved into the kitchen, pausing for a moment, before heading down the hall. That would be Gabe. Dani was ready for him when he reached the open door to the study.

"Can I talk to you for a minute?" she called out as he passed.

His steps stopped and he leaned back, bottle of water in hand, and peeked into the room. "What's up?"

She put a concerned expression on her face. "What's going on with you and Michelle?"

She'd tried to stay out of her brother's business, but the house was full of people now, and the arguments hadn't slowed.

Gabe took a careful step backward and came into the study. He closed the door, and stood, legs apart, in front of it. "What makes you think anything is going on with me and Michelle?"

God, she hated the alpha act men could dish out. "Don't treat me like I'm an idiot, you moron. I hear you two arguing every night. *Everyone* hears you two arguing."

"Couples argue. It's nothing I can't handle."

"Maybe I could help."

He laughed at that, but the sound was more sarcastic than jovial. "Did I miss your wedding?" He pointed the bottle of water at her. "Got some firsthand experience hidden in there somewhere?"

"Don't be a jerk. I'm only trying to help."

"Well, I don't need your help."

He turned for the door, so she tried again. "You know she's been flirting with Ben?"

It took a couple of seconds, but he once again reversed positions. He didn't speak.

"She took her clothes off in front of him last week," Dani informed him. "Did you realize that? Walking down the hall. And yesterday she was in the kitchen before he and Haley left, in a nightie that no one but *you* should see. It was embarrassing, Gabe. And completely inappropriate."

"I know. And we're all aware that she's angry with me," he explained. "She takes her anger out in really poor ways."

"Well, she needs to stop."

"And maybe you need to mind your own business."

Dani stood from the desk. "You are my business." Her voice rose. "Every one of you is. I've been here for the past fourteen years taking care of things. You can't just shrug that aside."

"Maybe we never wanted to be your business."

At his words, she froze. Then dropped to her seat. Was he serious?

"I didn't mean that," he said. And he actually looked apologetic. "Of course we were glad you were here. I'm just tired, and I'm not in the mood to argue." He held his hands out at his sides. "And I don't even know what we're arguing about."

She didn't get his attitude. Not too long ago they could talk about anything. They'd been close. It hadn't always been that way, but life had leveled out for them over the years. However, pretty much since the day she'd announced she was moving to New York, things had begun to change. His arguments with Michelle had escalated, and Dani sensed the distance growing between her and her brother every day.

She felt it with her whole family.

"I don't want to argue either," she spoke more calmly. "But I hate the thought of moving away, and leaving everything in a mess. And I'm afraid my going is what's doing it."

He stared at her then, and she could see his thoughts churning. Finally, he lost some of the steam in his stance. "Your leaving is not the problem."

"Then tell me what is," she begged. She needed to be able to fix things. "I just want to help because I care."

"I get that. Really. But it goes both ways. I care about you, too."

"Then why won't you tell me what's going on?"

He shook his head as if frustrated with a child. "Don't you get it?

I'm trying to handle this on my own—to leave you out of it—*because* I care. Because I don't want anything to get in the way of your leaving."

She rose once again, panic beginning. "What is it?"

When he didn't answer, she moved to stand in front of him. Her brother was tall and well built, but standing before her now, he didn't seem as solid as he always had. They'd relied on each other a lot through the years. She wanted to be there for him now.

"Don't push me out," she pleaded. "Tell me what's going on."

His jaw was hard, and she didn't think he would share anything with her. But when she put her hand on his arm, he broke. "Michelle wants to move," he told her, his voice cracking.

"With Jenna?" Fear swelled in her. He couldn't let Michelle take Jenna.

"With *me* and Jenna," he corrected.

"Oh." She blew out a breath. Then the meaning registered and her eyes went wide. *"Oh."*

"To the West Coast," he added flatly.

"But . . ."

They couldn't go to the West Coast. The orchard was here. He *ran* the orchard.

"I know." He nodded. "And I'll figure it out, I promise. I can hire a foreman, and still come back a couple of times a month, maybe more. I'd be here for harvest, of course. There are plenty of qualified people around to oversee things the rest of the time."

He wasn't going to run the business?

But it was their *family* business.

"Is moving what *you* want to do?" she asked. She couldn't imagine her brother anywhere but here.

He looked at her then, and she flashed back fourteen years. They'd been standing side by side at their mother's funeral. Her dad had his arm around Aunt Sadie, and the youngest kids were in front of the two of them. Cord had been on the other side of the adults with his girlfriend. But she and Gabe had stood apart from the rest of them.

They'd both felt the weight of the world on their shoulders that day. At the ages of eighteen and seventeen, they were no longer kids, and they'd understood that they had a family to think about. As the oldest siblings, they couldn't desert their family.

"I don't know," he answered, and she could see the truth of it. He'd been like her. He hadn't had options. "I'm not sure I've ever asked myself *what* I want to do with my life. No one has."

She stepped forward and wrapped her arms around her brother.

"You know I don't need hugs," he said drily. His arms remained at his sides.

"Everyone needs hugs." But she dropped her arms when he remained immobile. "We can figure this out. But let's include everyone in the decision. Maybe Jaden will want to take on more. If no one ever asked you, I'll bet no one ever asked him either."

"Dani—"

"We'll have a family meeting." She nodded, not letting Gabe stop her. "If Cord and Nate can't be here, then we'll call them, conference them in. Have you talked to Cord lately?" she asked. She'd tried Nate earlier today, but he was still avoiding her. "We should do this before picking starts, and from the looks of things I'd say that'll be soon."

"No, I haven't talked to Cord. And we start picking Wednesday. Some of the pickers got here today."

"So tomorrow night." She looked at her watch. "It's not too late. I'll call Cord and—"

"*I'll* call them," Gabe interrupted. He didn't sound happy with the fact, but he did sound resigned to it. "I'll set it up. Tomorrow night. Should we bring in Dad?"

"No." Dani shook her head.

Gabe lifted his brows.

"He's retired," she explained.

"And that's all? It has nothing to do with you being upset that he's marrying Gloria?"

"I'm not upset that he's marrying Gloria."

"Could have fooled me."

She stared stonily at him, but he merely stared back. She routinely forgot that he was more stubborn than her. Finally, she conceded. "Okay, fine. It wigs me out a bit," she admitted. "I know they've been together a long time, but I can't help but wish it were still him and Mom, you know?"

Gabe didn't agree, only stared. She sighed.

"I'll get over it," she promised. Mostly because she knew she'd have to. "But really, he's retired. He turned the business over to us. Let's let him have that. We can figure this out."

It took a few additional seconds, but Gabe's jaw finally eased. He shook his head in resignation. "*You* were supposed to be in New York before *I* figured anything out. You know you can't stay, right? Even if no one else in the family wants to run things. You're moving to New York."

"Of course someone in the family will want to run things. It's our *family* farm," she stressed. "But I don't get why you didn't include me to begin with." His omission hurt.

"Because I worry about you, you dumbass. You don't need another excuse not to go."

"I haven't been making excuses." Her voice rose with the denial.

Gabe once again glared at her. "We're all grown, Dani. Jaden's been an adult for years. You've made one excuse after another to stay here, and we won't let you do it anymore."

"No, I haven't," she continued to argue. Was he blind? "I had to stay. Dad needed me to take care of things. You *all* needed me. I had to make sure everyone was okay."

She'd promised their mother she would.

"We've been okay for years. And you're going."

When she didn't immediately reply, Gabe added, "We won't have the conversation if you don't promise me that. I'm serious." And he sounded serious. She couldn't remember ever hearing him be so firm with her.

"Of course I'll still go," she admitted. "But my boss is great. I could delay a few weeks—"

"No." His voice turned hard.

"I'm just saying. My new boss—"

"Will be thrilled when you're in New York. You can't stay, and you won't stay. You're leaving if I have to fly across the damned country with you and make sure you get off the plane."

It wasn't like she'd really had a choice of going before now, but she saw no need to argue the point further. "So you're saying that you're tired of me?" she teased, wanting to lighten the air in the room. It had grown too heavy.

Gabe scratched at the back of his neck in frustration, and he suddenly reminded her of their dad. Though their dad hadn't looked that worn out in years.

"No, sis." Gabe took her hands in his. "I'm not tired of you. Never. But you need to have your own life. It's time."

She suddenly understood this entire conversation. "And you need yours, too?"

His lips pressed together and he nodded.

She hugged him again, she couldn't help it. That time, his arms lifted to circle her loosely. He ended up patting her on the back. "Tomorrow night," she murmured into his chest. "And I'll still get on that plane in . . ." She peeked at the wall calendar and finished with "Seventeen days."

Oh, geez, she was leaving in only seventeen days. Nerves hit her again.

Gabe kissed her on the forehead and set her back from him. "I love you, dumbass. Knock 'em dead in New York, will you?"

She nodded. "I will. And I love you, too."

"Now, can you please try to enjoy harvest this year? It's the heart of us. Who we are. Slow down for once and take pleasure in it."

"I always take pleasure in it." And she didn't disagree. It was the heart of them. Some of the best times in her life had been during the middle of summer on their family farm. But slowing down wasn't an option.

"Enjoy it," Gabe stressed. "Because you're about to be a big-time New Yorker." He shot her a wink. "And who knows if *you'll* make it back next year."

"I'll be here," she told him defiantly. She couldn't imagine not being home for harvest.

"Maybe. But this year, treat it as if you won't."

He opened the door and walked out, and Dani stared after him. Fear gnawed at her. So much was changing. Gabe was moving to the West Coast? What would happen to the orchard? She'd held it together in front of him, but real fear rooted her feet to the floor. Her family—her world—was collapsing around her.

She needed Ben.

His strong face came to mind, and she wanted to go to him. Only, he wasn't there.

And for the first time in her life, she didn't think that ice cream or staring at the big Montana sky was going to soothe her heart.

She could text him.

Before she changed her mind, she grabbed her phone and tapped out a message: How are things tonight?

He answered almost immediately. Good. We went shopping again. She bought you something.

I'll love it.

You don't even know what it is.

I'll love it anyway.

Of course you will. You're good like that.

She didn't immediately reply, because she didn't know what else to say. She wanted to tell him about Gabe leaving, but that didn't seem like a text kind of conversation. But she also wasn't ready to let the connection drop.

Her phone chimed once again. I wish you were here.

She smiled. To take care of Haley?

LOL. No. Because you'd like it. And because you could use a break. Come down. Take a vacation before you start your new job. We can hang out down here for a few days.

Go to New Mexico with Ben? And Haley? She shook her head.

I can't just leave. I have work to do, and we start picking Wednesday morning. Plus, we're having a family meeting tomorrow night.

Everything okay?

A few things going on. I'll tell you about it when you get back.

Anything I can help with now?

The band constricting her heart loosened. You just did. She included a smiley face emoji. Thanks for the chat. Tell Haley I said hi.

Will do.

Her phone chimed once more as she set it down on the desk.

I'll be done here in a couple of hours. Call if you need to talk?

Unexpected dampness appeared in her eyes. I'm good. Thanks.

She put her phone down and dropped her face into her hands. She was so *not* good. How had it come to be that she got a little bad news and she couldn't function without talking to Ben?

That wasn't good at all. That was scary.

chapter eleven

B en stood face-to-face with the formidable set of double doors to his mother's seventy-five-hundred-square-foot Hollywood Hills mansion, and let himself go back twenty-four years to the very first time he'd been in this spot.

He'd been seven, and the last thing he'd wanted to do was move to California.

Especially when a stranger had picked him up at the airport to bring him here.

Today he was a grown man—a father—and had spent years in a rewarding and lucrative career. He'd reached impressive heights, won awards, gained international acclaim, and had people worldwide willing to pay big money for the opportunity to be photographed by him. He was somebody.

Yet standing there, he once again felt like that same seven-year-old kid. Hesitant, scared, and not wanting to open the doors and go in. As well as desperately clinging to the hope that his mother might show a little love.

Only this time, his wish was for that love to be directed toward his daughter.

"Are we going in?" Haley asked quietly at his side. She stood, hand in his, probably just as nervous. They'd decided on a quick detour back from New Mexico so she could meet her grandmother; however, since landing at LAX, Haley had fallen silent. Nothing about that had changed during the thirty-minute trip in the rental.

"We are going in," Ben confirmed. He glanced down at his daughter. "I just need a minute before we do."

He took in the very special outfit she'd picked out all by herself, and could already imagine his mother's response. Haley wore her new pink cowboy boots, carried a child-size green purse with a stuffed animal hidden inside, and had on a pink T-shirt and an orange tutu over her green leggings. The leggings and T-shirt matched her purse and boots respectively. This had been highly important.

She also sported a new hair bow with hearts on it that was half the size of her head. He'd had to ask the saleslady how he was supposed to attach that thing to her hair, and this morning he'd patted himself on the back for getting the job done.

Of course, it was crooked now, and her hair once again looked as though he hadn't bothered to comb it. But he was getting better. And Haley didn't seem to mind his lack of skills.

She pursed her lips as if in thought before nodding in a very grown-up fashion. "'Cause you're scared."

"I'm not scared," he immediately denied, but he saw that Haley seemed scared herself, and he had to admit that she had a point. "Maybe a little," he confessed. His daughter was smart.

"Me too," Haley said. "I think she might be mean."

At this, Ben had to chuckle. "She's not mean, sweetheart."

Just, maybe not exactly loving.

"Okay." Haley didn't sound like she believed him. "But can we go home soon?"

That was pretty much his thought, too. He wanted to go home soon. To Montana. To Dani.

But after a surprisingly good two days spent with his daughter, he'd been thinking about the fact that he had yet to introduce her to his mother. In fact, he had yet to speak to his mother since he'd learned Haley existed. Which was sad on both their parts. She had to have wondered about a granddaughter herself, given the rumors that had been flying.

So he'd decided a quick flyby could take care of the problem, and hopefully get them in and out without drawing attention to themselves. He'd called his mother's assistant, gotten an appointment on her schedule, and rebooked their flights.

And now here he stood. Too chicken to open the door.

"I'm tired of standing here, Daddy."

Before he could decide whether to laugh, climb back into the SUV, or knock, the door swung open.

"Mr. Denton," one of his mother's female staff greeted him formally, stepping aside to let them in. "Ms. Denton is waiting for you in the sitting room."

Haley's face turned up to his, her eyes round.

"That's not her," he said in a low voice and gave her a secretive wink. "Your grandmother is even scarier."

His teasing seemed to help, and the two of them moved together into the house. They arrived at the airy room with the twelve-foot ceilings that his mother often used for interviews, and as he'd feared, there was a reporter sitting anxiously on the settee.

"No," Ben said, the word coming fast and harsh. He turned, Haley's hand still in his, and immediately headed for the front door.

"Benjamin," his mother called out behind him.

"I warned you, Mother." He didn't look back. This was not an opportunity for a media plug, and he wouldn't let it be one. He'd made that clear to her assistant.

He reached the door, and surprisingly, his mother was only two steps behind. The reporter had not come out of the room.

"Ben," his mom tried again, "please. I didn't see the harm. He's from *People*."

She said the name of the magazine as though that was supposed to matter to him, and Haley inched closer, one small arm winding around his leg.

"And I don't see the good," Ben countered. "I made it clear, no press."

"It's not like it's a tabloid," she said, sounding exasperated.

He gave her a dry laugh. "And it's not like anything but you matters."

She was a piece of work. She stood before him, her shoulders pulled back and her hair and clothes prepped for a photo shoot, proving why she routinely still made the lists of Hollywood's most beautiful people.

Putting one last dagger in Ben's heart, she had yet to glance at her granddaughter.

Well, he'd tried. He could give himself credit for that.

"Good seeing you, Mother." He turned for the door.

"I'll send him home. Just come back in. I'd like to meet your daughter."

Ben slowly turned. Haley was more than his daughter.

"She's *your* granddaughter." He said the words gently, but with a stern point, and in a rare moment, Angelica Denton focused her attention on someone other than herself.

She took in Haley, at first looking horrified at the child's colorful choice of clothing, but then something interesting happened. Ben watched her eyes and the planes of her face soften. She must have realized that her granddaughter looked a surprising amount like her. And unlike seeing that same resemblance in her son, she seemed taken aback by it.

"Mom," he said. He was already here. He might as well stay. "Meet Haley."

Haley did not release his leg.

"Now you have about ten seconds to escort your guest out of the house," he added, "or we leave. And make sure he doesn't pass by us on his way out."

She nodded, looked at Haley again, and instructed another staff member to see the reporter out via the side entrance. All the while, Ben and Haley stood stiffly on the marble in the foyer. He looked down at his daughter and shot her a comforting smile. Once they had the all-clear, they moved through the halls.

It wasn't exactly a pleasant visit, but it was a visit. Haley met her grandmother. His mother met her granddaughter. And Ben was reminded of why he rarely sought out the company of his only living relative. There was nothing warm and fuzzy to be gained from it. No indication he was welcomed or wanted.

Just an item on a checklist.

It was good to ground himself in reality once in a while. He'd been on the verge of hoping there might be something more to her than seeking the spotlight.

Fifteen minutes later they were back in the rental and heading down the drive.

He looked into the rearview mirror. Haley hadn't said much while inside the house, and since coming out she'd said nothing at all.

"You okay back there?" he asked. He wasn't sure what to say or do. Maybe visiting his mom had been a mistake.

"I didn't like her," Haley announced.

Join the club.

"She's a little different," Ben acknowledged.

"Do we have to see her again?"

"Not if you don't want to."

He crossed through the security gates on the property, tossed the guard a wave, and turned onto the street. As he made the turn, he took another look at Haley. She'd gone quiet again, and she was staring out the window. The expression on her face ripped at his heart. It reminded him of those first few weeks. He'd been unable to break through to her, and she'd seemed constantly miserable.

"How about some ice cream?" he asked. They'd passed a creamery on their way in, not far from the house.

She nodded, but didn't take her eyes off the trees.

When he pulled into a parking spot a few minutes later, Haley finally turned her green gaze to him. "Can we go see my mommy now?"

Oh, shit.

"Well . . ." he stalled. He put the car into park and cut the engine. "How about you come up here and we talk about it?"

She nodded and he reached into the back to unbuckle her seat belt. After she crawled to the front, she surprised him by climbing into his lap. They'd made huge progress over the past couple of days, but this was a first.

She didn't say anything else, just waited for an answer, her eyes locked on his.

He took a deep breath and said the only thing he knew to say. "She's not coming back. And I'm sorry about that."

Haley didn't move at first, but he could see her thinking about his words. Finally, she asked, "Is she lost like Miss Dani's mom?"

He was completely inept in handling situations like this.

Which made him think about Dani's suggestion. He really needed to call that therapist.

He probably should have seen one himself as a kid.

"She's not lost, sweetheart," he began. "She's just . . . not coming back." Dani's words, warning him that Haley might be worried her mother had left because of her, echoed through his head. That she might fear making the same mistake with him. "It's not because of anything *you* did," he stressed to her. "Nothing at all. You were *perfect*. Your mother just . . ." He paused. What was he supposed to say? Has other things to do? Better things to do? He decided on another approach. "It's just you and me now."

Silent tears appeared and began rolling over her cheeks, and her fingers twisted in the tulle of her skirt. Ben did the only thing that came to mind. He wrapped both arms around her and pulled her to his chest.

They sat there like that for several minutes, and Ben couldn't help but worry he'd messed everything up. They'd probably have to start over at square one by the time he got them back to Montana. He just hoped Dani could help him fix it again. Thankfully, they'd return tonight.

After her soft sobs ended, Haley sniffled and sat up in his lap. She pushed her hair off her face and asked, "Can we get a dog, then?"

The shock of her words nearly had him laughing, but deep-seated fear kept him quiet. This wasn't over, and he'd been blind not to think about these issues before. He'd been too focused on simply getting her to be okay with him. But her problems were rooted so much deeper than whether he could be a good parent or not. He had to ensure she got the help she needed.

But to start with, if a dog would help . . .

"How about we look into getting a dog as soon as we get a house of our own?"

"We're getting a house?" she gasped. "Of our own?"

He'd meant renting a place, but yeah, why not buy a house? And why hadn't he thought of that before? Stability was what Haley needed. He nodded, excited with the prospect. He'd never had a house. "We're getting a house," he declared.

"With Jenna?"

Oh. Dang, the kid could burst a bubble faster than anything. "Not with Jenna, baby. She has her own place to live." How did he tell her that her best friend would be leaving her too?

They needed to get that dog soon.

"Can we talk about finding you some more friends?" he asked. They hadn't yet broached the subject about what had happened at the festival.

"I don't want any. I just want Jenna."

"Jenna will always be your friend," he explained. "But she may not always be *with* you. Especially when we get a new house."

Haley studied him carefully, and he could see her once again thinking. Her brow wrinkled the tiniest amount when she did.

"And you remember that Miss Dani is moving, right?" he reminded her. Might as well make sure she didn't forget that. "You won't get to see her, but she'll still be your friend, too. She'll call you on the phone. Or we can do FaceTime."

He hadn't asked Dani to call, but he knew she would. He liked that about her.

Tears appeared out of nowhere again, and this time Haley's bottom lip trembled. "I don't want them to go," she whined.

"I know, sweetheart." He stroked her hair. "I don't either. But we'll be okay. We have each other now."

"Are you going to leave, too?"

He shook his head because he couldn't get words out at first. "Never." The single word came out hard, and he hugged her tiny body to his. "Never," he repeated more softly.

Additional tears escaped from her now-spiky lashes. "My mommy left." Her voice wobbled against his chest.

"Yes, she did."

"You might, too."

"I won't, Haley. I promise you." He kept her tight against him, but lifted her chin to look at him. "I'll be your daddy and live with you and play with you for forever, baby. I promise you that."

"Will you play Barbies with me?"

Her question caught him off guard and he laughed. He nodded and pressed a kiss to her forehead. "I'll play whatever you want."

"I love Barbies."

"Then yes. I'll play Barbies with you. But wouldn't that be more fun with friends who are small like you?"

This got her attention, and she once again went into her thinking routine. The tears stopped, and her eyes wore a look that was too old for her. Finally she reached a conclusion. "I would like two new friends," she announced. "But only girls."

Relief eased the grip on Ben's heart. "Then we will find you two friends. Only girls."

"Okay. Let's do it." Her troubled features cleared, and she pressed both her hands to his cheeks before popping a kiss on his mouth. The move took his breath away.

She climbed out of his lap and turned a bright gaze to the store. "Can we have ice cream now?"

chapter twelve

A re you getting excited to leave, dear? Have you finished packing yet?"

"I'm very excited, Aunt Sadie. And no, not yet. But I'm close."

Dani closed her eyes as she lay on the boat dock that evening,
her cell phone at her ear, and lifted her chin toward the sky. The
lingering heat from the day warmed her cheeks as she tried her best
to be as relaxed as she hoped she looked.

In actuality, she was wound tight due to the upcoming family
meeting.

And because she had *not* finished packing. She still had to go
through the old desk in her bedroom, but she kept avoiding it for
fear of what else she might find.

"I'm so excited for you," Aunt Sadie said. "I know how you love
New York. But I do hope you plan on getting a place with a spare
room for when I visit."

Dani smiled at her aunt's suggestion, and pictured the two of them on that long-ago trip. Neither of them had been there before, and to a thirteen-year-old, New York City had seemed like the best place on earth. They'd done as much during the week as the trip had allowed, with plans to return the following summer.

A future trip had never happened, though.

In fact, Aunt Sadie had even quit visiting Montana. Up until then she'd stayed at the house several times a year. She'd claimed it was to give her brother and sister-in-law a break with the kids, but Dani had always imagined it was because *she* was special to her aunt.

But when the visits had stopped, no one had ever explained why.

"She's not traveling right now" was all her dad would say. But Dani had lived in fear that it was more. That Aunt Sadie had been sick.

Or just didn't want to see Dani anymore.

When she'd finally come back, it had been to help put their mother into the ground.

"I did find a place," Dani finally replied. She pinched the spot between her eyes and pushed the past from her mind. Aunt Sadie was firmly entrenched in her life now, and always would be. "As well as possibly a great roommate," she added. "However, if I sign the lease on that place, you and I might have to bunk together when you come out. There won't be an extra room."

"Well, then, maybe I'll just make Jonas splurge and put us both up in a fancy hotel. We can do research."

"Sounds like a plan to me." Aunt Sadie and her husband, Jonas, owned several boutique hotels, most of which were located in Colorado and Utah, but this wouldn't be the first time she'd taken a trip in the name of research. "Just give me time to settle in and convince my new boss that he didn't hire me for no good reason."

"You silly child. You've never believed in yourself as much as the rest of us do. It's about time you got over that, don't you think?"

Dani did believe in herself. But she was also realistic enough to see her flaws, and to know there was always room for improvement. "Silly or not, I'll be looking forward to seeing you. I'll take you to a Broadway show."

"Of course you will. And I'll take *you* to that fabulous little diner we found in Union Square."

Those had been two of their favorite stops on their trip. Dani was looking forward to revisiting both.

"So how about the boys?" Aunt Sadie's tone turned more serious. "Your father told me Nate didn't make it in again. He doing okay?"

Dani blew out a breath. "As far as I know he's fine, but you know how he is. Doesn't share much, and he definitely does his own thing. I've never understood why."

"Well, you know it was different for the younger ones."

"Yeah." There was a gap of several years between the twins and Jaden and the older three. "They didn't have Mom around as long as we did."

"Y-e-s," Sadie drew the word out, "but I . . . Dani . . . Sweetheart, what do you remember about your mother?"

Dani opened her eyes with the unusual question. "What do you mean?"

Her aunt went silent, which was odd for her. Usually on their weekly calls Dani couldn't shut her up.

With the empty air making her nervous, Dani filled the gap. "I remember how pretty she was," she started, then cringed at the description. The first thing she could say about her mother was that she'd been pretty? That seemed so superficial. "And she loved having kids." Dani hurried to get the words out. Her mother had told Dani that very fact on numerous occasions. Her kids meant the world to her.

But in trying to remember more, Dani was stumped at the lack of specifics that came to mind. She concentrated on Christmases and birthdays past. Her father showed up in her mind, along with her brothers. Even Aunt Sadie and Uncle Jonas. But she struggled to visualize her mother at all.

"She was a great mom," Dani finally said.

"Sure," Aunt Sadie agreed, but she didn't sound sold on the idea.

"And she died running errands I should have been doing," Dani finished with a bite to her words. If Dani had come home that weekend . . .

"No—"

"I don't want to talk about Mom." They'd argued before over who should have been doing what, and Sadie never saw things Dani's way. But the fact was, had Dani been home, her mother wouldn't have been where she'd been. She wouldn't have wrecked.

"The past is the past," Dani pointed out. "I'm moving to New York in a couple of weeks, and I intend to make my mother proud once and for all. That's all that matters to me now."

There were a few more seconds of silence, before her aunt agreed. "You're right. No need to bring up old hurts. So tell me, what's the first thing you're going to do when you hit the bright streets of New York again?"

The tension eased and they talked for several more minutes, and when they said their good-byes, Dani lowered the phone and stared at the sky. She'd been out there for the past hour, nervous about tonight, but the phone call had only made things worse. Had her aunt been implying something about their mother?

But what?

Footsteps sounded on the boards behind her, and Dani tilted her head back to look. Ben was coming her way, albeit seemingly upside down from her vantage point, and her heartbeat sped up. She couldn't stop the smile that spread over her face. "You're back."

He stopped right behind her, looking down into her face, and gave a heated smile in return. "I'm back." Then he shot a raised brow to the empty bowl beside her. "Was it a one-scoop or a two-scoop day?"

She made a face and pushed to a sitting position, taking in the sexy new cowboy boots on his feet. "I still can't believe you remembered that about me." She ran a hand over her hair, feeling ruffled at being caught stretched out on the dock.

"How could I forget?" he asked. "I mean . . . *gross*. You put chips on it." He lowered to sit beside her, and together they shifted so their legs dangled over the side.

"I see your point." She elbowed him in the ribs. "But really, it's good. You should try it that way."

"I'll take your word for it."

She glanced over at him then, and really, she tried hard not to stare. But, man, he looked good. And she hadn't seen him in two days. Almost three.

His hair was standing a bit on end, as if he'd run his fingers through it, and he didn't appear to have shaved since he'd left. He was quite . . . *rough* looking. Which somehow managed to tingle her toes. And made her wonder why she was suddenly so hard up for him.

"Want to talk about it?" he asked.

About her being hard up for him? She bit her lip. Wouldn't that be an interesting conversation?

But that's not what he meant. She glanced at the empty bowl.

"No need. How was your trip?" She changed the subject. "Haley still good?"

"Haley's great. In fact, I think this trip was just what we needed."

"I'm so thrilled to hear that, Ben. I told you she'd bounce back."

"You did." He grabbed her hand and held it in his lap. "But I did go ahead and make an appointment with your friend." He gave her a strange look before adding, "For both of us. We go in next week."

"Oh, Ben." She said the words softly. He struggled occasionally with knowing the right thing to do, but in the end he got it right. She slid her fingers between his and squeezed. "Janette is great. I'm confident that talking to her will only improve things."

"That's what I'm thinking, too." When she tried to untangle their fingers, he tightened his grip, and at her look, he twisted his mouth into a perplexed smile. "I missed you."

Her heart thumped. He'd missed her?

What in the heck was she supposed to do with that?

She would do *nothing* with that. "I don't believe that at all."

Instead of replying, he shrugged. Then he stared out at the lake.

There were a few boats still on the water this afternoon, and the two of them sat quietly together as several passed within view. One pulled a skier, and Dani suddenly found herself so hot she wished she were out on the lake with them.

Or maybe she should just jump off the dock and douse her head.

"So how's your week been?" Ben asked.

Lonely.

"Busy," she said instead. What was wrong with her today? "I took on a new client over the weekend, a fishing and hunting company opening up in Swan Valley."

"You're a busy woman." He peeked at her from the corner of his eye. "So you weren't sitting around pining for me?"

"Hardly."

He smiled at her comment, and tightened his fingers on hers. "Tell me about your client, then."

Delight filled her that he'd asked. "They're a start-up—brothers from this area—and they finally decided to put their money where their mouth is and follow their dreams. Yesterday we did a couple of planning meetings in the morning, then we drove out to the location in the afternoon. It was gorgeous, by the way. Amazing views of the mountains. Today I spent hours on the phone, and I think we've already nailed down a brand identity for marketing purposes. We should have the beginning ideas for a logo by the weekend."

Ben gave a low whistle. "Impressive."

She smiled at the compliment.

"You're going to be able to finish with them before you move?" he questioned.

"I'll get far enough. We'll map out a detailed strategy before I go, and hopefully the logo will be finalized. I may have to finish up a few things after I'm gone, but not anything I can't handle in the evenings. They wanted to move fast, but they also hired me with the understanding that my time was limited, especially starting next month."

Ben turned his green gaze on hers. "You'll be able to keep clients after you move?"

That was the part that stunk. "Not really. But I haven't been able to bring myself to part from things quite yet."

"Ah." He nodded as if he got it. "Changes. They can be both good and bad."

"That they can."

They both went quiet again, each in their own thoughts, and he tucked her arm under his. She noticed that their thighs were touching, but she had no idea which one of them had scooted closer. Or maybe it had been both.

As they sat doing nothing more than simply "being," it occurred to her that theirs was the only healthy relationship she'd ever had. Including the poorly-acted-out seduction routine she'd turned loose on him ten years ago. Even that had been better than any other man she'd been with. How sad.

She wondered what that said about her. Was she the problem? Or was Ben simply the solution?

She also wondered if she would be able to find this kind of comfort down the road. A relationship where she was an equal as opposed to a servant. Where the two of them talked.

And he listened.

She hoped so. Because she didn't want to be alone forever.

"So you took Haley shopping again?" She pulled herself from her thoughts, grasping at a conversation topic.

"I did." Ben appeared more relaxed than she'd seen him since he'd been back. "We had no meltdowns, and she talked nonstop. I'm calling it a victory."

"What did you buy?"

He held his feet in the air. "Besides boots?"

She grinned. "I like the boots. They suit you."

"Wait'll you see the cowboy hat she picked out for you. Just remember, you promised to love it."

"And I will. Sounds like you had a good time."

"You don't know the half of it. We also bought Barbies." He gave her an eye roll that was way cuter than he probably realized. "She came back so loaded down, I'll have to build her a closet just to store them all in."

"And I assume she's inside right now showing them to Jenna?"

"Couldn't wait to get back."

They fell into silence again, and Dani watched a fish jump in the lake. The tiny splash sent ripples spreading through the water.

"She also met my mom," Ben said. "We stopped off in LA."

"On this trip?" Dani's heart pounded with the admission. This felt big. "They hadn't met before?"

"I wasn't ready before. My mom is a lot like Lia."

"*Oh,*" she said, then wrinkled her nose with her next thought. "Maybe that's why you dated Lia?"

"Oh, geez, really?" He shuddered as if disgusted with the idea, then seemed to think about it. In the end, he merely shrugged. "Anyway, I surprised Mom with the visit, so she only had time to line up *one* reporter. Whom I got rid of immediately. In the end, I think meeting her brought Haley and me closer together."

"Bonding over bad mothers?"

He laughed easily. "Something like that. After a somewhat stiff conversation, Mom offered to put Haley in a movie. Haley's response was epic."

"And what was that?"

"She declared that she'd rather take pictures, like me."

Dani smiled along with Ben, and purposely bumped into his arm. She understood what that would have meant, and she loved that Haley had given it to him.

Leaning back, he braced his free hand on the dock, but kept his other wrapped securely around hers. Their clasped hands rested on his thigh, and her next topics of conversation vanished as she tried her best to ignore the hard muscle under their fingers. She picked at a loose thread on her jeans. One foot kicked back and forth over the water.

After another moment of pretending she wasn't aware of every breath he took, he squeezed her fingers, and when she looked back at him, he nudged his chin toward the empty bowl. "What's with the ice cream this time?"

She focused on the bowl.

Though they still had the family discussion to get through, she knew the outcome already. Gabe was leaving. And she was exhausted from the weight of worrying.

The backs of her eyes burned unexpectedly, making her quickly look away.

"Hey." Ben sat up. He put his arm around her. "What happened?"

She let her head drop to his shoulder. "My family is falling apart. And I can't figure out a single thing to do to stop it."

His arm clenched at her side. "What's going on?"

"I think Gabe is going to move away."

"Yeah?"

She looked up at him; his tone had been strangely casual. He also had a blank look on his face. "You knew," she accused.

Guilt flashed through his eyes. "He mentioned there were problems between him and Michelle. Not that we couldn't all figure that out," he muttered. "But he asked me not to tell you."

"Man code?" she asked sarcastically. She hated being left out of things.

"No. Just . . ." He lifted a hand toward her face as if to touch her, but in the end dropped it back to his lap. "I didn't know if I should. Gabe pointed out that they know you a lot better than I do. It made sense. Said he was protecting you."

She snorted. "That's his claim. Didn't want to worry me. Wanted me to stay out of it."

"I take it you're not?"

She smirked. "Cord should be in anytime. He caught a late flight. We'll call Nate when he gets here."

"Ah." He winked at her. "Big sister taking charge."

"It's what I do."

And for the first time, she didn't want to do it. She wanted someone else to handle things.

Ben's arm relaxed around her, and she once again tucked her head onto his shoulder. She'd missed this over the past ten years. "I've enjoyed us talking again," she said.

"Yeah." He stroked her arm. "Me too." After a pause, he added, his voice taking on a slight hitch, "Though I could think of a few things other than talking that would be nice, as well."

She peeked up at him. "Are you coming on to me again, Denton?"

"Would it get me anywhere if I were?"

Yes. "No."

She didn't need to let this go anywhere, she knew that. He was just messing with her. Filling time. It didn't make sense to even play with this kind of fire. Yet she stayed right there in his arms. And she almost purred when his fingertips lowered to trail along the outside of her thigh.

"Ben . . ."

"It's all good," he soothed teasingly, and she could see him holding in a smile. "This is only me comforting you, babe. You've had a bad day."

She snorted once again. "And you're full of it."

"Yeah." He smiled that smile she loved so well. "But it's the only way to get you in my arms."

She studied him then, pulling back a little, but not so far that he had to turn her loose. They'd had weighty conversations since he'd been back. Not unlike the one they were having today. However, today's seemed different. *He* was different. Had his trip with Haley changed him that much?

And just how much was he teasing her?

"Why do you want me in your arms?" she challenged. "You can get any woman you want."

"Does that mean I can get you?" He tried to pull her closer, but she held back.

"Come on, Ben. Be serious. You're just bored, and I'm handy. You never even showed interest in me back then until *I* made the move. I'd wager that you wouldn't show interest now if I hadn't back then."

He separated his arm from her body. "I didn't show interest because I was respecting you."

"You didn't show interest because you had plenty of better options to choose from."

"No." The word came out instantly.

She bit her lip.

He touched a finger to her jaw and lifted her face, and she couldn't make herself look away.

"Is that what you really think?" he asked. "Have you ever looked at who you are, Dani? And I don't mean on the outside, though Lord knows you're pretty damned awesome on the outside. Babe, you're the most beautiful woman I've ever met. You would end your world—you *did* end your world—for your family. And you did an amazing job of raising them—even though your dad should have done that himself."

"My dad needed me," she defended.

"I'm sure he did. And that he appreciates all you've done. But the truth is, it was his responsibility, yet *you* set aside your life to come home. To pretty much handle everything. And I know you'd do it again if given the same circumstances. You're honest and caring, sweetheart. You're smart. And you never treat anyone any way other than how you'd like to be treated. That's rare in people. You're a jewel. And it's *not* because you're handy."

His words spun around her, closing in on her the same way his arm had, and she found herself on the verge of tears once again. So few people ever looked at her the way he did.

"So no, it wasn't that I had no interest. It's that I was treated like a son by your father," he explained. The pad of his thumb grazed over her earlobe. "That Gabe was the closest thing I had to a brother. I couldn't take advantage of his sister." He gave a half smile. "But also because your brother would have kicked my ass. Or tried to. As would have Cord. Or hell, probably even the twins or Jaden. You had an army watching over you, sweetheart. An army protecting you. Your brothers would lay down their lives for you."

She nodded. She knew that. They'd had to rely on each other too much over the years not to be close. "We've been through a lot together," she spoke softly. "It wasn't easy losing our mom."

"I'm sure it wasn't. But I'd be willing to bet that wasn't all there was to it, either. You may be their *big* sister, but they're the men around here. And you're their *sister.* They'll have your back no matter what."

Was that why Gabe hadn't wanted to tell her about his plans?

She supposed it was, though it still annoyed her that he'd tried to leave her out.

"You're right," she said. "I know." They may have fought and disagreed over the years, but her brothers were her soldiers. Which was why she'd never minded staying. The six of them were a unit.

She just wished they weren't all flying solo these days.

But then, she was too.

"Did anyone tell you about Jaden yet?" Ben asked, his voice now hesitant.

"What about him?"

His eyes burned into hers for a long moment before he looked away. He groaned.

"What?" she asked.

"I don't want to tell you."

Which meant that she didn't want to hear it. Or maybe it was about Megan. Were they getting married?

She gasped. Was Megan pregnant?

Poor Jaden. That would certainly change his life.

But, a baby. How sweet.

Her phone chimed, and she glanced at it where it remained on the dock to see a text from Gabe. "Cord's here!" She practically squealed the words. She grabbed her phone and the empty bowl and rose. "I have to go." She hadn't seen Cord in a year.

She hurried up the path, leaving Ben to follow, and she put everything else out of her mind. Cord was home. She'd often felt that he'd taken their mother's death the hardest. He'd come upon the wreck minutes after it happened. He'd been the one to call for the ambulance.

He'd also been the one who'd changed the most afterward.

It had hardened him. Too much sometimes.

Therefore, Dani was even more protective of him than she was of the younger ones. Not that he needed the protection. Or allowed it. But she watched over him anyway.

She'd sent him care packages throughout college and medical school, and he was now set up in a private practice in Billings. It made her proud. But he hadn't softened over the years, and that bothered her. She hoped he'd someday find a woman who could help ease his pain. He deserved that.

"Dani."

She jerked to a stop just outside the back door and whirled to face Ben. "What?"

He trailed his gaze over her shoulder, and hers followed. Her family was waiting for her in there. They didn't see her yet, but she saw them. Gabe, Cord, Nick, and Jaden. Four strong, healthy, really good men. She'd helped in that. And she was proud of it.

And now she had to do her best to convince Jaden that it was his time to take over.

With a baby on the way, this could be a good thing for him. Bring a new generation into the family business.

Ben turned back to her. "I'll be around when you're done. If you need to talk."

She wasn't sure what she might need to talk about, but she appreciated the offer. "Thanks."

He took one final look at her family before leaning in and laying a long, hot kiss on her lips, catching Dani by surprise. Pulling away, he opened the door and strode into the house.

chapter thirteen

Dani stared at Ben's retreating back as he moved through the room and greeted her brothers. What in the heck had that been? Kiss her and then walk away?

Before she could even decide if she wanted to be kissed?

She growled under her breath. Men. They wore her out sometimes.

But also . . . *men* . . . When they came like Ben Denton, she could use a few more in her life.

She touched her fingertips to her lips. Because yeah, she'd liked it. And she hadn't needed additional time to figure that out.

"Dani," Cord said from across the room, and Dani forgot all about Ben.

She ran into the house and wrapped her arms around her brother. He immediately swept her up, lifting her to her toes. Unlike her oldest brother, Cord *had* been known to hug her on occasion.

Not often, which made them all the sweeter, but at least she occasionally got them.

When he set her on her feet, she was fairly certain she glowed. Her family was home. Most of them.

"I wish Nate were here," she exclaimed.

"I'm here, sis."

The words came from Gabe's cell lying in the middle of the coffee table.

"Nate!" She moved to the table, and stood looking down, her hands clasped in front of her. "Come home, you idiot. Would you do that for me, please? I'm desperate to see you."

Nate hadn't been home in more than two years.

A rumble of laughter came from the speaker. "I booked a flight today. I'll be home this time next week. Sorry I'm not there right now . . ."

"I know. You're busy. But next week will be great. I'll cook your favorite meal."

"Or maybe I'll cook yours."

"Right," she teased. As far as she knew, none of her brothers even knew where the stove was. They could only find the kitchen because it had a fridge in it.

She caught a gentle smile from Ben, who remained at the edge of the kitchen, then he winked and headed down the hall. She was left in the family room, standing in the middle of her brothers, and for the first time in a long while, she felt like everything was okay with her world. She had her family. She'd done her mother proud.

"So let's get to it," Gabe spoke up, reminding everyone of why they were there.

Dani nodded impatiently, and took a seat on the coffee table beside the phone. Everyone else settled on the furniture and turned to Gabe.

"So it looks like I'll be moving," he started.

The air went out of Dani's lungs, because even though she'd known it was coming, she hadn't been able to keep from hoping he'd change his mind.

She also noted that no one in the room seemed surprised by the announcement.

Seriously? They'd all known about this? Irritation tickled in her throat. She should have known he'd tell the boys before he told her. Or more accurately, he'd had no intention of telling her at all.

"Before I start looking for a foreman to be here when I'm not," Gabe continued, "I need to ask if any of you want to run things."

Dani looked, one by one, at her brothers, certain someone would speak up. Not Cord, of course; he was a doctor. But Nick couldn't be a bull rider forever, and he'd never left Montana on a permanent basis. Clearly he loved the area.

Yet he remained silent.

Then she turned to Jay and smiled. Did he really have a baby on the way?

"Jaden?" she asked when the youngest didn't look at her. "I thought you might want to take over. It would be a great opportunity for you, and we could bring you in more help since you'll be doing the books, too. And if you and Megan . . ."

She trailed off as she realized that no one at all was looking at her. In fact, they were making it a point *not* to look at her. Nerves tingled on the back of her neck. She was missing something.

"What is it?" she asked abruptly. She knew their nonlooks well enough to understand they didn't want to tell her something. "Is it the pregnancy? Ben told me."

That got everyone's attention.

"Pregnancy?" Cord asked. "Who's pregnant?" His eyes dropped to her stomach and his jaw hardened.

"Not me," she squeaked. She pointed at her youngest brother. "Jaden."

"Well, hell. I'm not pregnant."

"You know what I mean. Megan."

The room once again went silent, except for Nate clearing his throat through the phone.

"You knocked her up?" Nate's voice sounded in the room.

Jaden shook his head. "I did *not* knock her up."

"But—"

"And Ben told you this?" Gabe interrupted Dani.

She replayed her conversation with Ben, remembering that he hadn't actually told her anything. "Not in so many words, I guess. He said there was something about Jaden that you should tell me." She glanced toward the hallway. She could hear Ben and the girls playing upstairs, and assumed Megan might even be in there with them since she wasn't down here. "She's not pregnant?"

"No," Jaden answered. He rose from his seat and paced the length of the room.

"Then what do you need to tell me?"

This time, Nate didn't even clear his throat. There was only the silence.

"Come on, guys." Nerves had her bouncing the heel of her foot. "What is it?"

"Quit shaking your leg," Nate said from beside her. "You're rattling the phone in my ear."

"Sorry," she muttered. She forced herself to be still and turned to Jay.

"She's *not* pregnant," he finally replied. He took a deep breath. "But I am moving in with her."

"Dani," Gabe started before Jaden could say more. He ignored their younger brother's glare. "What he's saying is, he doesn't want to run the place either. He has other plans."

"What I'm *saying* is . . ." Jaden stressed his words, and Dani swiveled back to him. The glasses perched on his nose gave him a slightly different look than the rest of her brothers, yet he still had plenty of the Wilde characteristics in him. Meaning, he was full of stubborn. "That I'm not coming home at all," he finished.

It took a moment for his words to register. When they did, Dani rose from her seat. "You have to come home. You're taking over my job."

"I'm not. And I'm sorry I didn't tell you that before. I didn't even get an accounting degree."

She didn't understand. Jaden always ran a little more rebellious than the rest of them, yeah. Nothing illegal or out of control, as Nate had been known to do, but as the youngest child, Jaden often walked right along the edge of the line. He pushed the limit. He said things others wouldn't.

But to not come home? To not get the degree?

"He *did* get an accounting degree," Gabe added, his tone sounding exhausted.

"I minored in accounting," Jay corrected. "But my major is psychology. My *interest* is psychology. Which is why I'll be going to school in Seattle next fall, working on my master's."

"You're going back to school?" Dani asked, and for the first time since she'd come home to take care of her brothers all those years ago, she lit up with anger over what she'd done without. "I had a full ride to Columbia, and I killed it to come home," she said, her voice rising with her words. "Gabe got to go to school the very next year. All of you have gone on to do what you want. And don't get me wrong, I'm happy for each of you. But now, when I have the chance to go *back* to New York, to finally start the life I've always wanted, you're going to be so selfish as to continue on in school?"

"You could have gone back to school years ago," Jaden shot back. "No one asked you to stay all this time."

"And you could come home now and put in your time here."

Jaden ignored her response and faced Gabe. "And personally," he said to his brother, "I don't think *you* should have to go back and forth either. Unless you want to. You're moving to LA. Go live your life. We can find someone to run the whole thing. Living in the house could even be a perk, help with the cost of hiring out."

"No!" Dani shouted. She stood in the middle of the floor shaking her head. "No," she said again. "We can't just give everything to somebody else."

"We wouldn't be giving it to someone else," Gabe said, trying to soothe her. "It would still be our farm. Just not managed by us. And we would all still come home for harvest."

"But our house."

"Then fine," Jaden added, his frustration evident. "We don't have to include the house if that's a big deal. We can see how this works out first. Add it in later if we want to."

Dani looked wildly from one brother to the other. They all cut glances at her, but no one made direct eye contact. "I don't understand what's going on. Why won't one of you run it? It's Dad's legacy. It would break Mom's heart if she were here to see how things are falling apart."

They all remained silent.

"What?" she shouted frantically. She was still missing something.

"Maybe none of us want to do it *because* of Mom," Jaden suggested. His words stopped Dani in her tracks.

"Jaden—" Gabe butted in.

"What do you mean?" Dani asked.

No one answered.

"Gabe?" She turned to her oldest brother. "What does he mean?"

"Your memories are different from ours," Gabe said gently. "That's all."

"What memories?"

"Mom wasn't a saint, Dani." Jaden's voice rose with his words. "Not even close."

Nate cleared his throat.

"I never said she was a saint," she shot back.

"You haven't said anything about her for years except how proud we've got to make her," Nick pointed out. She faced him, and he went on, his gaze no longer breaking from hers. "You haven't let us change a thing in this house since she died, Dani. It's a shrine to her. Why do you think Dad moved out?"

Dani gaped. "That makes no sense. Why *wouldn't* he want to be in the home he'd made with the woman he loved?"

Cord snorted. So far that was his only contribution to the argument.

"What?" She whirled on him. "You don't think Dad loved Mom? Hell, maybe he didn't. Maybe that's why he's marrying Gloria now."

"Mom's been gone fourteen years," Cord interjected. "You think he's supposed to stop living because she died? Gloria makes him happy. They should have gotten married years ago."

"I know," Dani said, "it's just . . ." She hadn't meant to get on the topic of their dad, but now that they were, she couldn't help but continue. She pulled in a shaky breath. "Did he not love Mom?" It felt like that sometimes, though she'd been reluctant to admit it. The way he never talked about her. Dani couldn't remember the last time her dad had actually uttered her mother's name. It was as though she hadn't existed.

"Of course he loved Mom," Gabe answered. Cord snorted again.

Dani's temper flared. "Seriously, am I the only one who misses her? Who feels bad that her life ended the way it did? She didn't mean to die! We should have done something to keep the accident from happening. We should honor her better than we are."

A muscle ticked in Cord's jaw.

"Let's get back on topic," Gabe spoke up. "The farm. The house." He stood from his spot on the couch and looked at Dani. Her breathing was ragged.

"What am I not remembering correctly?" she asked the room. She would *not* let this go.

"It's not just that she *wasn't* a saint," Jay added callously. "She was a cold-hearted bitch."

Dani gasped. "She was not!"

"I may not remember it as clearly as everyone else, but I remember enough," he said. "She was heartless, Dani. She didn't care about us. That very fact has shaped my entire life. It's shaped all of us."

"Ask me how many times she ever came into our room," Nate spoke from the phone.

Dani stared down at the object. "What do you mean?"

"Never," Nick added. "No good-nights, no waking us up. She certainly didn't deign to come in and play with us."

"She didn't love us, Dani," Nate said. "She manipulated us. You most of all."

"No, she did not." Dani stared wide-eyed at her brothers, but no one backed her up. "Guys," she pleaded. "Come on. Tell him he's wrong. She would have done anything for us. That's why I'm here. Because I couldn't let her down. We can't let her down now. She—"

"She killed herself," Cord suddenly roared.

The room went deathly silent, and Dani saw Ben standing in the kitchen, his expression as shocked as hers.

"The kids," Ben started. He lifted a hand and pointed vaguely toward the ceiling. "They're in bed, but . . ." His gaze locked on Dani's, and she could see his worry for her before he shifted to Cord and then to Gabe. "Your voices are carrying upstairs," he finished.

Gabe nodded, muttered, "We'll keep it down," and Dani dropped back to the coffee table.

Cord rose from his seat and came over to sit beside Dani, and Ben quietly left the room.

"I don't understand." Dani's voice shook. "Why would you say that? You don't mean suicide?"

"I do." Cord didn't sound confused, but Dani knew he had to be.

"No." She shook her head. "It was an accident. She was running errands. She had a migraine."

"She wanted it to look that way," Cord told her. "But I was there. It wasn't an accident."

She stared at him. "You *saw* it happen?"

"No. I—"

"Then how can you even say that?" She was equal parts mortified and scared.

"We've talked about it before," Gabe spoke up, his voice grim. "When you look at the facts, she did it to herself, though we doubt she intended to go so far as to kill herself."

So many thoughts spun through her head all at once. She landed on the one she could best deal with. "You've talked about it before," she repeated. "Meaning, all of you. Without me?"

They'd all known Gabe was leaving, they'd clearly known Jaden wasn't coming home, and they'd also talked about their mother's death. Without her. Had they ever included her in anything?

She'd thought they were a team.

Yet clearly they weren't. Not with them keeping everything from her.

She shook her head again, her hands shaking in her lap, and Cord pulled her to his side.

"It came up a few years ago," he explained gently. "Most of us had reason to wonder, but we'd kept it to ourselves, because it sounded so crazy. Until Jaden told us what he'd learned."

Her eyes were so dry she couldn't blink. "What was that?"

"Narcissistic Personality Disorder," Jaden said from where he now stood by the fireplace. "Our mother was a classic example."

Gabe crossed his arms over his chest, but he didn't say anything.

"You've forgotten what she was like, Dani." This came from Nick. "After you came home, you went into a kind of frenzy to keep everything going, wanting the house to be perfect, us to be perfect. You wouldn't let anyone say a negative thing about her, so none of us ever questioned how things had been."

"Not that we would have questioned anything out loud," Nate added sarcastically. "We were masters at never admitting the obvious. She taught us well."

"I don't understand," Dani whimpered.

"Narcissistic Personality Disorder is more than simply being self-absorbed," Jaden explained. "Almost everyone has moments of narcissistic traits—being conceited, selfish—but our mother went beyond that. Hers was a mental disorder in which she had a deep-seated need to be the center of attention. All the time. At the cost of anyone and everyone around her. And she accomplished this by employing a lifetime of manipulating those closest to her."

"After the funeral," Nick jumped back in, "you went nuts if we didn't put her on some sort of pedestal. It was as if you couldn't remember what she'd really been like." He gave a little shrug and glanced momentarily at his feet. "Or maybe *we* were the ones remembering incorrectly—or so we thought. There were a lot of unvoiced questions for a long time. So instead of pushing back against you and all that you were doing for us, instead of bringing up memories of things we weren't even sure had happened, it seemed easiest to go along. We took our anger, and shoved it out of the way. And we let you do your thing."

"But it ate at us," Cord finished.

Dani remained close to Cord's side, but she looked over at Gabe. He had yet to contribute to this absurdity. He didn't agree with this, did he?

"So, you all knew from the beginning," she began, quickly sorting through everything that had been said, "or *believed* from the beginning . . . that Mom killed herself, yet you didn't think it was important to share that with me?"

"It was that whole don't-talk-about-how-messed-up-we-are thing," Nate explained.

"I don't know what you mean by that." She shrugged off Cord's arm and stood.

"I mean, we were the perfect family in public, Dani. Always. Mom looked the part. Hell, she played the part. The town believed in her sainthood. But at home? When the doors were closed? She fucked us all up."

Dani couldn't do more than stare at the phone.

"Even Dad," Jaden added. "For narcissists, it's all about them. She didn't have the capability to be empathetic toward any of us. Her world revolved around her, and her actions were based purely on getting what she wanted. We had to earn her love, yet that was impossible. It was worse with you because you're a girl—in direct competition with her as a woman."

Dani narrowed her eyes at Jay's words. She hadn't been in competition with their mom.

"I think even as small kids," he continued, "us younger brothers picked up on the fact that you got the worst end of things. You were her direct target. But it's not like she left the rest of us alone. Narcissists need everyone in their lives to revolve around them. They're known to pit siblings against each other to keep the focus on themselves. If you don't know if you can trust your brother . . ."—Jaden glanced at Cord and Gabe—"then you'll turn to your mother. Even a mother who twisted the facts whenever it suited her, simply to keep a cohesive family unit from forming, to make sure she was always the center of attention."

Had their mother done that to them?

Was that even possible? They *were* a cohesive family unit!

But . . . it hadn't always been that way.

Dani eyed Gabe then, who remained standing, arms crossed, several feet from her. He returned her stare, but didn't utter a word. He'd been their mom's favorite. She remembered that with sudden clarity. He could do no wrong. It had led to jealousy between them. Fights. Dani had hated him for a long time.

Had that carried over into his college years?

She couldn't remember. She only knew that at some point things had righted themselves between them. She'd thought their fights had come from the stress of all they had to handle together, but had it actually been latent rivalry built up by their mom?

Bits and pieces of other arguments flashed through her mind. Some between her and Cord, others as heated debates between Cord and Gabe. There had definitely been a time when the three of them hadn't gotten along. But wasn't that normal teenage behavior?

Finally, Gabe lowered his arms and loosened his stance. "Don't you remember how hard you tried to please her?" he asked. His words were spoken with only the tiniest hint of softness, and Dani could sense it was his way of reaching out. To help her see these "facts"?

"No." Dani shook her head. What they were saying wasn't right. Her mother had loved her. She'd loved all of them.

"You could make straight As in school," Gabe said, "but it wasn't all perfect hundreds, therefore you let her down. You won Miss Cherry Blossom, but she was ashamed of the dress you wore. Said it wasn't respectable and didn't represent a true Wilde. You—"

"Stop." Dani held a hand up in front of her. "I don't want to hear any more."

"She always claimed to have headaches," Nate said from the phone. "You had to take care of her. And us. You raised me, Nick, and Jaden, Dani. From the beginning. Never her."

"I—"

She was so confused.

"She pretty much stayed in bed the first few years of Jay's life," Nick added.

Dani closed her eyes as memories began to creep in, but she didn't like what she saw so she opened them again.

"Psychosomatic and emotionally needy," Jaden added when her gaze landed on his. "She faked illnesses to get what she wanted. She required attention to be directed her way. Always. But, she never handed any out. Why do you think I went into psychology? I had a mother who never mothered me. I needed to understand why."

She pressed a hand to her mouth as more pictures tried to push into her head. She didn't want to remember. She didn't want to know.

Cord moved to her side, but she jerked out of his reach, backing blindly away from all of them. She couldn't breathe. Nothing she'd done had ever pleased her mom. She remembered that now. Nothing. Her mom had hated her.

Yet, after Dani had come home from that trip with Aunt Sadie, her mother had decided that she and Dani should be best friends.

At first Dani liked it. If her mom was her friend, that had to mean that she finally liked Dani. Maybe even loved her.

Only . . .

"Oh, God," she moaned as more memories surfaced. The things that had been shared with her about her parents' relationship. She couldn't block the visions out. "No." She shook her head slowly. "NO." She wrapped her arms around her stomach and rocked in place.

Her brothers had all gone quiet, and she forced her eyes open once again. Each one of them stood, pain painted across their faces.

"We need to call Dad," Gabe said.

"Does he know too?"

Every one of them nodded.

"*God,*" she moaned again. "Why have you all kept this from me?"

"We were protecting you," Gabe answered. He had a phone in his hand. "We did the best we could."

"Stop it!" she shouted, throwing her arms up. "Just, stop it. I never needed protecting. I shouldn't have been excluded from things." She pointed a finger at Gabe. "And put that phone down. I'm not ready to talk to Dad yet."

He paused before slowly lowering the phone.

"Why do you think suicide?" She had to know.

All eyes turned to Cord.

He swallowed, then *he* moved off to stand by himself. His face was the hard steel he'd perfected over the years, but now the light had even gone out of his eyes. He looked like the shell of a person that Dani felt, and that scared her even worse. Whatever he was about to say, she instinctively knew it was why their mother's death had hit him the hardest. It was why he'd changed. And likely why he'd never change back.

"The first time she hurt herself was when you went to New York," he said. "I found her," he added. "I always found her."

Always?

Dani felt sick. She sank to the couch and pulled her feet onto the cushion. Wrapping her arms around her knees, she listened with horror to the stories her brother told.

Her mother had sliced the tip of her finger off that first time. They'd rushed her to the hospital, and the doctor had managed to save it. She'd wanted to call Dani to come home, but their dad wouldn't let her. She'd screamed at them for days to call Dani. Her dad had even removed the phones from the house until Dani had returned.

"That's when Aunt Sadie quit taking me places," she muttered to herself. "And coming to visit."

Cord paused, his eyes shifting to Gabe, and Dani suddenly realized another truth. She'd questioned for over a year as to why their aunt had quit visiting. She'd asked her parents—had even gone to her brothers for answers. No one had a clue. Or so they'd claimed.

But now she could see that they had, in fact, had a clue.

Their mother had hurt herself because Dani was off having fun, then the source of that fun disappeared from their lives. Every last one of them had likely known *exactly* why Aunt Sadie quit visiting.

Yet not a single word was ever uttered to her.

Had their mother accomplished that, too? Keeping Sadie away, as well as keeping her brothers' mouths shut?

Probably. If everything else they were saying was true . . .

The second "accident" had been after Dani's graduation, Cord explained.

Dani remembered. "Mom didn't make it to the ceremony because of a headache. Then she had an allergic reaction to a new medicine she'd taken. She had to go to the hospital."

"Where they pumped her stomach," Cord explained. "She'd swallowed a bottle of pills about five minutes before I was supposed to pick her up. She knew I'd find her in time to save her."

"We canceled my graduation party and spent the night at the hospital."

"All of us making *her* the center of attention. Just like she wanted."

The rest of her brothers remained silent. It was just her and Cord now, sharing what they remembered.

"The third time was the wreck," he stated flatly.

"You found her."

"She knew what time I'd be coming through there."

Surely her mother hadn't been that scheming. "But why do you think . . ." She quit talking. Her brothers were smart. Whatever Cord was about to say, she knew they hadn't come to the conclusion lightly. Her mother had committed suicide while trying to screw with their heads. And Dani had revered her for years.

She had no idea how she'd been so blind.

"She'd hit someone else," Cord said. "Totaled this other car. When I got there, Mom was sitting in the driver's seat, the air bag having deployed due to the tree she'd run into, and her seat belt locked into place. She was angry. She couldn't get out of the car because of the seat belt not releasing, and the air bag had left white dust on her outfit and given her a nosebleed. Also, her purse was on the floor and she couldn't reach it. Therefore, she couldn't 'fix herself' before the ambulance arrived.

"When she saw me, she informed me that the other car wasn't supposed to be in the way, then she said, 'Call Dani. Tell her to come home.'" Cord shook his head. "I refused."

Their mother had called the day before the accident to ask Dani if she would come home and take care of the kids if anything ever happened to her. Dani had never told anyone about that phone call because their mother had also begged Dani to fly home that weekend. She'd claimed a migraine coming on.

Dani had refused. She'd been invited to her first party as a college student, and she hadn't wanted to miss it.

Nor had she any desire to travel cross-country for her mother.

She remembered that conversation clearly now. She'd been thrilled to finally be away from home—away from her mother—and the last thing she'd wanted to do was come back and spend the weekend being made to feel less than enough.

Only, if she *had* come home, their mother would still be alive today.

She sat, unblinking, arms still hugging her knees, alone on the couch. Her mother had manipulated her until the end.

And she'd killed herself because of it.

"I went to check on the second vehicle," Cord continued his story. "I stayed with the other driver because she was young and pregnant and Mom seemed fine, but mostly because I was angry and I didn't want to go back over there. When the ambulances arrived, I watched the EMTs head to Mom's car. They began working on her, but then they just stopped. She'd died while I wasn't looking. Traumatic aortic disruption. The impact with the seat belt and air bag had caused a rip between the aorta and the heart, and she'd quickly bled out."

Dani remembered that part of it. A freak accident, the doctor had said.

Or was it karma having the last laugh?

Either way, their mother had died and Cord had stood by while it happened. Chances were good he felt he should've been able to save her.

"The pregnant lady?" Dani inquired about the other woman.

"Was fine."

She nodded. That's what she thought. "You couldn't have saved Mom," she told him. What could a sixteen-year-old have possibly done with an internal bleed that he didn't even know about?

His jaw tensed again, and she shivered at the hardness in his eyes. "That's just the thing. Probably I couldn't have. But the truth is, I'm not sorry I didn't."

And neither was Dani, though she'd forgotten that part until now, too.

She'd not been sorry that their mom had died.

She chewed on her lip before saying the only thing she could think of. "No wonder you never want to come home."

"It's a wonder any of us ever do," Nick added solemnly.

Dani looked at Nick then. He appeared as ripped apart as the rest of them.

"We come home for you," Jaden told her.

Tears slipped down her cheeks. "To protect me?" Because she'd been so out of touch with reality, she hadn't even remembered how destructive their mother had been. She didn't understand how she'd blocked that out for so long.

"Because we love you," Nate corrected.

chapter fourteen

The rest of the house had gone quiet, and it ate at Ben to sit in his room and wait them out. Dani's mother had killed herself? He would never have guessed that.

He'd hung out in the hallway after Cord's proclamation, long enough to hear the words Narcissistic Personality Disorder. Then he'd come into his room to google it. The stories he'd read over the past few minutes had turned his blood cold. It was hard to imagine a mother who not only didn't love her own kids, but also by turns ignored, bullied, criticized, and manipulated them, all to feed her own needs.

It made of him think of his own mother. And Lia.

He didn't think it was the same for them. He hoped it wasn't, for Haley's sake. Those two seemed more like they simply had no time for others rather than needing to use others for their own gain.

Dani's mother, though. She sounded like an emotional vampire. As if her children had been pawns in a very strange game of making sure the world revolved only around her.

He wondered how badly that had messed them all up. But he wondered most about Dani.

And what he could do to help.

Because he couldn't leave her alone to deal with this on her own. He'd already been playing with the idea of suggesting they see what this thing was between them. And yes, there was a thing. Even if they were both pretending it didn't exist.

He'd spent approximately sixty hours away from her over the past three days, and she'd appeared in his thoughts a surprising number of times. He'd missed her. He'd wanted to tell her all about his days with Haley.

Hell, he'd just wanted to talk to her.

So yeah, there was a thing. And he'd come back to Montana giving serious consideration to letting her know how he felt.

But now he couldn't tell her anything. What was happening out in the family room was far more important than his feelings, and it sounded like something that would have long-term effects.

Which meant, Dani was priority number one. This *thing* between them? This thing had to be forgotten.

His door suddenly opened, and Dani stepped into his room.

In the next instant he had her in his arms. Her hands lifted as quickly as his, closing around his waist and holding tight. She buried her face in his chest.

They stood like that for several minutes until her brothers' low murmurs registered from the other room. Ben shifted the two of them so he could quietly close his door. This was no time for one of her overprotective siblings to decide they needed to safeguard her against *him*.

She continued clinging without uttering a sound. She wasn't crying, and she was so quiet he couldn't even hear her breathing. But he felt her heartbeat against his chest.

He scooped her up, her arms going around his neck, and a whimper finally slipping from between her lips. Then he carried her to the chair in the corner of the room. After he settled them both on the cushion, she buried her face in his neck and her body began to tremble.

"Ben," she moaned.

"Shhh." He rocked her in his arms. "I'm here, baby. I've got you."

He crisscrossed his arms around her back, holding her close, and they sat like that for a long time. She never completely broke down, just let out the occasional sob. Finally, her body quit shaking and she lifted her face from his neck. Watery eyes sought him out.

"My mother," she whispered.

And he felt like he'd died.

Her gorgeous blue eyes pleaded with him. As though begging him to fix it. But he had no clue what to say. What to do. He'd been as floored as she. "I know," he finally muttered. He squeezed her to him and buried his nose in her hair. "I know," he said quietly once again.

"I hate my brothers," she muttered.

He gave a sad smile because he understood. She was a proud woman. She'd come home and taken over the care of her family, and they'd kept life-altering information from her. No doubt it had been done with the best of intentions, but now they all had to live with the outcome.

Her eyes were still on him, watching him carefully. The moisture had slowed, but the sadness remained abundant. He pressed his lips to each eyelid, one at a time, tasting remnants of tears and wishing he could do more.

"I need . . . something," she murmured, sounding lost. "I need . . . *you.*"

"You've got me." He hugged her tighter and resumed his previous rocking. "I'm not going anywhere." He would hold her until tomorrow if he needed to. Or longer. Whatever it took to make her not seem so destroyed.

"No." She shook her head and peered up at him. "Not like that."

He halted his movements. "What's wrong? Tell me and I'll fix it."

"I just need *you*," she stressed. "All of you."

"I don't—"

Her fingers touched his lips then, and he saw in her eyes what she meant. She was hurting. Desperate to feel something other than pain. And that something was him. Sex.

Pleasure.

Oh, Christ.

"No, babe." He shook his head while his lower body woke up. "That isn't what you need right now. Just let me hold you."

"Please," she begged, and he almost broke in two. The word was filled with so much misery. "Make love to me, Ben."

He stroked a hand over her arm, fighting with himself to do the right thing. "That isn't what you really want. You're just hurting."

"It *is* what I want."

"Babe." He momentarily closed his eyes. "You just turned me down out at the beach thirty minutes ago, remember?" He tried to tease her. "You wouldn't even let me flirt with you." He stroked the back of his finger over her heated cheek. "If I made love to you right now, you'd only regret it like you did the last time."

"I didn't regret it last time."

Her words were spoken clearly, and as bad a person as it made him, he desperately wanted to believe her. He desperately wanted to make love to her.

But he knew better. He remembered the past precisely.

"You disappeared from my bed that night, Dani. You were gone before I woke up. Gone the entire next day. I had to leave for school, and I didn't even get to tell you good-bye."

After he'd taken her virginity.

She shook her head. "I didn't regret it. I cherished it. I still do. But I was ashamed."

His eyes narrowed in surprise.

"I'd used you," she explained, the words spoken softly.

"You didn't."

"I did. I threw myself at you out on the dock, and after you turned me down, I still came into your room uninvited. I used you because I wanted to lose my virginity that night. Because I was tired of being different than other girls, and tired of not getting to do anything but be right here raising my brothers. And now I understand why I thought it was okay to do that. I manipulated you to get what I wanted because that's what I'd grown up with." Her brows scrunched together as if in contemplation before she groaned. "Oh, God. I'm just like her." She shook her head in denial and pushed at his chest. "I should go."

"No." The word shot out of him, and he pulled her back. "No," he said again, more calmly, while holding her steady in his arms. "To both of those things. You didn't use me. And you're nothing like her. Nothing, Dani. Listen to me. I googled 'Narcissistic Personality Disorder' after I heard Jaden say it."

"You heard?" she asked. She sounded mortified.

He swallowed his guilt. "Yes. I stood in the hallway and listened. But only for a minute. I'm sorry. I probably shouldn't have, but I couldn't just walk away. You looked so scared. I wanted to come to you. When Jaden mentioned what it was, I came in here to find out more. So I could help," he told her. That was what he wanted most right then, to help.

She blinked up at him and he noticed that her eyes had gone hollow. That was worse than being sad. "She manipulated people," Dani said. "She manipulated *me*." She licked her lips. "And I did the same to you."

"You may have behaved in ways similar to what you'd grown up seeing, but there's a world of difference in you and her. She didn't care about you. She *couldn't* care. You care about everyone." *Too much*, he often thought, but now he understood why. "And you came to me that night for a reason."

"Because I was tired of being a virgin."

He almost smiled at her blunt statement, but it wasn't the time for laughter. "Or because you were drawn to me, sweetheart." He pushed a strand of hair behind her ear and pressed a kiss to her cheek. Her skin was soft beneath his. "We've always been drawn to each other."

We still are.

"None of it is an excuse for what I did to you. I shouldn't have come in here that night. I shouldn't have taken off my clothes."

"Dani, listen to me. You didn't *do* anything to me. *We* made love. And I enjoyed the hell out of it. Every second of it. I only wish you'd still been in my arms the next morning."

He tucked her back against his chest, afraid she would leave him, and tried to force his own heart rate to slow. When she once again pulled back, he tensed. Her eyes were watering again, but no tears fell.

"I did too," she told him solemnly. "Enjoyed it. Every second."

"Then no more worrying, okay? Just let me hold you."

The instant he had her face back against his neck, she whispered, "I still want you to make love to me."

His heart seized, and this time he looked down at her with serious contemplation.

Could he do that?

"I'm using you again," she stated when their gazes met. "I know that. Maybe that's all I know how to do. But it's the only thing in my life that makes sense right now. *You.* You're what makes sense, and I need that. I need you." She reached up, and when her fingers trailed across his lips again, he damn near moaned out loud. "I need to feel like something in my life fits," she said. "And you fit me."

Ah, hell. He was going to do it.

And he realized that in doing so, he just might get his heart broken again. Because yeah, she'd broken it the first time. It wasn't like he'd been planning to stay back then, or even to carry on a long-distance romance, but he'd thought their night together was more than sex.

Then she'd disappeared. And he hadn't talked to her in ten years.

Before he could make up his mind, she pulled her shirt over her head and his blood told his brain good-bye.

"Dani," he warned. Her breasts were small in the pale lacy bra, the top curves capturing his attention as she pulled in breaths of air, and he remembered how perfectly she fit into his palms. How her nipples had pebbled at his touch.

It had been ten years, yet every detail rushed at him as if it were yesterday.

"Make love to me, Ben. Please."

"Babe. You don't play fair."

Her mouth reached for his then, and it was hot and seeking. Her tongue slipped past his lips as her hands held his head between her palms. And he wasn't innocent in the action, either. One hand slid to her rear. He squeezed the curve of her butt in his palm and groaned into her mouth.

Her behind had a way of making him restless even with the best of intentions, but with her in his arms and her mouth hot on his, his intentions were shot to hell.

"Dani." He tried again, thinking he had to say no.

But knowing that he wouldn't.

"I know what I'm doing," she told him. "And I promise, I won't regret anything." She leaned back and looked at him, her eyes serious. "I just hope you won't either."

Fuck.

He probably would.

"Don't you dare leave my bed while I'm sleeping this time," he demanded. "Not again."

A slight smile curved her mouth. "I promise."

Ben's mouth returned to hers, and Dani shook in his arms. He captured her head with his hands, replicating how she'd held him, and he took their kiss from heated to blazing. He possessed her. And she loved every second of it.

She had Ben again.

He devoured her only for a short moment, the scruff of his unshaven jaw scratching over her, intensifying the sensations, before easing up and sipping at her mouth. He moved to the tip of her nose to place a tiny kiss there, then headed farther from her lips. She groaned, nudging her mouth after his, but he refused to allow her to capture him.

As his heated breath came into contact with the shell of her ear, his hand skimmed down her body at the same time. Goose bumps lit on her skin, and her breasts begged for freedom.

"Ben," she urged. She ached to her core, but there was just enough awareness left that she understood the pain wasn't purely from longing. She hurt from what she'd learned tonight. "I love foreplay as much as the next person," she breathed out, "but hurry."

When his mouth touched just underneath her ear, she purred like a satisfied cat.

"Please," she begged.

"No hurry, babe," he told her as he trailed over her jaw. "Not tonight."

And though what she wanted most was to speed things up, if only to wipe the family meeting from her mind, she also wanted every single second that Ben had to offer. She was selfish that way.

He rose from the chair with her to his chest, and as he had the first time he'd carried her, he crossed the room. He put her on the bed, not bothering with the covers or lights, and simply came down beside her, refocusing on his mission.

His hands explored her body then. They skimmed over her jean-covered legs until reaching her feet, then back the way they'd come, his long fingers dipping between her thighs, taunting as his thumb traced the length of her zipper. Her body arched toward him, desperate for more, and her fingers slipped behind her back to undo her bra.

"Wait." The word stopped her movements.

Before she could do more, Ben had both her arms stretched above her head, their palms flattened together and his body running the length of hers. His head dipped, and his mouth closed over her left breast. She surged up once again.

"Ben," she moaned his name. "Seriously."

She didn't have a lot up top, but what she did have was sensitive. And with Ben's thigh now pressing into the apex of her jeans, she began a slow grinding rhythm against his leg while his mouth laved her breast.

She wanted more. And she really, *really* wanted it now.

When he separated his mouth from her body, the air touched the damp lace at the same time that his whiskers scraped over the very same spot. She moaned uncontrollably, and squeezed her legs around his thigh.

Then he sought out her mouth.

She took the opportunity to fight back. Her arms were still pinned, so she captured his bottom lip and sucked it hard into her mouth. His hands clenched against hers, and she felt his groan roll through his body.

"Babe," he growled the instant she turned him loose.

She answered by capturing his lip again, only this time with a nip of her teeth. He bucked against her.

"More," she insisted. "Now. I want to touch you."

He shook his head. "I can't let you do that yet." His words became breathless, and he once again sought out a breast. This time, her right one. She sighed in pleasure.

"Why not?" She thrust toward his mouth as he bit down on her, and her body shook to her toes. With his knee still between her legs, she thought she might be nearing the finish line already. Which really would be a shame. She didn't even have her pants off.

"Because the instant you put your fingers on me," he said, his words muffled against the lace of her bra, "I'm going to lose my mind."

She liked the sound of that, and she knew her smile advertised her gratification. "Maybe it won't be so bad to lose your mind," she suggested. She wrapped both legs around his hips and pressed into his erection.

"Oh, it won't be bad." He grunted as he pumped himself against her, their jeans blocking his entry. "But it'll be fast."

She laughed then, tossing her head back and letting him feast on her body. "This, Ben. This is what I need. Your hands. Your mouth." She sucked in a shaky breath as his lips found her neck. "Just . . . you."

Her tone changed with her final words, though she hadn't meant for it to. It grew serious. A bit sad. And she knew Ben noticed. He removed his delicious lips from her skin to look down at her. "You okay?"

She nodded and bit her lip. She hadn't meant to slow the moment down.

"I don't want to do anything to hurt you," he told her. "Ever." He brought her hands down, clasping them to her chest. At the same time he shifted to his knees and straddled her hips. He caressed one finger from her brow to her cheek. "I would never intentionally do anything to hurt you."

"You aren't hurting me."

"You're sure?" he asked. "This is really what you want?"

She nodded again. A lump had formed in her throat, making it hard to do anything else. The blockage was partially because she was moved by his concern, but equally because she knew there was this big *thing* she was hiding from at the moment. A thing she'd have to deal with later.

But she didn't have to deal with it right now.

Right now she wanted to feel. She *needed* to connect.

She was hiding behind the shield of sex, yes, but she was doing it fully aware. Allowing herself the temporary reprieve.

Pulling her hands free of his, she unbuttoned his shirt and slid her palms beneath the material. He sucked in air as her fingers connected with the heated ridges of his skin. Enjoying the moment, she took her time tracing the outline of his muscles.

When she scraped a thumbnail over his nipple, he shuddered above her.

"I'm supposed to be touching you," he ground out. But she noticed that he didn't hinder her movements.

"No one said you couldn't touch me," she taunted. She tweaked his nipple and silently dared him to replicate the move on her.

He accepted her dare, and within seconds he had her bra off and her breasts bare.

Their movements remained slow. Her mapping out his chest, pushing his shirt off his shoulders, and roaming her palms down his equally strong arms. While he took his time cupping and squeezing and pinching until she was coiled tight.

She liked this man's hands on her. And she liked the look of awe in his eyes as he touched her. He treated her—then and now—as if she'd given him a prize to be cherished. And that meant the world to her.

"Lock the door, Ben." At his hazy look, she added, "My brothers are in the other room."

"Ah, geez." He reared back, but she caught his wrists and put his hands back on her chest. She covered his fingers with hers. "We're not stopping," she told him.

"Your brothers will kill me if they find out."

"Then we'll be quiet." She stared at him. "But we're not stopping."

She didn't break eye contact as she squeezed his long fingers with hers, causing him to simultaneously tighten around her breasts. With the action, she surged into his hands once again, and he groaned in response. He nodded in capitulation. "We're not stopping," he agreed.

When he rose up off her that time, she knew he would be back. He headed for the door, and she tucked her arms beneath her head, taking the opportunity to feast in the glory of this man.

His chest was broad and strong, his back matching the front. And his shoulders looked lethal. The indentations at his waist, though, the ones that disappeared ever so temptingly right into the front of his jeans . . . they made her bold.

"Take off your pants," she instructed after he locked the door.

Her words stopped him, and then he smiled. It was that slow torturous movement of his lips that caused her to press her legs together every single time she saw it. His fingers went to his zipper.

"I like that smile," she told him.

"And I like you in my bed." The rip of the zipper sounded in the quiet room, and she touched her top lip with the tip of her tongue. But he didn't do anything more.

"Jeans, Hollywood," she whispered hoarsely. "Off. Now."

And off they came.

He stood ten feet from her, his erection behind the black cotton of his briefs, but the material most certainly did not hide anything. He was a big man, and the sight of him made her mouth water.

"Your turn," he told her. He didn't come back to her, just eyed her jeans, and she noticed that his breathing was as sketchy as hers.

She complied by inching her zipper down before lifting her hips off the bed and purposefully shimmying to get the denim to her thighs. His Adam's apple moved as he watched, so she let her fingertips slide ever so slightly between her thighs.

"Dani." His voice was as heavy as hers.

"Yes?" She kicked off the jeans, and lay there in nothing but a tiny pair of panties.

"You'd better be ready, woman." He picked up a duffle and rummaged around inside. "Because you've just pushed me across the line."

"I never did like those lines," she told him.

He tossed the bag aside and took a condom from the box he'd pulled out.

Then his teeth and fingers dragged her underwear down her legs, her hands shoved at his briefs, and somehow, one of them rolled a condom down over the very masculine part of him that she was so *very* interested in.

"Oh, my," she exclaimed faintly as she stared at him.

She lifted her eyes to his, noticing once again the look of awe that sat just behind the heat of his arousal. Then he leaned over and captured her mouth as he slid himself deep inside her body.

chapter fifteen

Ben lay in bed two hours later, his eyes following the shadows from the branches outside his window, while he listened to Dani breathe. She lay tucked against him, same as she had since he'd pulled the covers up over them and turned off the light, but unlike the past two hours, she was now awake. He'd felt the languor of sleep leave her body about five minutes earlier, but she had yet to speak.

Of course, neither had he.

He feared breaking the silence would send her running from his room. And since he'd only just gotten her back into his bed, he really didn't want her hurrying off.

He closed his eyes and faked sleep as he replayed the moments of making love with her.

She'd been fun, hot, and exuberant. And he'd been thankful.

But she'd also held back. She hadn't put everything she was into it, and he couldn't blame her. She'd found out tonight that her mother had not only manipulated her when she'd been alive, but apparently it had continued into death. Dani had been trapped in her own life, and her entire family had been aware of that fact. Yet, they'd done nothing to help her out of it.

He couldn't imagine the emotions she had to be processing.

Then there was the fact that she'd come to him when she was hurt.

That meant something to him, but he had no idea if she saw it the same way. He did know her well enough, though, to understand that she would be having second thoughts about her actions. He just hoped she realized it had been the right move.

She shifted against him, the sheet sliding with her naked body, and he fought the urge to roll over and bury his face against her warm skin. He wanted more. Once was not enough.

"You awake?" she asked.

He tucked in his chin and looked down at her. "Yep."

Wide eyes stared back in the moonlit room. "Have you slept?"

"Nope."

"Why not?" She covered a yawn with her hand, and moved out of his arms, tugging the sheet up with her. After she propped herself against the headboard, he studied the cotton covering her breasts and he told himself to lie. She didn't need to know the truth. It would only make him sound pathetic.

But he didn't.

Because he *was* pathetic when it came to her. "Because I didn't want to wake and find you gone," he admitted.

He'd lain there, eyes open, waiting for her to wake up and leave his side for the past one hundred twenty minutes.

She glanced at the bedroom door, and he recognized the facts. She wanted to go.

"You having regrets?" he asked.

"No." But she didn't look at him. It hurt.

"Want to go for a second round, then?" His question brought her gaze to his and he smiled. When she gave no response, he let the smile fall. "It wasn't a mistake," he told her.

"I know. I'm just thinking."

"Want to tell me about it?"

She stared at the closed door again, for five more seconds, then her shoulders slumped and she nodded in a way that reminded him of a child. Ben scooted over and brought her to his side—keeping that darned sheet modestly tucked around her—and wrapped her in his arms.

"She killed herself," she stated softly.

He closed his eyes with the words. "They're sure?"

He hadn't stuck around long enough to hear Cord's reasoning, but Ben couldn't imagine that statement being made without certainty. Dani nodded again, her hair brushing against his shoulder, and the slight fragrance of her shampoo drifting to his nose. She was leaned into him so that her head rested on his chest, and she quietly began talking, filling him in on the facts of her mother's death.

He caressed her arm as she told him the story, hoping the soothing motions would let her know she wasn't alone in this. He would help her get through it. And when she ran out of words, Ben's throat ached. For the first time in his adult life, he was on the verge of tears.

Dani sounded so alone, so hurt. And he had no idea how to help.

"Ever since they pointed out that I didn't remember things right, I've been bombarded with memories I'd forgotten," she said. "Some of them are horrible. And some just cruel."

She looked up at him suddenly.

"Dad spent years sleeping in this room, did you know that?" She shook her head before he could answer. "Of course you wouldn't know that. But he did. I'd hear him sneak down after everyone had gone to bed. That's how he figured out that I was sneaking out myself." Her words came out softer now and her gaze drifted away.

Ben didn't say anything, because he thought she might be talking to herself as much as to him. Walking through the past now in her head.

"He was already down here, so he'd hear me going out the back door, heading to the beach. Both of us just wanted to be away from *her*. But she came after him sometimes." She brought her eyes back to Ben's. "She'd tell me about that. How he wasn't a good man because she had to seduce him—her own husband—to get him to sleep with her." Her body shivered under the sheet. "And what could I say in return? If I said anything . . ." She paused, her gaze searching his before shifting and focusing on the middle of his chest. "If I defended him," she continued, her words now barely reaching his ears, "she got inflamed that I took 'his side' over hers. But if I agreed with her, she turned everything around. Suddenly he could do no wrong. How dare I say otherwise? I became the villain."

"That was her intent." He'd read that about narcissists. They needed to keep everyone off kilter, keep them confused. Dani's mother had wanted the focus to be on her.

Dani simply stared at him when he spoke.

"I preferred him to be the bad guy instead of me," she confessed, her words void of emotion. "So I kept my mouth shut, and I listened. Whenever she wanted to talk, whatever inappropriate thing she wanted to tell me. She told me about their sex life and the tricks she pulled. *How* she seduced him." The corner of her mouth lifted in a sarcastic tilt. "No wonder I did the same thing to you."

"You didn't do anything to me."

She rolled her eyes. "I did, and we both know it. Both times. But hey"—her tone turned mocking—"at least you didn't seem to mind."

In a quick move, Ben brought her mouth to his. He crushed her lips in a kiss filled with heat and misdirected anger. He needed her to see what was between *them*. To understand that it went beyond anything to do with her mother.

He needed to be able to fix this.

The kiss changed, though, turning slow and lingering, and he took his time tracing her mouth with his. He kept it going until they were both out of breath, both clutching at the other.

Only then did he pull back and look at her.

"*You* did nothing wrong," he growled out. His voice was laced with both passion and lingering frustration, and he almost wished Dani's mother were alive today so he could kill her himself. "She hurt you, and you needed *me*. That's all. And that's okay. It'll always be okay."

Dani didn't respond and he found himself wanting to shake her.

"Believe it, Dani."

"Ben, I'm too tired to—"

"You did nothing wrong." Fear pulled at him for her to understand. "We all have baggage, sweetheart. We all have crap in our lives. And we deal with it the best we can."

"You dealt with your baggage by avoiding your mother most of your life."

"Pretty much."

"That's so much healthier than me."

"Stop it," he demanded. When she didn't reply, he took her shoulders in his hands and got in her face. "You are not her. You are not like her. Say it to me."

Stubbornness shone back at him.

"Say it, Dani."

"What do you know about it? You haven't even been here! I might be just like her."

"You treat your niece better than her mother does. You treat my daughter better than her mother did. You run errands for anyone in town who needs it. You watch over your family like a hawk. You care about people, Dani. I hear you calling, checking up on others. I've seen you sad because someone is sick. I've seen you take them get-well baskets and balloons. Did your mother ever do any of that?"

His voice had climbed with his words, but he couldn't change that now. He only hoped no one remained downstairs to hear them arguing. But at least Dani finally seemed to be hearing him. He could tell she was sorting through his words.

When she still didn't answer, he did give her that shake. Just a small one, enough to bring her gaze back to his.

"No," she finally spat out. "My mother never did anything for anybody. She pretended she did. She would tell whoever would listen what a great person she was. All the good that she did for the world. But she was evil, and she never really did anything nice. I hated her."

Dani lowered her head with her last words, and wrapped her arms around his chest.

"And I was glad when she died," she whispered brokenly.

His heart ached for her. "Oh, sweetheart." He stroked her hair and held her close. "That's okay. You had a right. And you probably aren't the only one."

"I'm not," she cried. "But that doesn't make it better."

She clung to him then, letting hot tears fall from her eyes, and he simply held her.

After several minutes, when her sobs began to subside, he rocked them both back and forth. He wanted to do more, but also understood that this was going to be a process for her. It wouldn't be fixed overnight, and according to what he'd read, it was something she and her entire family would deal with for the rest of their lives. All he could do was be there to help her through it.

When the last tear was shed and she lifted her face, he kissed her again. This time, there was no anger driving the move. No frustration.

It was gentle and caring, and he knew that if she was paying the slightest bit of attention she would realize that it was more than a friend offering comfort. Because she was more than a friend.

But he didn't think she could see that.

Her lips clung to his, and he let his hands slip down to her back. But the instant he touched skin, she pulled away.

"I think I'll go to my room," she muttered.

He could only nod and remove his hands.

He clicked on a lamp and helped her find her clothes, smoothing her hair for her when she didn't do it herself, then walked with her to his door.

"We start picking at daylight," she told him. The night was over.

"I'll be ready. Haley's looking forward to it."

She nodded, then chewed on her lip, staring at the door instead of opening it.

"You okay?" he asked. He touched his fingers to the small of her back.

"I think so."

"Want me to walk you to your room?'

She peeked over at his teasing words, and a soft smile curved her lips. "Something tells me you'd try to stay."

He wiggled his brows. "I do have more condoms."

She laughed and patted his chest. "Thanks for tonight, Ben. But no."

Ouch. He supposed he had been officially dismissed.

Dani opened his door and walked out of his room without looking back.

chapter sixteen

Dani took a sip of her bottled water as she stood camouflaged between two trees, watching Ben heft a lug of cherries and carry it to the nearest bin. She pictured the muscles in his arms and back as he worked. Pictured them unclothed, of course. And pictured them right there in front of her.

She'd touched those muscles. She'd *licked* those muscles.

Then she pretty much hadn't spoken to Ben since.

In fact, she hadn't spoken to a single one of the men over the past few days.

It was day three of picking, and everyone was in their routine, going hard until early afternoon when the heat of the day often called a stop to the action in order to protect the tender skin of the fruit. The migrant workers carried their buckets strapped to their sides, their movements fast and efficient, since they got paid by weight of cherries picked. Jaden, Nick, and Cord were on tractor duty. They drove the trailers from the fields, through the cooling system that would keep the fruit crisp and firm, before depositing them in the barn. Full bins would be stacked and set aside until there was enough to be sent to the packing plant.

It was a well-functioning system, and Dani couldn't imagine not being a part of it.

She couldn't imagine her family not running it. But so far, no one had volunteered for the job. She'd considered doing it herself. It's not like she didn't know the entire operation. But she couldn't very well run the farm in Montana and live in New York.

Surely one of her brothers would decide to take it on. Because it was *their* farm.

She took another drink, and watched Ben as he went for another load. His job involved working directly in the fields, and Dani had been sneaking peeks at him all day. He emptied the cherries into waiting trailers, redistributed ladders from picked trees to unpicked ones, and generally did all kinds of heavy lifting.

And watching him wreaked all kinds of havoc on her tortured mind.

Because, though she knew she shouldn't have gone to him the other night, the fact remained that she *had* gone to him. He had a fascinating ability to get her mind off the topics eating at her, and she couldn't help but want to be distracted by him again.

And it only had a little to do with the fact that she was angry with her entire family.

Mostly, she just wanted to be with Ben.

But he fuzzed up her mind when she got too close to him, therefore she'd avoided him as rigorously as she'd steered clear of everyone else. She'd spent the past three days passing out cold bottles of water to workers, running fresh-picked cherries to the road stand that was being manned by Megan, or running cherries to The Cherry Basket for food to be made on-site.

The crowds up and down the road were heavy this time of year, and business was good.

Therefore she'd barely had time to work through the fact that her mother had devoted her life to making her kids' lives miserable before ending it in a pathetic bid for yet more attention.

Or how she, herself, had managed to block every last bit of that for more than a decade.

It had occurred to her that she should look into the disorder. She knew nothing more about Narcissistic Personality Disorder today than what Jaden had explained during their family meeting the other night. Understanding what was behind her mother's actions might help her to better deal with it, she got that. Possibly it could shed light on how to move on from this point in her life.

Only, she wasn't yet ready to move on. She didn't want to deal with more.

She was still processing the pain of her family leaving her in the dark.

Therefore, though she'd spent hours sitting alone at her laptop each of the past two evenings, she'd devoted that time to work. And she hadn't once typed the name of the disorder into a search engine.

"Miss Dani."

Dani jumped at the words, and forced her gaze from Ben's strong back to his daughter's sweet face.

Haley and Jenna stood just behind her, Mike at their side. A pink bunny rested in Haley's arms, and Gloria waited a few feet beyond the girls. She'd been watching the kids since harvest began while everyone else worked, and Dani had caught all three of them more than once plucking fat cherries straight off the trees.

Dani had given the girls bottles of water and instructed them to thoroughly rinse the fruit before consuming it, but she also remembered doing the same as a kid. And she had *never* taken the time back then to clean a cherry before popping it into her mouth.

"What can I do for you, sweetie?" Dani asked. She took in the girls' matching pink cowboy boots, Cinderella gracing the front of each.

"Will you be at dinner tonight? We're helping Miss Gloria cook, but we wasn't sure if you'd be there. We wanted to make your favorite food."

Guilt heated Dani's chest. She'd not only avoided talking to her family this week, but she'd avoided dinners, as well. Which meant, she'd barely spent any time with the girls at all.

"Do you happen to know what my favorite food is?" she teased instead of answering.

She really shouldn't skip it. She'd barely seen any of her brothers since they'd been home.

Haley looped an arm through Jenna's. "Grilled trout and baked beans," she announced.

"And corn bread," Jenna added.

Dani laughed. These two were so sweet.

If she stayed and ran the farm, she could see—

No, she couldn't. Jenna would be in California, and Dani wasn't sure where Ben and Haley would be, though she thought he might be seriously considering Montana.

But also, she couldn't stay because she had a job waiting for her in New York. As if she could forget that. Her whole life had been leading up to this point, and she wouldn't blow it now.

Only, she hadn't signed the lease agreement yet.

Everything was a tangled mess, and she'd essentially shut down over the past few days.

She couldn't stay that way for long, she knew. She got daily emails asking about the lease or if her broker needed to continue searching, and her new boss had already forwarded her background information on her first project. Everything was moving forward but her.

All she'd managed with any of it was to thank them and promise to reply soon.

Dragging her thoughts back from the deep trenches of her mind, she focused on Haley and Jenna standing in front of her with expectant expressions on their faces. She might be mixed up in a number of ways, but she couldn't let these two down any more than she already had.

"I'll be there," she assured them, and they showered her with exuberant smiles.

The girls skipped back to Gloria, and Dani remained where she was, watching the three of them head the other way as her mind whirled on all the many things she'd been processing that week. She grasped a branch above her head as she fought with one thought that kept pushing to the front of her mind. She wanted to talk to Ben. Maybe he could help her sort through things.

But she was afraid that talking to Ben wouldn't be talking at all.

And though not talking would be nice, it wasn't what she needed at the moment.

"I see you've missed me."

As if he'd read her mind, Ben spoke from directly behind her. Dani didn't even startle. She somehow wasn't surprised he'd come over. He would have heard his daughter's high-pitched voice. Thus, he would have seen Dani in the trees.

She lowered her arm and faced him. "You have quite the ego there, Mr. Denton. What would make you think that I've missed you?"

His gaze roamed over her face before shifting to the tree she stood under. "Because you're hiding in the trees."

"I am *not* hiding in the trees," she protested.

"*And* you've been watching me."

"You're out of your mind."

At his raised brows, she crossed her arms over her chest and shot him the same smug look. He just smiled.

"Fine," she muttered. She lowered her arms. "I watched you a little. But I've been watching everyone. And I'm not hiding. I'm resting in the shade."

"Then why not go to the barn? There's plenty of shade in there. As well as a fan."

"Because my dad's in the barn," she stated matter-of-factly.

And she was avoiding her dad.

His job this week was to oversee the loading of the trucks, but every time Dani had come within range, he'd turned to her with sympathy in his eyes. Which meant Gabe had told him about the conversation from the other night. If she got too near her dad, he would try to talk about it. And she most definitely wasn't ready to talk.

Not to him.

Ben studied her without expression for a moment before putting a twinkle back in his eye. He shook his head in denial. "Not buying it, sweetheart. Admit it. You miss me."

"Ben."

He took her hand in his and leaned in, and when his mouth brushed against her ear she shivered down to her toes. "Say it," he taunted. "I've missed you, Ben. I shouldn't have been avoiding you, Ben. I'll quit right now, and do whatever you want."

"Ben," she warned.

"I've missed you, too," he said, his tone turning sincere, and she understood that he was no longer teasing.

She locked her eyes on his, his face only inches from her own, and she saw the honesty of his words. He'd missed her. She didn't understand the connection between the two of them, but she did acknowledge it.

"Maybe a *little*." She stressed the last word.

"Maybe a lot."

At her pointed look, he gave her his hottest smile.

"Put that thing away," she grumbled. "And the fact that I might have missed you—"

"Do miss me."

She rolled her eyes. "It doesn't mean anything. The other night"— she shook her head—"it was just—"

"I know," Ben interrupted, his tone gentle. "It didn't mean anything. It was just sex—an outlet for your frustration. Or, that's what you've been telling yourself. But you're wrong." At her silent stare, he winked. "Take a walk with me tonight?"

"Oh, I don't think so."

"Quit thinking, babe. Just a walk." He leaned into her space. "Say yes," he urged.

She shivered instead. "It's complicated, Ben."

"I'm aware of that," he said all too knowingly. "I get it. And I'm here to help." His thumb slid over her wrist. "After the kids go to bed, just you and me. And just a walk." He pulled back and peered down at her, the devil once again dancing in his eyes. "Unless you have more frustration to get rid of . . ."

And with that, she thumped him on the chest. "Just a walk," she stated firmly.

"That's my girl." He put her palm to his mouth and pressed a kiss to its center. "I'll see you tonight."

He left her there, heading over to grab two ladders at once and move them to another tree, and when Dani forced herself to finally turn away, she saw Gabe watching her from a distance.

Her brother had been trying to talk to her for days, but she'd mastered the skill of avoidance. A skill she also remembered from the days following her mother's death. Don't talk about it, and it didn't happen? She supposed that was the way she'd played it in the past.

In this situation, though, she simply wasn't ready to talk about it. She was still too angry.

Gabe eyed her carefully now, before doing the same to Ben. But Dani didn't care what he thought or what he had to say about any of it. In fact, she only cared about one thing at that moment.

That she would be having alone time tonight with Ben.

"Excellent dinner," Dani's father announced later that night—for the third time in the past twenty minutes.

Dani didn't say anything.

"I'm glad you're enjoying it," Gloria replied, her voice a little too bright. "I tried to get Dani to sit this one out since we'd planned her favorite meal, but she wanted to help. She, Megan, and I work really great together."

The table went back to silent, and Dani caught Jenna and Haley exchanging confused glances.

The entire meal had pretty much been that way. Her dad or one of her brothers would speak up with some inane small talk, Dani ignored them, and Gloria filled in the gap. The kids had been quiet, Michelle hadn't come down due to a headache, and Megan and Ben looked as uncomfortable as two people could possibly look.

The evening had been nothing more than a waste of time.

"I went into town this afternoon," Megan contributed to the conversational void. "The library here is terrific."

"It's grown a lot since I was a kid," Jaden added.

Crickets chirped.

Dani wanted to speak to Megan, to be polite. But the longer she'd sat there thinking about who and what her mother was, how Dani had set her above the rest of them while at the same time her brothers and father had known differently . . . how they'd *kept* those things from her . . . she couldn't do it. If she tried to add to the conversation, she feared she would cry instead. Or scream.

She peeked at Megan, offering an apologetic look. The same was returned her way.

Then there was more silence.

Forks scraped against plates, Jenna slurped as she drank her milk, and Dani continued thinking about her mother. The woman wouldn't have allowed a meal to be this silent. Similar to Michelle—when Michelle graced them with her presence—Carol Wilde would have been filling them in on how amazing she was. She would also have called them out on their rudeness.

But Dani didn't feel like being polite. To anyone.

And since she'd figured out that she'd spent the majority of her life doing and feeling and acting the way someone else had wanted her to, she couldn't bring herself to fake it for the sake of good manners. Not tonight. No matter how rude that made her.

She did have a question burning inside her, though. One she decided it was time to ask.

Laying down her fork, she finally lifted her gaze to her father. The hope that flared on his face punched her in the gut, but she ignored the sensation. It wasn't time to move past this yet. He'd have to wait. Just like her.

"Did you know?" Dani asked, her words blunt.

Confusion flickered in his blue eyes. "Know?" he asked cautiously.

Cord shifted in his chair across from Dani.

"Did you know what Mom did?" Dani clarified.

The room went deathly silent for two seconds before Ben and Megan scratched the legs of their chairs on the floor by scooting them back so fast.

"How about we have dessert upstairs?" Ben asked the girls.

Haley looked up from the macaroni and cheese she'd been playing with. "In our bedroom?"

"I'll get it," Megan sang out. Gloria shot out of her chair to help.

Within thirty seconds, Megan had two dishes of cobbler in hand, Ben had both girls, and all four of them were hurrying up the stairs. At the sound of a bedroom door closing, Dani turned back to her father.

"Did you know her accident wasn't an *accident*?"

All the color went out of her father's face. "I talked about it with the boys at one point. We came to the same conclusion."

"Did you know before that?" she persisted.

"No, Dani. I didn't know. And I'm sorry—"

She held up a hand. "That's all I wanted to know."

"Dani," he said, but she returned to concentrating on her food as she contemplated whether she believed him or not. Probably.

But she was still mad.

"We need to talk," her dad tried again.

She didn't reply.

Every other member of her family had talked together about the fact that her mother had manipulated them their whole lives. The fact that she'd killed herself, if inadvertently. They'd talked, and they'd begun their own healing processes. But no one had talked to Dani.

As if she hadn't mattered.

As if there were no purpose for her being here at all.

But worse . . . how much had her dad been aware of as it was happening?

He'd slept down here for years. He'd avoided his wife as much as Dani had *wanted* to avoid her mother. He had to have known.

And what had he done to stop it?

He'd taken the boys and escaped the house as much as possible. She remembered that clearly now. There were always errands to run, chores in the field. And her dad always needed her brothers to help him out.

But what about her? Why had she been left here with that woman all by herself?

And then they'd allowed her to pretend for years that none of it happened?

They should have told her. Everything.

She shook her head slightly as she found herself fighting off tears once again. Her life was not only *not* what she'd believed, but she'd been completely alone in it, and she'd had no idea. How demeaning.

It left her wondering if they cared no more for her than her mother had.

"I think it's time to go," her father told Gloria, his words heavy with concern.

"What?" Gloria asked.

Dani's dad rose. "Come on. We're leaving. We're making Dani uncomfortable, and the morning starts early tomorrow. We should get home and get to bed soon. I'm sorry, Dani," he said as he stepped away from the table. "I would like to talk, though. We *need* to talk. Maybe in a couple of days?"

Dani didn't give him an answer.

"Well, okay." Gloria hummed under her breath as she rose and took her plate to the sink. "Just let me get the dishes real quick."

"Leave them," Max said. "They'll get done."

And with that single phrase, Dani went hot. *They'll get done?* By whom? Her?

Of course. Because they always got done by her.

Everything got done by her.

And then she remembered why.

If her brothers ever helped with the dishes—and she remembered a few times early on when they had—then after everyone was in bed, Dani's mother would get Dani back up and make her rewash everything. Sometimes dishes they hadn't even used that night.

Carol Wilde had been a mean, vindictive, manipulative woman who'd hated Dani from the day she'd been born. And the very idea of carrying any of that around inside of her made Dani's stomach roll.

"They may get done," she said, forcing the words out as she stood. "But they won't be done by me."

She escaped out the back door before her dad could, and had gone no more than fifty feet when she bent at the waist and threw up what little food she'd managed to get down.

"Dani!" Someone yelled to her from the house.

Instead of replying, she wiped off her mouth and disappeared between the closest rows of trees.

chapter seventeen

Two hours later, Ben stood at the top of the ridge that led down to the beach, watching Dani as she sat by herself on the end of the pier. She was a tiny form in the middle of vast surroundings, and he couldn't help but compare that sight to how he suspected she saw herself at that very moment. She had to feel small and insignificant in her own world. Her mother had been a narcissist. She'd manipulated Dani at every turn. And Dani's brothers had kept that from her. That had to be devastating.

Dani had unwittingly kept it from herself.

Moving again, he headed toward her.

He had to force himself not to run as he made his way down the slope. He'd missed her the past few days. And he hadn't liked her avoiding him.

He continued at a normal pace, but his gaze ate her up.

She'd changed into an orange sundress, and her hair was down and softly curved around her shoulders. The color of the dress perfectly complemented the sunset painting itself across the lake, composing the scene almost for him. It made him regret not bringing his camera out with him.

Her shoulders were bare—the heat had yet to evaporate from the day—and she had the hem of the dress pulled up and tucked between her knees. Her feet dangled off the end of the dock, but weren't quite touching the water.

As his footfalls reached the wooden slabs behind her, she glanced back, and when her gaze landed on the two bowls in his hands, he got the first smile he'd seen all evening.

"One scoop or two?" he asked, holding both bowls aloft.

"One." She reached out her hand. After he handed over the bowl, he retrieved a small baggie of chips—the edges of the baggie had been tucked securely beneath his belt—and held it up in offering.

"No, thanks," she said. "I'm good."

She scooted to the corner post then, put her back to it, and stretched her legs out so they ran parallel across the end of the dock. He joined her, sitting at the opposite post and facing her. His legs ran alongside hers, his booted feet reaching to her knees.

"You and your father okay?" he asked.

She held the bowl loosely in her lap, not touching the dessert, and rested her head on the wood behind her. Her head shook back and forth. "Nope."

"You think you'll get there?"

"I have no idea. But he said he didn't initially know Mom's accident wasn't an accident. Who knows what he was aware of before any of that." She blew out a breath and stared off in the distance. "It's not fair. Why did she hate me so much?"

Seeing her like this hurt him. "I'm no professional, but I'm pretty sure it had nothing to do with you." That's what he'd read.

"It feels like it had to do with me."

He could imagine that it did. "Maybe talk to Jaden about it?" he suggested.

At her heated glare, he gulped, but pressed on.

"He just majored in psychology. He might be able to help you make some sense of everything."

"Or maybe it'll never make sense," she mused. "Maybe she just hated me."

With that, she scooped up a bite of ice cream.

After taking her time to lick the spoon clean of chocolate, she wrinkled her brow and looked at him. "She put me on an ice-cream-free diet at fourteen for fear that my hips would get too wide." She shoveled in another bite. "As women, we had an image to uphold. Men wouldn't like a girl with wide hips."

She took a third bite while he eyed her hips.

"Your mother was wrong. I've never seen better hips."

She snorted as yet another mound went into her mouth. Once that bite disappeared, she relaxed back against the post, her shoulders curving into the wood, and blew out a breath. The chocolate was doing its job.

"I'll give you that tiny white lie," she told him, "but only because I don't think you make a habit of lying to me."

"I don't make a habit of lying to you, white or otherwise. And that wasn't a lie."

"Right. You, the man who makes a living photographing gorgeous models for a living, think I have the best hips you've ever seen."

"I *used* to make a living photographing models. And you do." At her raised brow, he gave a shrug. "I'm not a fan of skin and bones."

"Could have fooled me. You've sure dated your share of them over the years."

"Really?" He smiled at the jealous tone that had crept into her voice. "Don't tell me you're a tabloid junkie, Dani Wilde."

She didn't respond, just ate more ice cream.

"You are?" He faked a gasp. "Were you buying them looking for me?"

She gave him a smirk. "Cut me some slack. It's rare that a normal person knows someone who shows up in national magazines, even the trashy tabloids. So yeah, I've bought a few. And I bought them looking for you. It was fun keeping up."

The fact that she hadn't forgotten him over the years had him smiling even wider as he scooped up his own bite.

"Stop laughing," she muttered. "It's embarrassing. And I've had a lousy enough week as it is. I don't need rich-and-famous over there making fun of me."

"I'm not laughing. And I'm not famous—that's my mother. I just like knowing that you were checking me out all those years. Of course, I did talk to Gabe occasionally. You could have asked him what I was up to."

She set down her bowl—now empty—and leaned forward from the waist. Her eyes zeroed in on his. "I didn't want to talk to my brother about you," she said.

Her words made him hot.

He liked that she'd kept things between them private. He liked things between them *being* private. Yet he found as he sat there looking across at her, he would be okay with making them public, too. He couldn't stop thinking about her, and he couldn't stop wanting her. And he knew how stupid both of those things were, especially when he wasn't a big believer in forever and she would be heading to the other side of the country in less than two weeks.

But facts were facts. He wanted Dani Wilde.

"So you're no longer in the model business, huh?" she asked, as she once again relaxed back against the post. "That permanent? I thought since you and Haley had a good trip, you might decide to keep that going."

"It wasn't *that* good a trip." He put his own bowl down, a full scoop left in it, and scooted it her way. It stopped halfway between them, and he could see from the glint in her eyes that she wanted it.

With his toe, he edged it closer.

"Stop it," she moaned out. "My hips."

"Now you're just begging for compliments. Want me to go into specific detail about what I find most enjoyable about your hips?"

Her eyes widened. "No."

"Then take the ice cream. You want it, I can see it."

"I haven't had that bad a day. That's how I've managed to *keep* my hips from expanding over the years, by sticking to that rule. Two scoops only when it's a truly craptastic day."

He nudged the bowl within reach. "Break the rules, babe. I won't tell. And I promise, I'll still adore your hips."

She tossed him another smirk. But she also picked up the bowl. "I'll eat it only if you tell me why you won't be going back on the road."

"Because that's not the life I want for my daughter."

He studied the crystal-clear waters of the lake, focusing on a fist-size rock that was probably several feet below the surface even though it looked close enough to reach over and touch, as he thought about how true that statement was. He no longer thought in terms of his next great adventure. He ran everything through the what-would-be-best-for-Haley filter.

He could see taking her on the occasional trip, yes. But not for any of his previous types of contracts. He'd go to places that he wanted her to see. He could still do his thing, taking photos for additional books if this first one panned out, and Haley would get useful world experiences at the same time. Win-win.

"Plus," he added, bringing his attention back to Dani and watching closely as his spoon slipped between her lips. "I want to stick around here; it's good for Haley. I've already checked into preschools for the fall. And I'm going to do that book."

"Yeah?" She looked from the bowl to him. "Good for you. I think those are both excellent decisions. Montana has a way of taking care of people, you know? It gets in your blood. So what did you decide for the book? You going with people?"

He nodded. "I'm going with people." Though he still wouldn't include that picture of her.

But he would keep it close. He'd brought it out several times over the past week as he'd worked on the proposal.

"It'll be a bestseller," Dani predicted.

He chuckled at her loyalty. "I don't know about that, but I am looking forward to getting into it. I've already emailed a couple of agents with my ideas to get their feedback. I don't want to do just pictures. I want to discuss the techniques that went into each, of course, but also, I'd like to talk about the subject of the photo. *Why* I captured them. Why I did it the way I did." His passion for his idea got his words flowing. "I want to show that I'm more than just a good shot. There are reasons I framed each the way they are. Reasons I wanted to capture that particular person at that particular moment in time. I want the people who pick up my book to understand what I saw when I looked through my lens."

Dani had quit eating while he talked and simply stared at him now. Her scrutiny made him fidgety.

"What do you think?" he asked nervously.

"I think that sounds beautiful."

He brushed off her compliment. "That's the second time you've used 'beautiful' in relation to my work."

"That's because you're a beautiful person." She took another bite, taking her time before adding, "Haley's a very lucky girl. I hope you know that."

He didn't know that for a fact, but he had come to the conclusion that he made a much better parent than Lia. It had been days since he'd committed any sort of major screwup, and if the size of his feelings for Haley were any indicator, things would be okay with them. He could no longer imagine his world without his daughter in it.

"We went for our first appointment with the therapist this afternoon," he told her.

"Yeah? How'd that go?"

He shifted his gaze to watch the top curve of the sun slip behind the mountains. "I thought Janette was terrific," he told her succinctly. And he thought that she would probably help *him* as much as she would Haley. "Before the hour was up, Haley had opened up quite a bit. She informed Janette that she did not like her mother, and Haley learned that I'm not a big fan of mine, either."

The apples of Dani's cheeks plumped with a closed-mouth smile. "Another bonding moment?"

"Another bonding moment." He acknowledged the statement with a tilt of his head.

She set the remainder of the uneaten ice cream down, and her thoughts seemed to be drifting off.

"Maybe you should talk to her, too," he suggested. "She seems to be good with mother issues." He knew Janette was a personal friend, but Dani needed someone to voice her concerns to.

"Well, I certainly have those," she muttered.

She didn't, however, say that she would talk to her friend.

"How's that been?" he asked softly. "Any more memories creep up on you unexpectedly? Any new thoughts on the matter?"

She stared across the space at him, and he wished she were in his arms. "Yeah," she finally said. And that was the only word she spoke for several moments. Then her gaze lowered to the center of his chest. "It occurred to me that my dreams of moving to New York are all intertwined with hers."

"But *your* dreams are real."

Her gaze came back up. "Are they?"

"Dani," he began. Before saying anything more, he pushed to his feet and crossed the space. She dropped her legs off the dock, and as they had three nights before, they sat side by side, his arm around her, her head on his shoulder. "You went to New York as a teen, remember? *You* fell in love with the city. *You* had dreams of moving there. And you've worked hard to put that into motion."

"But did I do it only because I wanted to please her?"

That was a hell of a question. And one he hoped the answer to was *no*. "You're good at what you do," he pointed out. "Look at any of your clients. They're thrilled with your work. They give you glowing recommendations."

At her questioning glance he felt his cheeks heat.

"I've looked at your website," he admitted. "You've got an impressive portfolio. And huge words of praise."

She continued to watch him, unblinking, and he fought the urge to kiss her. If anyone ever looked like they needed to be kissed, it was her in that very moment.

"But my mother wanted to go, too," she said. "So did I want that only because of her?"

"Does it matter?"

"What do you mean?"

"Do you still want it now?"

"Of course."

"Then who cares what she did or didn't want? She's gone. She doesn't get to affect your life ever again." He held her to his side and pressed a kiss to her hair. "And you will impress the hell out of everyone in New York."

The sounds of insects filled the night. He'd worried for days that she would contemplate not going. Especially when he'd seen the unsigned lease agreement on the desk in the study. But that worry had stemmed from knowing that no one in her family planned to run the farm. It had never occurred to him that she might doubt her motives.

After several minutes longer, and with no daylight left around them, Dani finally relaxed and snuggled in tight against him. She wrapped her arms around his waist and brought her legs up on the dock, her knees bent out to her side. It felt right to hold her like that.

"Thank you for convincing me to come out here with you tonight," she said. "Talking to you gives me the ability to see the world better."

He closed his other arm around her. "I'm glad, babe. And ditto with the talking."

He shifted them both until his back lay flat on the dock. She remained in his arms, and he watched the stars as they began to pop out in the night sky. He couldn't stop the picture from forming of having Dani like this for years to come. The two of them out here, alone, hours after putting the kids to bed.

That kind of life would be nice. One like his grandparents had.

"Tell me about that box of condoms," she suddenly requested, sending his blood roaring.

Condoms? His body wanted to hear more.

"What about it?" he carefully asked. Because if she was suggesting . . .

They'd agreed this was just a talk.

"Didn't you pull it out of the bag you'd taken to New Mexico with you and Haley?"

"Yeah . . ."

She angled her face to his. "And . . . what? You were planning to party while your daughter was right there in the room with you?"

At her words, he grinned. And sadly, his body realized that this was not, in fact, a second invitation to remove her clothing. But he did think it was a second point in the jealousy column.

"I bought those at the airport," he told her. "On the way home."

Her brows pulled together in confusion and he laughed again.

"I was hoping to use them with *you*." He placed a tiny kiss on her upturned mouth. "And lucky for me, I did. I could even be persuaded to use another if you asked nicely."

Her gaze went to his mouth, and he held his breath. Then she shook her head, mumbled a barely coherent "no," and once again tucked her head against his chest. He sighed and thought of a long, cold shower. It had been worth a shot.

They talked for another thirty minutes, mostly about nothing, but the whole time she stayed right there in his arms. It had grown completely dark, but the many stars reflecting off the lake provided enough illumination that they could see each other well.

And what he saw now was her yawning.

"We should go in," he said. "Four a.m. comes early."

"Yes, it does. But at least we have a good time during the days."

"It's hard work, that's for sure."

"Respectable work." She looked at him. "I love that this is my family's heritage. I can't fathom the idea of parting with it."

"Has someone suggested you sell?"

"No. But if none of us are here, is there any difference?"

"I suppose not." He contemplated her words, seeing that yes, in fact, it was bothering her a great deal to leave home without a family member staying to run the farm. "Who's to say that something won't change down the road, though? You're not the only one suffering right now. Your brothers are, too. Maybe it's all too raw for them to consider coming back at this point. But that could change given time."

Those weren't simply words spoken to ensure she really left. He truly believed she wasn't the only one this place meant a great deal to. He'd had conversations with all of her brothers over the course of the week, some saying more than others. But what he'd seen was that each had their own burdens to bear. Now that the truth was out in the open, they could heal. They just needed the time to do it.

"I hadn't thought about it like that," Dani said softly.

"Then tell me this. Do you know exactly what *you'll* be doing ten years from now? Five years?"

She chewed on her lip before answering. "No. Any number of things could happen."

"And I'll bet your brothers don't either."

He didn't either. Though, with Haley now in his life, for the first time he could picture *who* would be in it with him. At least one person who'd be with him.

"Come on," he said. He stood and reached a hand down for her. "Let's get you in."

When they arrived back at the house, most of the lights were out, but Ben could see that Gabe was still in the living room. He watched them with a shrewd eye as they entered the back door, Ben's hand at the small of Dani's back, but he said nothing. Ben felt the heat of Gabe's stare until they'd rounded the hallway and disappeared from view, and only then did he think about Gabe's words warning him not to give Dani any reason to stay.

He knew he wouldn't give her one. Especially with the farm issues already weighing heavily upon her. She had to go to New York.

But he also couldn't stop himself from turning her to him when they reached her door.

"Thanks for tonight," he whispered. He touched the back of his fingers to her cheek, then covered her mouth with his.

Their kiss took its time, but that didn't keep it from being hot. Her tongue slid languidly against his, making him clutch the back of her shirt in his fist, and he matched her stroke for stroke. He needed to follow her into her room and wrap himself up inside her for the remainder of the night. Then he needed to do it again tomorrow.

Instead, he broke the kiss and put his forehead to hers.

Their heated breaths mingled, and he could feel her watching him, but he kept his eyes closed.

"Go in your room, Dani."

She didn't move.

He forced his eyes open and was met with the same desire pumping through his veins. Then he reached around her and pushed open her door.

"Go in your room," he repeated.

She pressed her lips together and nodded. But before she went in, she stood on tiptoe and brushed her lips against his cheek.

chapter eighteen

Dani slumped against her bedroom door the instant it closed, and put both hands to her mouth. Ben's kiss had almost done her in. It had certainly taken her mind off her woes.

And, wow, the man knew how to make a woman weep with pleasure.

Even though she'd wanted very much to ask for a repeat of Tuesday night, she was equally glad he'd ended things. She did not need to get any more involved with him than she was. It would be hard enough leaving in a couple of weeks. Letting herself get more attached? Stupid move. She had far too many other issues to worry about.

She pushed off the door, but startled at the sharp rap behind her.

Swinging it open, she found Gabe. He wore a snarl.

"What in the hell are you and Denton doing?"

"What in the hell business do you think it is of yours?" She put her hands on her hips and stuck her nose in the air. "Go to bed, Gabriel. And quit playing big brother. Because you're not."

She stepped back to close the door, but he blocked the opening with his foot. "I told him to stay away from you."

"And again, not your business." This time she stuck a finger in his face. "And not your right. Go take care of your own relationship and stay the hell out of mine."

She really wasn't a fan of cussing that much, not with Jenna in the house. It wasn't a good example to set. But her brothers had really riled her up. "What are you doing down here anyway? Surely you didn't think I had some sort of curfew and needed you to oversee it."

"I wasn't up because of you."

With his growled words, she realized what she'd seen when they'd come into the house and she'd been focused on ignoring him. Gabe had been up, yes, but he'd also had a pillow and blanket on the couch. He was sleeping down here.

The air went out of her lungs. "What happened?" she asked.

She stepped back, and after a quick glance toward the stairs, Gabe entered her room.

"Michelle kicked you out of your own room?" It wasn't even her house. What a witch.

He ran his hands through his hair, finishing by pulling at the ends. "I told her I didn't want to move to LA. I suggested Missoula. It's a larger city than Birch Bay, but close enough that I could maintain some control here at the farm. Maybe even stay over a couple nights a week."

"And I take it she didn't approve of that suggestion?"

"She threatened to leave tonight."

"Oh, Gabe." She didn't hug him, but she did call a silent truce. In all the years they'd been here holding down the fort together, many conversations had been shared. They'd been through a lot together, and they didn't always agree, but they'd learned to talk. They'd become tight. She'd missed that this week.

Of course, that didn't mean she wasn't still mad at him. Or that she wouldn't put something out there he might not want to hear. After this week, she would hold nothing back.

"You ever thought about the fact that Michelle's like Mom?" she asked.

Pain-filled eyes stared back at her. "You want to know *how* many times I've thought about it? I'd love to have a second child, give Jenna a brother or sister. But what Jaden didn't really go into the other night was something called triangulation. It's a way narcissists have of keeping their kids from getting along. Set one up higher than the rest"—he eyed her solemnly—"*me.* 'Golden child' is the correct term. Then blame others for everything that goes wrong. The narcissist stands in the middle and feeds lies back and forth to keep everyone from getting along." He shook his head as if disgusted. "She used us like that. I didn't believe it for a long time when the guys first brought it up, but Jaden made me see it. I'd played right into her hands. It was easier to get along if I was her favorite. But it hurt you. It hurt Cord. Hell, in the end it hurt me. Don't you remember how we fought back then? She'd even started it on the younger three, but she died before she managed *too* much damage with them. I'm terrified Michelle would do the same with Jenna and any sibling we might bring into the world. So I put my wants aside. Jenna will be an only child."

Dani put her arms around her brother.

"Dani."

"I know. You don't need a hug." She tilted her head to look up at him. "But did it ever occur to you that *I* might?"

Understanding dawned in his eyes and his arms closed tight around her. "I'm sorry," he told her. "We should have told you all of this a long time ago. We should have forced you to see the past the way it really was. But I went through some real pain accepting that she'd been this way. I didn't want that for you. I did think we were doing the right thing. I swear it."

"I'm sure you did. But do you know how used it made me feel to find all this out?"

"Used?" He reared back. "How so?"

She stepped out of his embrace. "I've done everything around here, Gabe. For years. *Everything.* What's to keep me from thinking that you didn't let that play into your decisions to keep the truth from me? You had a built-in housekeeper, a babysitter, and someone to cook your meals at night. Hell, I even washed your clothes and Michelle's, too."

"That's not why—"

"Are you sure? Because to tell you the truth, I'm not."

"I thought you liked to do that stuff. You always said you did."

She had said that. Many times. "Maybe I only said it because I was conditioned to. I remembered tonight that if you all helped me with the dishes, Mom made me redo them. Cleaning the house wasn't much better." She'd basically been her mother's servant.

Had she run around waiting on her family all these years because she was no more than a trained monkey? Did that play into why she'd only been capable of finding a man who expected the same?

She suspected *yes.* To both.

"How messed up *am* I?" she asked. "Maybe if I'd known the truth years ago I could have been working to fix myself. Instead . . ." She shrugged, and spit out yet one more curse word when tears appeared in her eyes.

Gabe reached out and pulled her back into his arms, and the tears released.

"I'm so sorry, sis. I never once thought about it like that."

"I know," she murmured. And mostly, she did believe that. But she'd thought about a lot of things that week. Things that left her confused about who she was. About what was really deep inside her. But after her conversation with Ben tonight—and now with Gabe—she knew she'd be thinking about things from a different perspective. Specifically that of her brothers. How badly had their mother affected them?

They'd known the truth all this time, but had kept it bottled inside. They saw the house as a shrine to a woman who hadn't loved them. Good Lord, she had to change things in the house before she left. Her actions had hurt them just as theirs had hurt her.

"We're all so screwed up," she said.

"There is no doubt about that."

"And I'm still mad at you," she pointed out. "Don't think you're off the hook."

He patted her back. "I've also no doubt about that."

"Shut up, you idiot." She pushed out of his arms. "Do you think any of us will ever be okay? We all have issues."

"Tell me about it." He glanced at the ceiling, his mouth a hard line. "I married our mother."

They laughed together at his words, though it was a woefully sad sound.

"She's not *as* bad as Mom," Dani pointed out, attempting to force levity into her voice. The attempt didn't work. "But if she leaves you, you can't let her take Jenna."

"I can promise you that. I'll live in LA forever if I have to, but Jenna won't be raised in a house alone with Michelle."

Dani simply stared at him then, thinking about their childhoods. So much hurt. So much lasting pain. "What are you going to do?" she asked.

"What can any of us do? Take it one day at a time. Maybe getting Michelle to a place where she enjoys living will change things. Possibly she's just spoiled rotten and not completely devoid of emotion."

"Well, that's looking on the bright side," Dani remarked. Her words were loaded with sarcasm. "But I hope it's true. Will you let me know if you need help?"

"No, because you'll be in New York. Have you signed that lease yet?"

She hadn't realized he'd keyed in on her stalling on the lease. And she wasn't exactly sure why she was stalling. "I'm just not sure she's the one."

He gave her a pointed stare and opened her bedroom door. "She's the one. Sign the papers."

Dani stuck her tongue out at her brother, and the two of them shared a real smile.

"Talk to Dad, too, will you?" he said. "He wants to make things right."

"We talked at dinner tonight." And she didn't know if he *could* make things right.

Gabe peered at her, letting her know that he was well aware there had been no real talking at dinner. "I know he made mistakes. He was far from perfect. But he loves you, he's worried about you. Talk to him, sis. Maybe together you two can begin to head down a different path."

The reality was that she did want to talk to her dad. Even while sitting at the table with him tonight, she'd wanted to *talk* to him. But she wanted the dad she remembered as a young child back. Not someone who simply wanted her to forgive him for his actions.

After learning about their mother, though, after letting the past replay in her mind, she'd wondered if it was even possible to have that dad again.

Dani paced the length of her bedroom, stopped, reversed, and retraced her steps. Then she did it again. Each time she made the same track across her floor, her gaze sought out the desk sitting in the corner all by itself.

Everything else in her room was packed up, and over the past couple of days she'd even moved quite a few things from the rest of the house into the attic. Items like family pictures that had their mom front and center. Her mother's favored chair, favorite knick-knacks. All pieces that, once Dani had started paying attention, she realized her brothers had avoided for years.

She'd avoided them too. She just hadn't noticed it.

But they were put away now. The house had less of a shrine feel, and she'd even spoken to all of her brothers. The six of them were working to move beyond this giant bomb that had been hanging over their heads for years, and they would eventually be fine. She hoped. They still had a long way to go.

She'd apologized to Jaden for giving him a hard time about continuing school, and each brother had taken the time to tell her *not* to clean something, or *not* to cook something. They'd come to the realization that she'd done all the work around here for years.

The only problem they hadn't quite figured out was that if she didn't do it, it didn't get done.

Dinner the past two nights had been takeout, and the sink was loaded with dirty dishes.

It killed her not to go in there and clean it up, but she also recognized that she had her own issues to deal with. And that meant she needed to put down the scouring pad and let the house get dirty.

It also meant ignoring the voice in her head telling her that her brothers wouldn't love her anymore if she didn't take care of them.

That was her mother talking. Her brothers weren't her mother.

She stared at the desk again. Yet another of her issues. She had to see what awaited her.

"Dani."

She looked toward her now open door to find her father, arms stiff, back straight, wearing an expression as though he were heading for the guillotine.

"Hello, Dad." The two words came out carefully modulated and precise.

She might have warmed to her brothers, but she had not let herself be in the same room with her father again. He'd been easier to avoid since he'd either been in the barn or at his and Gloria's place in town. But tonight, apparently, he'd decided to stick around here.

"Can we talk?" he asked. He didn't budge from the spot where he stood.

She nodded. She was ready for this talk. It had to be done.

"Come in." She waved him into the room and scanned the area for a place for him to sit. "Take the chair at the desk," she told him. She perched on the corner of her bed.

He entered, but took no more than a couple of steps inside before he held up a handful of papers. "When are you going to sign this?"

It was the lease.

Irritation bloomed in her chest. "Soon," she bit out. As far as she was concerned, it was none of his business what she did with it.

"You leave next week."

"I know when my flight is."

He thrust the papers at her. "Please, Dani. Sign them. You need to go to New York."

She didn't understand why everyone seemed so focused on her life all of a sudden. She would go to New York. Of course she'd go to New York.

She took the papers, tossed them on the bed behind her, and mulishly scowled at her father. Maybe she wasn't ready for this conversation after all, because she suddenly felt very unfriendly toward the man. "That all you wanted?" she asked.

His shoulders sagged then, and his hands shook as he clasped them in front of him. "No, that's not all I wanted." He crossed the room to stand in front of her. "I've talked to the boys several times this week, and I need to talk to you, too."

"Yeah?" She didn't give an inch. Seemed the more she'd forgiven her brothers, the angrier she'd become with her dad.

"I'm sorry," he started. "I know we let you believe things that weren't true, but we didn't intend any harm. It was . . ." He paused and coughed into his hand. "Well, it was just—"

"Easier to go along," she stated bluntly.

He looked surprised at her outburst, but the surprise was followed by guilt. The skin of his cheeks drooped along with the corners of his mouth. "Yes," he said clearly. "That's part of it. It's a shameful thing to admit, but yes. It was easier to go along."

"I probably needed therapy or something," she pointed out harshly, thinking of Ben's suggestion that she go see her psychologist friend. "You ever think of that? And I probably needed it long before Mom died. But instead, I've lived in a cloud of make-believe. Had just one of you set me straight, I might have learned to face life over the past decade. I might not be such a freaking mess right now."

He nodded. "Therapy probably wouldn't have hurt."

She laughed drily. "Dad, really, what are you doing in here? You aren't saying anything that I haven't already heard from five other people this week. You all screwed up. You kept me in the dark. Yes.

But you know what? I don't need your apology for *that*. I get that. No one meant any harm. Fine. Move on. But there *are* things I feel you owe me an apology for."

"For not having your back as a teen," he said solemnly.

"*Never.*" She stressed the word, coming to her feet at the same time. "You never had my back during those years. But you used to. I remember that. As a kid, I'd go out into the fields with you, or I'd ride up front in your truck as you ran your errands. I felt your love then, Dad. I think that even though I was confused and hurting, and didn't understand why my own mother didn't like me, I had you. And that was enough. But that changed. And that's what I don't get. You left me alone. With her."

Tears had come into his eyes during her speech, and he reached for her hands, holding both in his. She didn't return his grip.

"I had her in my ear twenty-four/seven," Dani continued. "Did you realize that? Did you know what she was doing to me? She told me things. Things a teenage daughter shouldn't know about her parents' marriage."

He blanched. "What do you mean?"

She let out another dry chuckle. Nothing about this was funny, yet she found herself wanting desperately to laugh. "Had you not been hiding from her around the clock, you might have seen what was going on," she said. "She treated me like I was one of her girlfriends." She squeezed her shoulders up as if to say it had been oh-so-fun. "She gossiped about her friends' lives, and we laughed and made fun of them behind their backs. She offered to buy me a boob job because I didn't quite measure up."

At his shocked expression, she nodded. "Yeah," she said. "For graduation. My very own size D. I had to fake a sickness to get out of that appointment. But worse than all that, she talked nonstop about you and her."

He gulped.

"I knew every argument you had, every time you disappointed her in some unfixable way. I knew you were sleeping down here, Dad. You'd sneak back upstairs before daylight, but I knew you were here. And I knew she slipped into the room many nights trying to get you to sleep with her. She desperately wanted another baby, only you wouldn't give it to her."

Her mother had told her over and over how she just wanted to give Dani a baby sister to love. Dani had never pointed out that she didn't *want* a baby sister to love. She hadn't wanted someone else she'd have to take care of.

She finally ran out of steam, and stood staring at her father, her breaths coming in gasping bursts.

"Not that I want to admit this," he began, his words slow and steady, his voice hoarse, "but if you want to understand what was really going on, I didn't want the last four kids that we had either— not that I'd ever change things. I love all my boys."

"I know you do." She thought of what Gabe had said about wanting to have more kids. Had their father been aware of what type of a person their mother was even then? That she would eventually try to turn their children against each other? "What do you mean, though?" she asked. "You knew what was causing the pregnancies."

His hands clenched hers tighter, and she maintained her lack of grip. "She didn't just manipulate you kids," he told her. And at this point he looked a little ticked himself. "She started with me. When you were toddlers, you adored her. Hung on her every word. She needed that kind of attention, and a new baby was the way to get it. But I refused."

"You're saying unplanned pregnancies?" Dani guessed.

"Amazing how many times birth control has failed in this house."

She couldn't believe she was talking to her father about his sex life.

"She had to be the center of her universe," he added. "Always. And if she wasn't, she was mean. Sadie pointed out a lot of things after Cord was born that I hadn't seen before. She was here helping take care of you, same as she'd done when Gabe came along, and she could see your mom in ways that I couldn't. Soon after, she made it a point to come around more. Eventually, your mother treated you worse than the boys. Some sort of payback for being female, I think. Anyway, it became clear that Sadie needed to devote her visits to you. Show you that you were loved."

"I'm pretty sure I'd be much worse off than I am now if I hadn't had Aunt Sadie in my life."

"I've no doubt you would be. I owe my sister the world for that. She made sure to take you under her wing. I couldn't change things for you, so she took it upon herself to counter as much of it as she could."

"But you told her to stop coming," Dani accused.

He didn't immediately respond.

"You did, didn't you? After New York. Or maybe Mom told her, but you backed her on it."

Guilt washed his features as he nodded, and she remembered thinking just last week that he hadn't looked this worn out in years. But he did now. He looked like a sad old man.

"Why?" She demanded an answer. That had been the pivotal point in their relationship. Things had changed afterward. "Why couldn't you stand up for me, Dad? Why send away the one person I was holding on to for sanity?"

"Because your mother intentionally sliced a knife across her finger due to your relationship with Sadie," he barked out. "What else was I supposed to do?"

"I don't know. Protect *me*? Make sure *I* was happy. That I was taken care of. Not let her keep hurting *me*!" She ended on a shout. Realizing her bedroom door was open, she moved to close it.

"And what if she'd left me and taken you and the boys with her?" He said the words flatly, but they hit her hard. "She told me she would. She already had a lawyer lined up." It was the same situation that Gabe was in now. He had to bend over backward to keep his wife happy or she might take Jenna and leave him. Geez, they were a screwed-up bunch. Every last one of them.

"Okay," she said more calmly. "I get that. I do. And yes, that would have been worse. But you didn't just push Aunt Sadie away, Dad. *You* left me too."

"I had to or she made your life even worse. She was jealous of you. By that point, everything you did and said was a challenge to who she was as a woman. You were becoming a real beauty, you were smart, you got to go to New York with someone other than her, and that trip was better than anything you'd ever done with her. And if I spent time with you? When I wouldn't even spend it with her?" He shook his head. "She turned her anger on you, baby girl. So I had to back off."

"You pacified her. Instead of fixing anything, you enabled her. Went along with all of it."

"I was weak. I didn't know what else to do."

"Hell yes, you were weak. You should be ashamed of those years. The boys disappeared from the house with you on a regular basis. You all got to escape her. I was left here any time I wasn't in school."

And even then, Dani remembered her mother occasionally showing up at the high school.

"I've hated you for a long time," she continued, her voice dropping to a shameful whisper. "Did you know that? But I didn't know why. I just knew that something had changed, and that it had hurt me badly." She crossed her arms over her chest. "Of course, I never let my true feelings show. Mom taught me well."

"Dani." He took a step toward her. "I'm so sorry."

She took a step back. "You should be. And sorry doesn't fix it, so keep it. Words are easy." She found that she couldn't forgive her dad as easily as she could her brothers. Her brothers had been victims, same as she. Their father should have protected them. All of them.

And he hadn't.

"Thanks for stopping by, Dad." She reopened her bedroom door. "But I think we've said all there is to say."

He didn't immediately go. Instead, he scratched at the back of his neck, and as he stood there she took in his age. He'd held up over the years, but he *had* aged. He was in his late sixties, and though he still should have plenty of years ahead of him, Dani suddenly envisioned standing at his funeral.

And she imagined what that would be like if she never forgave him.

The thought almost took her to her knees, but she fought the pain off. He was her dad, and she loved him. But she was not ready to forgive him yet. The old bastard would just have to hang on until she was. And that might be years from now.

Finally, he nodded and moved toward the door. When he got directly in front of her, he glanced back at the bed, at the papers she'd tossed in the middle of it.

"Go to New York," he said. "Prove to the world that your mother—that *I*—didn't keep you from your potential. You're amazing, Dani. And you have your life spread out before you. I'll do anything I can to help you have it. You don't even have to ask. I've a lot to make up for and I will. All I ask is that you let me try."

She swallowed the tears that clogged her throat and looked away from him. She couldn't stand seeing him hurting. And she knew that her rejection hurt him.

And deep down, she was glad for it.

"Sign the papers," he said again. "You're not staying here any longer."

"You're damned right, I'm not," she snarled. She had a life she deserved, and even if that meant their multigenerational business might fall apart, she was going to have it. She snatched the contract off the bed and signed on the dotted line. "Happy?" She held the signature page up for him to see.

He nodded, though he didn't look happy at all, and left her room.

After he was gone she closed the door, then she stood in the middle of the room, her entire body shaking, and she let her tears fall. Hot streaks tracked over her cheeks and rolled past her chin. She did nothing to stop them. Just let them fall.

She might have been too hard on her dad, she recognized that. But that's all she had to give at that moment. She was aware, though, that he was telling the truth about their mom. Dani and her brothers hadn't been the only ones manipulated in the family.

She pictured her dad with Gloria the night they'd announced their engagement. They'd been smiling and cuddling together in the living room, and Dani had wished it were her mother sitting there with her dad. But today she could remember clearly that her mom had never once showed authentic loving feelings toward her husband.

There had been smiles in public. Hugs and laughter for cameras.

But they'd all been fake.

Even as a kid, Dani had registered that, though she hadn't understood it at the time. Her mother's love had come with conditions. She'd been a master manipulator. An expert liar. And she'd been willing to do whatever it took to get what she wanted.

It terrified Dani to think of how much of her mother's behaviors *she* might have picked up. She'd finally looked Narcissistic Personality Disorder up, though. The Internet was a wonderful thing, and she'd spent hours the night before scouring sites. Her research indicated the prevailing thought was that the disorder wasn't genetic. That didn't mean she couldn't behave the same, though. That her brothers didn't have their own problems. They'd all grown up with that personality in the house. Of course they would have picked up some bad habits.

But the question was, were they reversible?

She supposed only time would tell.

Wiping her hands down the side of her jeans, she pulled in a deep breath, swiped at the tears on her face, and pushed that worry down for another time. Right now she had a desk to clean out.

Kneeling in front of it, she removed the tiara and the pink boa, then she pulled out the carefully wrapped package underneath. It was covered with parchment paper she remembered sneaking into the kitchen late one night to get, and tied with a red ribbon she'd once used in her hair.

These were the letters from Aunt Sadie after her mom had banned her from the house.

There had been no visits, and no calls, but Dani and Sadie had still written for a couple of years. They used the mailing address of a friend of Dani's so Dani's mother wouldn't see the letters. They'd filled a void for a while, given her something to cling to. But then her mother had found one of them when she'd been snooping through Dani's underwear drawer, and Dani had spent the next three weeks locked in her room. Supposedly she'd been sick.

Too sick for her brothers or father to see her.

After that, Aunt Sadie hadn't written anymore. It had just been Dani and her mom. Until Dani had been released from the grip of distorted "love" due to her mother's death.

Remaining in the drawer was one last item. She left it there.

It was a journal she recognized from the years after Aunt Sadie's letters had stopped. She remembered pouring out her feelings on the pages inside, and she recalled the burn of guilt that had scorched her each time she'd put pen to paper. But she'd had to have someone to talk to and that small notebook had been it.

She didn't want to look inside it. She wasn't sure she ever would.

Turning from the desk, she spent the next hour alone in her room, reading through the letters she'd once cherished. There was nothing all that incriminating in them, just two people who loved each other sharing details of their life.

There was a running theme throughout, though. Aunt Sadie had always made sure to tell Dani how special she was. How pretty and smart she was. Or whatever applied at the time. She'd been doing her best to build Dani up, even from a thousand miles away. Thank God for Aunt Sadie.

A soft knock sounded at her door and she pushed the letters off her lap to answer it.

Ben stood there, like life support.

"You okay?" he asked. His warm eyes drilled into her.

She tried to nod but all she managed was a blink. "I talked to my dad tonight."

"I saw him leave earlier." He grimaced. "I overheard part of the conversation. Want to talk about it?"

"Not really." She was too raw to walk through it right then.

"Want a hug?"

That brought a shaky smile. "Please."

He stepped inside her room and closed the door, then pulled her into his strong arms. Even though no more tears fell, some of the pain inside her eased. This man always knew when she needed him, and he knew what she needed the most. Right then, it was simply comfort. And his arms were the most comforting thing she'd ever met.

She held on tight for fear he would leave before she'd had enough, but she needn't have worried. He didn't let her go. She began to get the feeling that he would hang on for as long as she'd let him.

Finally, she loosened her grip and leaned back to peer up at him. "I signed a lease for an apartment in New York."

A shadow passed through his eyes. "Good for you."

When she didn't say anything else, just stood there wondering what to do next, he leaned in and pressed a soft kiss to her lips. He didn't push for more, and she didn't offer it. But she felt the strength of who he was through that one tiny touch.

She felt the strength of who they were.

After releasing her, Ben took in the scattered letters and the wadded-up tissues she'd gone through while reading them, then he took her hand and led her out of the room.

"Let's take a walk," he said.

It sounded like the best idea Dani had heard all day.

chapter nineteen

ate Tuesday afternoon, Ben found himself sitting with the Wilde boys just outside the main barn. Nate had come in earlier in the day, though Dani had yet to see him. She'd been in town since that morning, working on last-minute details with a couple of her clients.

But now, with the workday over and the pickers having headed to their temporary accommodations, Ben, all the brothers, and Megan were enjoying a cold beer and a handful of sweet cherries as they sat, propped back and feet up. Max had disappeared with the last truckload of cherries, and Jenna and Haley were up at the house with Gloria. They were having a playdate with Jenna's friend Leslie Roberts, and it was looking like Leslie might be the front-runner to becoming Haley's new other best friend.

Ben smiled to himself as he thought about his daughter and her strict requirements on friendship. She must be a girl, like pink, adore playing with Barbies, and most importantly, not eat all the ice cream.

Since going to the therapist for the first time, they'd been working on those friends, but Haley remained adamant that she only had room for two. He had caught her playing with several of the workers' kids throughout the week, though. And that hadn't seemed to cause her trouble.

"We'll be finished by this time next week," Gabe said from his nearly reclined position. He was leaned back on his elbows and staring at the blue sky.

"How do you already know that?" Megan asked. The girl had been right in the middle of everything since harvest began, taking an interest as though she intended to stay. Ben had noticed Dani take note of this herself, and he'd made sure to point out that, like Jaden, Megan would also be enrolled in a master's program come the fall.

Dani either didn't believe him, or no longer cared. She'd been different since her talk with her dad. Colder, in a way. But also happier. Less concerned with the orchard. More looking forward to New York.

"Years and years of doing it," Gabe answered. "Plus, we've made it through over half the trees." He took a long swig of his beer, eyed Michelle, who'd come out of the house in the distance, then returned his attention to the assembled crowd.

"Jaden mentioned a party?" Megan asked.

"Huge party," Nick added, raising his beer as if in a toast. "The pickers are ready to let loose by then, and they're the ones who cook. Great Mexican food, music, dancing. We bring in a local band. Wednesday night in the back lot, after all the trees have been picked."

"Only, this year will be different," Gabe added.

"Dani's going-away party," Nate said, answering Megan's questioning look. "She boards a plane first thing the next day."

Ben took a drink of his own beer then, and ignored his racing heart. Nine more days and she'd be gone. And he was thrilled for her. But, nine more days and she'd be gone.

Since he'd held her in her room Sunday night, they'd fallen back into the old pattern of nightly talks. Only, instead of sitting out at the boat dock, they'd been on the move. They'd traversed the orchard Sunday night, and the night before, she'd taken him to the neighbor's property to show him the perfect diving cliff.

They hadn't dived, of course. They were just walking. And talking. Like friends.

Except, he did hold her hand. And he wanted her more than ever. But there had been no kissing, and there had most certainly been no shedding of clothes. Maybe there had been a little flirting, though. He'd given it his best shot.

But even without the physical, Ben savored every second of his time with her.

"So, do I need to kick your ass?"

Ben brought his attention back to Gabe. "Excuse me?"

Everyone else had moved off, heading toward the beach. The day had been hot and long, and Ben had seen the ties of a swimsuit at the back of Megan's neck. She looked like a kid next to the older brothers, a foot shorter than them, but with Jaden's lesser height beside hers, she fit. She held his hand while Nick and Nate walked on the other side of her. Both men stood straight and tall, identical postures and looks. There was a bit more space between Cord and the rest of the group, but not so much as to make him seem reclusive.

Even as they moved away, Ben could see the fondness among the brothers, and he realized they'd seemed closer since the big family revelation. It had been the same with Dani the past couple of days. The Wilde family seemed to be healing. At least the siblings did.

"You," Gabe said tiredly, "and my sister."

"I don't know what you mean."

"You disappear with her every night, Denton. I have eyes."

Ben let a smile slip free.

"And that right there," Gabe added, sitting up and pointing with his bottle of beer. "Both of you. Smiling all the damned time."

"Hey, just because you got nothing to smile about doesn't mean we don't."

Gabe shut his mouth, silently acknowledging Ben's point, then finished off his beer. "She's leaving," Gabe reminded him. "Plane ticket is printed and stuck to the fridge. What are you doing messing with her?"

"I'm not messing with her. I swear. I like her, that's all. We're friends. It's always been easy between us. So yeah, I'm spending time with her, but like I promised you before, I won't give her a reason to stay. And I won't hurt her."

He didn't know if either of those things was completely true, but he did know that he'd cut off his own leg before asking her not to leave Montana. She deserved this. She had to go.

"Do either, and I'll have to hurt you."

Ben choked on his beer. "Like you hurt me sophomore year when I took out Heidi Mason."

A roar of laughter came from Gabe. The two of them had chased Heidi Mason all over campus before Ben had gotten her to say yes. Then he'd quickly discovered the error of his ways. She hadn't been . . . exactly . . . *stable.*

"You saved me on that one," Gabe acknowledged.

"You still thought you were going to kick my ass."

"And I still blame the beer. If I'd been sober . . ."

"Right." Ben grabbed two more beers and passed one to Gabe. "If you'd been sober, you would have simply been more embarrassed than you were."

"We were out of control back then," Gabe mused.

"In a good way. But only until you met whatshername that you dated for so long."

"Erica Alexandra Yarbrough." The softening in Gabe's tone showed his fondness for his former love. They'd dated for two years during college. "She's an elementary-school teacher now, not far from here. Ran into her at the bulk goods store one day. Teaches first grade."

"That so?" Ben eyed his friend, thinking about how fast he'd dumped Erica after he'd met Michelle. The man had been knocked on his ass by the big-city girl with big-city attitude. And now it was coming back to bite him in the ass. "You're really moving, then?"

Gabe cut his gaze over to Ben's. "To LA? Yeah. Before the school year starts."

"Sure that's what you want to do? There are other options." He gauged Gabe's reaction before continuing. The question didn't seem to offend, so he added, "I have money if you ever need it for a lawyer."

"I couldn't take your money."

"You also can't let your wife take your kid."

Gabe lowered his gaze, and Ben watched his chest rise and fall with a deep breath. They hadn't talked like this before, and Ben might be overstepping his bounds, but he also knew Gabe had to have floated the idea of divorce through his mind.

As a father now himself, Ben equally knew that scenario would bring with it concern for Jenna. Ben could no longer imagine his own life without Haley in it. He'd destroy anyone who tried to change that. And he suspected Gabe would do the same concerning his daughter.

But the thing was, twenty-first century or not, the courts often still favored the mother. High-priced lawyers helped with that.

"All I'm saying is," Ben added, "I have plenty. All you have to do is say the word."

Gabe nodded, his expression grave. "I appreciate that. I do. And yes, thank you, if the situation arises, I could make that call. As a loan. That's a weight off my shoulders, actually. But things have been better since I agreed to move. I'm encouraged. I doubt the move will solve all our problems, but I would prefer Jenna have two parents if she could. So I'll fight for this. And I'll move to LA as part of that fight."

"You're a good man," Ben said. If Michelle could get over herself and be a real mother, that would be best for Jenna. "Big change, though. LA is not Birch Bay."

"Tell me about it. And there's a lot to do before any of it can happen."

"Here." Ben reached into the pocket of his jeans and pulled out the keys for his apartment. He tossed the key chain at Gabe. "This'll take care of one of those things."

Gabe sat up. "What's this?"

"Keys to my place."

"Come on, I can't take this." He held the key chain out, but Ben refused it.

"I won't be using it," Ben said. "Stay as long as you want. It's a great place. Might even make your wife happy."

Gabe snorted under this breath.

"Seriously," Ben continued. "You might find that you hate the city. No use signing a lease until you know. Use it. Give yourself a chance to explore, figure out what area works best for you. And if you love it, then stay. Only caveat is, Haley and I get a bedroom if we come for a visit."

Gabe stared at the keys dangling from his fingers, then nodded. "Thanks." He shoved them in his jeans. "What're you going to do?"

Dani's car came up the drive then, and Ben straightened from his reclined position. "I'm going to stay here. I'm house hunting."

"That so? In Birch Bay?"

Ben watched as Dani exited her vehicle and looked in their direction, and his pulse reminded him that he was playing with fire. "Yep, here. I've talked to a couple of real estate agents, and have a few appointments set up for this weekend."

Gabe whistled under his breath. "Moving fast."

Dani climbed the steps to the deck and spoke with Michelle. "Nothing wrong with fast when you know what you want," Ben said. He glanced at Gabe. "And Haley needs stability."

"It'll help," Gabe agreed. He shot a look at Dani, and as he pulled out his cell and punched in a text, he added, "You're doing good with Haley. I can tell she means the world to you."

"That she does," Ben confirmed. Dani headed their way. "I'm a fortunate man."

About the time Dani reached the two of them, just when Ben was getting to his feet, her gaze locked on something in the distance and he was forgotten.

"Nate!" she shouted before taking off at a sprint toward her brother.

Nate had come up from the beach—likely whom Gabe had texted—and wore a smile as broad as Dani's. He scooped his sister up and twirled her around in a circle.

Gabe rose to stand beside Ben and the two of them watched the happy reunion together.

"Ouch," Gabe taunted. "And here you thought all she had eyes for was you."

"Shut the fuck up."

Gabe continued to smirk, while Ben admitted the truth to himself.

He may not break Dani's heart, but she sure as hell was going to break his.

Low voices came from Ben's room the following night as Dani neared the open door. It sounded like he was talking on the phone, but his tone was off. Not wanting to eavesdrop, and telling herself not to be nosy, she averted her gaze as she headed for the stairs.

She still caught a glimpse inside the room. And it wasn't a phone call at all.

Ben sat, legs crossed, in the middle of the floor—in the room where as recently as last week Dani had stripped off her clothes and begged the man to make love to her—and he was playing Barbies with his daughter. Neither noticed her, so she inched closer to the door.

It was cute. Ben marched Ken around on the throw rug, explaining to Barbie how pretty she looked and how he was such a lucky man to get to take her out to the movies. Mike, who'd become Haley's companion as much as Jenna's, was stretched out beside them while Haley patted him on the head.

"Will you take me to the movies someday, Daddy?" Haley's mouth curved at the corners, the tilt the exact angle as the one on her daddy's mouth, and she glowed up at him.

Dani lost her breath at the sight of them. He was so good for her. And she for him.

"Of course I will," he told her. "We'll make it a special day, just like Barbie and Ken."

"And we can have ice cream?"

He chuckled, the tone low and sexy, and touching Dani in her warm, dark spots. "Absolutely," he confirmed. "Chocolate?"

"Yes, please," Haley answered. "But it'll be a happy time, so we won't need the potato chips."

Dani held back a laugh in spite of the sad note, her gaze taking in every move made by the two. Along with now being a huge fan of her daddy's, Haley still followed Dani around, mimicking her actions, as well. Including her love of chocolate ice cream. So much so that Dani had upped the quantity purchased on her recent run to the store.

She would miss these two people when she left. Very much so.

As Ken opened the car door for Barbie, Ben caught Dani watching. His cheeks turned pink.

"Never thought I'd see the day," she murmured. Up until then, Ben may have bought his daughter the dolls, but he hadn't been so keen on playing with them.

"Jenna went to town with her mom and dad," he explained. "Someone had to step in."

Haley's head swiveled to face the door, her eyes as bright as her dad's were sexy. "Hi, Miss Dani. Did you want to play?"

Dani shook her head, not wishing to interrupt, but also almost desperate to join them. She had so little time left here, and her nightly walks weren't quite cutting it with Ben. Nor were her afternoon Barbie tea parties with Haley. She wanted more.

But such was life. And she couldn't have everything.

Ben patted the floor beside him with the perfect mixture of "come hither" and "come join the fun." He really had ramped up the flirting over the past week, though not once on their recent walks had he suggested anything more than holding her hand. Not even another kiss.

Which had frustrated her way more than she would have suspected.

"Come on," he told her when she still hesitated. "We need some-one to work the candy counter. You look like the perfect candidate."

He held out a dark-haired Barbie dressed in cutoff jean shorts and purple tennis shoes, and motioned to the makeshift counter they'd created from a cereal box. The top had been sheared off and the box turned upside down; the bright colors of the cardboard lent a party atmosphere to the "movie theater."

Aside from the counter, there was a white pillowcase draped over a large, propped-up book—she assumed it to be the screen—with a couple of Barbie-size chairs they'd swiped from Jenna's room perched in front.

With a smile that seemed to be attached to her heart, Dani entered the room. How could she say no to a daddy-daughter moment with two of her favorite people?

As she took the doll from Ben and settled in behind the "coun-ter," another question entered her mind. Why was she shying away from sleeping with him? From letting nature take its course? They had eight days left. They could be having a good time.

She wanted him. She was pretty sure he wanted her.

And they couldn't get serious because there was a clock ticking. It seemed the perfect scenario.

"Wait a minute." Haley suddenly jumped to her feet, Mike ris-ing with her. "Your candy girl should be *your* Barbie," she exclaimed. She dashed from the room and shot toward the stairs.

Haley had brought Dani a Statue of Liberty Barbie back from New Mexico, along with a pink cowboy hat. Both had ended up in the girls' room.

As feet sounded overhead, she turned to Ben. Her decision had been made. "I was thinking no walk tonight."

"No?" he asked.

She liked that he looked disappointed, and that he sounded even more so.

"But I like walking with you," he said. He reached for her hand.

"I like it too." Her body temperature rose merely from thinking about *not* walking with him, and she let her thumb slide along the pad of his hand. "I had another idea."

He studied her for a moment, not speaking, then his gaze lowered to her mouth. When his eyes lifted, his pupils had dilated. "Does this other idea still include me?" he asked.

Clearly, he was clueing in to her plan.

She nodded, and heat flooded her body.

His look turned pure predatory male, and she suddenly realized that he'd known exactly what he'd been doing since the day he'd brought her ice cream out on the dock. The man was an evil genius. He'd been seducing her.

Served her right, she supposed. It was his turn.

But she could learn from his technique. He wasn't nearly as obvious as she.

"My room or yours?" he asked, and she almost whimpered at the unspoken promises.

She swallowed. She should say his. She'd never had a man in her room—she'd never had a man at the house. And if they stayed in *his* room it would feel less personal.

But she found that she wanted to feel personal with Ben. Her time was limited, but as ridiculous as it was, she wanted those days to be as special as she could make them. Letting Ben into her space would do that.

"It'll just be us having fun, right?" she clarified. "It can't be more."

He swallowed as he watched her, and twined his fingers with hers. "Just fun."

She nodded. Her heart pounded. "My room," she said quietly as Haley returned.

Ben released her hand, but the flare in his eyes told her that he understood. It could be just fun, but it was also more. Their friendship made it so. She saw agreement in their depths.

chapter twenty

Several days later, Dani collapsed on her bed and stared up at the shadowed ceiling of her room. A light remained on in the bathroom, bathing them in a muted glow. Enough to make out the curves and angles of the man breathing heavily next to her.

"That was amazing," she panted.

A bead of sweat trickled its way under the bottom curve of one breast and headed toward the mattress as Ben rolled to his side. He reached out a large hand, wrapping it firmly around her waist, and pulled her to him.

"*You* are amazing," he mumbled into the pillow they shared. "And you're too far away."

"I'm trying to get some air. You wore me out."

A sexy hum came from deep in his chest as he nuzzled her ear. "If I recall correctly, it was you on top. You set the pace of that one. I was merely an innocent bystander."

She smiled. Yes, it had been her on top. A place she might return to before the next few days were over.

"But don't think just because you did so well, that's earned you a rest." He nipped at her earlobe while the hand at her waist began to glide lower. It didn't take a direct path, instead caressing and cherishing each and every spot it crossed. "I intend to keep you sweaty and breathing hard for a while yet."

She shifted to her side. "Are you saying you have no intention of me getting much sleep tonight?"

Not that either of them had gotten a lot the past few nights.

Ben drew a finger through the dampness at the top of her thighs. "Who needs sleep? You're leaving me in a matter of days. I have a lot to fit in before then." He nibbled along her jawline as the finger below wove deeper, the tip slipping just inside her heat, and her body once again sputtered to life. It shocked her that anything could reset that quickly after the round they'd just had.

"Then I guess I'll just have to go along with your plans," she conceded.

"I was hoping you'd say that." He bent over her then, using his mouth to seek out the hidden spots of her neck, and she angled her head to allow for easier access. She enjoyed the slide of his tongue over her body with the occasional teasing of his teeth along the way. He moved slowly, yet she could sense renewed desire already building.

"Sure you're up for going again?" she teased.

He growled against her as he pushed another finger inside her body. "I can't seem to do anything *but* be ready when I'm around you."

She laughed. She loved his hands on her. She loved every minute she had with him.

They'd spent a lot of time together over the past few nights. All of it hidden away behind her bedroom door. There had been a few hard and fast moments, but also some long, slow, draining ones.

And the thing that meant the most was that it never felt cheap. He always took the time to cherish her body. The man also had a talent for making her want more.

More than four more nights.

She groaned in pleasure at the things his fingers were doing to her, and involuntarily thrust against his hand. "I can't believe I get on a plane in five days," she moaned.

He rose over her then, settled between her legs, and without warning he pushed inside her. They both sucked in sharp breaths.

"I'm going to miss you, you know?" His words were spoken with heavy sincerity wrapped around a passion-fueled grunt, and they seemed to lodge right in the dead center of Dani's chest. "A lot." He pulled back and pushed in again. "Will you think about this when you're gone?"

"Oh, God, yes." She squeezed her eyes shut. Too much ran through her head to say one thing more. She just wanted to feel this man. Experience what he did to her.

Be amazed that he could satisfy her again so soon.

"Promise me?" He thrust once more.

He seemed to swell even larger, and she wrapped her arms tight around him. "I promise," she panted out. "Probably every night."

There were no more words spoken between them, but their movements said volumes. This was casual sex, yes, but there was nothing casual about it. They fit perfectly together. Their bodies in sync, as if the two of them had been doing this for years. They knew what each other liked, and what sent the other over the edge, without either having to speak a word.

And yes, Dani was going to miss him, too.

This man was important to her. Even ten years ago. She couldn't put words to it.

He gripped her butt in his hands and pumped hard, the softness of their lovemaking gone as she met him move for move, gasping from the sheer rawness of it all. At the last minute she opened her eyes. He was a thing of beauty, and she had memories to store up.

When her climax began to crest, she saw that his was too. Wanting the moment to be perfect, but unsure that was an achievable goal, she spoke his name.

Hot, drugged eyes met hers.

That was all it took.

With one last thrust, he caused her to splinter around him, the sensation of a million lights blinking to life pulsing through her body. She did her best to simply hold on as he followed her lead, shaking in her arms.

When they were both spent, he collapsed, heavy breaths matching hers, and immediately shifted so the mattress supported most of his weight. He kept a leg over hers, as well as an arm around her torso, and he buried his face in her neck.

"You . . . are . . ." he breathed out, but then chose to kiss her neck instead of finishing the sentence.

"You too," she whispered in return. Whatever he'd been about to say, he was, too.

After their heartbeats slowed, Dani found herself wide awake. Ben's breathing had evened out. It sounded like he was nearing sleep. But she couldn't even make her eyes close.

At the unlikeliest of times, her mother got into her head.

Dani could hear her now. It was sophomore year again, and Dani had brought home the one boy she'd dated in high school. He'd been on the academic team with her. They'd been friends since first grade, but sometime late in her fifteenth year, he'd begun looking like more than a friend to her. Surprisingly, the same had happened to him.

They'd gone out a few times, then she'd proudly brought him home for dinner.

She'd been head over heels for him already.

Is that the kind of boy you want to be seen with, Danielle?

It was as if her mother were in the room with her right that very moment, and Dani silently shook her head. The same way she'd done that night after her soon-to-be-ex-boyfriend had gone home. Her mother had given no explanation as to what was the problem. She'd simply thought him beneath what Dani could get.

You can do better than that. Why would you settle for less than you deserve?

But the thing was, before Dani had gone to bed that night her mother had pointed out that Dani didn't *deserve* anyone. No one could possibly love her.

Most memories came to her like that. Her mother's words contradicting themselves, her actions rarely making sense. Dani had even caught herself doing things in certain ways over the past week simply because her mother had once badgered her to behave in that fashion.

She didn't want to be her mother. She didn't want to *act* like her mother. Or believe her mother.

And she certainly didn't want to be locked in a world that had her mother in it.

"What's wrong?" Ben asked, making Dani realize that her body had grown taut and unyielding as she lay there. She forced herself to breathe normally, and concentrated on relaxing her muscles.

"Weird memories," she replied.

Ben lifted his head off the pillow. "Anything I can help with?"

She shook her head. She didn't think it was anything anyone could help with. The only hope she had was that once she made it to New York, the change of scenery might allow her mind to shut off the past.

"You need to get out of here," Ben said, as though he were reading her thoughts. "How about we go into town tomorrow night? A date."

She blinked at him as she reset her train of thought from moving to New York to going into town for an evening. "A date?"

They didn't date.

"You know, you dress in something hot and I shine up my boots."

"Your boots are new," she pointed out, but she did give him a small smile. The sound of his voice had a way of making her mother's recede.

"Then I'll shine up your boots," he offered. He pushed to his elbow. "Let's do it. Let's go out. Did I mention that Haley and Jenna are spending the night with Leslie tomorrow?"

"Jenna's friend?"

"Haley's now, too. She's filled one of her coveted friend slots."

"And they're staying overnight?"

"Yeah." A naughty twinkle lit his eyes.

"You think she's ready for that?"

His shoulders sagged. "Quit worrying about everything, babe. Yes, I think she's ready for that. Jenna will be with her. And if she isn't ready, then they'll call and we'll go get her. Leslie only lives five minutes away. But let's talk about you and me. I want to take you out. I'm tired of hiding away in your bedroom."

"But we don't date. We're just"—she waved a hand back and forth in between them—"this."

"We are this," he confirmed, mimicking her action with his hand before grabbing hers and kissing her fingers. "But we could be more."

"I don't have time for more, Ben. I'm leaving in . . ."

"I know. In five days. You don't have to remind me. But that's three nights of dates, if we want, and one going-away party. We have time. Say yes. Let's have some fun."

She'd thought they were already having fun.

But she eyed him as she considered his suggestion, uncertain what her hesitation stemmed from. She *would* like to get out of the house for an evening. That could be fun. And she'd love to get her mother out of her head for a few hours, as well. That could be exhilarating.

"We'd be letting everyone know what's going on between us," she said.

"You think they don't already know?"

They'd been trying to keep what they were doing just between them, but yeah, Dani knew they'd failed. If they were in the same room together, her brothers watched them like hawks. Gabe eyed Ben as if considering taking his head off.

No, it wasn't a well-kept secret. "No one has said anything," she retortd anyway.

He merely stared at her. "They know. Come on, let's go," he urged. "I heard Jay and Megan talking about a sports bar in town. They're going tomorrow night. Cord and the twins, too. We'll go with them."

"You want to go out *with* my brothers?"

"You'll be leaving soon," he reminded her. "Don't you want to spend more time with them before you go?"

"Using my brothers against me?" She shook her head as if disillusioned. "You play dirty."

He smiled. "I play to win."

She laughed then, and the pressure from her mother's words finally lifted. She did want to go out with Ben. And she wanted to hang out with her brothers. They'd all continued to smooth things over during the week—not including her father—and heading to the bar sounded like fun.

"Jay's going tomorrow because Sunday nights are line-dancing nights," she explained. "You up for some dancing, Hollywood?"

"With you?" He pulled her body back to his. "All night long, babe."

The bar was packed.

Dani stepped inside the front door, flanked by her brothers, Ben, Megan, and even Michelle, and peered through the low light, hoping to magically find a table where they could all fit. Instead of a table, she saw hordes of people. Locals, tourists, and a wide selection of the single men who were in the area for work. Young men who spent their days in the cherry fields, and looked for a good time at night.

She knew the group of them must make quite the sight, especially given that not a single one of the men with her was anything but drop-dead gorgeous. But if she hadn't already been aware of this fact, the many female heads now turned their way confirmed it.

Dani slipped her arm through Ben's.

"This is exactly what we needed," Gabe declared.

"I haven't been country-western dancing in years," Cord added.

Dani watched his gaze as it swept the room. He wasn't interested in the dancing so much as the dancers. He might be a tough nut to crack personally, but that didn't mean he sat at home all by himself in his spare time. Her second-oldest brother was a ladies' man, and always had been.

Dani now wondered how much the distance he kept between himself and women had to do with how their mother had treated him. Had she ruined everyone in the family for relationships? At least Jay seemed to be doing it right.

"Hey, baby." A scantily dressed woman sidled up to Cord as if he'd hung out a shingle advertising a good time. "Buy a girl a drink?"

And with that, Cord disappeared into the throng.

"So much for hanging with him tonight," Dani mumbled.

Nate laughed behind her. When she glanced back, she saw that he had a look like Cord's in his eyes. "I suspect our hanging out tonight involves seeing each other from a distance," he informed her. "But I'm glad you came with us."

His gaze landed on someone, and he shot his sister a wink. "Don't do anything I wouldn't do, sis." And then he, too, was gone.

"They're dropping like flies," she said to Ben.

"Can't blame them." He nodded at a group of five women heading their way. All of them wore skirts that barely covered their butts, and she could feel the buzz already coming from Nick.

"Good grief," she mumbled. It was a meat market.

"We'll catch you later," Gabe told her as the girls descended on the remaining dateless brother.

Gabe and Michelle moved into the crowd along with Nick and the five giggling girls. Michelle looked as hot as any other woman there tonight—probably hotter—but Dani was glad to see that her clothing was slightly more respectable than most. Not completely flaunt-your-assets-and-announce-your-intentions. Though some of her assets *were* definitely flaunted.

Her black dress had a nice plunge with a fair amount of cleavage and a hollowed-out back, and hugged her body tight. But it came to her knees with a statement of class instead of trash. If Dani wasn't still irritated with her for the way she treated Gabe and Jenna, she'd freely admit that her sister-in-law was quite gorgeous. She supposed *that's* what her brother had seen in her.

"I'm glad you came out with us," Megan said to Dani and Ben, as she and Jaden stepped forward to fill the space vacated by the others. "This is a great way to spend the last weekend with everybody here."

Dani had to agree. "Thanks for letting us tag along."

She took in her youngest brother, still looking as smitten as ever with his girlfriend, then held out a hand to him. "Dance with me, kid?"

Shock crossed Jay's face, and Dani saw Megan's smile widen.

"You think you can keep up with me?" her brother asked. "You *are* ten years older."

"I'm also wiser." Though that was probably not true. Jaden was a smart guy. "Come on, smartass, show your old sister what you've got."

She pulled Jaden to the dance floor, glad for the opportunity, and behind her Ben held out a hand to Megan. This was definitely what they'd needed tonight. All of them.

The two-step was the current dance choice, so she and Jay turned to each other.

Jaden was a few inches shorter than the other brothers, but still several inches taller than Dani. Only, with her heels, they were almost the same height. "I'm sorry about giving you a hard time about graduate school."

He eyed her. "You already said that. We've moved past it."

"Have we?" Because, though she and the rest of her brothers had been doing okay the last few days, more distance than she was comfortable with remained between her and Jaden.

"We have," he answered. He twirled her in time with the music.

"Then what's the problem?"

"No problem." His gaze trailed Ben and Megan as the couple passed them.

"Jay." She turned his face back to hers. "We have to be okay before I leave. Tell me how to fix it."

He pushed her around the floor for a few more seconds, not replying, then led them out of the pack and to the quieter back hallway. "We're okay," he assured her. "I promise. The issue is mine. I feel guilt for my part in things. Thanks to an early psychology class, and my own interest in the subject, I figured out what was wrong with Mom early on—way before college—and I brought that to the guys. That's when the conversation first started about what happened to her. I should have included you. I know that now. But I didn't, so I feel guilty."

Shock kept her quiet for an extra beat. She hadn't given the specifics too much thought, but she never would've guessed it to be Jaden who'd left her out. "It's not your fault," she began.

"Yes. It is. But the thing is, I excluded you on purpose. I knew Mom had been harder on you, that you were living in some kind of alternate universe, and I wasn't sure what you could handle or what you couldn't. I was wrong to be concerned. You can handle anything. You're the strongest female I know. And I should have known that all along. I just hope my actions haven't led to you now believing otherwise."

Her baby brother had always been more sensitive than the rest, but his words surprised her. "You're worried about me?"

"Did you think you'd cornered the market on worrying? We worry about you, sis. A lot."

His words brought tears to her eyes.

"Ah, geez," he mumbled. "Come on. Don't cry here in public."

"What's the matter? Afraid you'll get teary too?"

"I won't get teary."

But she thought, given the right circumstances, he just might. He was a great kid. And he felt things deeply—even if he had made the mistake of thinking she couldn't handle the facts. "I'm proud of you, Jay. A lot. You'll do great in school. Thanks for telling me this tonight."

He nodded. "I'm proud of you too. You're going to be a rock star in New York." He paused before continuing. "Will you do something for me, though?"

"Anything."

He took her by the elbow and moved them from the hallway out the back door. The wind caught her hair and whipped it into her face as the door clanged closed behind them. "See someone, sis. A therapist. You're strong, but . . . you lived with her disorder a lot longer than the rest of us. That affects a person. Way deeper than you might realize."

She stared at him, suddenly glad he'd brought it up. If she could talk to anyone in her family about this, it was him. "I've been remembering a lot lately. Some of it really bothers me."

"And some of it probably has affected your behavior," he explained. "Or the way you care about others. It's not genetic, but it is learned."

She thought of all her failed relationships. "Probably so."

"See someone. It'll help." He gave her a slight smile. "It helped me."

"You've been in therapy?"

"At school, yeah. And trust me. It helps. I was probably damaged the least of all of us, but not having Mom show affection got into my head. She yelled at me for wanting attention. Belittled me. I remember that clearly, as young as four, maybe three years old. She didn't touch me. She showed zero attention. That's why I went into this field. It's why I need to go further. But I want you to be okay, too. So will you consider it?"

"I will." Especially since her brother was worrying about her.

"Good. And we have to work on you and Dad, too," he added.

She groaned. "I'm not ready to work on Dad, Jay. I feel like he deserted me back then. And it's like I can only deal with one thing at a time. Right now, I'm dealing with me."

"He did desert you. But I don't think he really gets that. He loves you. He feels bad about everything. But he probably doesn't understand how *he* added to the problem."

"He's the one who should be in therapy," Dani mumbled.

"*You* should be too."

"I will. I promise." She wanted to get past this with her dad, but she needed to know that he wanted it, too. That he was willing to put in the work to get there.

And he needed to understand how his actions had impacted her.

"Would you talk to him about it, though?" she asked. That might actually help. "If he's seeing someone here while I'm seeing someone there, I'll know that he's putting in an effort, too. Because right now, I feel like he's just sitting around waiting for me to get over it. And Jay, I'm not sure I'll ever get over it."

Her brother took her hands. "You won't get over it, sis. But you will recover. I promise you. See a therapist, and work on yourself. You'll be fine. You'll be amazing. Not having Mom in your life now is the best thing you've got going for you. She hasn't been in your head in years. She won't ever be in your head again."

Except she was there every day right now.

"And yes," Jaden continued. "I'll talk to Dad. He contributed to the problem by continuing to allow it to happen. He needs to realize that and do his part to make it right."

"Thank you." She hated the whiny sound that came out as her voice.

"Also, I apologize for keeping everything from you for so long." He squeezed her hands. "But I apologize most for not including you to begin with. Our knowing, our talking about it together, was helpful. It solidified us in a way that you didn't get the opportunity to be a part of. And I regret that. I hope it doesn't mean we can't move past it, though. Be stronger because of it."

Dani nodded. His words were sincere, and that was all the apology she needed. "Thank you. No one has acknowledged that, just explained how they were protecting me."

"We were. But we went about it wrong. We should have done better."

The back door opened, and Ben and Megan stood there, music blaring behind them.

"You okay?" Ben asked. Concern filled his face.

Jaden let go of Dani's hands, while Megan looked on nervously.

"I'm good," Dani answered. At the stress marring Megan's brow, Dani wrapped an arm around her brother's waist and added, "Jaden was just telling me how much he loves me."

Megan beamed. Jaden groaned.

And Dani felt warmth settle in her heart.

They were good again. They would be okay.

Those ten minutes spent standing in the back parking lot with her brother tonight could turn out to be the most important ten minutes of her life. And for the first time since Cord had spoken the word *suicide*, Dani thought she might actually come out the other side of this all right.

The night before the party, Ben sat out on the dock with Dani after dark, both of them having a beer instead of ice cream. The ice cream had been put away for the past few days, as had the secrecy around their relationship, and Ben couldn't be more relieved.

Not having to confine their time together to only the night hours had opened up new possibilities for them. He'd sought her out during the days. Snuck kisses whenever he could. And even had a steamy make-out session under a cherry tree earlier that day.

They'd grown closer.

And Ben had begun to look at their relationship in a whole new light.

So tonight, he'd brought her down to the beach instead of dragging her off to bed. They had tonight and tomorrow night left, then she'd board a plane. He couldn't let her go without her understanding how he felt.

"I'm going to miss this sky," Dani said. She was sitting between his legs, her back to his chest, and her face tilted to the heavens. They'd been like that for an hour.

"I suspect it'll even miss you."

She gave a soft snort. "That makes no sense."

"I know. But it won't be the same without you here, sneaking off to stare at the sky."

"I'll have to fit plenty of that in on trips home, then."

"You think you'll be coming home much?"

She was silent for a moment, before shaking her head. "Probably not. I'll be busy. A new job is stressful," she added. "Then there's the fact that none of us will be living here. And me and Dad . . ." She trailed off.

"Nothing better there?"

"Not yet." She angled her head back farther, and turned her gaze up to his. "I'm hopeful, though. I noticed today that I didn't feel as angry toward him. I still haven't talked to him again, but the thought no longer makes me want to throw something."

He kissed the tip of her nose. "That's good. Improvement."

She shrugged. "It's better than nothing."

She went back to staring at the sky, and he closed his eyes. He couldn't just let her walk away from him for good, could he? Out of his and Haley's life forever? They needed more time.

"I wanted to tell you something tonight," he confessed.

"What's that?" Instead of looking at him, she turned to her side and snuggled in against his chest. He wrapped his arms tight around her and breathed in her scent. The mixture of the flowers from her shampoo, the smell of the lake, and the fresh air of Montana would forever remind him of Dani.

"That this isn't just sex for me," he said.

She went still in his arms.

"It's not just us having fun," he added.

"You know I'm leaving, Ben. I *have* to go."

"I know. And I'm not suggesting you don't. But you need to know." He forced his fingers to release the clench they'd formed at her waist, and thought about options. Long-distance relationship? More? "I care about you, Dani. A hell of a lot."

He watched her face when she still didn't look at him. Her expression never changed. He wanted to say more, but baby steps seemed the better way to go.

"That scares me a little," she finally spoke, and he let out a breath.

"It scares me a lot."

They sat there in silence for several minutes longer, him afraid to push, and her thinking who-knew-what, but he couldn't help but believe this thing between them was more for her, too. It might be hard for her to say it, to even admit it, but he'd spent many hours with this woman the past week. They'd shared tons of time over the course of the last month.

He felt it from her. They had a connection. Something rare.

Surely she could see the specialness of that.

Eventually, she spoke again, and her words sliced open his heart.

"I can't do more," she told him.

He closed his eyes once again. He had less than thirty-six hours to show her that she could.

chapter twenty-one

"I sure am going to miss you two." Dani hugged Mrs. Tamry, taking note of the frailness of her body, before turning her attention to Mr. Tamry. Dani had been thrilled to see them show up tonight for the end-of-season party, and even more so to realize they'd come out to wish her a safe new life.

As had many other people.

The sentiments had put a heaviness in Dani's heart all night, but at the same time she'd felt like she was being given permission to fly. It was euphoric.

"Be sure to watch your mailbox, okay?" she told the two. "I'll be searching New York for treats that I know you'll both love." She kissed Mrs. Tamry's weathered cheek. "And you take care of yourself. Don't be getting out and overdoing it by going to too many parties."

The older couple laughed, and Mr. Tamry put his arm around his wife.

"We had to come for this one. You're leaving us. Nothing could have kept us away."

"Well, I do appreciate it."

"You've done good, Dani," Mrs. Tamry added. She patted Dani's hand, her aged blue eyes showing pride. "Your mama would've been proud."

Dani swallowed, but maintained her smile. She didn't tell her friends that making her mama proud was now the last thing on her list. She was still her mother's daughter, after all. She hadn't had all those years of training to be perfect in public for nothing.

"Thank you," she said. "The best part is that I'm making myself proud."

And she was. She'd thought long and hard about whether this had been her dream or her mother's, and though she couldn't say with 100 percent certainty that her mother hadn't wanted it, too—everything was still too jumbled in her mind—she felt confident that it *was* her dream. She wanted it. And she'd worked incredibly hard to get it. Therefore, she would have it, and her mother was simply a nonissue.

She moved on from the Tamrys, talking to other townspeople who'd come out to wish her well. The manager from The Cherry Basket was there, as well as several of her local clients, and even her first-grade teacher.

It was a special night, and she owed this to her brothers. They'd made sure to invite the people who meant the most to her.

The band changed up from a raucous country tune to a slow song that pulled couples onto the freshly mowed dance floor, and Dani couldn't help but peek around for Ben. They hadn't talked since she'd come out. She'd either been busy chatting with one of the guests when he was free, or he'd been busy dancing with one of the locals when she was. It seemed attractive, single women had shown up in droves tonight, and Ben was being a darling to entertain them.

Or else, he was intentionally trying to make Dani jealous since she'd told him last night that she couldn't do more.

What had he been getting at, anyway? By this time tomorrow, she would be twenty-five hundred miles away. How could she possibly do more?

But she also didn't like him dancing with other women.

"Don't forget us back here in Montana, Dani Wilde."

She turned to find her very first client. "Harry," she murmured with fondness.

Harry Baker shook her hand before pulling her into his arms. His big body seemed to engulf her as he patted her on the back. Harry and his father owned a fishing charter up in Bigfork that had grown to be one of the area's premier tourist stops.

"I wouldn't be here without you," Dani told him when he stepped back.

He laughed. "We wouldn't be *here* without *you*. New York is lucky to get you."

She warmed at his praise. "Thank you. And I'm sorry I had to cut ties, but with the new job it was essential."

"I know. It had to be done. Life goes on and all that." He touched a finger to his hat, pushing it back on his head. Like several men there tonight, he'd traded in his baseball cap for his cowboy hat. It was their party attire. Some had even polished up their best boots. "You ever find yourself looking for clients again," Harry went on, "you call me. We can always use someone like you in our back pocket."

She agreed, and they parted and headed their separate ways. She'd made the final phone call today, and as of two hours ago, she had no remaining clients of her own. Which was scary. She'd worked hard for what she'd accomplished, but she knew she'd work even harder in her coming days.

Her gaze finally landed on Ben, and her heart turned over to see him dancing with Haley.

He'd also brought out a cowboy hat tonight. His grandfather's. The one that had been hanging in the study ever since he'd arrived back in Montana. It looked good on him.

Watching them, it was hard to imagine either Ben or Haley when they'd first arrived here. Haley had truly blossomed over the past few weeks. She talked nonstop, nothing seemed to scare her or slow her down, and she now had a running list of new friends she couldn't wait to invite to her new house.

And Ben. Dani pressed a hand to her chest. Ben was buying a house in Birch Bay.

Not yet, but he'd been looking.

That was something she would've never imagined from the big-city boy who'd only ever wanted to travel the world. He was an amazing parent, and he and Haley were both blessed to have each other.

"Aunt Dani?"

Dani looked down to find Jenna, dressed in her Sunday finest, peering up at her. "What is it, sweetie?"

Tears started. "I don't want you to go."

"Oh, baby." Dani quickly picked up her niece and held her to her chest. "It'll be okay. We've talked about this, remember?"

Jenna sniffled. "I know. But I'm going to miss you too much."

Dani began swaying to the music, Jenna still in her arms, and smiled at Ben when he shot her a wink. "Did your daddy tell you about your Christmas surprise?" Dani asked, putting her mouth close to Jenna's ear. "I'm not supposed to tell."

Which wasn't really true, but Jenna loved learning about surprises.

"No." She sniffled again.

"He's going to bring you to New York during your Christmas break from school," she told the girl. Dani and Gabe had talked about it, and with the move to LA, along with losing Haley and Dani, it seemed Jenna might need something special in the coming months. "How about that?" Dani asked. "We'll go see the big Christmas tree at Rockefeller Center, and we'll ice-skate. And we'll go shopping. That sound good?"

Jenna nodded, but her face still said she'd rather nothing changed. "I might like that," she finally got out. Dani once again hugged her niece tight in her arms.

"I suspect you will. And I'll enjoy seeing you. It'll be almost as much fun as moving to California," she added, faking confidence. Jenna had not been handling all the pending changes well, so Dani and the rest of her family had been playing it up. "I understand you'll also be going to Disneyland."

"I don't want Disneyland," Jenna suddenly wailed.

Dani saw Michelle watching from the other side of the dance floor, but she didn't seem overly concerned with her daughter. She had been sticking to Gabe's side this evening, though. For the most part. At least she wasn't ignoring both of them. Of course, Michelle wasn't one to cause a scene in public. Plus, she was getting her way. They would be moving in a couple of weeks, therefore she had reason to be less of a witch.

"You don't want to go see Cinderella?" Dani asked her niece.

This dried the tears. "I do want to see Cinderella."

"Well, she's at Disneyland."

Jenna seemed to think about that, and finally, sent her aunt a questioning look. "Will there be a prince there?"

Dani smiled. "Most likely there will be several."

"I do want a prince," Jenna informed her. And with that, the world righted itself.

Dani continued swaying with the girl in her arms while watching Ben do the same with his daughter. His gaze was also trained on Dani. They'd had a lot of fun together these last few days, and she wanted to be in his arms right now. Whether they could do more or not, they did have tonight. And she would miss that man like crazy come tomorrow.

The song ended, and Dani set Jenna on her feet. "We'll call each other every week," Dani promised. "And everything will be okay because we'll all still love you just as much as we do today, right? Me, Uncle Cord, Uncle Nick, Uncle Nate, and Uncle Jaden. All of us."

"And Pops and Gloria?"

"Yeah, baby. And Pops and Gloria."

Dani *had* spoken to her father tonight, but only briefly. It had been a tiny step in the right direction, but they had a long way to go yet. The distance would help. It would take the immediate pressure off. They could talk a couple of times a month, and with some effort, she thought she could one day have her father back.

All five of her brothers suddenly moved toward the trailer being used as a stage, and one by one they climbed aboard. The band stopped playing and all eyes turned to them. Dani got teary as she looked on. They were proud, good men. And she'd played a huge role in that. Her next thought was of her mother, which she promptly suppressed.

Her third thought was that she wished they could all be here together again. Forever. That was her real dream, to have her family right here in Birch Bay. And *her* right there with them.

But maybe deep down she'd always known that would never happen.

"May we have your attention, please," Gabe announced up front. The few who hadn't already quieted stopped talking immediately.

"Thank you." Gabe looked around the crowd. "I know this party's been going for a while already, but we wanted to take a moment to welcome you. Usually tonight is reserved for all the many hardworking people who've helped make Wilde Cherry Farm a success, but this year is a little different." He squinted his eyes and peered into the crowd. "Dani?"

Dani grinned. What were they up to? "Yes?" She raised her voice to be heard.

"Would you get up here, please?" This voice was Cord's, and Dani snickered at the feminine sighs of pleasure at the deep rumble. His was the deepest voice in the family. Add that to his way-too-good-looking exterior, and she understood the moans.

Poor girls. They didn't stand a chance.

She made her way through the crowd and to the trailer, where Nate and Nick reached out and helped her up.

"This here," Gabe started, putting his arm around her shoulders, "is one tough lady. Our big sister has held our butts to the fire more times than you can imagine over the years. She's helped hold this family together, and she's done it at a huge cost to herself. So tomorrow, with all of our blessings, she starts a new page in her life."

More cheers sounded, and Dani fought off tears.

Ben grinned at her from the crowd, and Haley and Jenna stood together at his side. The smiles on the girls' faces overshadowed the sadness she knew they felt over her leaving.

Her dad and Gloria linked arms as they watched on, their pride clear.

And Michelle stood, arms crossed, looking bored.

"We're proud of you, sis," Nick said into the mic. "You were a pain in our ass most of the time, but you've always been consistent."

Laughter bounced through the crowd.

"You didn't let us get away with anything," Nate added. Then tossed in a wink. "As far as you know."

Everyone snickered.

"And we're way better people today because you were in our lives," Jaden finished. His words—and gaze—were sincere, and she went to him and gave him a huge hug.

Standing with Jay, she took in the rest of her brothers. They sure knew how to make a girl feel appreciated. *Thank you*, she mouthed to all of them. She couldn't have described the enormity of her love for her family at that moment if she'd had to.

"And with that said"—Cord once again took the mic—"we wanted to give our sister a going-away present from her little brothers. Something she could remember us by."

A present?

She eyed them, suddenly not trusting whatever they were about to do.

And she was right not to.

In a flash, they picked her up while several of the pickers rolled out a giant vat of cherries that hadn't made the cut. If the skin was broken or if the stem got separated from the fruit, it couldn't be shipped.

But they didn't make a habit of putting those cherries in a person-size tub.

And they sure as heck didn't put them in a tub and smash them!

"Noooo!" Dani thrashed in their arms, but they merely laughed at her efforts.

"We love you, sis. But this is payback for all the times you're driven us crazy," Gabe said.

"And there were a lot of those times," added Jay.

"Don't forget us when you're a big, bad New Yorker," Nick began, and Nate finished up with "but go blow the socks off everyone out East."

And with that, Cord took her from the rest of them and dumped her into the vat of cherries.

chapter twenty-two

The last rays of color disappeared from the sky as the music started back up after the band's break, and Ben grew anxious waiting for Dani's return. Her brothers had wrecked both her hair and her outfit, but it seemed she'd been gone an awfully long time for repairs.

He was tired of waiting. And he was finished dancing with anyone but her.

If she didn't show back up soon he would go to the house and find her. And if that happened, neither of them would be returning to the party at all.

Familiar laughter hit his ears, and he followed the sound to find Michelle talking with a man who appeared quite pleased with the attention. She'd been at Gabe's side for most of the evening, seemingly on her best behavior, but she stood now, distanced from everyone else, just her and this man. And then Ben realized who the guy was. Ben had seen Michelle talking with him at the bar Sunday night. Or, rather, *flirting* with him.

Ben hadn't said anything at the time, assuming it to be harmless. She'd had a few too many to drink, but she and Gabe had seemed to be having a good time.

But damned if she and the man didn't look awfully chummy tonight. Which pissed Ben off.

His friend was changing his entire world—their child's world—for her. And she still flirted with other men?

Not on his watch.

The sea of people parted as he crossed the middle of the dance floor. When he reached Michelle's side, she glanced up at him and her laughter slipped.

"Dance?" he asked. It wasn't really a question.

"I'm in the middle of a conversation, Ben." Her flirting with *him* had ended a couple of weeks ago—thank goodness—and she looked at him now as if he were mud on her shoe.

"Your conversation is over." Without waiting for a reply, he took her wrist and moved them toward the dance floor.

"Ben," she gritted out, as she tugged against his hand as subtly as she could. "Let me go."

"Not until you hear me out."

"About what?"

"About you," he said. He swung her into his arms and smiled as if he were thrilled to have her there. "And your marriage. Smile so people don't figure out that we're arguing."

A bright smile lit her mouth. "Stay out of my marriage."

He swung her out and back, rewrapping his arms around her to have her right up against him, and put his mouth to her ear. "I can't do that. You're married to my friend, yet you routinely seem to forget that."

"I don't—"

"Here's the deal," he interrupted. "I have money."

With his statement she stopped struggling against his touch, and he gave her some space. They remained together, however, both dancing to the beat, and to the casual observer they would look like any other couple having a good time.

"I have a *lot* of money," he clarified with yet another fake smile.

He'd known she would listen to that, because he'd overheard her telling a girlfriend this week about "her" new LA apartment. The woman was a money-grubbing, coldhearted bitch. And Ben would do whatever he could to protect his friend from letting that destroy him.

"And if I have to use every last cent of it to pay for *your* divorce," Ben continued, "and to make sure Gabe gets custody of *your* child"—he stared straight into her eyes—"you'll get nothing."

"You have no right to talk to me like that."

He ignored her. "You either start treating your husband like the good guy that he is, quit flirting with any-and-everyone, and pay attention to your daughter, or I'm going to rain hell down on your head."

His speech shut her up. And honestly, it shut him up, too. He hadn't been planning on saying all that, but he found that he meant it. Gabe was a good guy. His friend. And even though Ben hadn't seen him in years before this trip, Gabe had opened his home to him without question the minute Ben had needed it.

That kind of favor had to be returned.

He and Michelle swooped around the dance floor, they smiled, they pretended a grand time.

"You can't threaten me like that." Michelle finally got her voice back.

Ben once again pulled her to him. "If that's what you believe, then go on about your business tonight. Flirt. Hell, sleep with the guy. That'll help my fight."

"I don't cheat on my husband."

"No?" He wasn't sure if she did or not, but if she hadn't already . . . "If I hired someone to follow you, would that hold up?"

She stopped dancing, her breathing hard, and looked him up and down. "How dare you?" she spat out. Venom shot from her eyes, and he began to suspect that their ruse of enjoyable dancing was about to be up. Which was fine. He didn't want her near him any longer.

"Your husband is by the band," he told her. "Ignore your new friend, and don't leave Gabe's side again tonight. Or that apartment I've just set you up in is history. As is the life you're hoping to fake your way through once you're in LA."

She eyed him, anger rolling off her, and without a word turned and walked away.

Standing behind her was Dani, and Ben immediately forgot about Michelle and everything she'd done to piss him off. Dani was back.

She was dressed, now, in a flowing skirt of turquoise and white that hit just above the knees and dipped longer in the back. Her own set of cowboy boots were on her feet, and there was something flimsy and clingy draped around her chest. He gulped. He couldn't wait to take that off her.

She also had on the pink cowboy hat that Haley had brought her from New Mexico. Ben couldn't help but smile at the contrast the hat made with the sex goddess thing she had going on in the light of the bonfire.

"Well, hello, darlin'," he murmured.

Her brows shot up. "Where'd you pick up that accent, Hollywood? It come with the hat?"

He tipped his grandfather's hat at her and winked. "Maybe. Or it might be because I've officially turned in my Hollywood card. Handed my apartment keys over to your brother the other day."

"Yeah?" She glanced in the direction that Michelle had gone. "That why you were dancing with my sister-in-law?"

"Ah, babe." He reached for her as the band started a new song. "I do love your jealous streak."

"Please." She made a face. "I am so not jealous."

"Well, I am." He pulled her into his arms. "Dance with me, woman. I think you've been in the arms of every man here tonight but mine."

She gave him a throaty laugh, but she also twined her arms around his neck. Her body fit snug against his. "I seem to be a popular girl. Not that you've been standing around by yourself."

"Oh, there's that jealous thing again," he murmured.

She softened and warmed in his palms, but her massive eye roll kept the mood light.

"You look beautiful tonight," he told her. He stared down at her and made a point of capturing her lower body tight against his. At the sight of her he'd started to get hard, and he wanted to make sure she knew it.

Her eyes widened in pleased surprise.

"Of course, you're beautiful every day," he added. His hand was on the small of her back—the shirt she wore left the skin there exposed—and his fingertips took a quick dip under the material of her skirt to sweep across the top curve of her butt. "But tonight you're glowing."

She wiggled at his touch, and he grew harder with her movements. Short breaths came from between her parted lips. He had her ready to do more than dance.

"I guess it comes with taking two showers for one party." Her words came out breathless.

God, he wanted this woman. Right now. And he didn't want to let her get on that plane tomorrow.

"They love you, you know?" he said. "Your brothers."

"I know." She nodded. "And I even realize that they showed that tonight. In their own way. But good grief."

He put his mouth to her neck. "Well, I liked it. It got you back out here like this." He nipped her just underneath her ear, and her breasts pushed into his chest.

"Rein it in, big guy," she whispered. "We have a party to get through before any of that can happen."

"Too bad," he murmured. But he put two inches between them, because it would be a long night if he had to spend every remaining moment of it erect. He captured her hand, and wrapping her fingers in his, brought their hands between their bodies. "Want me to take you to the airport in the morning?"

"No need. Cord's got a flight out, too. He has a rental, so that'll make it easy."

There would be absolutely nothing easy about her leaving in the morning.

The volume of the music picked up as the band neared the end of the song, and Ben took a moment to spin Dani away from him. He needed a second to breathe, and he'd never been able to do that with her so close.

When he brought her back, she tilted her face up to his.

"I love being in your arms," she said.

He couldn't do this. He absolutely could not do this.

He couldn't let her get on a plane and never look back.

Once again, he closed the distance. "Dani," he started. He could see everything he was feeling, everything he wanted, right there in her eyes. She felt it, too.

"I—"

"Dad." Haley tugged on a belt loop, cutting off his words, and he and Dani both groaned.

Dani made a move to step away, but he tightened his grip, keeping her in his arms. His daughter had the worst timing in the world.

"Yes, Haley?" he answered, careful not to show his frustration.

"Daddy," she said, "Leslie says her doggie is having puppies and I can have one. Can I? You told me we would get me one."

When he didn't answer in the first second, she asked, "Can I?" once again, and he chuckled at both her unbridled enthusiasm and his unfit state. His daughter might be the death of him. Either that or Dani.

"Can we talk about this later?" he asked.

"But I need to tell her yes or no."

He kept him and Dani swaying together, not wanting her to forget where they'd been, and all the while looking down at his daughter. She was literally bouncing, and he couldn't get over how different she was.

"Yes," he told her. "You may have one." He'd give her anything she wanted, but there would be logistics to work out. "You'll have to wait a few weeks after they're born to bring it home, though. Puppies need their mothers for several weeks."

She nodded, her face a mixture of confusion and trust, then was off, heading back to shout the answer to Leslie and Jenna, along with several additional girls who'd joined the trio. He also heard her inviting every one of them to her new house to play with her dog.

Ben brought his gaze back to Dani's. "Can you believe she claimed to only want two friends? What have I turned her into?"

"She's the life of the party."

"Thanks to you." He put his cheek next to hers. "Thank you for suggesting the therapist. I think Haley's actually going to be all right."

And he was, too. Because he'd finally figured out what love was.

Dani pressed her cheek more firmly to his, but she didn't say anything. Ben kept them dancing.

"How's the house search going?" she eventually asked.

"Great. I got an email earlier today from my agent. She sent pictures of a property on the lake not far from here, and it's gorgeous. If there are no issues, it could be the one."

It was a place where he could picture Dani and himself.

The song stopped, and she stepped back.

"No," he said. "You're dancing with me for the rest of the evening. Only me," he stressed. "I want you in my arms."

"But there are people here I haven't seen yet," she said. "They came to see me."

"I don't care." They'd just have to do without, because he couldn't handle another second with her anywhere but in his arms.

When she didn't agree, he tried the only thing he knew to use. His smile. He knew she loved his smile.

At the attempt, a curve of her own lifted the corners of her lips, and she returned to his arms. "You don't play fair, Hollywood." With one finger, she traced the creases that ran alongside his mouth. "You know this smile can bring women to their knees. You could get anything you want with it."

He clasped his hands behind her back. "And what if what I want is you?"

At his serious question, her mouth flattened. Her gaze turned uncertain.

The sound of silverware tapping against an empty beer bottle pulled their attention to Gabe, who once again stood on the trailer. Michelle and Jenna were at his side.

"Can I have your attention once more?" Gabe shouted through the microphone.

After the crowd hushed, he continued. "As you know, we've had another successful crop this year, and it's in no small thanks to you."

Cheers went up, and a couple of men snagged their wives and pulled them onto their laps. These people worked hard, and they played the same way.

"I couldn't be more proud. Thank you all for the hard work, for the great effort, and for another terrific season." Gabe reached for Michelle's hand. "But I also wanted to let you know that within the next few weeks, Michelle, Jenna, and I will be moving, and I'll no longer be the man in charge."

Shock echoed through the crowd, and Ben saw Max making his way to the trailer.

"Don't worry." Gabe held up his hands. "I'll still be back for harvest next year. We all will. You can't get rid of us that easily. But I *won't* be running the day-to-day operations." He stepped aside to make room for Max. "I trust you might recognize our new manager, though," Gabe added. "It's not like he hasn't done this before."

"Dad's coming out of retirement?" Dani whispered in shock.

Ben was as astounded as she.

"Thanks, son," Max said. "And as Gabe said, I, too, thank you all for your hard work, and I hope each of you will be back next year—when hopefully the crop will be bigger and better than before." He winked at Gabe. "I can't have this guy showing me up. But also, I hope you're not too sorry to see me back up here."

Choruses of disagreement sounded. Everyone loved Max.

"We've had a lot of changes in our family recently," the elder Wilde continued. "Dani's got a job in New York we're all proud of, Gabe is going to California. And that left a hole in our family."

He looked at Dani now, and Ben felt as if far more was being said than what the workers would hear.

"I couldn't leave our farm without family to run it. It means too much to us."

"He's trying to fix things with me," Dani said softly. She reached for Ben, and slipped her hand into his.

"And I won't let our family down." He swept his gaze over the crowd. "Not everything is perfect in the world, but it's up to us to fix it when we mess up."

A few questioning gazes passed through the crowd, but no one said anything.

Max looked at Dani again. "Don't worry about our legacy, Dani girl. You go do what you've waited your life to achieve. I've got this. For as long as I need to."

He didn't say a lot more after that, but the heart of it had been said. They might be heading down different paths, but their family was still here. Their farm. The thing they could always count on.

When Max left the trailer, Ben turned to Dani and lifted a brow.

"That helps," she confirmed. The music started, and without encouragement she returned to his arms. "Dance with me, Ben."

And so they danced.

But after three more songs, Ben couldn't wait any longer. He brought Dani's face up to his. "You do know that I love you, right?"

Her feet stopped moving to the song. "What?"

He urged her to continue following his lead, sliding them back in with the crowd. "I love you," he said again. He pressed a kiss to her temple. "That can't be a surprise."

"Ben . . ."

"It's a good thing, Dani." He leaned back and looked her in the eye. "*We're* good."

"But why would you tell me that?" Her words came out blunt. "Why now? I'm catching a plane *tomorrow*."

He swallowed around the fear that rose up. Putting his heart on the line, he found, was no easy feat. "I'm telling you because I don't want it to end here, babe. Haley and I could catch a flight in a couple of weeks. We could come out with you."

Her jaw dropped. "You want to do a long-distance thing? Won't that be too confusing for Haley?"

"I want to do a permanent thing, Dani."

Confusion crossed her brow.

"I'm saying that Haley and I will move to New York. For you." She didn't respond, so he added, "We'll follow you. Because we love you."

Her forehead wrinkled even more, and if he wasn't mistaken, it was in horror. This was most definitely not going as he'd envisioned.

"Haley needs Montana," Dani told him. "You're buying a house."

"Or it could be a vacation home. A place to visit. To come see your family."

"My family isn't even going to be here."

"Come on, your dad isn't going anywhere. And you know the others will come back. The house could be our chance to be here in Birch Bay when we want to, but not have to be underfoot of everyone else. It could provide you the opportunity to work on your relationship with your father. To continue being close with your brothers."

She took a step back. "Do you even know me at all?"

"What do you mean?" He realized that they weren't moving, and everyone else kept bumping into them. One couple even tried to dance between them.

Ben took her arm, and moved them off the dance floor.

"I need to go to New York." Dani made the statement as though he weren't aware of the fact.

"And I'm not asking you to do anything different."

"By myself."

The words seemed to echo in the night. *Oh.* She didn't want *him* there.

"I'm too messed up," she explained. "Don't you see that? What if I'm like my mother?"

"You know you aren't."

"No, I don't." She inched backward. "How could I know that? I don't even know who I am."

"And you can't figure that out with us around?"

"No."

They stared at each other in silence until she added, "What if having you around causes me to fail at my new job?"

That didn't even make sense.

"What if I become more focused on *you*?" she continued, her voice rising slightly. "On Haley?"

"You know me, Dani. I wouldn't let that happen." He was the one person who'd never tried to dump everything on her. He didn't understand why she didn't see that.

She shook her head again. "This is my last chance. The job is all I've got, and I can't screw it up."

The job was all she had?

Anger began to hum inside him. "And us being there would screw it up?"

"I have to focus on me," she said. The words fell flat. "Not my family. Not you. And not Haley. I can't take care of her right now."

"I'm not asking you to take care of her," he said, his voice increasing to a level above hers, and more than one couple turned to watch.

"Not in so many words, but you know I would. It's what I do. It's what I was taught to do. Plus, this thing between us . . . it was supposed to just be fun." She whispered the last sentence. "You knew that all along. I told you. That's all it could be." Her voice shook, but she didn't look like she thought she was saying the wrong words.

But that wasn't all it had been. He opened his mouth to contradict her, only, he made himself stop. Had it truly been nothing to her? He found that hard to believe. But then, what did he really know about love, after all? He hadn't even believed in it until a few days ago.

He had to pull himself back before he made an even bigger fool of himself. "My mistake," he gritted out.

"I'm sorry, Ben." And that quickly, she was done. She glanced around, like she was just remembering where they were. "We have guests. I need to mingle."

In the next instant she was gone. Out of his reach.

Someone stepped beside him and Ben turned with a confused mix of shock and anger.

It was Gabe.

"I told you not to sleep with her again," her brother said.

What the hell had just happened? "Don't worry," Ben assured him sarcastically. "She kicked my ass for you."

He couldn't believe he'd been nothing more to her than a good time.

Gabe remained silent, watching Dani alongside Ben. She laughed with another couple from town, played with a toddler belonging to one of the migrant families. And at no point did she look back at Ben. As if completely unconcerned that she'd just stomped on his heart. And certainly not seeming in the least like hers was broken.

Because it apparently wasn't.

"It comes from our mom, you know?" Gabe finally said.

"What does?"

Gabe nudged his chin toward Dani. "That show she's putting on."

Ben watched for a moment longer. "Doesn't look like a show to me."

It looked like she was owning the crowd, same as she always did. Content, in charge, and looking forward to her next challenge.

Had this really been one-sided all this time?

They watched Dani continue charming the crowd for another minute before Gabe turned to Ben. "Then you're not looking close enough."

chapter twenty-three

B en lay in the middle of his bed later that night, still confused.
And still more than a bit angry. He'd replayed every moment of
the conversation on the dance floor with Dani, several times, and he
couldn't figure it out. It was as though any emotions—any *feelings*—
she might have had toward him had turned off with a single click.

The rest of the night had continued, with her laughing and talking with others, acting as if nothing were wrong. The entire family
had partied, they'd bid the workers good-bye until next year, then
the group of them had walked back to the house together.

Dani put the girls to bed, since she would be leaving before they
got up—Ben had heard her promise to sneak into their room in the
morning for a good-bye kiss. Then she'd gone to her room.

She'd promised *him* nothing.

Nor had she even said another word to him.

A faint light appeared around the edges of his door as he lay there, and he held his breath. He listened, unsure if it was Haley, or if Dani had decided to break her silence. But one thing was for certain. He would not be the one to speak first.

The door opened wider. "Are you awake?"

He closed his eyes. It was Dani.

His anger moved from a simmer, right to the edge of boil. "I am," he bit out.

"Can I come in?"

"Dani . . ." He didn't know what to say. If anything could possibly be said that would matter at this point.

"Just to talk," she begged. "And maybe . . . I don't know. Could I stay in here for a while? I'm going to miss you, Ben."

What the fuck was wrong with the woman?

"Never mind," she said into the silence. Her voice turned to a whisper. "It was wrong of me to ask."

The door was almost shut when he opened his mouth. "You can come in."

He might regret it—he would *probably* regret it—but they didn't feel finished yet. He had to let her in. At least to hear what she had to say.

"You're sure?"

He could see her now. She was beautiful.

And he loved her.

He moved over on his bed, and she settled beside him—still in the outfit she'd worn to the party—and lay flat on her back. She didn't touch him, nor did he touch her.

After several minutes, she spoke. "I'm sorry," she said simply. "I was distant with you after we talked tonight. I didn't mean to be, but I needed to get away from our discussion."

"To act like nothing had happened? Like we hadn't just broken up."

He could see her turn her face to him in the dark. "Were we ever really together?"

Once again, he found himself surprised at her words.

"I grew up pretending the world was okay," she explained. "That I was loved. Only, I wasn't loved and it was never okay."

Ben rubbed a hand over his face and noticed that it was shaking. She'd had a crappy upbringing, he'd give her that. But still . . .

"I know that's not an excuse, but that's part of why I have to do this on my own. I don't know how to have normal relationships."

"You have them with your brothers every day," he pointed out. "I've seen it."

"But they're a part of me. They're part of both the problem . . . and the solution. I think. If there is one. I can be more real around them because they get it, they were a part of it. Yet, because of them, I also feel as if I've been in a black hole for most of my life.

"I'm hurting," she continued. "I don't feel normal, and I don't know how to fix it. I don't know if I can fix it. To me, love is tied around *me* doing for everyone else." She rolled to her side. "Don't you see that? I don't know how to do anything else, and if you're there in New York with me, I might be just like I've been here my whole life. And I don't want to be that anymore."

"But love doesn't come from what you do for others. You know that. You get that."

"Logically, yes. Yet at the same time, my entire existence has *been* that. My mother didn't love me if I didn't take care of her. Or my brothers. Or the damned dishes."

"That wasn't love."

"But it's the love I was shooting for. It's the only kind I knew. And even these last two weeks . . . when I've known who my mother was, how she manipulated me . . . while being mad at my brothers and my dad . . . I've worried the whole time that they're going to quit loving *me* because I quit taking care of *them*."

He didn't get it, but at the same time she was making a weird kind of sense. "You know they still love you, babe. They'll always love you. You know the difference in your mother's conditional love and reality now. You *know* what love is."

"Do I?"

He didn't answer because he didn't know what else to say.

"I'm sorry," she said again.

And again, he didn't respond.

Instead, he rolled to face her and silently tucked her against him. He got that she was trying to explain things, but he couldn't get beyond her so callously reminding him that they were nothing.

That he'd been nothing but a good time.

He wanted more, and he'd wanted it with her.

And he was hurting too damned much to give anything more than an inch at the moment.

Ben woke to an empty bed just as the sun began peeking through his bedroom window. He was still on his side, the way he'd been when Dani had been in bed with him, and he rolled to his back.

Was she gone?

"Thank you for letting me be in here last night," she said from the other side of the room.

She hadn't left yet.

He rolled back to his side and saw her sitting, back straight, on the edge of the chair in the far corner of the room. She looked as if she'd been waiting for him to wake up simply so she could leave. He supposed that was better than having left without a word.

"I'm glad you came in," he told her. And he was. He hadn't slept for a long time last night because he'd been thinking about everything she'd said. He'd been *hearing* everything she'd said. And it had finally begun to make sense.

She felt she had to fix herself *for herself* before *they* could be together.

He could respect that. His childhood may not have been great, but it hadn't been a series of manipulations either. The impact of that was foreign to him, and before he'd finally fallen asleep, he'd understood that he had to let her go.

He could only hope that she would eventually come back.

Rising from the bed, he crossed to her and went down on one knee. He reached for her hand.

"I love you, Dani." He said the words clearly. Because he did love her. He knew that. "And those aren't just words. I love you with my whole heart. I think it began that first summer, and after all this time it hasn't let go. I see you for the person you have the potential to be. I don't see your mother, and I don't see your walls. I see behind all that, and when I look at you, I'm looking at a beautiful, capable, loving human being who just wants to be loved in return. So yeah, those words are real. And I get that you need boundaries right now. I get that you have to work through things by yourself." He pressed a kiss to the back of her hand. "So go do what you need to do. See someone. *Please.* You're right. This is what you need. But the thing is, I'll be here when you're ready."

"You can't wait for me," she pressed.

Pain lanced through him. "Babe. You've got to give me something. I can't do it all for both of us."

"I'm not joking." She cupped his cheek as a thin beam of sunlight reached into the room and touched her face. "You need a woman who can commit to you. Someone who can be there fully.

Haley needs a mom. A woman who you won't have to worry might be manipulating your daughter," she said in a low tone. She shook her head. "You can't wait for me. I'm not coming back."

He felt like he'd been punched in the gut. "Do you not love me?" he forced himself to ask.

"Buy the house, Ben. Go on with your life."

"Do you not love me?" he repeated, the words coming out hard. He locked his gaze on hers, and what he saw ripped him apart. Because even after all this, he'd still thought she cared.

"I don't even love me," she said.

She rose from the chair then, and he didn't utter another word as she stepped around him and crossed the floor. Nor when she silently slipped out of his room.

chapter twenty-four

Two weeks later

T hank you all for the party." Bette Turner poked her head into the break room one last time, placing her half-eaten cake on the small table. Her Gucci pumps and crisp, black pantsuit provided her the same formidable power that Dani assumed she'd shown at BA Advertising for the past twenty-three years, and Dani couldn't help but picture the woman in her same clothes, scooping up the grandbabies she was moving to the middle of Indiana to enjoy. "It was a lovely surprise."

The colleagues who'd worked the closest with Bette moved in for a final hug. It was rolling down to the last minutes of her last day before retirement.

Dani liked the woman, but having only known her for two weeks, she stayed out of the way, giving the time to the other employees. Instead, she remained by the high-rise office window, staring out over the late-Friday afternoon mayhem of the city down below. Twenty floors up, the people on the streets looked tiny and the sky close enough to touch.

The sad part was that the sky was white. She hadn't seen a blue sky in two weeks.

"Dani," Bette said from the door. "It's been a pleasure. Keep up the excellent work."

Casual laughter followed her as she and the others made their way down the hall, leaving Dani alone in the break room. The cake that had been purchased for the party remained in the middle of the table, and a tub of ice cream sat melting beside it.

She moved to put the ice cream away, and found herself cleaning up the kitchen. It had become her daily routine, to tidy the small area before going home.

"Thanks for starting the cleanup." Kendra returned to the room with a handful of used paper plates. "Bette just left, as did most everyone else."

The majority of her colleagues had better things to do on a Friday evening than stay late at the office. Dani had been privy to the conversations. A final night out with husbands and kids before the start of school next week, a hot date with the new guy two floors down. A couple of people were even heading out of town for one last end-of-summer weekend at the beach.

Dani would be working. She'd done a good job so far, but as the newbie, her nerves remained on edge. She wanted to ensure she got noticed.

"Did you want the rest of the cake?" Dani asked as she closed the lid to the box.

"Oh, no." Kendra looked at her watch. "You take it home with you. I have a train to catch to my boyfriend's place as soon as I leave here. We're visiting his parents in Hartford for the weekend."

Kendra grabbed a rag to wipe down the table, but Dani took it away from her. "You go on," she said. "You have a long drive. I'll finish up here."

"I couldn't . . ."

But Dani saw the desire to do just that in Kendra's eyes.

She motioned to the door. "Go. I've got this. I'll be here for a couple more hours, anyway. I want to get started on the Eaton project."

"You're sure you don't mind?"

"Positive." Dani nudged the woman toward the door. "Enjoy your weekend."

Kendra's face lit, and she gave a quick nod. "Thanks, Dani. You're the best."

Left alone in the room, Dani finished cleaning the space, cut a piece of cake to take home to her roommate, and wrapped the remainder in plastic wrap before putting it in the freezer. One of the women with kids might want to take it home next week, so she'd leave it for them.

Then she switched off the lights and returned to her desk.

Thirty minutes later, the building had grown silent and Dani sat alone at her desk. Which was nice—being alone. That was something she'd gotten little of since moving to New York.

She had a roommate, there were after-hours drinks and meetings, and the city was constantly full of people—everywhere. There was so much going on all the time that she had yet to find a spot to sit and think without at least a hundred people already there, all sitting and thinking. It was exhausting.

And it made her miss home.

And Ben.

She thought about the night of the party again. And the morning after.

The last thing she'd meant to do was hurt Ben, but when he'd started talking about love and coming out here, she'd panicked. She'd been holding on to the moment when she could get away from her life. Escape the pressure of having the memories of her mother in her head day in and day out, and turn her back on the strain of every member of her family watching her to make sure she was okay.

She was fine. She would remain fine, that's what she did. But she'd needed to get away.

And Ben's suggestion to come with her? Something like that had never once entered her mind. It had scared her.

Do you not love me?

She pictured the pain in his features when he'd asked the question. She hated herself for causing that pain.

But how could she love him? She'd told him the truth. She didn't love herself. She didn't know what a normal relationship was. She was a mess, and neither he nor Haley deserved that in their lives.

She'd said no for his own benefit.

"Love the work for the Falcon brand, Dani."

She looked up from her desk to find her boss standing in her doorway. "Thanks, Bill. It's a great company to work with."

"They're already talking about signing a longer contract. Because of you."

The words encouraged her. She'd thought she'd been impressing, but unwanted worries continued to creep in at all hours of the day. Those worries often came with her mother's voice, and had managed to layer in way more self-doubt than Dani was comfortable with.

"Keep it up," Bill added. "You're very good. I can see you going places with us." Her mother's voice disagreed with him. "I'm glad we talked you into coming on board."

Dani nodded at the praise, and after wishing her a good weekend, Bill departed.

She picked up her phone, her fingers automatically scrolling through her contacts, before realizing what she was doing. She was about to call Ben.

She'd had the desire to share all kinds of things with him over the past two weeks, and as she'd done every day, she found his number and spent several minutes staring at it. She wanted to talk to him. To hear his voice. To tell him about her day.

She wanted to ask how Haley was doing.

School would be starting soon. Was she continuing to adjust well?

There were so many things Dani wondered about, but she didn't have the right to ask. She didn't even have the right to call. No matter how much she simply *needed* to talk to him.

He'd declared his love, and she'd walked away. There was no recovery from that.

Changing gears, she pulled up Jay's number and sent him a text. She might be out of her brothers' daily lives, but the physical distance now between them had brought them closer than ever before. She'd talked to each of them at least once a week since she'd arrived in New York—even reclusive Nate—and Gabe and Jay more than that.

Her phone buzzed in reply. Jay was good. He and Megan were in Seattle, and had signed a lease on an apartment today. He would begin looking for a part-time job, starting tomorrow.

Dani smiled fondly at the message. Her baby brother was growing up.

Putting her phone down, she returned to the work open on her computer, and spent the next two hours prepping for the coming week. As she finally finished for the day, her phone rang.

It was Gabe.

"Hey, moron," she answered in her customary way. The distance between Gabe and her had disappeared. They talked again. Shared things. And she was pretty sure he missed her.

"Hey, dumbass. How's New York?"

"Noisy." She rose and went to the window, and Gabe chuckled in her ear.

"A bit different than home, huh?"

"Some." Surprisingly, she'd found that, though she did enjoy the city, the energy, the people . . . it wasn't quite what she'd built up in her mind. "You about to head out?" she asked.

Gabe and Michelle were moving to California that weekend.

"Just finished packing up. But that's not why I called. I wanted to talk to you about something before I left."

"What's that?"

She squinted as she stared down at the street, trying to make out whether the grilled cheese vendor remained on the corner or not. She would love a grilled cheese sandwich before going home.

"Dad," Gabe said in her ear. "He and Gloria would like to move into the house, and I'm in agreement. I'd prefer it didn't sit empty."

Dani had also talked to her dad since being in New York. Once. It had been a polite conversation. They were trying. "Sure," she said now. "Someone should be there."

"If it bothers you, then say so."

"It's his house, Gabe. He can live there if he wants."

"It's everyone's house."

Which, technically, was true. Her dad had deeded the house to all six kids when he'd retired and moved out. The house and the business belonged to them.

"Gloria might change it up," Gabe hedged.

Nick's words telling her that the house was a shrine to their mother came to mind. "Tell her to have at it." That was exactly what needed to be done.

They talked for several more minutes. About Birch Bay, New York, California, and his family. Jenna was doing good. Michelle was being Michelle.

Gabe didn't bring up Ben and Haley, and she didn't ask.

"Jenna misses you," he told her.

"I miss her too." She crossed the room and shut down her computer. "Can't wait for you to bring her out for Christmas."

"Can't wait to bring her out there. Christmas in New York? Sounds like a dream. Michelle will love it. And by the way . . ." His tone changed, and Dani said up straight, wondering what was coming. "Thank you for all you did over the years. Did I ever really say that? We should have done more. Hell, we should have done *something*."

She started to give him a hard time, but instead, took the compliment the way it was intended. With sincerity. "Thank you," she said. "And you're welcome. It was truly my greatest pleasure to be there for everyone. Even if . . ." She didn't finish.

"Even if we went about some things wrong," he added.

She nodded, feeling suddenly melancholy and missing her family even more.

"I'm glad you were here," Gabe told her. "We love you, sis. And we're proud of you. *All* of us."

Meaning their dad, too.

"I love you too," she added. "*All* of you."

They hung up and she pulled her purse from the drawer, intending to go, and her gaze landed on the small notebook tucked underneath. It was the journal she'd pulled from the old desk in her bedroom back home. She'd brought it to New York with her, but she had yet to open it.

She did, however, retrieve it from the drawer daily . . . and stare at it.

Then she'd put it away without cracking the cover.

She pulled it out now, and placed it on the desk in front of her. Her phone buzzed and her heart leapt at the hope that it was Ben.

She really had to stop doing that. Ben would not be calling her, texting her, or caring about her ever again.

It was another text from Jay.

Just talked to Gabe. He forgot to ask. You scheduled that appointment yet?

They'd been checking on her regularly. Was she seeing a therapist yet? Did they need to make an appointment for her? Jay had even gotten recommendations from past professors who knew people in New York and emailed the names and phone numbers to her.

Her brothers were truly worried about her. Which made her feel . . . odd.

Special, yes. They loved and cared about her. Just as she did them.

But all the attention directed her way added additional stress she wasn't used to. She was supposed to be the one who took care of them.

Not yet. She really didn't know what she was waiting for.

Dad's been twice already.

She ran the edge of her thumb over the spine of the journal before typing a reply. He's okay with it?

Seems to be. He's putting in the effort, sis. Now you.

She drew in a breath. I will. I just needed to settle in first. New job, and all. I've been busy.

You're avoiding. You're scared. Stop it. Want me to make the appointment for you?

If she'd needed another reminder of how their positions had reversed, this was it. Her baby brother was now taking care of her. Or trying to. That meant something to her.

That meant it was time to get her butt into gear and face the past.

She flipped open the journal to the first page.

I hate my mother.

The words were as real to her today as the day she'd written them in her early teens. As well as the guilt for her feelings. A daughter wasn't supposed to hate her mother.

Nor was a mother supposed to hate her daughter.

If her own mother couldn't love her, how could anyone else?

She pulled the paper that contained the numbers Jay had sent her out of her purse, and drew a circle around the one she'd researched and decided she liked the best. Then she sent one more text to Jay.

I'll call and leave a message right now.

"Don't forget my lunch box, Daddy." Haley swung her legs back and forth from the stool at their kitchen island as Ben rushed around gathering up the items he would need for the day.

"I fixed it for you last night," he reminded her.

"You put the cookies in there, too?"

"I did." He stopped his hurried motions and took the time to drop a kiss on the top of his daughter's head. They'd been in their new house for one week, and today was the first day of school. He seemed more nervous than she. "Did *you* remember to put your notebook and pencils in your backpack?" he questioned.

She smiled brightly as she nodded. Her legs continued swinging and her brand-new backpack hung low on her back. "I gots all the pencils and all the crayons."

Ben stopped then, his laptop in hand, as well as his camera, and took the time to really look at his daughter.

And then he thought about those words. *His daughter.*

She was 100 percent his. The custody agreement had come through last week, and he'd heard no additional word from Lia or her lawyer. It was a done deal.

Haley continued with her therapist two days a week, and probably would for a while. But she was good. She had adjusted. And so had he. He was the single father of a school-aged child. She would turn five next month—there would be a big party for all the new friends she planned to make in school—and in thirty minutes he'd drop her off for her first day of kindergarten.

A little over two months ago he'd been on a shoot on the other side of the world, his most pressing matter being whom he would sleep with next and where he wanted to travel to in his downtime, and today he was a homeowner and a single father.

Wow.

"Did we need to go?" Haley asked. She pursed her lips with the question, seemingly having no concerns at all.

"Yeah." He nodded. "We need to go. Put your cup in the sink and go wash your hands."

She did as she was asked while Ben finished packing his camera equipment. According to his agent, a book deal was looking good. And though he needed to get to work on that, he'd also volunteered his time as a photographer for a local magazine. He and Haley were becoming part of the community. They fit.

He only wished there wasn't a hole left in both their hearts.

But as Dani had insisted, he wasn't sitting around waiting for her. He was moving on. Slowly on some levels, but he'd put her to the back of his mind.

Or, he tried to.

He bustled Haley into the car, and ten minutes later pulled up in front of the school.

"There's my teacher!" Haley pointed out the window. "You don't have to take me in, Daddy. My teacher can."

He still got out of the car. Because she was four. He couldn't very well leave the engine running and simply drop the kid off.

Her teacher saw her and headed their way with a welcoming smile. "Miss Haley," the teacher said. "It's so good to see you again."

Haley giggled. "You had to see me again. It's time for the school."

They'd met Miss Wiggins at new-student orientation last Friday. The woman was fresh out of college, and looking forward to the challenge of a roomful of five-year-olds.

Haley grabbed her backpack from the floorboard. "Kisses, Daddy," she demanded, and he bent down and both gave and accepted a kiss. Then she took her teacher's hand and she was gone.

And just like that, his brand-new daughter was already growing up.

"I'll pick you up right here as soon as school is over," he called out.

She glanced back at him and waved, and the smile on her face would forever be a part of his heart.

Leaning against his SUV, he watched until she got inside. Haley would be fine.

He just didn't know if he would be.

With a shake of his head, he circled the front of the car and climbed back into the vehicle. When he pulled out onto the road his phone rang. And as ridiculous as it was, his heart beat fast at the sound, hoping it was Dani. His heart did that every single time the phone rang.

He glanced at the number on the car screen, but no. Not Dani. It was never Dani.

But it was a number just as surprising.

He pushed the button to connect. "Hello, Mother."

"Ben," she said. "I'm glad I caught you."

He hadn't talked to his mother since he and Haley had made their impromptu visit to LA. "Just getting started for the day," he told her. "What can I do for you?"

Their conversations had always been polite and cordial, and he saw no reason to change that now. Even if she had no desire to know Haley. It was a nonissue. She'd never had any desire to know him, and yet, he'd turned out okay.

"I've been thinking, Ben. I'd like to get to know my granddaughter. Might I come for a visit?"

He very nearly rear-ended the car in front of him.

"You want to come here? To Montana." He thought of the last time she'd been in the state. At his grandmother's funeral, camera crew in tow.

"Just me," she added, as though she could read his thoughts. "No cameras. No reporters."

He'd never known of his mother wanting to go anywhere without cameras or reporters.

"I might have to bring a bodyguard," she added. "I learned that the hard way once."

"Why?"

"Why do I want to come there?"

"Why do you want to come here? Why alone?" he asked. "I doubt you even know how to go anywhere alone. And why now? What's changed?"

She grew silent, and while he waited he checked his watch. He needed to be at the magazine office in ten minutes.

"I know I wasn't a good mother, Ben," she finally said. "I understand that. Why do you think I asked my parents to raise you?"

"Because you didn't want me," he blurted out.

"I suppose it might have looked that way."

"Might? Come on, Mother. You visited me maybe twice a year those first few years. And I'm not sure why you even did that."

"I visited because I wanted to see you," she told him. "You were my son, and I loved you." At his silence she added, "I still love you."

"You don't understand love." He got that now. Because, even though Dani had left him, he'd loved her. And Haley? He couldn't put into words his feelings for his daughter. His mother had never felt anything like that toward him.

"Your grandparents were kind people, Ben. They tried their best with me, but I was different. I'm not as nurturing. And that was fine with me. Then you came along. I couldn't take care of you the way they could, so I asked them to raise you. I thought you might stand a better chance that way."

"You asked them to raise me so that I didn't get in the way of your career."

"Well, yes. That too. But that's because I knew that my career would always come before you. I didn't know how to change that, but more importantly, I didn't want to. And I suppose I should apologize for that, but I can't change who I was. At least I tried to give you a good childhood."

He thought about his time with Grandpa. "My first seven years were very good."

"I know."

"The rest weren't."

"I know that, too. But Ben, were they bad? Or were they just not good enough?"

She had a point. "What's it matter now, Mom? I'm grown. I have a daughter of my own, and I no longer need your approval."

"It matters because I'd like to get to know her."

"But you just said you can't love."

"I said I do love. Just differently. But the thing is, I've thought about Haley every day since you were here."

His heart thudded. Then it occurred to him that his mother's shock at her own feelings now meant that when he'd been a kid, she *hadn't* thought similarly about him. Which hurt. Even if, deep down, he'd always known that fact.

"I missed out on a lot with you," she said. "And that's my fault, and I freely admit I didn't mind it at the time. But I don't want to miss everything anymore. I have a granddaughter. Did you know she looks like me?"

His mother was changing? It sounded like it. The very idea had him going mute.

"I won't come if you say no," she told him, "but I want you to know that I *would* like to get to know her. I'd like to get to know you both, actually."

It wasn't that easy.

Calling up with a casual "I'm sorry" and expecting to stroll back into his life? Possibly at his daughter's expense?

His mother had hurt him. She'd never wanted him. And he'd always been aware of that.

"Let me think about it," he finally answered. He didn't want to act irrationally. "I'll talk to Haley. If she says no, then it's no. But Mom, if she says yes, and one single camera shows up—"

"It won't. Just me. I swear it."

He couldn't handle more rejection. He'd had enough to last him a lifetime.

And he didn't want to screw anything up for Haley. They'd come too far. She was his number one priority.

But if she had a grandmother who actually cared, didn't she deserve that?

Honestly, he didn't know.

"I'll get back to you," he said.

chapter twenty-five

A six-pack of squirming black-and-white puppies wiggled in the makeshift bed that Leslie's father had created for them in the back corner of his garage, and Ben watched through the lens of his camera as Haley bent, hands on knees, and examined each one closely.

"This is my favorite," Leslie said, pointing out the fattest of the bunch. Its tiny stomach rounded on both sides of its body while the puppy worked her way back to her mother's teat.

"I don't like that one best," Haley determined. "I like that one." She pointed to the smallest—the runt of the litter—and nodded her head decisively. "It's the most beautiful."

Leslie's father gently lifted the pup in question. "This one is a boy."

Haley's mouth twisted as though she was fighting the urge to change her mind, but then she looked straight at Ben, her eyes wide and guileless. Ben snapped off a shot. "My daddy is a boy, and I like him, so I'll take the boy."

Ben captured two more photos before she turned back to her new puppy.

"His name can be Montana," she declared. "'Cause I love it here."

"I like that name," Leslie agreed.

Several minutes of petting later, Mr. Roberts lifted the puppy from Haley's lap and returned it to its mother. "You can visit him anytime you want," he explained, "but he has to stay here with his mama until he's eight weeks old."

Haley nodded. "My daddy told me. That's why he brought his camera. So I can see him anytime I want."

"Sounds like a great plan." Dean Roberts glanced at Ben. "I'll leave you guys alone so Haley can get to know him a little better. Just give me a yell if you need anything."

He disappeared in the office off the back of his house, and Leslie and Haley both bent, hands on knees once again, peering in at the dogs.

Ben took more pictures.

Haley had been in school for a couple of weeks now, and in addition to Leslie, she'd acquired several new friends. So many, in fact, that the sleepover planned for her birthday might not happen. Not unless he could figure out the logistics of chaperones. He was doing okay these days taking care of Haley, but he couldn't imagine a house full of girls just like her—with him the only adult.

"Can we talk about your birthday party?" Ben asked as the two girls continued petting the puppies.

Haley looked up at him. "I done invited everyone."

"Haley," he began. Crap. "I'm not sure we can do a sleepover."

"Why not?"

"Well, how many friends did you have in mind?"

"All of them."

Which amounted to around ten, depending on the day.

"I can't take care of ten girls at once, sweetheart. Not all night long."

"My mama could help," Leslie volunteered.

Her father might have something to say about that. But before Ben could voice his opinion, Leslie ran off to ask her mom.

"Haley," Ben said again. "We might have to only let Leslie stay overnight this time."

"But that's not what I want."

"I know, but sometimes we can't get everything we want." He'd learned that several times throughout his life. Most recently with Dani. More than a month had gone by, and still no word from her.

"But—"

"We'll talk about it later, okay?" Both Leslie and her mother were heading their way.

"Hello, Ben," Linda greeted him. "Good to see you again. Hi, Haley. Did you pick out a puppy?"

Haley beamed. "I did. And I love him already."

Linda chuckled and turned to Ben. "Leslie says there might be a problem with the party?"

"I was just explaining how everyone staying overnight might not be possible this year. I'm not sure I can properly oversee ten girls."

"Well, maybe some of the other mothers and I could help," she suggested. "I'm sure we could work something out. Your house is big, right? We could stay over with the girls. Make it a hybrid grown-up/kid party."

A house full of five-year-old girls *and* their mothers? He didn't think so.

"I'm sure Brandi Smith's mom would be there," Linda added. As if that would be an enticement. It wasn't. Brandi Smith's mom had been after him since learning he was the son of Angelica Denton.

Not what he needed.

"Let me think about it," Ben suggested. There had to be another way.

"Sounds good. Just let me know how we can help." She winked at Haley. "We'll do whatever we need to make sure this one has a great day."

Haley preened in front of the woman, thinking she'd won the battle.

"Leslie," her mom said. "Time for your piano lesson." She turned to Ben. "It's good to see you again, Ben. You and Haley stay as long as you want and play with the puppies."

After they drove off, Haley turned pleading eyes up to his. "Please, Daddy?"

She could be so sweet when she wanted to. But was it worth putting up with Brandi Smith's mom?

"We'll figure it out later," he promised. He put his camera down and lowered to sit on the concrete floor beside her. "Let's play with Montana for a couple more minutes, then we have to go."

He plucked the tiny pup out of the straw, and after stroking its black head, gently placed him in Haley's waiting hands. As he did, he thought about the time he'd asked his own mother for a dog. She'd gotten him one—she'd had her assistant pick out the perfect pedigreed pup—along with a dedicated dog trainer.

Not the life he'd ever want for Haley.

"You thought about your grandmother anymore?" he asked. They'd talked about the request to visit after his mother had asked, and so far Haley was unenthused. But they had FaceTimed with her. That had gone over well, and Ben had been able to see for himself that his mother really did seem to care. It was comforting to know that she did, indeed, have a heart inside her polished and shined shell. "You think we should invite her to come see us?"

Haley peered up at him, her forehead forming the tiny line it took on when she thought hard.

"Could we FaceTime with her and show her my puppy?"

"Sure," he said. "We can try. She might be busy right now, though." He pulled out his phone, but didn't make the call yet. "But it might also be nice to see her again."

She rubbed the pad of her finger between the puppy's ears. "Would we have to do it at our house?"

When they'd talked about it before, he'd gotten the sense that his daughter didn't want her grandmother coming to their house. Not yet. It was a protective measure, her therapist had told him. Their home was her safe place, and she was guarding what she was comfortable with—not easily opening herself up to rejection.

He could understand that completely.

And then he got a better idea.

"How about we go to California to visit her, and while we're there, we can go see Jenna?"

Haley's eyes went wide with excitement. "We can see Jenna?"

She missed her friend so much. They'd video chatted, too, but it wasn't the same as having her friend in the same room with her.

"We can even stay with them."

Haley started to jump up, then realized she still held Montana. Ben took the dog and placed him gently back in his bed, and Haley shot to her feet.

"Can we leave now?" she asked.

He laughed. "No, baby. Not now. We have to see when your grandmother will be home, and if Jenna will be. But if they'll all be around, we'll go this weekend. How about that?"

She nodded vigorously. "I'd love that. I haven't seen Jenna in forever. Could we go see Dani too?"

The air went out of Ben's sails. As she'd done since the day Dani left, Haley continued to ask about her several times a week. She couldn't understand why her friend had simply disappeared.

"Oh!" Haley suddenly shouted. "Let's FaceTime with Dani. She needs to see Montana."

"No" immediately came to his lips, but he found that he was as near-desperate as his daughter to talk to Dani. Or, at least to see her. He'd forced himself not to ask Max about her any of the times he and Haley stopped by the house, but he needed to know that she was okay. Maybe then he could move on.

Maybe ask out Brandi Smith's mom.

No.

He would never move on that much.

But he could use Haley as an excuse to see Dani. If she would take his call.

"Sure," he said. He pulled up Dani's number instead of his mother's, then he passed the phone off to his daughter.

Standing, he moved out of range of the camera, but where he could still see the screen.

Dani sat facing the Gapstow Bridge on the south end of Central Park, a brand-new journal open in her lap, pen in hand, when her cell phone rang.

Relief washed through her. She was supposed to be "processing" feelings from when her mother had been alive, and she'd been struggling to figure that out. Processing was not the same as talking about them. Or thinking about them. Processing meant feeling them.

And she didn't particularly *want* to feel them.

She closed the journal and pulled her phone from her purse. Only to pause at what she saw.

Ben was calling her.

Actually, Ben was FaceTiming her.

Ben!

Her breathing went erratic as she stared at the screen. She so wanted to talk to him.

With a steadying breath, she pushed the journal off her lap, focused on looking "normal," and pressed the button to connect the call.

Haley appeared on her screen.

"Miss Dani!" the girl shouted. "I've been missing you so much!"

"Oh, baby." Tears sprang to Dani's eyes. She was processing *these* feelings, that was for sure. "I've missed you, too. How are you?"

"I'm fine. Why didn't you call me?"

"Oh. Well . . ." She gulped. What should she say? I broke your daddy's heart and figured he didn't want me talking to you? I was too chicken to call?

I didn't deserve to talk to you?

She had to quit with the negative talk. Her therapist had been all over her about that.

"I've been really busy, I guess," she finally said. It was lame, but Haley wouldn't understand the truth. "How are you, sweetie? Did you start school yet?"

Her head bobbed up and down. Ben had put her hair into pigtails, and they bounced with her movements. "I did start school, and I love my teacher. Her name is Miss Wiggins. Isn't that a funny name?" She giggled, pausing only for a couple of seconds. "And I got more friends. They're going to spend the night for my birthday. And here's my puppy!" The camera swung in a blur until it landed on a litter of puppies, all cradled together.

Dani's heart slammed against her ribs. Ben was getting Haley a dog.

The camera swung back. "He's a boy," Haley said.

"He's gorgeous. What's his name?"

"Montana. And I got a new house, too."

"Did you? I wish I could see it." Which wasn't a lie. She'd love to see the house Ben decided to buy.

She'd love to see Ben.

"It's so beautiful," Haley enthused. Her eyes were wide with excitement. "I have my own room, and my daddy put stars on my ceiling, just like in Jenna's room." Her words cut off, and Dani watched a tiny frown appear on her mouth. "Jenna had to leave."

"I know, baby. But, I'm sure she'll come back to visit sometime. Or you and your dad might go to see her."

Haley's nod was less enthusiastic than before. "We are going to go see her . . ." She paused and turned away from the camera to ask her dad when they were going. Dani barely heard Ben's voice in the background before Haley returned to the call. "Soon," she finished. "We're going to see my grandmother, too. But we can't take Montana with us yet. He has to stay with his mama."

"You're going to see your grandmother? In California?"

"Yes. But I don't know if I like her or not. I didn't last time. But Daddy says we'll go see her again to see if I like her any better."

Dani so wanted to talk to Ben. Were he and his mother getting along better? Who suggested the visit? She stared hard at the phone as if doing so would make him appear on screen, but all she saw was Haley's face.

"Did you want to talk to my dad?" Haley suddenly asked.

Dani didn't immediately answer, instead waiting for some sign of Ben. He didn't appear. She knew he was there, though. Just out of sight of the camera. Listening to them.

Not wanting to talk to her.

"I'm fine just talking to you," she answered. Which was a lie, but talking to Haley was more than she'd expected.

"He let me use the FaceTime," Haley explained. "I called it all by myself. I've gotten good at it 'cause me and Jenna talk all the time."

The phone swung around again until it landed on the top half of the puppies.

"Did you want one?" Haley asked behind the camera. "Leslie has five more."

Dani laughed softly. She missed Haley. She missed Montana— the state, not the puppy. "I probably don't need a puppy. I don't have room in my apartment. It's too tiny."

"Can I see it?"

"Well, I'm not home right now. I'm at the park."

Haley gasped. "I went to the park last week. Do you have swings?"

"No. No swings where I am right now." Dani stood and moved so that she could put the bridge in the shot. "But there's this bridge. It's very pretty with the water running beneath it." She moved again, and framed the tops of the trees and what could be seen of the New York skyline. "And there are lots and lots of buildings here."

"That's so pretty," Haley gushed. She looked away from the camera again. "Daddy, isn't that pretty? Could we go see Dani and go to the park?"

Dani held her breath. He wouldn't come there. The last time he'd offered she'd told him no.

She heard the rumble of his voice again, but as before, she could make out nothing.

Haley returned. "Daddy says I got to go."

Sadness welled up inside Dani and she looked down at her journal. Maybe she should process these feelings. Especially since she was about ten seconds from crying them out. "Thank you for calling me, sweetheart. I loved it so much. And I miss you," she added. "Lots."

"I miss you, too. Next time I'll show you my house."

Would Ben let her call again?

She hoped so.

"That sounds terrific," she said sincerely. "I'll look forward to it."

The phone disconnected, and Dani dropped to the ground. Everything inside her screamed that she'd made a mistake in coming here. She wanted to go home.

She wanted to see Haley. And Ben.

She even wanted to see her dad.

But the logical side of her reminded her that this was where she belonged. She had her dream job, and she was in the city where she'd always wanted to live. She'd made it.

It was simple homesickness. Because she'd done the right thing in coming here.

Her therapist had explained that her leaving the home she'd grown up in had been healthy. It was her way of moving on. She'd separated herself from her mother—the house representing her mother—and because of that, she was already ahead in her recovery process.

The next step was to accept the fact that she not only didn't have a mother *now*, but that she'd missed out on both a childhood and a mother her whole life. At least, in the traditional sense. Her life had been merely an illusion of normalcy. However, that didn't define her future. It didn't mean she couldn't move forward.

If she wanted love, if she wanted to be "mothered" . . . that would be on her. She had herself for emotional support, and she could handle that. She got that. One day she'd be good at that.

Only, today . . .

Today she wasn't quite finished grieving the loss of what she'd always wanted. A mother's love.

So yes, moving here had been good. She needed to be here.

Even if she did often yearn to be firmly planted back in Montana.

chapter twenty-six

October 31

A handful of kids in Halloween costumes dotted the sidewalk as Dani rushed from the subway station to her brownstone apartment on the Upper West Side. It was Friday night, she'd been one of the first out of the office, and she'd just come from her therapist—who'd declared she was making steady progress on her road to recovery.

Of course, she understood that recovery would be a life-long process.

But things were improving. Her job was good, and she loved her roommate. Her days were settling into a new kind of normalcy. To put it bluntly, her life was looking really good.

And Aunt Sadie would be arriving at her apartment any moment.

Entering her small foyer minutes later, the first thing Dani heard was Aunt Sadie's laughter. Hurrying down the hallway, she turned into the small kitchen to find her aunt and her roommate already hitting it off.

"Dani." Aunt Sadie turned, pleasure in her eyes.

Dani rushed into her aunt's arms. They hadn't seen each other in well over a year. "I'm so glad you're here." Her words were muffled by her arms, now wrapped tightly around her aunt's neck.

When they parted, Aunt Sadie simply took Dani in, and after several long seconds her still-sturdy hand patted her on the cheek. "You look good," she said. "Strong."

"I am strong, Aunt Sadie." She kissed her aunt. "And good."

"It was lovely meeting you." Dani's roommate Beth held out one hand to shake, the other wrapped around her ever-present mug of coffee. "You two have a great time in Times Square this weekend."

Dani and Sadie had a hotel room rented just off Broadway, and they planned to live it up.

"You should come with us," Sadie offered.

"Really," Beth began, "I couldn't intrude. Plus, I'm looking forward to my own little weekend vacation. No roommate." She winked at Dani. "You wouldn't believe how much trouble this one is."

The three of them laughed at Beth's teasing, then Beth excused herself and disappeared into her bedroom. Aunt Sadie turned and once again looked Dani up and down. Dani did the same. Sadie's stylish outfit was trendy and up to date, her hair remaining a fabricated light brown. Little about her hinted at her actual age. Dani was lucky to have this woman in her life.

"The city agrees with you," Aunt Sadie said.

"Yeah." Dani nodded. It was what she'd needed. It was allowing her to heal. "I think it does."

"And Jaden says you're doing great in therapy?"

"I am. It's been really painful at times, and I've cried a lot." She thought of the journal where she'd spent so many hours processing her feelings. "A *lot*. But the thing is, every tear that I shed seems to clean out more of the bad and make room for good."

"That's terrific, sweetheart. I'm so happy for you. And I understand your dad is seeing someone too?"

"Yeah." Their conversations had gotten easier over the weeks. It made her wish to go home so she could see him in person. "We're doing good, too. We're getting there."

"I'm thrilled to hear it." Her aunt pulled her in for another hug. As she released her, she pointed to the tabloid article stuck to the fridge. "Now, tell me about this."

Dani's gaze went to the picture in Los Angeles captured last month of Ben, his mother, Haley, and Jenna. They'd been seen at a restaurant known to be a place more for children than for adults. Haley had told her all about it in one of their weekly phone calls. But what could she tell Aunt Sadie concerning why it was stuck to her fridge? Aunt Sadie knew about her relationship with Ben.

She knew that Dani still missed Ben.

And she remembered him from his college days. She'd been in town for harvest a couple of the years that he'd been at the house. She'd liked him.

"Beth thinks it's fun that I know them," Dani said, fudging the truth.

Her aunt's perfectly lined brows lifted. "This is here because of Beth?"

Dani shrugged.

"Oh, sweetie. I'm sorry that didn't work out."

"Me, too." Everything about their relationship had been perfect except for her.

They put aside thoughts of Ben and headed for their hotel, and once checked in, hailed a cab to the restaurant. They were saving the trip to their favorite café for tomorrow. Tonight's reservations were more upscale. The food was delicious, the company sublime. And the view of the city spectacular. Aunt Sadie seemed to have the best time.

While Dani spent most of it staring out the window at the darkened sky.

After dessert, they walked off some of the calories as they made their way back to their hotel, but instead of going in, Aunt Sadie wanted to do more. The night was just getting started.

"You must love this," Aunt Sadie said. She had her face tilted up, taking in the bright lights of the many billboards.

"I do," Dani agreed. She followed her aunt's gaze. She *should,* anyway. She'd claimed it was exactly what she wanted.

Only, most of the time, she found herself less than enthused.

"It's everything I remembered," she confirmed.

Her aunt brought her gaze back to Dani's. "Then why the long face?"

"I don't have a long face."

Aunt Sadie pointed to a darkened window in the corner of the building beside them, where Dani could see their reflection. She had a long face. She looked sad.

"You miss home?"

"I love my life here," Dani defended. "It's what I've always wanted."

"Sure it is, but wants can change." Her aunt slipped an arm through hers. "And it's okay if they do."

Dani didn't reply, instead thinking about Sadie's words. *Had* her wants changed?

She had changed, that was for sure. For the better. She saw reality more clearly these days, and she faced things head-on. There was no more living in a make-believe world.

But had her desires changed?

She wasn't sure.

She'd spent the past two and a half months focusing on her job and her therapy sessions. Little else. She'd come to New York with a purpose, to build a life for herself. And she'd been working hard to meet those goals.

Her family relationships continued to strengthen, and her personal happiness grew daily.

Only, she always missed Ben. And she always missed home.

And she hadn't allowed herself to stop and think about whether her wants had changed.

Checking her watch, she saw that it was nearing time for Haley's call, and pulled out her phone. The background picture was a shot of Jenna standing between two princes at Disneyland, her smile stretching from ear to ear, and Dani passed it over to Aunt Sadie. "Did you see this? Jenna found a prince."

"Two of them." Aunt Sadie gazed at the screen. "That smile tells a story. She's a good kid."

"Yes, she is. And I miss her like crazy."

There would be a few minutes before Haley called, so Dani motioned to the bleachers above the TKTS booth. "Do you mind if we sit? It's time for Haley to call, and I promised her I'd show her the city."

Aunt Sadie cut shrewd eyes to Dani. "You talk to Ben's daughter?"

"Every Friday night." She said the words casually, as if weekly chats with an ex lover's daughter were normal. But there was nothing casual about the butterflies that flapped through her insides every Friday night before the phone rang.

She talked to Haley, and she loved it. But she always wished for more.

"Do you talk to Ben?" Aunt Sadie asked.

Dani shook her head. Not once.

The phone chirped, and the butterflies took flight. Dani smiled. Then the elation dropped. Gloria was FaceTiming her?

She answered to find that, in fact, it was not Gloria. Haley was using Gloria's phone.

"Hi, Dani," the girl squealed. "Do you like my costume?" The phone was pulled back to show Haley in head-to-toe Cinderella gear.

"You look marvelous," Dani told her. "Did you trick-or-treat yet?"

"I did. Daddy took me and Leslie. I'm at the house with Gloria and Pops now."

"What are you doing there?" Haley had taken to calling Dani's dad Pops just like Jenna did. Apparently they saw each other a lot.

"Daddy has a date, so I'm spending the night."

Dani completely lost the ability to speak.

Haley didn't seem to notice, and continued chattering on, while Aunt Sadie reached over and took Dani's free hand. Haley showed her the tub full of candy that had been acquired that evening, the decorations Gloria had on display on the front porch, and the clown outfit Pops had worn while handing out candy.

Ben was out on a date.

Overnight.

Dani's heart hurt so badly.

Several minutes later, after somehow managing to carry on a partial conversation and show the girl pieces of New York, she hung up the phone and slid it back into her purse. Her hands shook.

"Are you okay?" Aunt Sadie's gentle voice wrapped around her.

Dani nodded, but she wasn't okay. Ben was on a date.

"You can't have expected him to wait forever."

"I wasn't expecting him to wait at all." She swallowed. Her eyes blurred with tears.

"But you'd hoped?"

She shook her head and the first tear slipped free. "I couldn't hope that, Aunt Sadie. How could I? I was so dysfunctional when I left. He didn't need that in his life."

"Maybe not," her aunt acknowledged. She patted Dani's knee. "But how are you now? You seem better."

She was better.

But did it matter? Ben had moved on.

And the reality was, she *was* still messed up. She would never be truly healed.

She thought of both journals currently sitting on the dresser in her bedroom. One was from her teen years. It had flooded her with guilt when she'd first found it, but today it made her mad. It made her hurt.

But she no longer felt as though she'd been in the wrong for writing the words she had.

The other had become the place she'd allowed herself to feel over the past couple of months. It often seemed like blood had been shed as she'd written on those pages, but the blood—the tears—had freed her in a way she'd never imagined.

How was she now? Had her wants changed?

She was good. And quite possibly yes.

But could she do anything about it, was the question.

Or was it already too late?

"You going home for Thanksgiving?" Aunt Sadie tactfully changed the subject.

"I don't know." Dani leaned back, putting her elbows on the riser behind her, and stared up at the black night. If she went home for Thanksgiving, she'd get to see the stars.

If she went home, she might get to see Ben.

"I wonder if any of the boys will be there," she questioned. She hadn't asked them yet.

"I understand they're all planning to come home."

"Really?" Dani straightened on the seat. It had been years since everyone had been home for the holidays.

"Jonas and I plan to, as well," Aunt Sadie added with a tender smile. "We're all hoping you can make it."

Her whole family would be in Montana for Thanksgiving? She had to be there.

And maybe . . .

Her stomach twisted into a knot. Was it too late to want more with Ben?

Could she consider new wants?

She loved her job here. Her roommate. She even loved the city—or . . . she didn't *hate* it. But she couldn't just walk away from the commitments she'd made here. Could she? She had clients who asked for her by name. She'd have to break a lease.

But in Montana . . .

She looked at the sky again. And she pictured Ben's face.

How much had she already lost?

And was any of it salvageable?

She nodded, returning to her aunt's question. The decision to go home for the holiday was easy. "I'll be there. I wouldn't miss it."

The harder question was, would she go home seeking more?

chapter twenty-seven

B en scrolled through the pictures on his laptop to find the one he wanted to work on next, and as it loaded he sipped his cup of coffee. He zoomed in, taking note of the details in the subject's eyes. It was a woman in her early forties. She'd posed for him a couple of years ago. She wasn't a professional, just someone he'd met at a coffee shop similar to the one he sat in today.

He'd been taken with the woman's eyes, as well as her entire face.

Her bone structure hadn't been perfect, but she was one of those people who was more beautiful because of it. He'd caught her unsmiling, and the shot seemed to invite people in.

"Can I get you anything else, hot stuff?"

Ben looked up and shot Karen an easy smile. Karen was a server he'd taken out a couple of times. Working on his book in the coffee shop most days, he'd become friends with her. So when she'd invited him to a Halloween party last month, he'd decided it was time to do more than spend his evenings staring at the lake. The date had gone well, and he'd asked her to the movies the following weekend.

That had been fine, too.

But then he'd cancelled on her at the last minute the previous Saturday. He felt bad about that.

"I'm good," he answered now. "Still working on my coffee."

She pulled out a chair and sank onto it. "How about something . . . that you can't get here, then?" she asked, seeming embarrassed. It was endearing.

"Like . . . an omelet?" he teased.

She laughed. She was pretty—blonde, trim, maybe five-six. And she was nice. He'd been in here with Haley a few times after picking her up from school, and if Karen was on the clock, she always made it a point to stop and chat with his daughter, usually bringing her a place mat to color.

"I wasn't really thinking an omelet," she admitted. Dimples flashed in her cheeks. "Maybe dinner? Thought you might be free this weekend."

She seemed to hold her breath as she waited, and Ben forced himself not to immediately decline. They'd had a good time together. It's just that he hadn't been overly eager to do it again. He'd rather spend his evenings with his daughter.

He hadn't *hated* it, though. He'd merely been neutral.

But maybe he needed to reconsider. Push it a step further. Probably he should actually kiss her before writing her off.

Only, he had little desire to kiss anyone.

"There's Haley," he pondered out loud. She'd been his excuse for cancelling last weekend, claiming a babysitter emergency.

Of course, there had been no issue. He and Haley had both ended up spending the evening with Max and Gloria, instead of

Haley being there by herself. Gloria hadn't asked about the change in plans, but she'd given him a look as if she'd known.

As if it had something to do with Dani. Which it did not. He was over Dani.

Or, he'd like to be.

But with Dani's regular conversations with Haley, he'd found that getting over her was harder to do than he'd anticipated. He'd watched her throughout the weeks. Every time Haley and she talked. He'd stood off to the side and drunk in the sight of her the way an addict might his vice. She looked good. And the last few calls, she'd seemed different.

More confident. More settled.

More satisfied.

Which made him wonder if the satisfaction came from personal changes in her life . . . or from a man.

The thought of her happiness coming from another man filled him with a level of jealousy he couldn't have anticipated. Especially after more than three months of her being gone. It irritated him that he even cared.

But the fact was, he did care. She'd hurt him. And then she'd moved on.

While he'd remained in Montana spinning his wheels.

"We don't have to *go* anywhere," Karen proposed. "I could come to your house. Haley could be there too." She gave a hopeful shrug. "I'd cook."

He didn't want her at his house.

Actually, he didn't want any woman there.

So far, other than Gloria—and all of Haley's friends—he'd only had men inside his home. He felt protective of the space.

Haley's birthday party had turned into a boys' night-slash-girls' party. The dads had all piled into his media room while the girls had overrun the remainder of the house. Plenty of chaperones had been on-site, but not one of them had been a woman.

It had been a really great time, and there was talk of a repeat next year. Without the girls.

But was he ready to have a woman at his house now?

He thought of Dani once more. She was gone. He'd lost her. He knew that.

He had to move on, in heart and mind, as well as in body. It was time.

Just not at his house quite yet.

"Dinner," he said before he could change his mind. "But I'll find a sitter, and I'll take you out."

Karen's smile grew bright. "Great. Tomorrow night?"

"Tomorrow night."

"I'm looking forward to it. And tell Haley I said hi, will you?" She rose, and tossed him one last smile before heading to another table.

Left standing in her place was Dani.

Son of a bitch.

"Hi, Ben," she said, and hot anger shot through him at the flare of hope her presence caused.

"Dani." He schooled his features into an emotionless mask. "What are you doing here?"

"Thanksgiving," she murmured. "Everyone's coming home." Her hands twisted together in front of her as she glanced at Karen, and Ben watched her eyes, trying to figure out what she was thinking. Why she was in the coffee shop.

Why she stood before him after three wordless months.

She'd never once asked to talk to him when she'd been on the phone with Haley. Nor had she even asked *about* him. Had he meant nothing to her?

But then, hadn't she made it clear she didn't love him?

She turned back to the table, and he forced himself to loosen the clench of his jaw.

"And I'm here in the coffee shop because I needed to see *you*," she said. "I was hoping we could talk."

He didn't want to talk. He didn't want to see her. He didn't want to want her.

Only . . . *Fuck.*

With a slight nod, he motioned for her to go on, giving silent permission for her to say her piece. He would hear it, and then he'd make sure she left.

Dani stepped closer. "I'm sorry I hurt you, Ben." Her eyes softened with her words. "I never wanted to, and I've felt bad about it since I left. But I do maintain my belief that I had to go. By myself," she added softly, almost apologetically. "I've learned a lot over the past months. I have a better handle on who I am. Who I want to be." She licked her lips. "And what I want in the future."

He stared at her and forgot to blink. What did she want?

"You needed me to know something once before," she continued. "And today I'm here because I need *you* to know something too. That I've missed you."

No words came to mind. He did force himself to blink, though.

Then Karen passed through his peripheral vision, and he let his gaze follow her as his brain screamed at the injustice of Dani's words. She missed him. What did that mean? Was he supposed to care?

Did she think he'd pack his bags and head to New York now? After all this time?

Because he wouldn't.

He didn't need her anymore.

As he continued to focus on Karen, he had the quick thought

that Karen was the type of woman he needed. She was cute and normal. Nice.

And she wouldn't make him love her, then rip out his heart.

He returned his attention to Dani, taking note of the overt glances being tossed their way from surrounding customers, and shut down the quickening of his pulse. He didn't care that Dani had missed him. He couldn't care.

"You've been gone a long time," he said. He didn't adjust his voice for politeness.

"I have."

"You told me to move on."

Her bottom lip slipped between her teeth and she nodded. "I did tell you that."

"That's what I'm doing."

For a moment, she glanced down at her hands, and he thought she'd leave. He'd won. She would not stand there and verbally shred his heart.

But then she looked back up, and he saw the determination in her eyes. "Could we find a more private place to talk, do you think? There's more I'd like to say."

His instinct shouted *no*. They didn't need privacy. He didn't want to hear what she had to say.

Only, he was an idiot when it came to Dani. Anyone watching the two of them could probably see that the mere sight of her brought him to his knees. She made him want to hope, and he couldn't help but selfishly drink her in. He wasn't ready for her to leave yet. Even if that meant listening to whatever else she had to say.

Standing, he motioned with his head, and together they moved to a more quiet area by an empty booth in the back corner. Neither of them sat.

He crossed his arms over his chest.

"I *have* missed you, Ben. A lot. And Haley." She chewed on the corner of her mouth. "But I also came here today to tell you that I can love you now."

Ben's heart clenched. "You can love me now?" he repeated. Ire rose inside him. "Well, thanks so much."

The woman drove him crazy.

"What I'm saying is," she began, the tightness of her mouth showing her frustration, "that I love *me* now. Or, I'm learning to. Therefore I can be capable of loving *you*. I tried to explain that before." She made a face before adding, "I probably didn't do a good job of it. I wasn't completely sure I knew what I was talking about, anyway."

"Dani." He held up a hand. "Just stop. You've been gone for over three months. Am I supposed to care at this point? What the hell does that mean, anyway? Capable of loving me?"

"It means . . ." She stopped talking when Karen passed by, leading a customer to a nearby table. Karen's gaze sought him out, and he couldn't help but let his cling to hers. He needed to *not* need Dani at that moment.

He needed to not need her ever again.

Because her words were already reaching inside him. Seeking out more than he thought he wanted to give.

"Never mind," Dani murmured. "I get it. I'm too late." She pressed her lips together and eyed Karen one last time, her chest rising and falling with steady breaths before turning back and staring directly at him. "I came here because I wanted another chance, Ben. *You're* what I want in the future. That's the other thing I figured out in New York. I don't want to give up on us. But I see that option is off the table. I'll be around if you ever want to talk."

She turned, then, and as she had the last time he'd seen her, she walked out of his life.

And as he had before, he let her go.

Two seconds later the spot before him was empty, and his head felt like it was spinning in circles. What in the hell had just happened? She wanted him back?

She could love him now?

What did any of that mean? *Did* she love him? Did he care?

Did *he* want *her* back?

And what had she meant about being around if he wanted to talk? Was she here for the week . . . or for longer?

And again, did he care? He'd just moved on. *Today.* He'd made a third date with Karen. He intended to kiss her. Maybe more. He was over Dani.

Only . . .

She could love him now.

She wanted him back.

His chest deflated. He couldn't get his hopes up. Not again. Not for Dani. His heart couldn't take another beating.

No. He shook his head, ignoring the renewed looks from customers. He'd stick with Karen. They had a date tomorrow night. That was enough. Karen was safe.

And that was all *he* wanted.

The smell of warm bread greeted Dani as the front door of her childhood home opened later that afternoon.

"Dani!" Gloria gasped and Dani gave the older woman a little hey-I'm-home smile. "Come in. Please." Gloria ushered her inside the house. "Your dad is in the family room. You're earlier than we expected. He'll be so pleased to see you."

Dani had shown up at the house, without calling or even telling anyone she planned to return to Montana before next Thursday, but as she'd driven up the driveway in her rental, it had occurred to her that this was no longer her home. She'd moved away. And her dad and another woman had moved in.

Her dad and the woman he loved—who loved him back—had moved in.

That was the pertinent fact. And it made her happy.

But still, it was their home now. She couldn't very well just traipse in the back door as she'd always done. Especially not when the air between her and her dad had not been fully cleared.

Therefore, she'd found herself standing on the front porch like a stranger. And she hadn't liked it one bit.

As she made her way down the hallway, she caught a glimpse inside her open bedroom door. The colors were brighter in the room, and there was a new bed in there, as well as matching, breezy curtains hanging at the windows.

"It's still your room." Gloria patted her on the arm. "It just needed a bed."

Dani nodded, unable to speak. The changes weren't bad . . . just different.

When she came into sight of her dad, he rose from the recliner. "Dani." His surprise was evident in his voice. As well as not a small amount of nerves. "What are you doing home already?"

She wasn't sure how to answer. Honestly?

Instead of immediately replying, she took in the room. It was different, same as her bedroom. For starters, there was a lovely flowered armchair in the space where her mother's chair had once sat. Dani had removed her mother's chair before leaving, and the new one looked very much like something Gloria would pick out. It complemented her dad's recliner nicely.

The colors had been changed in here too. The room had a softer feel than ever before.

Happier.

And there was a basket of kids' toys sitting by the fireplace. She assumed it was there for Haley.

As she noted the changes, Dani could sense the nerves coming from Gloria.

"It looks good in here," she finally said, including the other woman in her gaze. "Really lovely."

"I was worried I might have changed too much," Gloria hedged.

"No." Dani shook her head. "You didn't. It's needed this for a long time."

Her mother was now completely gone from the space, and seeing that had the strange effect of allowing Dani to breathe much more freely. Thus making her decide to answer her father's question with brutal honesty. It was time to move beyond their issues.

"I'm home because I missed it." She faced her dad. That was part one of the truth.

The lines on his face eased, and he crossed to her. They'd had several conversations over the past few months, but talking from twenty-five hundred miles away couldn't compete with face-to-face.

"I'm home because this is where I belong, Dad. I'm not healed—I won't ever be 'healed'—but I am better. I can't forget, but I can forgive. And you're my dad. Your life wasn't easy either, I do understand that. You were a victim in your own right. So I'm here bearing an olive branch. I hope you'll accept it and hold out one of your own."

He did better. He pulled her in for the best hug of her life.

She clung to him as if she would never again get the opportunity to do so, and she noticed that his embrace felt the same. Their distance over the past months had been needed, but it had also healed.

"I'm so sorry, Dani girl. I should have done better for you." He took her by the shoulders and pulled her out from him, and she noticed Gloria quietly slip out of the room. "I shouldn't have let you stay here after your mother died," he said. "You were in school. That's where you belonged."

"You tried," she said. She now remembered him and Aunt Sadie trying to talk her into returning to New York. "I recall those conversations. But I'd cancelled my scholarship before I ever came home, Dad. I couldn't have gone back if I'd wanted to."

"We could have fixed it, and I should have. I could have raised the boys myself. Or hired a nanny. You deserved your life."

Yeah, she had. But he wasn't fully at fault.

She took a moment to fortify herself with a breath before pushing forward. "I needed to be here, Dad. I didn't know it at the time, but I needed you all as much as I thought you needed me. Also . . ." She paused and pulled in another breath. "I'd promised Mom that I would come home if anything ever happened."

At his questioning look, she told him about the phone call the day before the wreck.

"I refused to come home that weekend," she explained, "but I also promised that if you all ever needed me, I'd be here. I was loaded down with guilt after the wreck, and nothing could have stood in my way to fulfill that promise. It was my chance to make her proud. I wanted my mother's approval."

Her dad shook his head, his eyes drawn with sadness. "You never needed her approval."

"And I never would have received it. I get that now. But in my head, that was it. The one and only opportunity I would ever have again. And if I didn't succeed?" Dani shrugged. "Then she would never love me."

Dani understood that her mother never had loved her, and had she lived, never would have. And she understood that those lack of feelings had nothing to do with Dani. Her mother *couldn't* love anyone. That fact was sad, but her mother's lack of ability did not alter who Dani was.

"I came home back then, and I took over your life," she told her dad. "And I apologize for that. I pushed you out. Possibly I even made you feel similarly to how Mom once had."

"No." The word burst from his lungs. "Never. Dani, this wasn't your fault."

"I know. But I took the spotlight and I made sure you all needed *me*." She laughed lightly. "I'd developed a few unhealthy traits of my own while growing up. If I kept everything spotless and on schedule, everyone in school, then you all had to be proud of me. I put myself at the center of our world. Quite similar to Mom, only in a different way."

"You're nothing like her."

"Only, in some ways I am." And she was working on that. "But I do understand my own behavior better now. As well as yours."

He nodded. "I've learned a thing or two myself. I shouldn't have allowed you to be kept in the dark about your mom's accident. That only hurt you in the long run."

"No, you shouldn't have."

"And I certainly should have stood up for you well before then."

She agreed with his words, and it still hurt that he hadn't.

But the hurt was remembered pain, and didn't include the facts she'd learned. She wouldn't play the it's-not-fair game any longer. That got her nowhere, and she was finally starting to move past it. So as she'd told her father when she'd first come in, she could forgive. He hadn't intended any harm.

"I added to the problem by burying my head in the sand," he continued. "My actions hurt you. And I can't change that. I can only apologize." He took her hands. "And swear to you that I'll never stand aside and allow anything to hurt you ever again. I love you, Dani. And I thank you for coming home and allowing us to have this talk."

He'd offered to come to New York to see her last month, to talk. But she wouldn't let him. She'd made it clear that when they saw each other again, it would be her call. She'd needed that control. But today she simply needed her dad.

"One more hug?" she asked.

He held open his arms. "All the hugs in the world."

When they separated, Gloria had returned with warm bread and cookies, and the three of them took a seat. Dani filled them in on New York and her job, telling them of a few trips she'd taken for BA. But what she didn't immediately share was that she'd quit her job. That she was home to stay.

Her dad talked about the orchard. Pruning had started, and they were looking into new cooling machinery for the next season.

It was mundane talk mostly, but it was nice. It was great to be home.

She keyed in on the toys by the fireplace. "Are those for when Haley comes over?"

Gloria's gaze turned to guilt. "Yes," she answered, the word coming out quick. She motioned to the small pile of dog toys nearby. "And when Montana comes with her."

Dani's dad shook his head. "That dog's a runt, but he acts like he's as big as his name."

They talked for a minute about the house Ben had bought just up the road, and Dani learned that her father and soon-to-be stepmother had been there. It apparently had a majestic view of the lake and the mountains. Which made Dani wonder if Karen, from the coffee shop, had seen that particular view.

And if it had been first thing in the morning when she opened her eyes.

"So you guys keep Haley when Ben goes out?" Dani continued down her path of torture. Hearing the facts of Ben's love life would only cause her pain, but she needed to face it. He'd moved on. She hadn't wanted to believe it, but her trip to the coffee shop had proved otherwise. He'd been unable to take his eyes off the other woman.

"We do." Gloria's hands fidgeted in her lap.

Dani opened her mouth to ask how often, and if it was always overnight, but decided at the last minute that she didn't want to know. That kind of pain she could do without. So instead, she nodded, expertly changed the subject, and the three of them acted as though her heart weren't bleeding right there in front of them.

Eventually, the conversation turned back to New York. In fact, Dani steered it that way. Time to face the facts.

"I didn't like New York as much as I expected to," she confessed.

"What?" Her dad and Gloria spoke at the same time.

Gloria leaned to the edge of her seat. "We thought you loved it."

"And I thought I would."

"You didn't like the job?" her dad asked.

"Actually, I loved the job. And I was really good at it."

"So, what happened?" He looked as shocked as she'd been when she'd come to the realization that she intended to go home. New York had been her dream. For forever. She was supposed to love it.

Only . . . she loved home more.

"Did you know you can't see the stars in New York?" she asked. "And the Hudson River is no Flathead Lake."

Her humor was lost on them, so she stood from her seat.

"I was running away," she admitted. "New York wasn't really the dream. I needed to be away from Mom, and it just so happened, New York was the one place I'd visited that gave me something better than I could get here. That's why I fell in love with it. It's why I applied to Columbia. It's why I never let the idea go. I needed the escape. But take everything else out of the picture"—she paused and shook her head—"and I would have regretted being there all this time. I would have missed seeing everyone grow up. And as annoying as they can be, I love my brothers. I'm glad I was here with them."

"Oh, Dani," Gloria whispered. She had tears in her eyes. So did Dani's dad.

"I've finally found myself," Dani told them. "And I don't need New York to be who I want to be. I just need to be here."

Her dad nodded in approval. "I'm glad you're home."

"What will you do now?" Gloria asked, and Dani couldn't contain the smile.

"I've already put in calls to my old clients. I'll soon be renting an office in town."

Gloria came to her then, and gave Dani a hug. She kissed her cheek, and Dani squeezed the woman tight. Her own mother had never showed her as much love as this woman had in this single moment.

"I'm glad I'm home too," she told both of them. "I'm ready to start the rest of my life."

"I'll fix your room up for you," Gloria told her.

"There's no need." Dani's words stopped her before she made it out of the room. "I've got a hotel room for tonight, and tomorrow I'll start looking for a place of my own."

"Dani, it's your room," Gloria assured her. "Your house. You're always welcome here."

"I know."

"Do you?" Her dad stood. "Because I feel the same way. Or we'll leave if you want to stay but don't want us here."

"Dad." She swallowed as her emotions threatened to suck her under. "It's *your* house. Not mine. And no, you aren't leaving. But it's not because of you that *I'm* not staying. I need my own place. I need my own boundaries." She touched his arm. "I need to not have the pressure of too many memories in this house," she finished softly.

He hugged her again, and that time it didn't feel so much like desperation on either of their parts. It felt like healing. It also reminded her of being a kid. When her mom hadn't been around.

Her dad had tried so hard to love her back then. She knew that. He just hadn't always been able to show it.

Standing in his arms now, it occurred to her that she'd once thought her mother had deserved more from her dad, but that hadn't been the situation at all. Her *dad* had been the one getting the short end of things.

"You deserved more from her, Dad," she spoke against his chest. "We all did. But you too. I hope you and Gloria are happy together."

He kissed the top of her head. "Gloria makes me very happy. But this moment is my favorite."

Tears fell from both of them, and Gloria hurried off for tissues.

When Dani straightened and made to leave, her father pointed a finger in her direction. "Don't ever come through the front door again."

She agreed. "It's a deal."

Gloria stood, her hands at her mouth, seemingly thrilled with the outcome of the visit. "Will we see you before Thursday?" she asked.

"I don't know yet. I have a lot to do. Getting my business back up and running. Finding a place to live. I'll be here early Thursday morning, though. I'll help cook dinner."

Gloria's smile widened. "No need. The boys are cooking. All of them. It was their idea."

Dani's gaze shot to her dad.

"I got roped into it." He didn't sound upset by the fact.

"Who among you all even knows anything about cooking?" she asked.

"To hear Nate tell it," Gloria began, "he's quite the chef these days."

"Nate?" Dani was struck dumb. The most difficult one of them all?

"That's his story."

She looked from her dad to his fiancée, and a comfortable smile of her own began. Her brothers—and her father—intended to cook Thanksgiving dinner for them. That was an event she never would have imagined.

But it was also something she found herself very much looking forward to experiencing.

"In fact," Gloria began, "I'm glad you made it in early. Sadie and I were thinking we'd do it up right. Girls' night Wednesday night in Missoula, not coming back until Thursday. We'll stay out of the boys' way. I hope you'll join us?"

"Girls' night?" Dani echoed.

"Your dad's paying."

A chuckle slipped past her lips, and she gave her father one last hug. "Then I'm in."

chapter twenty-eight

The knock came at Dani's Main Street apartment door just after seven Tuesday evening, and her first thought was that whoever it was had to be looking for someone else. No one knew where she lived. But then, Birch Bay wasn't that big. Probably anyone who wanted to find her could.

But who would want to find her?

Her next thought was, *Ben*.

Her pulse sped up as she set her unfinished dinner on the side table and shoved her laptop off her thighs. She hurried to the door, checking herself in a wall mirror as she went—on the off chance that she was right—and pulled herself up short when she reached the door. What if it *was* Ben?

She hadn't talked to him since she'd sought him out Friday, and she knew that he *had* gone out Saturday night. This knowledge came from her dad and Gloria being on babysitter duty. Though thankfully, it hadn't been overnight.

Still, it probably wasn't Ben on the other side of her door.

But just in case . . .

She calmed her nerves, said a silent prayer for him to be standing there, and pulled open the door.

"Aunt Dani!"

Jenna lunged into Dani's arms, and Dani had to admit, that surprise might just be better than if it had been Ben. "Oh, sweetheart." She hugged her niece tight. "I've missed you so much."

Over Jenna's head, Dani took in her brother. Tall, dark, and handsome.

And exhausted.

"What are you doing here?" she asked him, as she pulled back and drank in the sight of her niece. Three and a half months, and she'd swear the girl had grown half a foot.

"Jenna didn't want to go to the house until she saw you."

Dani smiled broadly. "Well, I'm glad she did. I'm way more fun than Pops and Gloria, anyway." Jenna giggled as Dani tickled her ribs.

Dani had filled her oldest brother in on her whereabouts when they'd talked a couple of days, she just hadn't expected him to pay her a visit. Nor had she anticipated them arriving in town this soon.

She moved aside and let him into the small one-bedroom she'd lucked out in finding the first day she'd looked, and peeked behind him as he passed. No Michelle. She'd thought they were *all* flying in for Thanksgiving.

"Michelle . . ." She let the question fade away.

"Mom didn't come with us," Jenna informed her. Dani's eyes went back to her brother's.

He lifted a shoulder. "Had a couple friends she wanted to hang with this weekend."

So, Michelle hadn't changed. It remained all about her.

"Well, that only means you get to eat more turkey," Dani teased Jenna. The girl giggled again, causing Dani to do the same. Jenna had yet to let go of her aunt, her thin arms twined around Dani's neck, and it was one of the greatest feelings in the world. Now that Dani was back for good, she only wished she had her brother and niece permanently there with her, as well.

They settled on the small couch and recliner that had come with the apartment, and when she caught Jenna eyeing her half-eaten burrito, she passed over the plate. "Have at it, kiddo."

Jenna dug in. "We didn't get dinner yet."

Gabe explained that they'd come straight from the airport after more than one delay due to weather. Thunderstorms in California, and early-season snow moving through Idaho.

"You want something to eat?" she asked Gabe. "I could fix something real quick."

He looked at her tiny connected kitchen before shaking his head. "No, I'm fine." When he turned back, he asked, "So, you're really back for good?"

"I am. And along with this spectacular little living arrangement, the office below me is mine, too. The whole setup is for sale if I decide down the road that I want to buy."

He eyed her peculiarly. "You might buy the building?"

"Who knows? I've already reclaimed my previous local client list, and I've been up and running for only two days. I can't take on work from major companies until the noncompete clause I signed with BA expires, but I have enough work for now. And in the future? Why make it just my thing? I could expand. Hire an assistant and another marketing exec. Create a real business."

It was something she'd thought about since deciding to come home. She not only had local potential, but long distance as well.

She'd made a name for herself in the field, and she intended to expand on it.

She'd bring in a receptionist to start. That way clients would no longer get a recorded message instead of a live person when she was in meetings. She wanted to be official. And professional. She wanted to do it right.

She'd loved running her own business before; but now she intended to make *it* the dream.

"And this is what you want?" Gabe asked, still sounding stunned. She'd told no one her plans until she'd gotten back. "What happened to New York?"

Ah. It wasn't just Jenna who'd wanted to stop over and see her. Her brother had had to see for himself that she was okay.

She grinned at him. "I'm good, Gabe. Trust me. Never better."

He nodded slowly. "I see that."

"You see a difference in me? After only ten minutes?"

He nudged his chin toward the kitchen. "I don't think you've cleaned up in there all week."

She laughed at his observation. Mostly because it was true. There were dirty dishes stacked in her sink, as well as on the counter beside it. She'd developed an aversion to cleaning. "I've worked really hard on me," she told him. "I'm ready to live in the future instead of the past." She winked at him then. "And my future might just include a cleaning service."

"Dani." Gabe simply spoke her name as he once again took her in. When he seemed to believe what he saw, he added, "You're really good."

She nodded. "I really am." She'd never been more pleased with herself or her life.

Wonder filled his features as he scanned over the remainder of the tiny space she'd rented for the next six months. Sure, she'd prefer something larger, but at the moment she didn't need larger. Her focus was her business.

And Ben.

But her options looked slim when it came to the man she wanted in her life, so the job currently got all her attention.

"You talked to him yet?" Gabe asked.

Her smile faltered. "Now, why'd you go and ruin a perfectly good reunion?"

He just looked at her.

"I talked to him Friday," she told him. Gabe was aware they hadn't ended on the best of terms, though she'd given him little to no details. She had no idea what Ben might have said. "He's seeing someone," she added.

"Who's seeing someone?" Jenna jumped into the conversation. The burrito was gone, with only traces of sauce left on her face.

Her dad reached over and tapped her nose. "Go check out Aunt Dani's bedroom, sport. See if she even has a bed. I'll bet she doesn't."

Jenna laughed, and hopped down from the couch to determine the state of Dani's bedroom.

When she disappeared from the room, Gabe turned back to Dani. "Did you tell him you're back for good?"

She shook her head. She hadn't seen the point.

"He should know."

"Why?" she asked. "He made his lack of interest clear when I spoke to him."

"He was hurt before."

"Of course he was hurt. I left him." She swallowed. "And he wanted more. I messed things up, and now he's moved on."

"But you had to mess things up. You *needed* to go."

That didn't seem to matter in the grand scheme of her relationship with Ben.

They could hear Jenna laughing from the bedroom as she bounced on Dani's bed.

"Tell him," Gabe said. "It might matter."

She stared at her brother. She wanted to believe him. Because she hadn't been joking with Ben. She wanted a second chance. She wanted *him* in her life.

But she struggled to see that happening at this point.

"So, what are you saying?" She spoke in a teasing voice, hoping to lighten the mood and get the attention away from all she'd lost. "That you now *want* me to be with your friend? Because the last time I checked, you didn't want him anywhere near me."

Gabe rose from the chair. "I want you to be with someone you love."

"And you think I love Ben?"

Jenna came skidding into the room. "She does have a bed, Daddy. And a television too. I turned it on, but couldn't find the good shows."

Gabe turned a fond eye to his daughter before returning his gaze to Dani. "I think you do."

Damned perceptive brother.

"I think you did when you left, and that hasn't changed."

"I had too many issues when I left," she argued.

He eyed her. "But the feelings were there."

Dani's jaw clenched as she stared at him. She wanted to say more, yet at the same time wanted to say nothing at all. Yes, maybe she had loved Ben when she left. But she'd still had to go. If she hadn't, she wouldn't be where she was today. She wouldn't be ready for more.

But how did she go about winning back the man she loved, when the last time they'd had a real conversation she'd walked all over his heart?

"Anyone tell you he'll be at the house Thursday?" Gabe asked.

It took a second for his words to have meaning, and when they did, Dani rose to stand beside him. "What?"

Gabe nodded and picked up Jenna.

Ben would be at the house? Thursday? For Thanksgiving?

Would his girlfriend be there, too?

Panic threatened to take hold, and when she caught her hands shaking, she shoved them in her jeans. "Why?"

"Gloria and Dad invited him. He's always been like family," he reminded her.

Right. It wouldn't be the first holiday Ben had spent at their house.

"They invited who, Daddy?" Jenna turned her daddy's face to hers, and Gabe placed a kiss on her forehead.

"Your best friend," he answered her.

Jenna gasped. "Haley? Where's she gonna be?"

"With Pops. At the house."

"Then let's go. I haven't seen her in forever."

Gabe winked at Dani. "Lost out to a five-year-old, sis." He turned back to Jenna. "You won't see her until tomorrow. You and Haley get to go shopping with Aunt Dani and Gloria, and then you get to spend the night in a hotel with a pool."

"While you cook, I understand," Dani interjected.

She'd tried hard to keep the hurt out of her voice, but she'd picked up on a key fact from her brother's words. The women would be taking the girls with them . . .

Which meant that Ben would be free for another overnight date.

"That's what I hear." Gabe stepped closer then, and in an unprecedented move, wrapped Dani in a huge hug. He muttered into her hair, "It's good to see you again, sis. It's good to have you back where you belong."

Though her heart was breaking over Ben, it was full of love for her brother.

She wasn't sure Gabe was aware of it yet, but he was different, too. He and Jenna were closer, and he seemed to care less about the state of his marriage. That was both sad and a little joyous. Dani had grown tired of watching Michelle walk all over him.

He moved to the door with Jenna, but looked back before heading out. "Tell him," he repeated.

The thought sent her heart on a race, but she just might. Because whether he was spending his nights with another woman or not, Ben was worth fighting for.

Dani led the caravan of cars back to the house the late Thursday afternoon, with Aunt Sadie in the vehicle with her, seated in the passenger seat of Dani's sedan. Dani had her own car back now—her dad had gone with her to return the rental to the airport earlier in the week—and she glanced in her rearview mirror to see the empty spot where a child's safety seat had been strapped in for more than four years. Today, that seat was in another vehicle.

Both Jenna and Haley were riding with Haley's grandmother, who'd been waiting for them outside the mall last night.

Angelica Denton was even more beautiful in person than in the movies.

She'd flown in with a bodyguard, and had rented a Cadillac Escalade for which her bodyguard also served as driver. Haley and Jenna had been taken with the idea of riding around with a "driver" whom they didn't even know, and according to Gloria, this had been fine with both Ben and Gabe. She'd called to check once they'd found out that the elder Denton would be accompanying them.

Megan had also come in with Jaden yesterday, and she and Gloria were pulling up the rear of their three-car procession.

They'd shopped, dined out, had their nails done, and gotten the girls' hair styled.

They'd even ended up having their pictures taken a couple of times by people who recognized Angelica, and that morning they'd requested a late check out of the hotel and spent the day by the pool. All in all, it had been a great trip. The time away couldn't have been more relaxing. Especially knowing that a houseful of men were back home preparing dinner.

Only, Dani had been stressed.

Because Ben was at the house. And she had every intention of talking to him.

She only hoped it wouldn't have to be in front of another woman.

"It was a fun day," Aunt Sadie mused.

"Yeah." Dani put the car in park, but didn't move to unbuckle her seat belt. She left both hands on the steering wheel and stared straight ahead.

"You okay?" Her aunt asked. She had her belt off, and her hand on the door.

Dani shook her head. She was so *not* okay.

Everyone else passed their car, heading for the back door, and still, Dani sat. Aunt Sadie pulled her hand back and clasped her fingers together in her lap.

"This about Ben?" she asked carefully.

Dani nodded. "I just need a minute."

"Okay. I'll sit with you."

A small smile came to Dani's lips. "I love you, Aunt Sadie. No matter what's going on, you're there for me, aren't you?"

"I've always tried to be."

"And I appreciate it. Very much." Dani leaned across the front seats and gave her aunt a hug, and as she did, it was as if the strength from the other woman transferred to her. Her family had her back.

She loved that about them. "Let's go in," she said. She wasn't ready, but at the same time, it felt like she'd been looking forward to this her whole life.

She had a man to win back.

They got out of the car, and moved to the house, and through the back windows Dani could see her brothers, her father, Uncle Jonas, Gloria, Megan, Ben's mother, and the girls.

No Ben.

And no girlfriend.

She and Sadie stepped inside the house to controlled chaos. Her brothers saw her, and all came over to greet her, welcoming her home. She'd never felt so much love. And amazingly, the house smelled like Thanksgiving—turkey and dressing. With not even a hint of burned food.

Impressive.

She shed her coat while the guys moved back into the kitchen, where each had a task that needed tending. Watching them, Dani forgot all about Ben. She focused, instead, on her brothers. Nick and Cord seemed at a loss as to what to do, but did take instructions well. Jaden wasn't a total reject, Gabe was on about the same level as him, and Nate seriously was in charge. The man even wore an apron around his waist.

Jenna and Haley attempted to help them out, and Dani's dad and uncle were on dish duty.

Dani suddenly wished she had the camera Ben had carried around all summer. This was a shot that would win the hearts of millions of women, if they could only see it.

And then Ben came down the hall.

He was alone.

He stared across the room, his eyes on hers, but he didn't speak.

And Dani simply couldn't do it. She reversed positions, and headed in the opposite direction. "I forgot something in the car," she mumbled when Aunt Sadie looked in her direction, then she fled out the back door. She needed one more minute.

She needed to breathe.

Stepping into the cold air, she realized she'd come out without her coat, but she didn't let that slow her down. Taking the stairs, she played along with her ruse and went to her car. She'd said she left something in there, so she'd find something to take back inside with her. And by the time she did, she'd have herself back under control.

But, damn. She'd forgotten that she'd always kept her car as clean as she'd once kept the house.

Opening the back door, she leaned inside and peered at the floor. Jenna had sat back there a lot. Surely there was something stuck under one of the seats that she could use.

She shivered as a burst of cold air slid up the back of her shirt, and reached a hand under the passenger seat. When she landed on something fuzzy, she pulled it out. It was a piece of purple fluff from Jenna's princess wand. It would have to do, because she was now freezing her rear off.

When she straightened from the seat, Ben was there waiting for her. With her coat.

Ben held Dani's coat out for her, and couldn't stop himself from soaking the woman in as she silently turned and slid her arms into the sleeves. Good Lord, he'd missed her. The time apart had eased the memory of his loss, but now that she was back? All he'd thought of over the past six days was her.

When he got Haley ready for school—he'd wondered if Dani was out of bed yet.

When he'd taken Montana out for a walk—he'd wanted to know if Dani was walking on the beach.

And when he and Karen had been out Saturday night.

He'd desperately wished for it to be Dani.

Karen had wanted more; he'd been going too slow for her. So he'd kissed her.

And he'd thought of Dani the entire time.

Karen had not been pleased to be taken home early. But he couldn't worry about that now. Dani was back. She wasn't out of his head. And he had to find out what that meant.

She took her time buttoning her coat, and when she finally faced him, he felt as if the light had come back on in his world. Damn, he didn't mean to still love this woman.

"Rumor is that you've set up shop in town," he said. He'd heard that all week. *Dani Wilde is back, and it looks like she's here to stay.*

"I've rented a building on Main," she confirmed. Her face remained passive.

"The two-story with the vacant apartment on top?" Not that he'd driven by trying to figure it out. Much.

She gave a small nod. "No longer vacant."

"So what does that mean?" he asked.

Her throat moved as she swallowed. She glanced toward the house and back to him, then finally she spoke. "It means I'm home, Ben. To stay."

Both elation and frustration sailed through him. She was home. To stay.

He either had to get over her—*fast*—or he had to be prepared to chase her until he caught her for good. There was no middle of the road on this for him. And he feared there was really only one path he could take.

He just wasn't sure if he was prepared to take it.

"Why?" he asked.

"Why am I home?" She looked at the house again, and this time she chewed on her bottom lip. Then she peered through the dark in the direction of the nearest field of trees. Then toward the beach. When her gaze came back to his, he felt as if he'd traversed the grounds of her family's orchard with her. "Because this is where I belong."

"Seems fickle. A short time ago New York was where you belonged." His words were harsh, but he couldn't help it. And he didn't care. The last time they'd both been here she'd told him she didn't love him.

He didn't want to love her either.

"New York *was* where I belonged," she answered. "Three months ago. One month ago, even. But not anymore. I don't need the escape anymore." She shook her head. "I'm not healed. I won't ever be healed. Childhood scars remain forever. But I am better. I'm mentally healthier. I can function in the world I live in without having to create make-believe barriers to keep it from being too hard, and most importantly . . . I *want* to function in the world I live in. But I want to do it in *my* world. My home. Here, in Montana. I want my own life. I want to love. And I want to be loved. So I'm back. For good."

He swallowed the words that rose to the top. He'd loved her. He'd offered her all of that.

But he also remembered how she *had* needed to go. She hadn't dreamed that up, and he was honest enough to admit that he'd understood it. He just hadn't like it.

And he'd watched her change over the weeks through her phone calls with Haley.

He got what she meant when she said was better. She was. He'd just never been able to figure out if the changes had come about because of her, or due to someone else. And that ate at him. That terrified him.

"Did you meet anyone in New York?"

Her brows shot up. "You mean a man?"

"Yes."

The laugh that slipped out of her was dry. "No, Ben. I didn't meet anyone. You're the only one who's been dating. You're the one with a girlfriend."

He didn't acknowledge or deny her words. Yes, he'd gone out. No, he didn't have a girlfriend.

"You told me to move on," he said.

"Yeah. I'm aware of that." She shivered as she stood in front of him. They remained slightly behind the open car door, but that wasn't enough to keep the wind from whipping around them. Even with a coat, it was too cold to be outside. Snow was moving in, and an arctic blast had arrived first.

"Get in my car," he said.

She motioned toward the house. "It's time for dinner."

"Dinner can wait. We need to talk, Dani. And it's cold out here." When she didn't move, he added, "We can't talk in the house. Every one of them would be listening to us." He held out his car keys. "Get in my car, and I can at least run the heater to keep us from freezing to death."

With a small nod, she headed for his car.

And with sudden clarity, he realized that he wanted to take her to his house.

He'd refused to let Karen come to his home, but he wanted Dani there. He needed to see her there.

He got in the vehicle, and started it up, and when he put it into gear she barely acknowledged the action. It was as though she'd known he would take them somewhere. Possibly, she understood where they were going.

chapter twenty-nine

Dani sat stiffly in the front seat of Ben's SUV as he made the five-minute drive to his house. The instant he'd put the car into drive, she'd known where they were going. Which thrilled her. She wanted to see his home. Only . . .

When the house came into view, nerves ignited in her stomach. She turned to him, apology in her heart, but she had an issue with this. "Have you brought your girlfriend here?"

She didn't think she could go inside if he'd had another woman there.

Ben didn't answer. Instead he focused on maneuvering in the narrow driveway.

When he reached the side of the house, he parked facing the lake, shifted out of gear, and stared straight again. "I don't have a girlfriend."

Dani snorted, and Ben shot her a irritated look.

"Dad and Gloria babysit for you," she said. "I overheard you making a date."

"She's not my girlfriend."

"Fine," she grumbled. "Has your bed-buddy been here?"

"Dani, for Christ's sake. I thought you might want to see the house. I *want* you to see the house." He motioned to the side door. "Do you want to go in or not?"

She shook her head. Right or not, her jealousy won out. "Not if another woman has been here."

Yes, she'd told him to move on. And she'd meant it. She hadn't thought she would be back. She hadn't thought she'd ever feel less than abnormal.

But she was, and she did.

And the very thought of Ben making love to another woman inside the house he'd once suggested could be theirs brought bile to the back of her throat. She stared at the large house sitting quietly in the dark.

She could move on from him dating. If she wanted him, she'd have to.

But did she have to see where he'd taken another woman?

"Take me back to the house, please," she requested.

He turned off the car.

"Ben." She whipped around to him. "I asked you to—"

"No!" he shouted. "No one has been here. No woman. I couldn't stand the thought of it. I only wanted you here, don't you get that? It's you, dammit. Only you. Yet I'm so hurt, and so angry, that *you* may not even be enough. I don't know. But I want you to see my house." His voice lowered with his last sentence, and she gave a hurried nod before climbing from the car.

Did that mean she could hope?

Ben unlocked the side door, and led her in through the kitchen. His house was warm and inviting, and her dad had been right. In the daylight, there would be spectacular views from his back windows. But even with the enthusiastic greeting from Haley's dog, Dani struggled to feel welcome. Not with Ben standing so stiffly beside her.

She followed along behind him as he showed her the house, her coat still on, and her arms crossed over her chest, and she appropriately complimented the spaces that she saw. It was a fabulous home.

It was a place she could see herself in.

What had he meant, exactly, that it was only her? Did he still love her?

"Why did you come to the house tonight?" she asked. That question had been burning in her mind since Gabe had told her Ben would be there. Why would he come? Either he was over her—and had truly moved on—or . . .

What?

He wanted to see her?

He wanted to have this talk?

They stood in Haley's room now, and as Dani looked out over the lake, Ben looked at her. "I came because I was invited," he answered simply.

"Yet you knew I would be there," she pushed back. She didn't turn to him as she spoke, instead maintaining her visual on the dark night beyond the window. It was easier than facing him. "Why did you come?" she repeated.

"Because I couldn't stay away."

She finally looked at him then, her gaze drawn to the hollowness of his eyes. He didn't want to care about her anymore; she could see that inside him. But he did.

"I came because, whether I want to admit it or not, we're not finished. I need answers."

She nodded. "And are you getting them?"

He took her in, and for the first time tonight he seemed to look deeply enough to actually see her. He stared into her eyes, took in the twist of her hands and the protective barrier of her coat.

She believed that he saw her fear.

That he might see how terrified she was of losing him for good.

"You said you could love me now," he told her.

"I do love you now."

His gaze heated, but he said nothing else. The look, though, it empowered her. Telling him that she loved him hadn't been as hard as she'd thought. And the way he was staring back at her . . . she began to truly hope that all might not be lost.

"It's the real kind of love," she went on. "Not the kind where I want to wash your clothes or do your dishes for you. As a matter of fact, I'll be fine if I never do dishes again." She forced herself to loosen her stance and lowered her arms. "I love you, Ben. The right way. But I also love me. So to go back to your earlier question at the house . . . am I back? Yes. Forever. No matter what happens between me and you."

All she could do then was wait.

She'd laid her cards on the table, and her heart was in his hands.

A muscle ticked in his jaw. "You don't need New York?"

"No."

"Just like that?"

She pulled in a breath and blew it back out. "It wasn't *just* like that. I spent three months in therapy. I've worked really hard on myself. New York was my way to not be around my mother. To not *be* my mother," she stressed. "But I'm not her. And I believe that now. So no, I don't need New York. I had a job I loved here. I like working for myself. I enjoy helping my clients. I don't need anything else." She paused before adding, "Except you."

"Christ," he mumbled under his breath. "You . . ."

He stopped trying to talk and just looked at her. She stared back, doing her best to show him anything at all that he needed to see. She was here. And she was his, if he would have her.

She could be forever.

"Damn, Dani."

He pulled her to him then, and a moan of relief slipped out of her. His mouth found hers, and she clutched at him. His lips were hot and seeking, and they clung to her with the same desperate need that she felt. She didn't want to ever let go.

Only, the kiss ended too soon.

She whimpered when he pulled away.

"I love you," he ground out.

She nodded as tears filled her eyes. "I love you. I'm so sorry, Ben. I never meant to hurt you."

"I know." He pulled her back to him and just held her. "I do. And I see how good you are now." He looked down at her. "Yet still the woman I love."

"Do you think we could date?" her voice quivered. "See where this could go?"

He laughed. "Babe. I know where this is going to go. So before we commit to doing anything, there's one more thing I need to get off my chest."

"Oh, God," she groaned. "You slept with her." Pain sliced through her.

"What?" He shook his head. "No. I've slept with no one but you. Shit, Dani. I forced myself to kiss her after three dates, and that ended it. It's *only* you. Always you. I don't want anyone else."

She nodded, loving his words. "Then what do you need to tell me?"

He took her hand, and he led her from Haley's room. Turning outside the door, she followed him down the hall until they reached another room. When he pushed the door open, she saw that it was the master bedroom. It had the view. The stars were bright enough that even in the dark she could make out the lake and the surrounding mountains through full-length windows. A deck sat outside a set of French doors, and Ben took them to it.

The wind remained cold, but he stepped behind her and wrapped her in his arms, and she would forever be warm enough. They gazed at the water together, and he pointed out his beach. And his boat dock.

"That spot right there," he said into her ear. "If we do this, I'm eventually going to make love to you right there." He turned her to him. "*And* I'm eventually going to ask you to marry me."

She stared at him. She couldn't breathe.

"We stop here if you aren't ready for that," he told her. "Because I won't lose you again. I can't. I can't have you in my life for a short time, and let you walk out of it ever again. So if we do this, you have to be prepared to say yes."

She nodded. And tears fell. She couldn't have asked for anything more.

"When you ask me," she began, her voice no longer shaking. "I promise I'll say yes."

He kissed her for real, then, and it didn't stop after a few seconds.

chapter thirty

Two and a half weeks later, Dani, Haley, and Jenna were in the
den at Ben's house while Ben had disappeared upstairs to his
bedroom. Both girls were out of school for the holiday break, and
Ben had offered to bring Jenna to the house for a few days, to allow
the friends to spend some time together. Thus, the four of them
had just returned from LA where they'd visited Ben's mother
before heading to Disneyland. Haley had never been to the park,
and since Jenna wasn't getting her Christmas trip to New York,
they'd all spent the past two days riding rides and hanging out
with princesses.

It had been fun. But exhausting.

Now they were back in Montana, with Gabe and Michelle
planning to arrive the following week for their dad's wedding, and
once again, everyone would be home at the same time. This time
for Christmas. Dani couldn't wait to see them all.

"When's Daddy gonna get done?" Haley complained from her spot in front of the fireplace. Ben was unpacking clothes he'd recently had shipped from California, and making sure he had a suit to wear to the wedding.

"He'll be down soon," Dani answered. She closed the top of her laptop, deciding work could wait, and took in both girls with their newly purchased Cinderella dolls—including pumpkin carriage and glass slippers—spread out all over the floor. "Did you need him for something?"

"We need him to be our prince," Jenna replied, holding up the prince doll.

The girls had talked Ben into purchasing pretty much every Cinderella accessory available while at Disneyland, including a tall, dark, and handsome prince.

"How about if I be the prince?" Dani asked. She rose from the sofa and moved across the room.

"You can't be a prince, Miss Dani," Haley said. "You're a girl. You're a princess."

Dani chuckled. "I guess I am. But I could pretend until your daddy gets back."

Haley and her dad were close these days, and though Dani never felt like a third wheel, she was always aware that she wasn't yet an official part of their family. But Ben had promised her that day would come. She just had to be patient.

And though it had been less than three weeks, her patience was wearing thin.

They saw each other every day, their connection was as strong as ever, and she had no doubt he was the love of her life. She wanted to marry that man, and soon.

As in, today, if they could make it happen.

But instead of marrying her prince, she would play one with the girls.

She lowered to the floor, and the three of them began acting out the fairy tale. Haley and Jenna took turns being the evil stepsisters—as well as being Cinderella—and Dani deepened her voice an octave and became the handsome prince.

As they played, she watched both girls that she loved so much. LA had been good for Jenna, if for no other reason than it had brought her and her daddy closer together.

It might not save her brother's marriage, but it had given him his daughter.

"What did you ask Santa for Christmas?" Dani asked them both.

Jenna looked up from dancing Cinderella around the ballroom floor with the prince. "More dolls," she said. "I need more princesses and princes."

"Me too," Haley agreed. Then the girl bit her lip and sent Dani an angelic smile. "I wanted to ask for a new mommy, but I already have you."

"Awww, sweetie." Dani's heart soared. She stood and circled the toys to pick up Ben's daughter, and hugged her tight. As she squeezed the little girl, her gaze landed on the photo Ben had framed and placed on the mantel. It was of her from years ago, lying on the dock late at night. He claimed it was his favorite picture.

The clock beside it began to chime—it was noon—and Jenna gasped from the floor.

"Cinderella has to leave the ball before her carriage turns into a pumpkin." Jenna hurriedly ran the doll to the carriage while Dani and Haley watched from above.

And then Haley sucked in a sharp breath.

Dani lifted her gaze at the sound to find Ben standing in the doorway, all tall and hot in a sexy tailored suit, and she completely lost her breath herself. He was magnificent.

"Daddy, you look like a prince."

Ben smiled, the smile that made Dani squeeze her thighs together, and he crossed the room as the clock continued to chime. In the story, time was running out, but as Dani stood there looking at the man she loved, with his daughter snuggled in her arms, she knew that their time was only just beginning. They had the rest of their lives to be together.

He stopped in front of them. "What do you think?" he asked Dani. "Do I look prince-like?"

She slowly nodded—while her thoughts went way past naughty. With the trip to California, they'd had precious little alone time lately, and she could sorely use some. She so wished the girls weren't in the room at that moment.

"Very much so," she murmured. She needed to get that man alone.

From the gleam in his eyes she could tell that he knew exactly what she was thinking.

"Good." He took her hand in his and kissed her fingers, one at a time, and Haley giggled in her arms. Montana let out a bark, and Jenna put down her dolls to watch.

Then Ben dropped to one knee and pulled out a ring.

"He *is* a prince," Jenna whispered.

Ben looked up at Dani then, love shining from his eyes. "What do you say, babe? Will you be my princess? I know it's only been a few weeks, but I can't wait any longer. I love you. No more living in town in that tiny little apartment. I want you here with me. Where you belong. Will you marry me, and be mine and Haley's forever?"

Haley held her breath, and Jenna froze in her spot on the floor. Dani could sense their anticipatory gazes, but neither said a word. They wanted to see the fairy tale come true.

So did Dani.

Instead of answering, she put Haley down, then she lowered to her own knees and faced Ben. She cupped his jaw in her hands, and kissed him tenderly, his touch filling her with love and promises, and she knew that she could never be luckier.

She'd found herself, as well as the man of her dreams.

"I love you," she told him when they pulled apart. "A love as huge as the Montana sky we sit together and look at every night. And yes, Ben. The man of my dreams. I'll marry you. I'll be your wife, your princess. I'll be whatever you need me to be. I'm yours. For the rest of our lives."

"I just need you to be you."

She nodded. She could do that.

She would do that with pleasure.

Holding out a trembling hand, she gazed on as Ben slipped an incredibly huge diamond on her finger. She took it in, kissed him one more time for good measure, and turned her gaze to the kids.

They smiled with bright anticipation in their eyes, but for once, they were speechless.

"Looks like I already got what *I* want for Christmas," Dani told them. She winked at the girls, and kissed Ben once more. "I got my prince."

Acknowledgments

This book was originally written back in 2011, and in its first iteration it was shorter, simpler, and . . . just okay. Then my agent sold it, and I quickly had to make it longer, more complex, and . . . much better! The speed with which this had to be done caused me great heartburn (and I suspect before it was done my agent had some of her own), along with a huge loss of sleep. But in the end, I love this book. I love the setting, the family, and I love the drama. And yes, I did eventually get some sleep.

Thanks to Nalini Akolekar for selling the book, to Maria Gomez for buying the book, to Chuck Henry for letting me know there were cherry orchards in Montana, to Keena Kincaid for walking long distances on the beach to help me figure out what I wanted to do to make it "bigger," and to Anne Marie Becker and June Love for participating in last-minute brainstorming to help me get the final scenes just right (when my brain was too tired and I couldn't do it myself!).

And a special thanks—the most important thanks—to my copy editor, Diane Sepanski, for going above and beyond to help me get this story just right. You know what having you work on this book meant to me, so I won't go into it here. But thank you. A million times thank you. And huge, huge hugs. I'm sending you a gorgeous bouquet of flowers (in my head) right this very moment. I hope you enjoy them!

As I said, I love this book. It's special to me for a number of reasons, and my fingers are crossed that readers will love it, too. But mostly, I hope this book touches someone who needs to know that they're not alone.

Narcissistic Personality Disorder is real, and doesn't always get the attention it needs. People are damaged by the words and actions of a parent or loved one, and they may never understand why. Adult children who've lived with this disorder may continue to wonder for their entire lives if it's just them. Did they do something wrong? They may always assume it's *their* fault.

But it's not. And you're not alone.

You're a survivor.

You got dealt a rotten hand in life.

But you *can* move on.

There are resources available on the Internet and books on this subject in libraries and bookstores. I urge you to read up on this disorder whether you think this is something you've lived with, personally, or not. You might discover a piece of information that's the key to helping a friend. A nugget that'll make him or her suddenly not feel so alone in the world.

And you might discover a wealth of information to help *you*.

I felt drawn to write this book, and I can't even explain why. But my sincere hope is that it'll shed light on a disorder that is still relatively untalked about. Women—men—should not feel they've done something wrong to be undeserving of a parent's love. They shouldn't have to suffer because someone else didn't have the capacity to love them.

One last note: Due to the length of time that can realistically be covered in a romance novel, Dani's recovery period in this book was portrayed at a speed which, for most, would be unattainable. (Additionally, NPD often engenders a family fracturing that was beyond the scope of this novel.) As I stressed in the book, recovery is a lifetime journey, and simply getting to Dani's level of function would likely take well more than a few months. There are many steps to work through in the process. And many setbacks to be expected along the way. But with determination and the healthy willingness to face your hurts, it can be the best path you've ever traveled.

For more information on Narcissistic Personality Disorder, an excellent book to read is *Will I Ever Be Good Enough?* by Karyl McBride, Ph.D. Additionally, included is a short list of websites referenced during the writing of this book:

http://www.narcissisticmother.com
http://www.willieverbegoodenough.com/
http://parrishmiller.com/narcissists.html